TOM BEDLAM

ALSO BY

GEORGE HAGEN

THE LAMENTS

TOM BEDLAM

George Hagen

SCEPTRE

First published in the US in 2007 by Random House

First published in Great Britain in 2007 by Hodder & Stoughton
A division of Hodder Headline

The right of George Hagen to be identified as the Author
of the Work has been asserted by him in accordance with the
Copyright, Designs and Patents Act 1988.

A Sceptre Book

1

A CIP catalogue record for this title is
available from the British Library

978 0 340 92112 8

Printed and bound by Griffin Press

Hodder Headline's policy is to use papers that are natural, renewable
and recyclable products and made from wood grown in sustainable forests.
The logging and manufacturing processes are expected to conform
to the environmental regulations of the country of origin.

Hodder & Stoughton Ltd
A division of Hodder Headline
338 Euston Road
London NW1 3BH

For my three muses:
Sophie, Brooklyn, and Lola

My son – and what's a son? A thing begot
Within a pair of minutes, thereabouts.
A lump bred up in darkness.

—THOMAS KYD

PART ONE

TURNING THE OTHER CHEEK

It is quite possible that Emily Bedlam was simply a very good woman, but to her son, Tom, she appeared insane.

She was the embodiment of Christian virtue. 'God Bless!' she would say to the surliest stranger with a giddy and well-meaning smile. When she received a fearsome oath in reply, Mrs Bedlam held no grudge. She tried again the next day. And the next.

She never spoke in scorn, nor did she gossip or disparage her neighbours. She provided for her only son through her employment at Todderman & Sons Porcelain & Statuary, and remained faithful to her husband though he had deserted her many years before.

Never had the boy met a woman as selfless and self-effacing. She had been robbed, sworn at and gossiped about, but she always turned the other cheek. Since Tom had never seen an angel, he was tempted to assign his mother's virtues to a category of folk he *had* seen on the rough city streets – the simple, the touched, the witless.

In Vauxhall, south-west of the City of London, Tom accompanied his mother to the factory every morning. Through the wrought-iron gates and across a windswept courtyard, they would pass Mr Todderman greeting his employees from a parapet on the second floor of his domain. Behind him, two smokestacks from the factory released a black smear across the London skyline, while next to him, the cripple, Brandy

Oxmire, clutched a slate for the purpose of marking down absences and latecomers.

'Morning, Mrs Bedlam!' her employer shouted.

'God Bless, Mr Todderman!' came the gay reply, 'and thank you for Mrs Todderman's shoes!' Then she'd pause to display the gaudy red-leather shoes on her feet.

Todderman acknowledged them with a weary growl. 'It was a pleasure, Mrs Bedlam.' She'd been thanking him for his wife's castoffs for weeks, even though he'd subtracted a small fee from her wages in compensation for them.

'You need not thank him,' Tom had whispered many times.

'Nonsense, Tom,' replied his mother. 'D'you know what these shoes are worth? If nobody acknowledged a good turn, just imagine what an unkind city London would be.'

Tom needed no imagination. He'd seen their tenement landlord turn out folk on the second of the month for missing the rent; there was always a supply of desperate faces at Mr Todderman's gates looking for work; and of course, there was the daily unkindness of the street – the strangers who mocked his mother's patrician manners because she wore secondhand clothing, the neighbours who joked about her married name, and the factory biddies who told his mother to bless herself, for she needed more blessing than they did.

Was she stupid? No, for there was a solid Christian philosophy behind her disposition. Three dog-eared Bibles on her bookshelf confirmed it: *Do unto others as you would have them do unto you;* and *Whosoever shall smite thee on thy right cheek, turn to him the other also.*

But as Tom accompanied his mother through the glazing rooms and the clay shops of Todderman's factory, he couldn't prevent her cheery greetings to her co-workers. 'Morning, Esther! Hello, Mary! God Bless, Bonnie! . . . Oh, Mrs Mudd, you look *very* nice today!'

The replies were rare. As for Mrs Mudd, her pudding face – round, mottled, and grimy at the edges – didn't acknowledge the compliment; she grunted and spat, striking the heel of one of Mrs Todderman's precious shoes with a milky clod of phlegm. Mrs Mudd knew her workmate was more valued and chose to believe that it was not Mrs Bedlam's skill with clay but her genteel accent that earned her a shilling more a week.

'You're disgusting!' Tom cried in his mother's defence, but Mrs Mudd shook off the nine-year-old's protest with a sneer.

'God Bless, Mrs Mudd,' said his mother faintly as she wiped her heel and took a seat at her bench.

'It doesn't help that you forgive her so easily,' the boy whispered.

'It was a mistake, my love,' his mother replied. 'What sort of world would it be if we took offence at every mistake?'

Would Mrs Bedlam's blithe philosophy change the world for the better? Tom looked doubtfully at Mrs Mudd. She was a notorious slut who tried to shock his mother with her spitting and raunchy language. He never forgave a remark he had heard from her lips: 'What a pathetic 'un with that barmy smile, every bloody morning, and a son who's never seen his father!'

Mr Todderman made a considerable profit from reproducing the delicate figurines that were popular in Paris and Dresden, and Emily Bedlam had a remarkable talent for imitation; she could fashion anything from the fine white porcelain clay – miniature duchesses, dukes, swans, amorous goatherds and coy shepherdesses. Each delicate figure subtly echoed Emily Bedlam's own naïve features.

Ten hours a day, his mother laboured here. Above, a skylight admitted the occasional ray of sun, reflecting a million tiny white particles. It was always snowing in the porcelain factory; everybody had a cough; and the mucus was always milky white.

When Tom was ten, he was employed to run errands between the various departments. Mr Todderman needed a few boys of Tom's size, small enough to retrieve pieces at the back of the kiln and navigate the warehouse without damaging the stock. Tom did many odd jobs, taking messages to the glazing shops, the furnaces, the accounting department, and fetching pieces from the cramped underbasement, where racks and racks of identical dukes, duchesses and shepherdesses (not to mention the busts of Her Majesty, Queen Victoria) were stored for shipment.

On the factory rooftop, where silt rained down from the two billowing smokestacks like black hail, Tom took refuge from Mr Todderman's heavy-lidded scrutiny. On this roof he surveyed the grimy streets of Vauxhall, the muddy brown ribbon of the Thames, and the grander vista of the City of London that lay beyond Westminster Bridge.

'Looking for your papa?' Brandy the cripple grinned. He had followed Tom up there this morning.

'Well, I won't find *yours*, will I?' Tom replied.

Brandy was an orphan. His right foot had been mangled in an explosion in the kilns when he was fourteen. Dubbing him Brandy for the scar tissue over most of his face, Todderman used him as his eyes and ears about the factory. The cripple's distorted face on the parapet every morning also assured the other workers that their employer had some tender, fatherly spirit in him.

'Todderman'll gimme this here factory when he dies, I reckon,' said Brandy, pausing to stoke a little white clay pipe.

'He has a nephew. You'll get nothing,' Tom replied.

'I have a living,' Brandy declared, squinting as the wind changed direction and black smoke wafted down from the stacks, showering particles across his distorted features. 'What did your father ever give you? Only a name I reckon!'

Prompted by such challenges to learn more about his father, Tom might as well have asked the miniature dukes and shepherdesses for an answer. His questions to his mother rarely elicited more than an assurance that she was legally married to Mr William Bedlam, that he was away on business and would return someday hence. Then Tom was reminded not to listen to the gossips. 'Do you think I'd take a name like Mrs Bedlam for no reason, Tom? I married for love, and gave up much for it,' she would say, though she would never explain the nature of her sacrifices.

And what kind of a man had married a righteous woman like his mother? Was Mr Bedlam righteous too? Or did he stray from the flock? None of Tom's many questions were answered to his satisfaction. The reply was always the same: 'I wouldn't be telling stories about your father, Tom,' she said. 'He toils under God's blessing, same as the rest of us.

And if you can't speak pleasantly about a person, it's best to say nothing at all.'

Because his mother considered tact one of the prime virtues and would reveal nothing more about her past *or* his father's present circumstances, Tom sincerely hoped that William Bedlam would make his appearance soon and speak for himself.

A WISH GRANTED

THE ROOM THEY SHARED WAS IN A TENEMENT THAT LEANED AGAINST Todderman's factory. There was an imploring quality to the structure; its cracked windows dimly reflected the sky, and its front door was ajar in the same way that the mouth of a bitter man gapes open. The bricks were caked with black silt from the smokestacks next door, the stairway was a fresco of grubby finger marks, and the steps were dusted with fine porcelain powder. Every inch of this building bore the stain of Todderman's factory, as did most of its tenants. Rooms were divided and subdivided as necessity warranted. A hole in the floor of the entrance hall tripped unwary visitors. Tenant outrage over the building's condition matured into apathy and her offspring – acceptance and wilful damage. Every week the hole grew; perhaps somebody thought that improvement would come about only by making the structure even more squalid and treacherous.

In one corner of the tenement room Tom shared with his mother, he would press his ear to the wainscoting, listen to the visceral clamour of the building, and try to make sense of it, just as he listened to the beat of his own heart with his fingers pressed tightly to his ears.

It was a wet autumn evening in London. The cries of the eel fishermen could be heard echoing across the muddy Thames at high tide as Mrs Bedlam counted her savings. Her system was simple: she collected her coins until they could be exchanged for paper money, then the note would be deposited in one of her Bibles, a one-pound banknote for each chapter. Currently, the Bible contained twenty-five pounds. When she reached Revelation, Mrs Bedlam expected to have enough money to move to the country with her son. Far from the white dust that collected in milky tears in the corners of their eyes, far from the stifling black smoke in the skies, far from the filth that contaminated the streets, and the offal house nearby, Tom could have an education, and his mother could raise chickens, a cow, and perhaps some sheep.

'It won't be long until we're living in the country, Tom,' she promised with a frail, giddy smile. 'And it won't be long until you go to school.'

Tom said nothing; this promise was all too familiar. With his ear against the wainscoting, he identified the footsteps of his neighbours in the same way a country boy quickly distinguishes the call of a wren from that of a curlew.

Mr Bottle, for example, always dragged his feet slowly up the stairs in anticipation of the verbal taunts he would receive from his bedridden and demented daughter.

The Limpkin children stampeded to the second floor with peals of laughter. The entire Limpkin family could be seen outside the building on the twenty-ninth of any month offering up their pots and pans, furniture, clothing (and sometimes Mrs Limpkin's pastries) in a desperate attempt to raise funds for the rent.

Mr Hull, whose head hung below his muscular shoulders, ascended the staircase with bovine snorts much as the Minotaur must have stalked Theseus in the labyrinth. Tom had learned about the monster from Oscar Limpkin, a boy Tom's age, whose fertile imagination was matched by an incredible grasp of mythology.

Suddenly Tom heard *new* footsteps. The pace, the weight of each tread and the agility of the person were unfamiliar. Usually he expected a shout and a curse as every newcomer misjudged the widening hole in the foyer – but today this obstacle was nimbly traversed without even a scramble.

As Tom changed his position by the wall, Mrs Bedlam looked up from her counting. 'Who is it, Tom?'

'A man, I think.'

'There's a new man on the fourth floor,' suggested his mother. 'He works in the furnaces. Dear me, such an awful place.'

But Tom's ear remained pressed to the wainscoting as the strong footsteps came up the first flight, paused on the landing, and proceeded to the second.

A stranger always took a moment to consider the smells emanating from sixteen households, the trick step (seven up from the landing) that promised a bruised shin, and the spokelike shadows of the banisters on the grubby walls; but this person proceeded up the second flight without such contemplation. It seemed obvious to Tom that he knew somebody here. But what surprised Tom next was the silence that greeted the second floor, *his* floor. There was no creak from the spinster's door, and no sound from the Limpkins', whose children could be counted on to greet any creditor with shrieks of hostility (and any friend with jubilant cries).

Tom rose from his bed and stared at the crack at the bottom of the door. A pair of feet blocked the dim red glow of gaslight. For a long moment they remained in place, as if their owner were staring directly through the wooden door at Tom.

A sudden *rat-a-tat-tat* on the door was made with a flourish, like a stage knock.

The sound startled Emily Bedlam. Like a jointed doll pulled rigid by a string, she became taut, eyes wide, mouth trembling. She snapped the Bible shut and hid it among the other books on a shelf while casting one tentative glance in Tom's direction. Then, hurriedly preening herself, she went to the door to release the bolt.

WILLIAM BEDLAM

HE WAS TALL, WITH A SHOCK OF SILVERY HAIR AND A BLACK WOOLLEN overcoat, the high collar thrust up to his ears. His silhouette was distinct, and his nose ramrod straight – a prominent profile, handsome, even in the dim gaslight.

Tom watched his mother open the door a crack. There was an urgent exchange between her and the visitor; Mrs Bedlam was firm, but the visitor persisted; his voice was, by turns, explosive, cajoling, merry, and despairing until she relented and withdrew, permitting him entry. In the next instant, the stranger sprang across the room and knelt by Tom, assuming both his height and an absurdly innocent expression.

'Hello then,' he said, in reaction to Tom's scrutiny.

It seemed to Tom that the man was pretending to be a boy. Not a very convincing one, but the sort who gets laughs on a stage. The man rubbed his nose carelessly, tousled his own hair, and playfully flicked his ear with a finger. 'Who have we here, eh?' he said. 'What's yer name?'

Tom stared at his interlocutor, puzzled by such mockery, and puzzled also that he needed to identify himself in his own home.

'You named him Tom, remember?' Mrs Bedlam replied.

'*Tom*, yes – *of course*!'

The fellow stood up slowly, now mimicking Tom's serious expression. 'You must be ten years old. Good heavens!' He frowned. With a tilt of his silver mane, he bowed, sweeping one hand elaborately while offering the other. 'William Bedlam at your service!'

The man's coat was drenched, and his boots whistled through their damp stitches; yet even in this condition he seemed most concerned with Tom liking him. Bedlam spoke to his wife in an obvious stage whisper. 'What's the *matter* with him?'

'Nothing,' replied Mrs Bedlam. 'Say hello, Tom!'

Bedlam patted his chest to assure Tom that he was flesh and blood. 'I'm yer father, my boy! I'm your chum. Bill Bedlam!' When the boy didn't respond, Bedlam gave his wife an accusing glance. 'Why's he staring like that?'

'Well, he's never seen his father before,' Mrs Bedlam explained.

Bedlam dropped to his knees, winked at the boy, made a grand show of pushing up his sleeves, and reached carefully behind Tom's ear. Something appeared in the man's hand. 'Well now' – he chuckled – 'you're not quite the goose that laid the golden egg, but—'

Tom examined the dull farthing that had been drawn from his ear. He knew this parlour trick. Mr Todderman pulled twice this sum from Tom's ear at Christmas. Still, he recognized the intent, if not its value, and offered a brief smile.

'*There!*' said Bedlam. 'A sense of humour, just like his father!' He added with a wistful glance at his wife, 'and his mother, once.'

Mrs Bedlam didn't acknowledge the remark. She had not said much since the man entered the room, and Tom wondered if, being at a loss to say anything good about him, his mother was remaining mute on purpose.

'Oh, we had good times!' Bedlam said in answer to his wife's silence. 'Admit it, Emily!' He tipped his head at Tom, encouraging the boy to rally with him. 'Your mother and I, we had such good times!'

Now Mrs Bedlam folded her arms, and Mr Bedlam reacted as if she had spoken volumes. He turned to Tom. 'She hasn't told you much about me, I reckon?'

'She wouldn't tell me *any* stories about you,' Tom replied.

'Stories! Well, *I'm* the storyteller in the house!' said Mr Bedlam. 'I could tell you stories that would curl your toes, Tom! Know what I am? I am an actor. D'you know what that is, Tom?'

'Yes,' the boy replied. 'Pantomime. *Puss in Boots.*'

'Better than *Puss in Boots,*' said his father. 'I play kings! Princes! I perform before *hundreds* of people, Tom!'

Bedlam directed his son to pay attention and withdrew a folded sheet of foolscap from his pocket. He presented it to him with a teasing flourish. 'Open it up!'

It was a theatre broadsheet featuring Bedlam's likeness wearing a crown. *Astounding King Lear!* 'There I am,' Bedlam whispered in reverence. 'King Lear. The greatest of Shakespeare's kings, Tom. The *greatest.* That's *your* father, Tom. Keep it, it's yours.'

Since it was made clear that this was a document of extraordinary importance, Tom presented it to his mother, who mixed some flour paste, dabbed it upon the corners of the foolscap, and pressed it flat against the grubby wall.

THE EVENING PROCEEDED with a meal of porridge mixed with vegetables. Mr Bedlam praised his wife's cooking, ate three helpings, and scraped the pot clean. In return, Tom's mother administered a cautious affection for the man; she wrapped Mr Bedlam's wet coat about the stove to dry, put his boots on top, and gently chastised her husband for lacking gloves.

'You must take care of your hands, Bill. Remember how you chafe in the winter? Your fingers are raw as beef.'

Bedlam smiled wistfully at his wife and began to recite a limerick:

The bird that deserts his own nest
Is a fool, and to this I attest:
My loss is eternal,
My future infernal,
But the wife I abandoned is blessed!

Mrs Bedlam looked pained by the verse, and Bedlam quickly put his hand on hers. 'You're too good to me, Emily,' he said, 'considering.'

In spite of Mr Bedlam's assuring words, Tom saw the uneasiness between his parents. When the conversation failed to take root, Mrs Bedlam asked her most direct question: 'What brings you here, Bill?'

Bedlam replied by averting his eyes and shaking his head. Then he said, 'Why, the comfort of my family, Emily!' As if expecting her retort, he added, 'I regret, Emily, deeply regret, that I've sacrificed domestic happiness for my calling.' Then he described his tour across England, the enormous success of *King Lear*, the applause of the crowds, and the praise he'd received in newspapers.

'When was this?' inquired Mrs Bedlam.

With excessive pride he replied, 'Why, only five years ago, Emily, and I'm *still* recognized on the street. "There goes Bill Bedlam!" they say. "An astounding King Lear!" What I'm saying is that it's not all for naught that I went my own way. I am an actor, an artist, not an average man by any means, and not a man to be judged by other men's standards!'

Stung by this remark, Mrs Bedlam folded her arms, and Bedlam realized that he had contradicted his earlier regrets. 'Oh, Emily. You *know* what an actor's life is like! I've *suffered* for my profession, believe me.'

'You were always welcome here,' she replied gently. 'In sickness and in health – as you vowed once.'

This silenced Bedlam for a moment. 'I'm ashamed, Emily. But I was an actor when we met, and I am still one now, and in all likelihood—'

He paused, took her hand tenderly, and kissed it without finishing his sentence. He frowned at Tom. 'Your mother's a good woman, Tom, a *very* good woman. You know that, don't you?'

Tom nodded. To see his father holding his mother's hand was gratifying enough, but to hear his mother's praises sung was quite another. Observing his father's affectionate gestures, Tom forgot ever having doubted his mother's wits. The sight of his parents in this sublime domestic tableau warmed his heart – for a moment, all seemed right in the world – and a timid smile appeared upon his face.

'And it just so happens that I've got good *prospects*, Emily.'

'Prospects?'

'Title role in a production of *Julius Caesar* here in London. With top billing, I stand to make a good deal of money!'

'Oh, Bill,' Mrs Bedlam replied. 'How wonderful! I've been so worried about Tom's schooling. Perhaps now he'll have a—'

Bedlam nodded vigorously. 'Of course, Emily! And when I have paid back my investors, Tom's education will be first—'

Mrs Bedlam lowered a plate. 'Your investors? You mean you are the producer *and* the top billing?'

Bedlam nodded proudly. 'I have realized a simple fact: God helps those who help themselves!'

'Amen,' she softly replied. Bedlam glanced cautiously at her, adding that it was a virtue to be ambitious, but she didn't reply – this comment appeared to refer to an old argument. His eyes flickered to Tom, and he remarked again on the fine meal and removed a long-stemmed pipe from his pocket, put the tip in his mouth, and made a considerable fuss of looking for his tobacco pouch.

'Stolen, I'm sure,' he muttered. 'I passed a man on the stairs and I'll wager he—'

'On the stairs?' said Tom, for he had heard no one else on the stairs.

'Probably on the street,' corrected his father, 'a city of ne'er-do-wells. But perhaps a neighbour might lend us some tobacco. Do us a favour and beg me some, Emily. If I go to the Limpkins, they'll have me recounting my successes for hours!'

In his mother's face Tom recognized her determined optimism at work again. 'Of course,' she said. 'And poor Tom hasn't had a moment to talk with his father.'

Almost immediately upon his wife's departure, Mr Bedlam's vulpine gaze turned to the room, to the items stacked on the shelves, and his conversation became abstract. 'Your mother's a good woman, Tom, a fine and good woman. God bless her. She takes good care of you?'

'Aye,' Tom replied.

'Of course she does,' said Mr Bedlam. His attention strayed to the cluttered kitchen shelves; tipping his pipe up and down thoughtfully, he peered into the jars that were stacked on a small table by the potbellied stove. He lifted his coat, checked that it was dry, then threw it over his shoulders.

'Why don't you stay?' asked Tom, fearing that his father was about to leave.

Bedlam looked blankly at him. 'Stay? Stay where?'

'My friend Oscar's father stays at home. Why don't *you*?'

Bedlam smiled at the boy's sincerity. 'I am a poor player, Tom. I strut and fret upon the stage. It's no life for a family. I'm better off on the road, and you're better off here. But when my fortunes improve, Tom, *you* shall be the better for it!'

Losing interest in the kitchen, Bedlam now scrutinized Mrs Bedlam's bed. He slipped his fingers under the mattress and made a show for Tom of testing the bed's softness. Then, eyeing the door, Bedlam leaned towards his son with a conspiratorial gleam.

'Bless her, she's been saving her money for us. Y'know that, don't you? For when we're all together again.' Bedlam waited for Tom's reply.

Tom nodded. 'In the country, yes.'

'Aye.' His father smiled. 'In the country.'

Tom echoed his smile.

'Yes, indeed. Saving up for the country.' Bedlam raised his empty palm. 'Watch carefully, Tom—' With a flourish, he produced a folded banknote from between his fingers. He passed the note before Tom's eyes, savouring the boy's fresh respect. 'I was going to add this *one-pound note* to her savings. Perhaps you know . . . where she keeps them?'

'Aye.' Tom nodded.

'And where would that be, lad?'

HIS TRUE CHARACTER

WHEN MRS BEDLAM RETURNED WITH THE TOBACCO, SHE FOUND Tom seated alone in the room.

'Where is he?' she asked.

'Gone, but he'll come back,' Tom promised. 'He said so.'

'Gone?' repeated Mrs Bedlam. She turned to the potbellied stove and saw that the coat and boots were missing.

'He left us money,' said Tom. 'And he's bringing more when his play opens.'

'Money?'

Mrs Bedlam quickly knelt by the bookshelf, removed the Bible, and then uttered a cry.

'Oh, Tom.' She sighed. 'Did he ask you where our savings were?'

'Yes.' The boy nodded. 'He had a pound note to add to them, so I told him where you kept them. He said he wanted to make sure we had enough.'

Mrs Bedlam flipped through the Bible's empty pages.

'He expects to make hundreds of pounds, and then we can move to the country and I'll have an eddication!'

Mrs Bedlam pressed her hand to her heart. To Tom, it was a sentimental pose, like the ardour of one of her shepherdesses.

'He'll be back soon,' Tom assured her.

His mother didn't move for a moment. 'Of course he will, Tom,' she finally replied, clasping him to her breast with the most miserable smile.

THOUGH SHE STILL GREETED friends and strangers alike with her giddy smile, there was less joy in Emily Bedlam's demeanour after Bill Bedlam's visit. Her confidence in the goodness of man had suffered a grave setback. In subsequent days, a stranger with the luck to be greeted by Mrs Bedlam often didn't know whether he had been blessed or cursed; such was the ferocity with which she delivered her *God Bless*es.

Meanwhile, Tom began to dream of his father's success on the stage, for he was certain that this would bring his family together. Surely, if William Bedlam made his fortune, he would come home, and Emily Bedlam's love would be justified.

So Tom looked for his father's face everywhere, pasted on foolscap, perhaps with the words *Astounding Julius Caesar!*

But a full year passed without any sign of a production under way. Instead, Emily Bedlam continued to work at Todderman's factory, and Tom continued to escort her every morning.

As Bill Bedlam's likeness yellowed and curled upon their wall, Mrs Bedlam let it remain a silent testament to her husband's questionable character; but it served only to reinforce Tom's perception of his father as a figure of prominence. Long after he had forgotten the man's awkward efforts to win his affection, Tom remembered his ramrod nose, his handsome figure and his charm. Tom was sure that, somewhere out in the world, William Bedlam was playing kings and princes.

AN EDUCATION

UNTIL THE LOSS OF HER SAVINGS, MRS BEDLAM HAD BELIEVED that an adequate (though by no means ideal) education could be gleaned from the Bible. Beginning with Genesis, she had taught the boy his alphabet. From Adam to Zillah, Tom learned his letters. The Bible was also Tom's source for geography and history. He didn't know where France was, but he knew that the river from Eden divided into four – Pishon, Gihon, Tigris and Euphrates; and he didn't know the kings of England, but he knew that Lamech was the son of Methuselah, who was the son of Enoch, who was the son of Jared, and so on. Such matters, however, seemed irrelevant within the walls of Todderman's factory.

One morning, when Tom neared twelve, it became obvious to his employer that the boy could no longer fit into the crawl spaces behind the kilns, or make his way through some of the tighter passages. Todderman summoned Tom to his parapet and handed him a letter sealed with red wax. 'To whom is this letter addressed, Tom?' he said.

After reading the name of the addressee and the street aloud, Tom proved himself a capable messenger. He was to deliver invoices in the city.

Quickly, he learned his way around London, from Westminster to Paddington, and Finsbury Square to Whitechapel. He knew which streets were busy and which offered quick passage. Sometimes he dawdled on the way back, knowing how much time he could tease out of his errands.

One day he went walking along the Thames Embankment, where the workers gathered at lunch. The street entertainers were out in large numbers to take advantage of the crowd. A man played a flute while two monkeys danced at his feet, and farther on several acrobats constructed a human pyramid to the watchers' enormous applause. Still farther, a man stood upon a crate, holding up a small sign, which read, SHAKESPEAREAN SOLILOQUIES. His silver hair and pike-straight nose immediately caught Tom's attention.

'Tom? Good heavens! What luck!' cried Bill Bedlam. 'Come to me, lad!' he cried, dropping his sign and giving the boy a hearty embrace. 'This calls for celebration!' After leaving his crate and sign in the safekeeping of another performer, he led Tom down a side street.

'Come, lad, ask and you shall receive! What'll it be?'

Buoyed by his father's greeting, Tom glanced about the busy stores and noticed the pastry shop directly before them. It was a genteel establishment, with a large window at which many people were seated. Peering in at the counter, he saw an array of lemon tarts. 'A tart, perhaps?' he said.

'A tart!' echoed Mr Bedlam. He immediately dug into his pockets and, having taken tally of what was inside them, removed his hands slowly.

'Here's the thing about lemon tarts, my boy.' He frowned. 'The one thing you *don't* want is a lemon tart. Did you know that it stunts the growth? I suspect not. The effect of this poison on the body is most obvious in the petite figure of our own Queen Victoria.'

To make his point, Bedlam composed a limerick:

There once was a queen quite absurd,
With a passion for pastry and curd,
She ate three small portions,
And suffered contortions,
That reduced her dimensions one-third!

'The poor creature!' Bedlam continued. 'If she were not a monarch, she would be on parade in a circus for tuppence a showing. Tragic, eh? What I propose is something guaranteed to give you long life *and* a healthy disposition.'

'*Those* people are eating tarts,' Tom countered.

Bedlam, however, removed a green apple from his satchel; it was pitted with holes, bruised, and unimpressive, in spite of the furious polishing it received from Bedlam's sleeve.

'Yes, and they shall shrink, Tom,' he said. 'You, on the other hand, shall attain a respectable height, live a longer life, and thank me for it one of these days!'

Reluctantly, Tom accepted the apple, though it reminded him of the dull farthing he had received the last time they met.

'Tell me about your mother. Is she well?'

'She is as well as usual,' Tom replied. 'Did you put on your play?'

'Not yet, lad, but I have good prospects,' his father replied. 'And when my ship comes in, so will yours!'

Bedlam proceeded to describe his standing in the theatrical community. He was clearly adored by his audiences, admired by his fellow actors, and sought after by producers. Success was merely a matter of time.

'I'd like to see you play a king or a prince,' Tom said.

Bedlam promised that Tom and his mother would have the best seats in the house at his next production. 'You have my word, Tom,' he said and, embracing the boy, went on his way.

WHEN TOM TOLD his mother about his encounter, she listened but expressed no joy at her husband's promises. Tom couldn't understand why.

'He expects to be on the stage in a few months,' Tom explained.

'God bless him,' his mother replied with more condemnation than kindness.

BY THE TIME TOM was fourteen, there had been no more news of Mr Bedlam. True to his father's prediction, however, Tom gained many more inches, which he attributed to the avoidance of lemon tarts. He had more mature interests and desires now, and had refined the technique of eluding his responsibilities in pursuit of these impulses. It was a wonder that he still had a job, for he was never available when he was needed, and when he wasn't needed, he was always up to mischief.

'Where's Tom Bedlam?' cried Brandy Oxmire when Todderman sent him to find the boy. Brandy roared for him past the sweat-soaked men shovelling coal into the furnaces, past the workshops of the potters straddling their wheels as they drew jug and bowl from primeval clods, past the glazers, spattered and half-demented from using their leaden potions, until he arrived on the rooftop, with London spread out before him – a thousand towns of steeples, town houses and higgledy-piggledy tenements dappled with sun and smoke.

There, Brandy dug into his pocket for his thistle-shaped clay pipe, but finding his leather tobacco pouch empty, he cursed, stuffed the pipe into his pocket, and let out another roar for the idle boy in case his employer might be listening.

The only place Brandy had missed was the factory cellar, a quiet tomb where rows and rows of freshly fired porcelain pieces stood white and still – a line of stiff-shouldered earls no taller than a boy's hand, two score duchesses with raised noses and milky white décolletage, dozens of delicate horses poised on rear hooves and fifty milkmaids with coy smiles.

In a dark corner, two figures were nestled on a heap of sacking. Tom Bedlam placed his hand on the warm, pink breast of Sissy Grimes.

'Tom,' she murmured in warning, but the boy smiled innocently. She was a pretty creature. She worked in the sunlit studios where the glazing was done. Sissy's job was to paint the identical smiles on the lips of the milkmaids – perfect copies of her own tempting and elusive pout. But when his hand strayed below her waist, Sissy's body went taut, and suddenly she slapped him, not once but three times.

'I love you, Sissy,' he said, gasping.

But she was already fastening her buttons, her fine eyebrows knitted together and her own milkmaid mouth firmly set. 'Love!' she muttered.

'Honest,' he added. But her head tossed sceptically, and her elbow almost knocked the shelf that supported the porcelain earls.

'Take care, Sissy.' Tom gasped, fearful that, if one piece fell, the whole row would shatter and Todderman would have his skin.

'*You'd* best be careful, Tom Bedlam!' Sissy's eyes bored into him. 'You're only a boy.'

'But I *do* love you,' he replied, perhaps with more emotion than he meant, in defiance of that increasingly unkind stare of hers.

'Love.' Her scepticism reappeared. 'A man who loved me would get me away from here,' she declared, indicating with a glance the dusty timbers of the cellar and everything above, including the smokestacks.

'I'm going to marry you,' he vowed.

'Oh, Tom.' She sighed, tied up her hair, then shook her head at him. 'If I married you, I'd be stuck here forever. I don't want to turn out like your mother.'

Tom might have defended his mother if Brandy's uneven footsteps hadn't approached. He snatched a basket of figurines while Sissy busied herself by spreading the other items on the shelves.

'Gone deaf, Tom Bedlam?' muttered Brandy, his deep breaths enough to make the little salt and pepper shakers tremble. Then he noticed Sissy. 'What are you doing down here with *her*?'

'See here, Brandy, you'll upset the whole works,' chided the boy as the cripple glared at him. 'Sissy was helping me bring some pieces up to the glazers. A dozen milkmaids. Now you watch – one breath in the wrong direction and there'll be nothing standing. What'll Mr Todderman say then, eh?'

The cripple stopped breathing; with hands raised, he tried to turn around, but his hip grazed one shelf, and a small puppy dog rocked. Tom caught it before it fell, and Brandy groaned.

'No harm done, Brandy; lucky I was here,' he scolded. Sissy slipped up the far stairs without a backwards glance.

After Tom took the basket to the glazers, Brandy gave him his next task. 'The master wants you to deliver an invoice to Belgrave Square. And on your way, Tom,' he added, softening his tone as he tossed the boy a coin, 'get us some t'baccy.'

Tom loved the distant errands. On those rare moments when the weather and his duties collaborated, he slipped into the more genteel crowds – gentlemen in their top hats and day coats, women in gaily coloured frocks and bonnets – and imagined himself a man of leisure with money in his pocket to spend as he pleased. For a moment he forgot his oversize shoes, oily black breeches, woollen shirt, threadbare cap, and the grimy canvas bag slung over his bony shoulders that contained one invoice from Todderman & Sons Porcelain & Statuary. That was, until he brushed against a barrister in a handsome black morning coat, who took offence and swiped at Tom's ear with the ball of his fist.

After delivering the invoice to the gentleman on Belgrave Square, Tom remembered Brandy's demand. He decided to go out of his way, across St James's Park, to a shop on the river near the shipping companies where Virginia tobacco was sold and where, coincidentally, there was always a crowd and a show to be seen.

Today, a man with a deep voice and a small body stood upon a wooden crate, pamphlets in one hand, Bible in the other, and predicted the '*end of the world two weeks hence!*' His name was Paddy Pendleton, and his face might have been carved from granite, full-lipped, with deep-set eyes and a big puss's nose and whiskers. When the Bible became too heavy, Mr Pendleton would take hat in hand, flick back his mane, and temper his tirade to make a plea for pennies for orphaned children. Once an adequate sum for a meat pie and a pint of ale had gathered in his hat, it would return to his head, the Bible would rise, and the subject would return to the darker matter of Armageddon.

The next act that caught Tom's attention was a new one. A sizable throng gathered around a rope stretched between two lampposts while a figure in a white dress and parasol attempted to cross from the first to the second post. The performer's jerky, exaggerated movements seemed futile at first, but it became obvious to Tom that this was a comic performance intended to provoke laughter and derision.

Two strangers to the event spoke behind the boy.

'Good heavens, is that a lady?'

'Only if I'm a lady too,' said the other with a laugh, noting that the 'lady' had very broad shoulders and hairy fingers.

The figure now executed a backward somersault and landed back on the rope, petticoats tumbling. The bonnet fell to the crowd, revealing the acrobat's face – a swell of silver-white hair tied back in a ponytail and a familiar nose.

'It's a bloke!' cried a sailor to one of his companions. Rude laughter burst from the group.

Tom worked his way through the crowd until he was close enough to examine the fellow in petticoats in closer detail.

It was unmistakably the face from the broadsheet on his wall. The man executed three somersaults on the wire and displayed enough dexterity to earn applause and a generous offering of coins. But instead of playing kings and princes, Tom's father was reduced to playing the fool.

Whatever elation Tom felt at seeing his father was muted by disappointment; quietly, he eased himself away through the crowd, hiding his face for fear of being recognized by the performer.

MRS BEDLAM'S NEW CONDITION

It happened one cold spring morning. The sun had lost its jaundiced hue as a fresh wind blew across the courtyard of Todderman's factory. Emily Bedlam was walking with Tom towards the yawning factory doors when Mr Todderman greeted her from his place on the parapet.

'Good morning, Mrs Bedlam!'

'*Up yours*, Mr Todderman' came the reply.

Todderman blinked at her. 'Beg pardon, Mrs Bedlam?'

Mrs Bedlam responded with her familiar smile, gentle and kind as ever. 'Why, I said *God bless*, Mr Todderman, just as I always do!'

Surprised, Tom looked at his mother, but she showed no change in expression, no indication of malice or anger. Perhaps the wind had changed the sound of her voice.

But when they walked through the glazing workshops, it happened again.

'*Up your arse*, Mrs Mudd,' cooed his mother.

Putting her meaty fists to her waist, Mrs Mudd growled, '*What did you say to me?*'

But Mrs Bedlam had the same good-hearted look on her face. 'Just what I always say, God bless and keep you, dear!'

Baffled by this curious exchange, the woman didn't know whether to believe her own ears or the pious figure before her.

Tom left his mother at the pottery bench, feeling a peculiar sense that justice had finally been done.

The news travelled quickly through the factory. All day, Mrs Bedlam was uttering the most shocking greetings, and yet she seemed unaware of it. And when challenged with her own words, she replied with such innocence, and even indignation, that her inquisitors backed down. There was no doubting Mrs Bedlam's goodness – for many years they had mocked her for turning the other cheek, ridiculed her innocence, and mimicked her kind words. This was either the devil's work or the sweet revenge of an addled mind. Her victims could respond with shock or pity, but it was impossible to think ill of the poor creature.

'Have you any idea what you're saying?' Tom asked her that night.

'I'm not saying anything that I don't usually say,' his mother replied. 'I only mean goodwill; surely people can see that!'

For the next week, a series of increasingly astonishing epithets poured out of Mrs Bedlam's mouth whenever she greeted people who had betrayed her. It was as if her brain had decided to mete out the justice her decency would not. Her greetings to friends were as sweet as ever, but when she met any souls who had wronged her, her greetings were delivered in the foulest language.

On three successive days she called Mr Todderman a flesh barnacle, a cankerworm and a dog-hearted scoundrel.

Fearing that he would be a laughing stock in front of his employees, Todderman chose not to address her at all, but when he made the mistake of meeting her eye as she passed him in the hall, she curtsied. 'Ah, Mr Todderman, *may the devil brand your backside with the face of your wife*!'

He'd have fired her on the spot, but she did such fine work, and for so little wages – the abuse he suffered was worth it.

When Mrs Mudd realized that all of the other women were laughing to hear her abused, she confronted Mrs Bedlam. 'Listen here,' she said, '*I never said nothing behind your back!*'

'Oh, Mrs Mudd,' said Mrs Bedlam sweetly, '*if your mouth isn't opening and closing all day, then the hole between your legs is!*'

These words spread through the pottery workshops, the glazing rooms, the kilns and furnaces, and eventually spilled up and down

Procession Street. Suddenly, it was Mrs Mudd who was leered at by strangers, while Emily Bedlam was treated as an oracle. Folk asked for her opinion on the honesty of their neighbours, their doctors and grocers, and Emily issued unvarnished replies, though moments later she couldn't remember a word of what she said.

Finally, however, she made a tearful confession to her son: 'Tom, I'm afraid my mind is going,' she cried. 'My mouth says one thing while my head thinks another!'

'Nobody thinks ill of you,' he assured her.

'How can that be?'

'Well, on account of it being only certain people,' he said. 'People who *deserve* it. Brandy told me it was *God* talking through you, telling people what they deserve to hear.'

His mother looked horrified. 'God would *never* say such things! It's awful what's happening to me, and I don't know what to do!'

Tom didn't know either, but he feared a dreadful irony: that the true sign of his mother's encroaching insanity was that she was finally speaking her mind.

HE SETTLED HIS MOTHER in bed one evening with assurances that it would pass. It felt strange to be giving her advice for a change, and Tom wondered what he would do without her if indeed her mind was going. The image of Bill Bedlam earning pennies for walking a tightrope in petticoats was not reassuring.

Then Tom remembered Sissy's dismissive remark: *I don't want to end up like your mother, do I?* Both of his parents were spiralling down in their own miserable trajectories, and it frightened him.

Presently, his mother asked Tom to read to her.

Tom opened Genesis and read, 'Now Adam knew Eve his wife, and she conceived and bore Cain.' He paused, hearing the Limpkin children. They were running up the stairs emitting high shrieks and joyous giggles.

'I wish I had a brother,' Tom remarked.

'You had one, Tom,' his mother replied softly. 'An older brother, but he died at birth,' she added.

'What?' Tom replied, surprised.

'I didn't say anything,' Emily answered, her face becoming fearful that she'd uttered another blasphemy.

'You said I'd had a brother.'

Mrs Bedlam denied it, drew up a blanket around her shoulders, and directed him to put a chunk of coal in the potbellied stove.

The next day at work, Tom recalled his mother's remark. Perhaps, if he put the question to her again, her new 'condition' might yield more answers.

He waited until she was settled in bed the following evening. When she seemed tired but coherent, he rephrased his question. 'Mama, tell me about when you married Mr Bedlam.'

'Oh, Tom, we hadn't an easy life. My father wouldn't permit me to marry Mr Bedlam even though I loved him. He said he had a "weak character".'

She paused to savour those words.

'Actually, Tom, his character was worse than "weak", but I was as stubborn in my way as my father. He was a brewer by trade, and very successful. Success makes some men believe they know everything. They will not let others make mistakes that *have* to be made. My father warned me that Mr Bedlam had no capacity for work, and if I married him, it would be without parental blessing, and support.'

This prompted Tom to wonder if his mother would disapprove of Sissy, and what she would do about such a marriage. Then it occurred to him that the matter was irrelevant as Sissy already disapproved of Tom as a husband.

'But you married him?'

His mother nodded. 'From that day on I never spoke to my family. Bill and I made our way through that first year living all over London, scraping by so he could do his theatre acting, and I eventually found work at the factory, you see, because I had a gift for shaping clay. So, your father performed, and a newspaper printed that he was one of the best young actors in London, and he carried that article around in his pocket until it fell to pieces from being quoted.' She sighed. 'As though a piece of paper granted him privileges – the right to be idle, to wait for reward, success and his rightful place on the stage – but it didn't, you know. It was all just talk.'

'When was my brother born?'

His mother blinked at Tom. 'Why, Tom, you have no brother. Whatever gave you that idea?'

THE TRUTH HAD TO BE teased out slowly. Emily Bedlam's pride and decency were entwined so tightly with the circumstances of her marriage to Bill Bedlam that she would allow only a portion of her story to escape on any particular evening. But Tom persisted, and over a succession of nights, the following story emerged:

'One day, Tom, I felt I was with child, and I told your father so, and he became very upset. He knew, you see, that we could go without meals and sleep in odd places as two but not as three. A baby needed a home and a father with steady work. He wasn't ready for that. He knew that his acting days were numbered, because how could *I* work with a baby to raise? He even went to my father for help!'

'And what did he say?' asked Tom.

'My father told him he would support the child only if Bill left me for good – you see, *that's* how much he hated the man: he'd rather see me disgraced, raising a single child alone, than support an idle man.

'So there we were,' Mrs Bedlam continued, 'with a baby due soon, and I'm working up until I feel the labour pains coming, and your father broods in silence in the corner of the room while the midwife fusses over me. It took your older brother a day and a half to be born – as if he wasn't sure about his future in this world. But when he arrived he was the most beautiful little thing, with a full head of brown hair and the sweetest little face, and eyes as bright and curious as two stars. And your father wouldn't touch him. I believe he looked at that baby and saw his career ended.'

Mrs Bedlam looked sadly at Tom. 'When a baby comes, everything changes, Tom. A man can't be selfish any more. He has a baby to protect, and a child's future to consider. There's no living day to day or week to week any more. A steady living was what we needed. I told him that, and your father greeted that medicine like a dose of tar water.' Mrs Bedlam sighed. 'Well, I'd been awake for two days minding my baby, and I was tired, Tom, so I fell asleep for almost a day.' Then she uttered a groan and wiped tears from her eyes.

'When I awoke, snow was falling on the windowsill. The room was cold, and the stove was dark. I knew the midwife must have been dismissed. Then I saw your father stamping the fresh snow off his boots. He'd been out, and when he saw me looking at him, he took my hand and told me how sorry he was, but the baby died. He'd been out to bury him.

'I thought I'd never get over it, you see, Tom, but your father showed it worse than me, for in a few months his hair had grey streaks, and by the next year, when you were expected, he was almost completely silver at the top.

'I thought it was his *regret*, you see, changing his hair, but' – she paused – 'then he went about his life as if nothing had happened.

'Two months before you were born, Tom, I saw your brother in a dream. He was a little boy, but I recognized him, for his eyes were the same, like two stars, and he said something strange to me. "Mama," he said, "keep the baby in your arms and never shut your eyes, don't sleep, until you're sure he's safe." '

'What did he mean?' asked Tom.

Mrs Bedlam shook her head. 'I don't know. But I forgot the dream, you see, until the day you arrived. When I saw your little face, Tom, all creased and wrinkled and your eyes opened, I *remembered.* And though your father begged me to sleep, I lay in bed with you in my arms, my eyes wide with worry.' She looked at Tom. 'I thought that, if I slept, you might perish like your brother.'

Here his mother stopped and asked for a drink of water, and Tom poured her a cup from a jug – it was one of Todderman's, with a Chinese design; the glaze had bubbled into a froth at the rim. He had sold it to Emily Bedlam for a quarter of its normal price and taken the money out of her wages.

'I held on to you,' she continued, 'and I did not sleep for three days until I simply couldn't keep my eyes open. And when I finally passed out, your brother appeared in my dreams again, and he cried to me to wake up. I opened my eyes, found myself alone. The window was open, the room was cold, but I could hear the cries of a baby – *your* cries, Tom. I went to the door and heard a fuss on the stairs.'

Mrs Bedlam described stepping out of her door to see all her neighbours peering over the banisters, watching Bill Bedlam, who was dressed in his greatcoat and holding his shrieking newborn.

'Where are you going, Bill?' she cried.

'Why, to find a doctor, of course. The baby is *sick*, Emily! *Terribly sick!*'

At this point there were interjections from the spinster, Mr Bottle and the Limpkins, arguing that the baby was hardly sick and that they'd never heard a newborn cry with such powerful lungs.

'Well, your father insisted you were dying,' said Mrs Bedlam. 'But I knew differently. I held out my arms for you, Tom. Your face was crimson, your little red hands shivering with cold. With the eyes of all the neighbours on him, your father handed you back to me, his face ashamed.'

Mrs Bedlam's expression darkened. 'I couldn't read his mind, Tom, I just knew that he had fearsome thoughts, and that my dream had saved you from a walk through the streets in the cold air. Who knows what might have happened to you then?' She shut her eyes to clear such thoughts from her head. 'I nursed you until you were quiet, and then your father left.'

'He left?'

'For good.'

'Why?'

'He said I didn't trust him, that I thought the worst of him. He said he was innocent.'

'Innocent of what?'

His mother's expression became cautious; her eyes avoided her son's persistent stare.

'I don't know why the room was cold, Tom. Or why the window was open, or why your father didn't wake me to feed his baby boy. I won't accuse any man of ill when I have no reason. I only know that I was woken by a dream, and your brother probably saved your life that night.'

His mother drifted off to sleep. Tom found himself stroking her forehead and wondering, if he mentioned this story in the morning, whether she would acknowledge a word of it.

THE NEXT MORNING they were trudging through the snow to Todderman's factory when Tom remembered his question. 'Did he have a name?'

'Who, Tom?' his mother replied.

'My brother – before he died.'

'You had no brother, Tom,' she replied. 'Whatever gave you that idea?' She seemed indignant, as if he had made an unkind remark. They paused at the threshold of the factory, kicking the snow from their shoes against an iron post.

Above, Tom noticed Mr Todderman's face duck from the parapet as soon as he recognized Mrs Bedlam.

Tom frowned and wondered whether his brother was in heaven looking down at his predicament. It was some consolation to have a sibling (if only in theory) to share the burden of his mother's madness and his father's desertion.

THE LIMPKINS

At some time we all covet a place in another family, or a respite from the darkness of our affairs. There were times when Tom wished his father had succeeded in stealing him from his mother's bedside, if only to deposit him in the care of the next-door neighbours.

The Limpkins led a cluttered, debt-ridden and astonishingly loud existence. Their children spilled out of the tenement half-dressed and barefoot, often filthy, and frequently hungry, yet they always seemed to be happy.

It was to young Oscar Limpkin that Tom confided his mother's story. Oscar was like a brother to him – they were the same age and bound by years of pretend games, jokes and a shared passion for fiction. Oscar fed Tom a secret supply of Dumas, Scott and Cervantes to relieve his biblical diet. They re-enacted sword fights in the stairwell, banished each other to lifetimes behind the bars of the banisters, and laid siege to the top floor, where the smell of the Witters' cooking was as vile as the sulphuric horrors of Hades. Oscar was an incorrigible romantic and a ham; he cast himself as all three musketeers, or Don Quixote de La Mancha, while Tom played the faithful consort or squire, or the surgeon who arrived in the nick of time to dress the hero's near-fatal wounds.

Oscar's younger sister Audrey was a compassionate girl who seemed always to be minding the Limpkin baby, a pink bundle called the Orfling.

His real name had been forgotten, but the nickname suited him. He had a bobbing head, enormous eyes, and a runny nose, and he was always being set down and forgotten – part orphan, part changeling. When he wasn't bleating from hunger or asleep, he was gazing at the chaos of the Limpkin household.

When Audrey could escape her duties, she played another swordsman in their games, which, as they grew older, became more complex. Oscar devised the rules of battle: there were mortal wounds, requiring a cure of love or religious transformation, and injuries, which resulted in a limb becoming inactive. Tom would narrate the sword fights between Audrey and Oscar, dispensing aid to both as they received competing wounds. Audrey began to insist on collapsing in Tom's arms; then she would beg for a kiss to bring her back from death's edge. Tom considered such demands inappropriate – Audrey was as innocent as Sissy was sophisticated, and as flat-chested as Sissy was voluptuous. Her nose was red and pointed – she was still so much a child.

'Please, Tom, one kiss and I shall live,' she would murmur breathlessly.

'But I haven't wounded you yet!' shouted Oscar. 'Tom, just bandage her up and get her back into battle!'

It was Oscar's rule that only a stab to the heart constituted victory. He used an old pan lid as a breastplate, which made him as invincible as Hercules – and insufferably confident. To balance the sides, Tom would coach Audrey. 'Look,' he said, 'you must stab him sideways, in the *armpit.* It's the shortest distance to his heart.' When Audrey struck her brother under the arm with her broom handle, Oscar issued a bloodcurdling howl that drew all the panicked neighbours into the stairwell and immediately embarked on an extended death scene, which required Tom to administer a lifesaving elixir, but only in short doses while Oscar dictated the distribution of his worldly possessions to an array of countesses and damsels (then staged a miraculous recovery). Afterwards they would wreak vengeance on the washing lines in the shabby courtyard until the toothless spinster squawked from her window, spitting a rain of curses upon them.

One evening, while his mother prepared dinner, Tom persuaded

Oscar and Audrey to re-enact the story of his own birth, with Audrey playing his mother, Oscar his father, and Tom the ghost of his brother. But the game offered no catharsis for him because Oscar spoiled the ending by attacking everybody with his sword instead of following the plot.

'Start again, Oscar!' insisted Tom. 'Audrey must rescue the baby first, or there's no point in the ghost warning her.'

'It's no fun if I can't kill someone,' Oscar protested. At this moment, Audrey, always the conciliator, gently suggested that Oscar take vengeance *after* he had handed over the baby.

'All right,' her brother conceded. 'I'll surrender the Orfling, but *then* I'll hack all the neighbours to pieces!'

The toothless spinster could be heard slamming her door shut in answer to this proposal.

Tom adored Mr and Mrs Limpkin. They were always hugging him and tousling his hair; he received more physical affection from them in one visit than his mother gave in a month. He overlooked their inability to dress or mind their children. They always mixed up the names of their little twin daughters, Elsie and Eloise, and it fell to Audrey to mediate the girls' squabbles and nurse their injuries, whether real or imagined. Mrs Limpkin was a tall, full-breasted woman, whose pale skin, red nose, and perpetually anguished demeanour reminded Tom of the cuddlesome white rabbits in wire cages at the street market. She never spoke harshly and went about making dinner with a twin anchored, like a lemur, to each of her feet.

Mr Limpkin, a clerk, was a long-boned fellow with a narrow face and saddlebags of skin beneath his eyes; an unkempt spray of grizzled hair shot wildly from his temples. When he wasn't joyously bouncing his children (and anybody else's) upon his knee, he spent his evenings poring over invoices on a small wooden desk while wringing a handkerchief into the most agonized contortions.

'Oh dear me, oh dear, dear me!' he would cry as Mrs Limpkin staggered about the kitchen.

'What is it, dear Mr Limpkin?' Mrs Limpkin cried, handing the Orfling to Audrey in time for him to spew a streak of sour milk across the poor girl's shoulder.

'We face a surfeit of creditors, my dear, and a paucity in our accounts receivable,' said Mr Limpkin, throwing his face into Mrs Limpkin's apron while the children around them wailed and the baby emitted an earsplitting shriek.

Tom and Oscar took refuge under the dinner table. 'I wish *my* father walked the trapeze,' Oscar whispered. 'Then I could join him, and leave everybody else at home.'

'It's not a trapeze,' Tom corrected. 'He wears petticoats while he walks the tightrope quite close to the ground, in fact.'

'How peculiar!' replied Oscar with delight.

'I don't think he's ever coming home again. And my brother is probably in heaven,' said Tom.

'How tragic!' replied Oscar. He envied the element of drama and secrecy in Tom's life as well as the peace and quiet of the Bedlam home. 'Perhaps we could change places,' he suggested, 'like Lucentio and Tranio, or something!'

When Tom was invited to dinner, Audrey took great pains to be seated beside him and kept offering him things from her plate, though he always declined. Audrey irritated Tom, but she also made him feel loved (as when she re-enacted the role of his mother in the stairwell) and ashamed of himself (with her dismayed expression when he refused her a healing kiss).

Poor Audrey smelled of sour milk – from the curdled white lumps hiccuped on her shoulder by the Orfling. If Oscar engaged Tom in a conversation, Audrey would whisper into his ear her plans, which included their marriage and twelve children (all girls).

Tom was fascinated by the love between Mr and Mrs Limpkin; it was a long-suffering, embracing, cuddly, messy alliance; and though financial ruin beckoned at the door, they were united against the world. Any rift in the Limpkin household was quickly mended by Mrs Limpkin's warm-breasted embrace.

By contrast, Mrs Bedlam's affection was offered rarely, her alliance with his father nonexistent, and the bond between husband, wife and son existed in name only.

Tom certainly couldn't be blamed for imagining his adoption by the

Limpkins. He also dreamed of being nestled with Sissy Grimes amid the potato sacks, his hand on her breast. Finally, he imagined bringing his brother back to life through some fantastic miracle, for he dearly needed someone with whom he could share the doubts, questions and riddles of his own existence.

THE LEMON TART

ALMOST A WEEK AFTER HIS MOTHER'S REVELATION, AUDREY LIMPKIN paid a visit across the landing to Tom's door. When he answered, she placed a gift in his hand with a timid smile.

'What's this?' he asked.

'Open it,' she replied.

Tom unwrapped the paper to find a small, homemade lemon tart. 'I don't want it,' he said.

Audrey's smile collapsed. 'Don't you?'

'They stunt your growth.'

The girl's eyebrows converged. 'They do not.'

'Oh yes,' said Tom. 'The queen ate them, and she's tiny.'

The effect of Tom's rejection was obvious: Audrey unravelled the pink ribbon she had placed in her hair and scratched at her shoulder, as if to remove a streak of baby vomit. 'I don't believe you,' she said defiantly.

'My father told me so.'

Audrey raised her chin. 'Have you ever eaten one?'

When Tom admitted he had not, she pounced on his reply. 'My dad eats them, and he's six feet tall.'

Tom was perplexed by this information.

'Taste it,' she said. Then, urgently, she pressed it into his hand. '*Please*, taste it!'

Tom raised the tart to his lips and took a bite. His face registered dismay. It was delicious – absolutely delicious, both sweet and sour – as was the realization that his father had denied him such a pleasure. He swallowed the rest of it rapidly.

Audrey watched as Tom picked every tiny crumb from his shirt and emptied the last morsels into his mouth. Then, she tempted him with another. 'But this time,' she said, 'I want something in return.'

'What?'

'A kiss,' she said. 'On the lips.'

He agreed.

She returned quickly with another wrapped tart. Tom took it, and Audrey raised her face to him, closing her eyes. Tom delivered payment and disappeared behind his door. Audrey stood quietly in the hall, savouring her reward. She licked her lips, as if to catch every lingering remnant of the kiss, and with ardent satisfaction, returned to her family.

THOUGH THE TART COST Tom only a peck on Audrey's mouth, it was now worth far more. The second one went into his pocket. He took it to work the next day, determined to exploit the pastry for its utmost potential.

'For you, Sissy, if you'll give me a kiss,' he said when they were alone together.

'Oh, Tom,' she cooed, 'there ain't nothing more delicious than lemon tart.'

She reached for it, and he drew back the treat, leading her behind the rows of coats and shawls hanging from pegs on the wall of the workshop. Soon they were in near darkness, concealed in the smells of other men and women, and wool dampened by the morning's rain. As Tom placed the tart in her hand, he felt her breath on his cheek.

Then, Sissy gave Tom a kiss no boy would forget. She pressed her lips to his, parted them slightly – simulating the kiss she had been given by an aggressive boy in the warehouse – pushed her tongue against Tom's in a probing circle; then, as quickly, she pulled back, leaving Tom with his eyes closed, and his loins throbbing. Her grey eyes glittered triumphantly as she assessed the desire she had provoked.

Tom leaned towards her for another kiss, but she pressed her hand to his chest with a ruthless smile. 'Bring me another tart.'

So, when Audrey Limpkin gave Tom another tart, he rewarded her with the kiss he had learned from Sissy Grimes.

'Oh, Tom.' She sighed with such ecstasy that he felt another throb in his loins, for Audrey had accepted the kiss in the very way he *wished* Sissy would, with a sigh that provoked him to smile foolishly for days afterwards. And Tom had given Audrey the kind of kiss that inspired a girl's heart to speed up while time – in fact, the whole world's chaotic spin – seemed to slow down to a breathlessly rapturous crawl.

It explained the whole riddle of life.

But after the fourth lemon tart, Sissy still refused to retire to the packing basement, with its dark recesses and soft bags of wood shavings. Why? Because her older sister was abandoned at the age of sixteen and expecting her second child.

Sissy had no intention of being another Mrs Bedlam.

BILL BEDLAM'S UNDOING

William Bedlam was at the mercy of the weather. On sunny days, large crowds gathered to see him walk the tightrope. And their generosity was as infectious as their laughter. He had noticed that more than half the crowd would toss him a few coins on a sunny day, while on overcast days they were far less generous. The show was the same; the performer, the danger and the talent were no less remarkable, so why the shallow pockets? Perhaps the damp cooled their generosity – or maybe it was the cost of coal. He knew better than to berate the crowd for this inconsistency; instead, he prayed for sun and made the best of those days when the heavens cooperated.

So after two weeks of rain, he was relieved to have a fine day in late February to perform. People spilled out of the shipping offices at lunchtime to gather around the wooden coffee stalls, baked-potato carts, and oyster vendors. They congregated on the wharves to absorb the scant radiance of a wintry sun, have a smoke or a pint of brew, or merely peer at the human parade – any reason was good enough to stop and stare.

As Bedlam set up his rope between two dock posts, he issued a nod to his neighbour, the doomsayer Paddy Pendleton. Bedlam then donned the grubby skirts of his wedding gown, parasol raised, bonnet secured, and tottered on the rope in merry imitation of an arthritic dowager.

The first and second performances were a tremendous success, the crowd alert, good-humoured and generous. But by the third, a new element was loose on the wharf – the prowlers, the pickpockets and their decoys. One fellow, with a mouthful of teeth and tobacco, and a ripe, rude lip, wearing a boatswain's whistle on a chain around his neck and a cap on his head, took position a few feet from the rope. His lieutenants radiated a short distance through the crowd, then gave him a nod.

As Bedlam performed one of his somersaults, the fellow rested one hand on the rope and yawned a stage yawn. 'Me muvva can do better than *that*, mate! . . . And she's *blind*!'

This provoked a scattering of laughter. Bedlam ignored it, but the boatswain, intent on his mission, waited for the next somersault and strummed the tightrope with his stick, causing Bedlam briefly to lose his balance.

Their eyes met.

'Oops!' remarked the boatswain with full-cheeked amusement.

Bedlam seemed to recognize the fellow. 'Ladies and gentlemen, I advise you all to check your pockets; it appears that an undesirable element is in our midst!'

This provoked a number of hands to seek their wallets and purses, and a few hands to retract – their owners suddenly gazing innocently upwards, perhaps in evocation of more heavenly virtues.

'You insult me, sir?' replied the boatswain.

'On the contrary, *you* insulted *me*, sir,' replied Bedlam. 'Perhaps you'd care to join me on the rope, unless of course, your *blind mother* is available!'

This provoked laughter, and a flash of malice appeared in the boatswain's eye. But before he could respond, Bedlam continued his act, calling to the crowd for objects to juggle. A woman offered a limp bouquet of forget-me-nots, a man presented his boot, but nothing more was offered, so Bedlam tiptoed across the rope and seized the boatswain's hat.

With laughter, the crowd grasped the irony of this gesture while the boatswain glowered, faced with a dilemma, for his mockery was now part of the show, which provided a fine distraction as his confederates proceeded with their darker purposes, though it was at the expense of his hat – or, shall we say, his *dignity* – spinning arcs through the air with the forget-me-nots and the boot, first clockwise, then in the reverse.

With a final flourish, Bedlam cast the forget-me-nots back to the woman, blowing her a kiss, then delivered the boot to the man. But the crowd was waiting to see what transpired between the boatswain and his antagonist: the former's visage now portended murder, and nothing excited a crowd more than that.

Bedlam spun the hat into the sky, caught it behind his waist, and kneeling on the tightrope, presented it to its owner with an open palm. It was a peaceful gesture. There were *aahs* of disappointment, and then his audience dispersed as Bedlam extended his own hat for coins.

'Here, *I've* got something for you,' murmured the boatswain, reaching up with his stick, which parted at the handle to reveal a knife.

Bedlam must have sensed a threat, because he attempted to stand on the tightrope. This may have saved his life – for the arc of the boatswain's blade was trained on his belly, but Bedlam moved back so swiftly that the assassin pierced his right calf instead, ripping a long, red seam from knee to anklebone, and Bedlam fell, swaddled in the now bloody bridal gown, while the boatswain dodged away.

ABOUT A MONTH LATER, Tom was sent to retrieve a small statuette of a shepherd boy. Todderman had ordered the item from France (where it was all the rage and thus worthy of urgent replication in Britain). After Tom had wrapped the parcel safely in wood shavings and sacking, he went looking for his father. He had decided that Bill Bedlam should know about his mother's perplexing condition. After completing several rounds of the performers, he recognized his father's neighbour, standing on a small wooden crate, doling out admonitions to passersby. Since Mr Paddy Pendleton had predicted that the *absolute end of the world* would occur a considerable while earlier, Tom stopped to inquire about the change of date.

Pendleton didn't miss a beat. 'My calculations were offset, dear boy,' he replied, 'by an increase in the faithful, a *blessed increase*, mark you. You may imagine my relief.' He extended his appeal to a lady in a grey dress with a bustle. 'And if you open your heart to the Saviour, madam, perhaps we can postpone the apocalypse, or alas, I fear we will be damned by June the third at the very latest,' he warned, slipping the pamphlets into a pocket and now holding out his upturned hat. '*Give, that God may see ye are merciful*, and withhold the mighty apocalypse that will take down our fair city like Sodom, Gomorrah and all the godless souls that lie within its unnatural walls!'

When Tom inquired after the tightrope artist, the colporteur lowered his pamphlets.

'Mr B-b-b-bedlam?' replied the robust fellow, displaying a startled frown. 'He succumbed, my boy, in a tragic accident!'

'Accident?' repeated Tom.

'It is one of the most grievous risks of public life – one's vulnerability to the wretched sinners of this city, the criminal and the murderous element!'

Pendleton placed his hand on his heart, adapting Mr Bedlam's fate to his own travails as a public orator. Meanwhile, Tom, whose own heart felt about to jump out of his chest, interrupted to urge the evangelist to explain what had happened to his father.

The details took an agonizing length of time to draw from Mr Pendleton, as pauses were required for him to hawk his pamphlets, press the gentry for donations, and remind passersby of the revised date of Doomsday. But the important facts were that Pendleton had helped Bedlam to a rooming house not far from the river. Since the hooligans accompanying the assassin had robbed Bedlam of his day's earnings, the services of a doctor were not to be found, though Mr Pendleton had eventually engaged a fellow in the tavern next door who claimed to be a dentist. Upon sight of Bedlam's bleeding leg, however, this fellow had passed out and, when revived with a few drams of whisky, proceeded to sew the cavity.

'For ten days – feverish, wretched, and consumed by pain – he tossed in his bed like Jonah in the stormy sea,' explained Pendleton, 'and when, in charity, I paid for the services of a *real* doctor, Mr Bedlam was advised that the damaged leg would be his undoing if he did not have it removed.' Pendleton shuddered, placing his hand on his heart in memory of the lost limb.

'So it was done. With a poker, they sealed the, eh, *matter*, and after several weeks, he rose, like Lazarus, to walk among men, due in no small part to my prayers, I'm sure.'

Until this moment, Tom had managed to contain himself, but this was too much. 'He is my father, Mr Pendleton. I beg you to tell me where he is now,' he cried.

'Cast out, my boy, just yesterday, for failure to pay board.' Pendleton sighed. 'The economics of recuperation are harsh indeed.'

'But how *could* he pay? Surely the landlord—'

'The landlord understands only *one thing*, lad. The beginning of the month and what comes with it. All else matters not.'

'What will he do now?' wondered Tom. 'How can I find him?'

Pendleton shook his head. 'A few months, my boy, is all we have left on this earth. It hardly matters what your father does. I urge you to pray for him, and for humanity!'

WHEN TOM TOLD his mother about his father, she said a prayer for him, and the matter might never have been discussed again. Oscar, however, sensed that something was up and pried the news out of Tom. The Limpkin boy couldn't resist a good story; in a matter of hours, the entire factory resonated with talk about the matter. Folk in the furnace room claimed to have seen Bedlam crawling the streets, still wearing the tattered and bloody bridal gown, begging with a tin cup. Others suggested that his career would surely be ruined and predicted his suicide.

Oscar Limpkin disputed this. 'He could still play pirates. Plenty of them had wooden legs!' he declared and conjured an image of Mr Bedlam sporting a new leg of carved ivory, with a knife, a compass and a shiny doubloon secreted in one of its many compartments.

Brandy told Tom that he was sure Mr Bedlam was in hot pursuit of the man who had stabbed him and that the other's leg would be taken in retribution for the loss of his own.

Mrs Bedlam would entertain none of these rumours. Tom noted that she included his father's health and salvation in her prayers that evening.

'Perhaps he's with family?' Tom proposed.

Mrs Bedlam shook her head. 'Your father was an orphan,' she said. 'No relations. A stray cat.'

Tom shivered. He and his mother were little more than strays themselves. 'And you have only a father?' he inquired.

Mrs Bedlam nodded. 'My mother died when I was young. And my father was so intolerant that I considered myself lucky not to have uncles, aunts and cousins who may have been blessed with his temperament.'

WHEN EMILY BEDLAM began to complain of headaches, Tom put aside his concern for his father. She started missing work once or twice a week and claimed that the slightest noise rang like a hammer against her skull. 'What is that din?' she would moan as a horse passed by.

She would huddle in a foetal position with a sheet wrapped around her head to block out light and sound. When her son arrived home in the evening, she resembled a turbaned apparition – cross-legged on the bed, silhouetted by the dying light of a blue sunset, her head swathed in linen.

One morning she tossed and turned, complaining of a ceaseless drumming sound. Tom could hear nothing until it occurred to him that his mother's heartbeat was probably the source of her torment. Mrs Limpkin visited, bringing soup and bread. Gently, she prepared Tom for the possibility that his mother was suffering from a disease of the brain.

When Mrs Bedlam could get out of bed, Tom would lead her to the factory. Friends and foes alike steered clear of her now, for she truly resembled a Delphic sibyl, a stick in one hand, the upper part of her face wrapped in linen, revealing only an odd, beatific smile. Once Tom settled her at her potter's bench, she worked on the clay, never missing her quota. She removed the linen from her eyes for the last details – the petulant smiles, delicate hands, lacework, and ruffled collars – then shrouded herself again to shape her next creation.

RUMOURS OF WILLIAM BEDLAM'S fate had one beneficial aspect; his status as husband and father was validated. With everybody talking about him, a taboo had been lifted. Tom, however, was filled with dread at the possibility of the man's exit from the world. Was he to be the only member of his family left alive?

Audrey often found him sitting alone with his legs dangling through the banister, eyes red and his shoulders low – a picture of sorrow. When she lavished her sympathies on him, offering him a kiss, Tom was disconsolate.

'I know it's much the same thing,' he confessed, 'having a father who's never home and not having a father at all – but it would feel so much worse if I knew he had gone for good.'

'Oh, Tom,' she cried, 'I wish we could adopt you; if Father didn't fret so about his accounts, I'm sure he would welcome you into our home, and Oscar would be glad of a friend, and I . . . well, I would make you lemon tarts every evening, and we could marry as soon as Father permitted it!'

Audrey's sweet remarks didn't allay Tom's fears, but they did assure him that he was loved. As for the future, Tom prepared himself for the likelihood that he would be an orphan before his fifteenth birthday.

AN INCIDENT CAUSED Tom to reconsider his plight. One day at the factory he observed Mr Todderman catch Brandy Oxmire having a t'baccy break on the roof. It astonished him to see the tiny man fly at Brandy like a harpy, striking about him with stinging blows from his own walking stick while the cripple whimpered but barely raised a hand to defend himself.

'Why did you let him abuse you?' Tom asked later. 'You're twice his size!'

Brandy shrugged. 'He's like a father to me, I s'pose. If I defended meself, I might hurt him. You can't hurt your *father*, can you now?'

Tom decided he was better off without any such figure in his life, then changed his mind again when he caught sight of Mr Limpkin sitting with Oscar on the tenement steps one evening. The gangly clerk was teaching Oscar the lyrics of a rude song out of his mother's earshot, and Oscar looked both shocked and thrilled by his father's confidence.

One evening Tom watched the Witters making their way to the top floor, Mr Witter's hand resting affectionately on his son's shoulder for support. It was another pleasure denied him by Mr Bedlam's strange fate.

Even Mr Todderman made a remark about Tom's father one day: 'Awful luck, your father has; one can only hope he doesn't darken the family door with it.'

When he had put his mother to bed (for that had become his ritual now), Tom watched the streets from the window for signs of William Bedlam's new incarnation. He imagined him as a ghostly phantom in a dark coat, bent on revenge for his lost leg and, alternately, as the buccaneer pictured by Oscar reeling about on a leg of pure ivory. In the mornings, when Todderman peered from the parapet at his minions, Tom half-wondered whether the factory owner was intent on scaring the man away too.

There was an odd exchange one brisk morning in April. Mrs Bedlam was sick, complaining about the pounding in her temples. Tom stayed at home to tend her. He had made her breakfast but found her asleep when he brought it to her. He peered out the window and saw Mr Todderman perched behind the red-brick parapet staring at an elderly man in a blue frock coat who stood on the opposite side of the street.

The man must have been about sixty, stocky, red-nosed, with a curly thicket of white hair bursting out from beneath a cream-coloured top hat. He wore fashionable striped grey trousers and shiny black shoes. His attention was fixed on the workers passing from the tenement into the gates of the factory; he examined each woman's face thoroughly, as if in search of someone. Todderman seemed to take offence at the man's scrutiny and barked an inquiry as to his intentions.

THE FACTORY COURTYARD carried sound with all the clarity of an amphitheatre. From Tom's window perch he could hear the man's sharp and dismissive reply. 'None of your business, sir!' Then a coach rattled by, and nothing could be heard for a moment, though the man clearly conveyed his disgust for the premises by sweeping his hand from the foundation stone up to the stain of smoke disappearing over the rooftops.

Todderman answered with a more provocative hand gesture.

The gentleman, however, ignored Todderman as more workers passed through the gates; his scrutiny remained devoted to the women, and he peered at each face with his hands poised at his sides, fingers spread, in preparation for some sort of appeal if the right one should pass by. None of Todderman's epithets could distract him from this task, and only when the courtyard was empty did the gentleman finally turn his attention back to the proprietor on the parapet.

He tipped his hat to Todderman with a bitter smile, and this time, his words rang out across the cobbled street. 'May you rot in hell, sir!' he cried.

A FEW DAYS LATER, spring announced its arrival with a weeklong torrent of rain. Todderman's factory roof sprang leaks in a myriad of places, and Tom was dispatched to stand buckets wherever water collected. He spent his days darting about the floors, from the sculpting benches to the glazing shops to the warehouse, emptying buckets out of the windows. He had never seen so much water. His mother started murmuring about Noah's flood, and it being the end of everything. Tom recalled Mr Pendleton's prediction and assured his mother that they had at least until June.

The deluge unsettled London's social order. Many citizens were forced out of inundated homes, and the homeless sought refuge in higher, more fashionable parts of the city. The rich complained about a flood of vagrants in their neighbourhoods, while the poor coped with the water itself.

The tenement building sprang its own leaks. The Witters complained of the ceaseless drips from their ceiling, but those at ground level endured the worst of it. The hole in the hall floor became a whirlpool until the basement filled. Clothes, furniture and other possessions were ruined by mildew. The water would not leave; it turned foul. Tenants retreated up the stairs and slept on the landings to escape the creeping mould. Tom and his mother could hear their downstairs neighbours chattering and complaining on the second-storey landing most evenings, their bedding spread about the steps, their laundry hung from the banisters. One fellow brought up his stove and cooked sausages outside the Limpkins' door.

When, after a week, the rain ceased, water still lingered in pools on the first floor, mould crept up the wallpaper in black streaks, and the smell of mildew seeped through every crack. The neighbours below inched their way up the stairs to escape it. Mrs Bedlam boiled nutmeg and cinnamon to drive the odour out of their little room. With his ear against the wainscoting, Tom slept in fear that the neighbours would eventually advance through his door.

Early one morning he heard a heavy step on the stairs that sounded like no neighbour he knew. It was matched by the cautious thump of a stick, or some other wooden support. After a lengthy pause, there was another step, and another thump. The isolation of each sound suggested a creature unused to stairs, perhaps even unused to walking, and this scared the boy; he had a suspicion, of course, that this was the visitor for whom he had been waiting.

All of a sudden, Tom feared for himself and his mother. If it was his father, what horrible form had he taken? And what would he steal *this* time?

Tom listened to the visitor ascend the first flight, then navigate the turn to the second. There followed a lengthy silence.

The boy rose to shake his mother awake, but she was not in her bed. It was then that he realized she was already up, standing in the darkness, listening. 'I hear him, Tom,' she whispered.

They peered at the glow of gaslight beneath the door. Suddenly, a single obstruction appeared – one foot, and one foot only. Tom's heart leaped into his throat; he fought to breathe, chest pounding, knuckles trembling, and he let out a cry.

'It's all right, Tom,' said his mother. 'I'll answer the door.'

GRATITUDE

'WHAT ARE YOU STARING AT?' BEDLAM ASKED MISERABLY. 'HAVEN'T you seen a man eat before?'

Tom conceded to himself that his father's mood was justified; Bedlam shivered beneath a blanket while his wet clothes warmed on a rack beside the potbellied stove. His eyes were hollow, fingers raw and trembling from the damp cold, and his white hair was matted, greasy and receding at the temples. How much of this was age or the ravages of his recent infirmity, Tom didn't know. But he couldn't take his eyes off the man.

'He's entitled to look at his father,' Mrs Bedlam replied.

Bedlam frowned. But the food was beginning to take effect, and he signalled the return of his sense of humour with a wink.

'Much obliged for this, Emily . . . Much obliged. Hadn't eaten in a week. You've saved my life, you have.'

He paused to relish the sensation of food in his belly, and then his eyes surveyed the room and arrived at Tom again.

'Look at 'im! So tall. Soon be as tall as me.' He presented the empty bowl to Mrs Bedlam for another helping, but she shook her head. 'The rest is our breakfast.'

Bedlam seemed about to get angry, but again, he caught Tom's eye and instead smiled wistfully. 'For what we've received, may the Lord make us truly thankful,' he murmured and winked again. 'Look at you,

Tom. Nimble too, I reckon. Think ye could walk the rope?' His eyes settled on his son in expectation of an answer.

But Mrs Bedlam interrupted. 'I won't have him do that.'

'It's work.'

'He's *got* work.'

'In a *factory*?' Bedlam sneered. 'What about the open air?'

'Honest, regular, dependable pay – even when it rains,' said Mrs Bedlam.

'Honest? What's more honest than risking your life, madam!' cried her husband. 'He'd be an artist of the tightrope. Not like regular folk. A performer, a presence on the stage, a master of balance and grace!' Bedlam began directing his pitch with full intensity at the boy. 'We're not land-bound, lad. We roam the clouds, we fly, we touch the angels!'

'You almost took room and board with the angels,' added Mrs Bedlam. 'What happened to those lofty aspirations of yours – the stage and so on?'

Bedlam's expression became haughty. 'The world's a stage, my dear. People *like* to see children on the tightrope. Big crowds. Big receipts. There's no telling what people would pay to see Tom—'

But Mrs Bedlam finished his sentence: '—fall. Because *that's* why they watch.'

Mr Bedlam's humour vanished, and cold fury appeared in his eyes. 'I never, *ever* fell, madam.'

Without reply, Mrs Bedlam looked at his knee, beneath which, braced by a leather harness, was a rough wooden peg. 'Tom will grow up to be a gentleman,' she said. 'Not a *beggar*.' Her expression was bitter, and directed squarely at her husband. Bedlam looked at Tom, who looked away, sensing the man's humiliation.

'Shame on you, Emily, for saying such a thing,' said Mr Bedlam. 'How dare you disgrace me before my protégé?'

'Your *protégé*? You deserted him. As a father, you're a disgrace; as a gentleman, you're a failure; as a husband, you're nothing but a burden!'

Mrs Bedlam had never spoken with such clarity before, and Tom was surprised. She pressed one hand to her head, as if to soothe a headache, but there was no mistaking the disgust on her face.

Rising from his chair, Bedlam whipped his clothing from the rack around the potbellied stove where it had been drying. He dressed himself without speaking and, once dressed, struck the floor with his wooden leg – it echoed loudly like a gavel in the small room, and he proceeded to argue in his own defence.

'Know this, Tom Bedlam: I am not the man she describes! There are two sides to every story. And one day, perhaps when you have a wife' – here he glared at Mrs Bedlam – 'and a son, you will understand. You will think kindly of your father. And, in spite of Mrs Bedlam's slings and arrows, mark my words, you will feel gratitude to me . . . *Gratitude.*'

This last word was delivered to his wife, but it seemed directed at the world at large.

The solemn echo of the wooden peg marked his departure. Down the stairs, *thump* by *thump*, it rang. Tom listened as the sound mingled with the other noises of London in the early morning – the cry of gulls, the clatter of wooden carts on the cobblestones, and the steady rhythm of horses pulling cabs, the calls of hawkers, tradesmen, and a wailing infant somewhere in the crowded tenement. Then the steam whistles of the factories of Vauxhall summoned the minions in a cacophonic blast, erasing his father's progress.

Mrs Bedlam collapsed on the bed, her reserves of energy and lucidity spent. She sent Tom to work that morning without her.

All day long, Tom heard his father intoning *gratitude.* The meaning, implicit in its repetition, was that he had misjudged his father.

'DO YOU EVER FIND, Oscar, that your parents see things in exact opposites?' Tom inquired later.

'All the time,' Oscar Limpkin declared. 'My mother says we're a happy lot, my father replies that we're miserable. That's why I'm getting a job.'

'A job?' Tom asked.

'Selling newspapers,' said Oscar. 'I shall bring the day's facts home and settle the matter of happiness once and for all,' he promised with a gleam in his eye. 'One day I shall be a reporter, Tom, and I shall know what goes on in London, from the finest mansions to the most depraved cellars. Then I shall expose the corrupt, free the oppressed and champion the truth!'

What was the truth about William Bedlam? Tom wondered. Some families lock up the liquor, or the savings; the Bedlams were miserly with the truth. In refusing to speak of her husband for the majority of Tom's life, Emily Bedlam had denied the boy his right to assess his father's character and measure himself against the man. The few details that Tom had teased from her as her mind became feeble merely perplexed him. Had his father really killed Tom's brother? Had there been a brother? Or was Tom simply the unfortunate product of two adults with equally flimsy grips on reality?

Emily Bedlam did not rise from her bed after Mr Bedlam's visit. Her illness took a turn for the worse, and Tom was spared such existential questions while he dealt with her care and worked the hours necessary to sustain their small household.

THE FURNACE

TOM GAINED SEVERAL INCHES IN THE SUBSEQUENT THREE MONTHS, and his voice dropped. Mr Todderman rewarded him with a new job, working in the furnaces, shovelling coal. In proportion to these changes, Tom's view of life contracted. As he was paid more, he began to understand the virtue of money, and the relative poverty of freedom. Wandering around London lost its appeal in comparison with feeding the eternal fires at Todderman & Sons Porcelain & Statuary. He shared the coarse jokes of his furnace mates, who talked about the pleasures that sustained them – drink, women, and more drink.

His mother's condition did not improve. Mrs Limpkin sat with her once in a while so that Tom could take a night off. Even the gap-toothed spinster took a turn at Emily's bedside.

Tom saw more of Sissy Grimes, whose perspective changed in kind; she still dreamed of leaving the factory, but she had to accept its one virtue: the newly strapping figure of Tom Bedlam.

As for poor Audrey Limpkin, she pined for Tom dearly, and her expressions of love became impossible for him to ignore. When he returned from work, his dark hair caked with coal dust, his skin fiery red and his boots grey with ash, she was always there to greet him. If he was late and the stairs were empty, he knew he would see her face peeping from the Limpkins' door as he stepped upon the landing. Her greetings were always giddy and sweet, and when she had coaxed from him a summary of his day, she would tell him of her own, minding the Orfling while Mrs Limpkin baked and sold her tarts to the workers at Todderman's.

'Tom, there's something wrong with the baby,' Audrey confessed one night. 'He hasn't grown in a year. He won't walk when other children his age are running, and he babbles while they talk – it's the strangest thing.'

'Is he eating?' asked Tom.

'Anything mashed.' She nodded. 'His teeth haven't come through, yet he's such a happy child, Tom. He never cries – he's a little joy, crawls around looking at things on the floor. Just the other day, when I was short of money at the grocer, he held out a sixpence. I don't know how many days he'd had it in his fist.'

'I'm sure he'll catch up,' Tom said. 'He has to *want* to walk, and speak. When he's ready, he will.'

Audrey smiled. 'You're going to be a doctor one day, Tom. You *think* like one.'

'Oh, Audrey.' Tom laughed. 'Doctors need an education; I'll be here forever.'

But Audrey's expression contradicted his despair; she looked at him as if surveying his mortal coil from beginning to end and saw only his potential. 'No,' she replied. 'I don't think so. I've a feeling you'll surprise yourself.'

The confidence of this remark belied his impression of Audrey as a weak, mousy girl. She was changing, and there was, in her spirit, a resilient flame. All at once she pressed her hand to her breast, then kissed her finger and touched it to his lips. 'I see you in far-off lands. A doctor, respected and admired, with lots of children of your own,' she said.

TENDING THE KILN FIRES for twelve hours a day had burnished Tom's taut muscles with sweat and coal dust. Though he strode home looking as filthy as the other stokers, his figure became tall without being beefy and his expression furtive. The job required no thought – hoisting up coal with a *hep* and a *haw*, and knocking the cast-iron doors shut with the butt of his shovel – a constant, mind-numbing repetition. Sometimes his mother heard the sound of his labour as he slept. Tom could tell when a furnace needed stoking just by holding up his palm to feel the heat emanating from the iron door. As his movements were confined to the furnace, his fantasies contracted. He could no more imagine himself being a doctor than he could hawking newspapers. He had rent to pay, a sick mother, and no money even for a doctor.

In the midst of this meagre lot, with his wings clipped and his dreams stunted, Tom turned to Sissy Grimes. On his day off, they would walk out together. She would link her fingers in his and touch him seductively. Their conversations, however, were never lewd. Sissy was thinking ahead.

'I see us in a little house, Tom, with pigeons cooing under the eaves.'

'What about in some far-off land?' suggested Tom.

'Oh no, Tom,' said Sissy. 'I could never be away from my sister and mother. Besides, they have awful diseases in those places.'

'Once I thought of being a doctor,' said Tom.

'Don't be silly,' Sissy replied, resting her hand on his firm shoulder. 'Doctors don't have muscles.'

As Sissy gauged her effect on him, Tom exercised considerable self-control. He desired her but feared her capricious nature. He dreamed of her white cheek against his and imagined himself entwined with her naked body. Sissy took advantage of his caution, tempting him with kisses from her flawless milkmaid's mouth; she presented herself to Tom as the only uncharted territory worth exploring and, by running her finger along the curve of her breast, caused him to tremble with lust.

One evening, below a pier, while the boatmen sang profane arias across the misty Thames, Tom and Sissy shared several bottles of ale and overcame their inhibitions upon a bed of crushed mussel shells. While they kissed, he worked feverishly to remove the many layers of her underwear until his fingers felt the round of her bottom. She sighed encouragingly as his hand rode her hip bone and descended to the warm mesh between her legs, but then she pushed Tom's hand away and sank her own fingers in place of his. Confused by his limited role, he watched as her breaths became quick and shrill, her back arched, and she suddenly uttered a long and satisfied sigh.

Realizing bleakly that he had served merely as the inspiration for her pleasure, he glared at her.

'Did you have fun, then?' he inquired.

Sissy's expression was defiant and unashamed. 'I've let no man touch me the way I let you, Tom. And you're not even my husband.'

'Here, then—' he said, steering her hand into his own breeches. 'I'll do you the same favour. I've let no woman touch me here either.'

Sissy balked, however. 'Goodness, Tom, it's like a piece of knotted rope you find on the beach. I won't have anything to do with it!'

'Then some wife you'll make,' he said bitterly.

Sissy lowered her skirts and started for home. Tom tagged miserably after her, wondering if the carnal pleasures he'd heard so much about in the furnace room were merely a cruel joke passed down from the old fellows to the young.

After he had seen Sissy home, he returned to his building, a little drunk and much disgusted. Audrey was on the second floor, her legs dangling through the banisters. She eyed him with a look of betrayal.

'You're late,' she remarked.

'Yes,' he said.

'A good time?' she inquired.

'Not really,' he confessed.

Audrey's face was a storm of jealousy. She struggled to keep her composure, then forced a remark she'd been practising all day long: 'That Sissy has a reputation. For your own good, I hope it wasn't her you wasted your time with.'

'What reputation is that?'

'Oh, what an awful creature she is. I've heard that she leads boys on with the most shameful performance.'

'Performance?' replied Tom sharply. 'Who says?'

'Well, my mother hears everything from the men *and* the women,' she answered. 'Apparently Mr Todderman has a nephew who is very interested in her, and she catches his eye when he passes her' – Audrey paused to be sure that he grasped the full implication of her account – 'by touching her own person suggestively. She's ambitious, Tom; and she might inherit Todderman's factory if her plan works.'

'Audrey!' Tom laughed. 'That's just talk!'

'Is it?' she replied. Then she traced her finger about the curve of her breast in mocking imitation of Sissy.

'I can't imagine she'd do that in broad daylight,' he replied weakly.

'Well, I've heard she's done worse when it's *not* broad daylight. She's an awful creature, Tom. I hope you have nothing to do with her!'

'You shouldn't be spreading stories,' he declared and disappeared into his room.

Racked with jealousy, poor Audrey kicked her feet against the stairs and stamped back to the hue and cry of the Limpkin household.

TOM FOUND HIS ROOM dark that evening. Ravenous, he consumed a bowl of cold porridge while he brooded over Sissy's ambition. He had no doubt that Audrey was right. He couldn't compete with Todderman's nephew.

A sound from the corner gave him a start.

His mother was talking in her bed.

Tom put his hand near her cheek; he felt the heat of a fever, like Todderman's furnace, a raging one.

He whispered to her. His mother turned her head, and though she stared directly at him, she showed no recognition. 'What of Tom's education?' she murmured.

'Mother,' he whispered several times; when this failed to rouse her, he tried addressing her as Mrs Bedlam, and finally Emily.

'Who is it?' she asked, looking around, though her head didn't move.

'It's Tom,' he replied.

'Tom?' she repeated curiously, as if his name came strangely to her lips.

'Your son.'

'My son? Turn your head!' she said suddenly.

Tom turned away, and she pointed to his neck.

'You're not my son. He had a little red spot below his left ear. Mr Bedlam took him from me and buried him. When I woke up, I saw the man stamping the snow from his boots, and then his hair turned white. White with sin. My poor little baby gone. My little baby. Just below his left ear, a little red spot.'

This repetition, and the unnatural glow in his mother's cheek, propelled the boy to seek help, not for her but for himself, for he felt the most selfish panic. Was he to be orphaned tonight?

Tom rapped on the Limpkins' door. Mrs Limpkin appeared and immediately sent Oscar out (in boots, nightshirt and Mr Limpkin's coat) to summon her cousin, a young doctor in Whitefriars. Audrey kept Tom company, patting his hand and whispering assurances. Mrs Limpkin put cold compresses over Mrs Bedlam's forehead in an attempt to bring down the fever.

'Try not to worry, Tom,' whispered Audrey.

'How can I?' he replied. 'She's talking madness. She has forgotten my name. She thinks I'm a stranger.'

'Perhaps it's the end, Tom,' Audrey said. Mrs Limpkin issued her daughter a shocked frown. But Tom nodded, sensing that she was right.

Audrey kept Tom company that night, and in the morning, the doctor examined Mrs Bedlam and declared that she had a swelling in her head.

For the next three days, Tom's mother lay in bed, sleeping for long spells, then waking in a state of delirium. She was blind now. Audrey took turns with the twins caring for her. Tom returned in the evenings only to find that his mother didn't know his name. The raging fire in her cheeks perplexed the boy, for it was the most colour he could remember her having, making her seem more alive than ever before, though it also seemed unnatural on her normally grey features.

'I saw my father this morning,' she said. 'He was standing across from the factory gates in his striped trousers, looking for me. He always looks for me.'

'Your father?' Tom asked.

'I was too proud.' She nodded. 'He begged me to leave Mr Bedlam. Couldn't. Stubborn.' She laughed weakly. 'Just like him. If I die . . .'

Her ramble ceased. 'Paper, Tom, and a pencil. *Fetch it for me!*'

She scribbled a note, folded it, and asked Tom to close it with sealing wax. The letter was addressed to Shears Brewery, a familiar location; Tom had seen the brewery carts driving past with that name painted on them. But the possibility that he was related to such a wealthy enterprise seemed too good to be true. 'You'll send this, Tom,' she said, 'if I pass away. This will get you your education. Do you understand?'

'Yes,' he replied.

'Put it in your coat pocket,' she said.

EARLY THAT MORNING, in the darkness, Tom heard his mother talking. Gibberish, it seemed at first. He rose, lit a candle and saw her eyes fixed blindly in space. 'He's not sick. Listen to him cry!' she insisted. 'Give him back to me!' she demanded, as if Tom were his father. Her hands stretched out to Tom, fingers quivering. 'Give him back to me!'

'Mama?'

'Give him back to me!' she wailed. *'Give him back!'*

Her pleas continued until Tom, now desperate to calm her, bundled his own coat into a shape resembling a small baby and offered it to her. 'Here he is,' he whispered.

Mrs Bedlam's stricken expression softened. 'My baby?' She clutched the bundle to her breast and then smiled briefly. But her face hardened, and she gave Tom a wretched stare. 'I'll never forgive you for killing my child! And when the time comes, I'll search heaven for him. Search every baby in heaven until I see him.' And here Mrs Bedlam pointed to the left side of her neck. 'I'll know him because of the spot, that little red spot. I'll find the poor abandoned creature!'

Then, with the bundle clasped tightly in her arms, she sank slowly into her bed, sobbing, and closed her eyes.

TOM CONSOLED HIMSELF by watching the rise and fall of her breast – assurance that she remained in his world. But he must have drifted off eventually, because the next thing he became aware of was a change in the colour of the room. The sun had not risen yet, but the walls were suffused with a cold blue light. His mother was still clutching the bundle, her eyes wide open, fixed on the window, the faintest smile on her lips.

Tom approached her bedside. He gently removed the bundle from her grip and, with trembling fingers, pressed her lids closed.

He ached in silence. He had expected tears to come, but none did. Of course he loved her, but for as long as he could remember he had borne the duties not just of son but of confidant, companion, advocate, nurse and defender. With the burden of those responsibilities lifted, Tom felt a pang of relief – and, with it, the tears fell.

He rose, dressed, shook the bundle until it became his coat again, and set out. He walked the empty Vauxhall streets as the sun rose, wearing his new circumstances like a fresh set of clothing. He wept as he walked, consoled himself and wept again.

As he passed the great gates of a brewery, Tom recognized the name: *Shears*. Recalling the note his mother had written, he retrieved it from his pocket and placed it under the wooden gates.

There, he thought. I've done my last errand for her. Tomorrow I shall be responsible only for myself.

He found enough money in Emily Bedlam's Bible to pay for her burial. The matter was resolved swiftly. She was buried in a cheap plot. The Limpkins attended, with Oscar speaking in place of a clergyman because none could be found. Sissy did not appear, but many of the women from the pottery benches came, including Mrs Mudd, who apparently wished to make sure that her verbal tormentor was gone for good. Mr Todderman sent Brandy Oxmire with a beautiful piece of white granite to mark Mrs Bedlam's grave.

The following day, Tom returned to work in the furnace room. Mr Todderman assured Tom that he would keep his job, and explained that the headstone was not a gift but an item to be paid for in instalments over the next two years. It was then that Tom realized his employment was secure for as long as he owed a debt to Mr Todderman.

TOM VISITED SISSY in the glazing workshop, but she would not look him in the eye. Her skin was as pale as porcelain. Shame suited her beauty.

'What d'you want?' she said finally.

'I didn't see you yesterday at the funeral.'

'I warn't invited,' she replied.

'Everyone was invited.'

'I hate funerals,' she replied, pursing her lips.

Tom was hurt, but she was a delicate creature, he decided, and perhaps the ceremony would have been just too much for her to bear. He vowed to work as hard as he could to pay back the money for the headstone so that he might save for a wedding befitting his sweetheart.

That evening Tom returned to the tenement building to find Audrey on the landing, with her ear pressed to his door.

'Tom,' she whispered. 'I believe your father's waiting for you inside.'

'My father?'

'He has been arguing with a stranger this last hour.'

'About what?'

'*You*, Tom!' Audrey replied urgently. 'I believe this other man is your benefactor. Perhaps this is your chance for an education.' She smiled. 'Know what you want, Tom, and ask for it.'

MR SHEARS

WILLIAM BEDLAM GREETED TOM WITH A MERRY AND ASSERTIVE CRY. 'There he is, my son, my heir! My dear boy, what a tragedy! What a sadness! Oh, you poor lad! Your *poor* mother! An *unfortunate* creature! A *fine* woman, a *good* woman, pious and dedicated and, oh, the *tragedy*!'

Before Tom could reply, Bedlam staggered towards him and half-fell into his arms in what was meant to be a consoling embrace. 'It's true, blood *is* thicker than water! What joineth here let no man cast asunder!' Bedlam began to sob upon Tom's shoulder.

Unmoved by the man's dramatic display, Tom's other visitor regarded his father with narrowed eyes and openmouthed derision. Each time Bedlam uttered another remark, the elderly man's mouth would open again, as if he couldn't believe the performance.

'I am Horace Shears,' he said, extending his hand to Tom.

'Poor Tom,' Bedlam interjected, 'you wouldn't know yer own grandfather from Adam.'

Shears glared at Bedlam. 'I am hardly more of a stranger than *you* are, sir!' He turned back to Tom. 'I am your mother's father, Tom, your grandfather and, regrettably, this man's father-in-law!'

'What can I do for you, sir?' Tom replied.

'It is what *I* can do for you, Tom, that matters!'

The man's clothing was familiar – a blue frock coat, striped grey trousers, and shiny black shoes – this was the man Tom had seen shouting to Mr Todderman at the factory gates. Mr Shears slipped his thumbs into a pair of worn leather braces – the only part of his outfit that seemed incongruous and workmanlike. Some men who rise in station or income will cling to some vestige of their former status. The braces reminded Tom of his mates in the furnace room. Shears's curly white hair hung thinly about his scalp; he must have been at least twenty years older than Bedlam, and his face was pugnacious, with a broken nose and a short forehead.

Bedlam leaned towards Tom. 'Yes, indeed! It's what *he* can do for you!' he echoed, which caused Shears to sneer at him.

Bedlam's smile faded.

'Well, my boy,' said Shears. 'I promised your mother many years ago – when she first took up with this man – that if she were to quit his company, I would take care of her and any child she might have.' He paused and clasped his hands. 'A stubborn girl, she refused my advice. I don't blame her none. I'm stubborn, myself.'

Bedlam sniffed, as if that wasn't the half of it.

'But my Emily soon learned that Mr Bedlam was as fine a breadwinner as he was a devoted husband!' Shears continued. '*Pride*, my boy! *Pride* prevented her from asking my help.' He dabbed his shiny forehead with a handkerchief and ran his thumb up and down one of his leather braces. 'Now I am without a daughter and you are motherless.'

Here Shears paused and put his hand tenderly upon Tom's shoulder. Bedlam grasped the other shoulder. 'There, there, Tom,' he muttered.

'You are my only grandson, Tom,' Shears continued, his voice becoming thick and muddy, 'and I have the assets to secure a decent future for you. It is my wish to provide you with the education you will require to go forth as a gentleman someday.'

Tom thanked him, and Bedlam immediately interjected with a point of his own: 'As I was saying to Mr Shears, before you arrived, Tom. I am your guardian, and as such, Mr Shears should address his intentions to me. And all finances—'

Shears bared his teeth at Bedlam with exasperation. 'You, sir, merely wish to skim money from the gift horse!'

Bedlam turned indignant. 'How *dare* you, sir? How dare you trespass and make accusations?'

'I'm offering the boy an education, which you have denied him with your foolish pursuits! You'll have no money from me!'

The two went at each other while Tom recalled Audrey's advice. When a brief pause stilled their volley, he spoke up. 'I accept your offer, sir!'

Both men turned to him with surprise.

'Well then.' Shears nodded. 'So be it, Tom. I shall make the arrangements.' He reached out to the boy and patted him gently upon the neck – as a man might caress a horse. Then, pleased to be done with Mr Bedlam, Shears bade him a quick goodbye.

Bedlam turned to Tom, frowning. 'Astounding! A stranger walks into a boy's life and claims kinship!' He cocked an eye at his son. 'I don't blame you, Tom, for accepting his terms, but the arrogance of the man!'

Now Bedlam rubbed his hands and took the vacated seat.

'Look, all I meant to say was that I wanted the best for you. Before I spoke to him, Mr Shears wouldn't have considered your education. He'd have had you working for him at the brewery for the rest of your life.'

'Really?' Tom wondered how a brewer's work compared with shovelling coal – almost any prospect seemed an improvement on that.

Bedlam nodded. 'Fortunately, I was here to argue on your behalf, Tom. You'll get a fine schooling, and all I ask is a little gratitude.'

'Then I thank you, sir,' Tom replied.

His father assumed a frown and dismissed his son's reply with a regal wave. 'Don't mention it!'

TO HAMMER HALL

A SCHOOL WAS RECOMMENDED TO MR SHEARS, AND ARRANGEMENTS were made for Tom's enrolment in time for the new term. His grandfather issued Tom a generous stipend for clothing and books, which Mr Bedlam claimed, warning Tom that the city was full of criminals and such a large amount of money required safekeeping. Father and son spent a day shopping together, with Tom expressing his preferences and Mr Bedlam suggesting cheaper alternatives. By the end of the day, Tom had several parcels to carry and noticed that his father had accumulated a few of his own.

Mr Shears settled his grandson's debt to Mr Todderman for the headstone. Tom was amazed that a two-year obligation could be wiped out with a piece of paper and a handshake. Afterwards, his grandfather took him to dinner at a fine restaurant where waiters served wide platters of partridge and lobster, leg of lamb and quail. Tom had his first cut of mutton, which was so rich (for a boy accustomed to porridge at breakfast, dinner and supper) that he was kept awake all night by his busy stomach.

Their conversation was cautious; Mr Shears said very little. Tom's few comments seemed to remind the man of his daughter, and every few moments he would pause to wipe his face with his handkerchief.

'I have arranged for a coach to take you to Hammer Hall – that is your school,' he informed his grandson. 'Your father seems to wish to accompany you. I had planned to do so myself, but I cannot bear the man's company and will, instead, visit at a later date.'

'I shall look forward to it, sir.'

Mr Shears squinted at him. 'Will you, Tom? I am a stranger to you, but I promise we will be good friends before long. I'm not your father, but I shall assume his responsibilities, his debts and obligations. You and I are bound by flesh and blood, my lad!'

Mr Shears slapped his knees in anticipation of their new relationship.

'Thank you, Mr Shears,' Tom replied.

'Don't call me that, boy! It's a name for strangers.'

'What should I call you, sir?'

'Grandfather!' He laughed. 'How's that?'

TOM SAID GOODBYE to Sissy in the factory courtyard as the workers' shifts changed. Above them Mr Todderman sat, flanked by Brandy, pipe in mouth, releasing small white puffs of smoke that rose in stark contrast to the great billowing darkness emanating from the chimneys some thirty feet above.

'Perhaps after your eddication, Tom, you'll come back and buy the factory,' Sissy whispered, 'and I'll be your wife.'

'Perhaps.' He smiled.

'I'll be waiting for you, Tom,' she warned, her eyes lingering on him with wounded grace. 'Don't forget me.'

'I could never forget you, Sissy,' he promised.

And he meant it. Her grey eyes and petulant milkmaid's mouth would haunt him for years.

Tom received smothering embraces from Mr and Mrs Limpkin, and a tender one from Audrey, while the Orfling drooled on her shoulder.

'I shall write to you, constantly, Tom,' Audrey promised, 'and when you next see me, I shall be much, *much* older!'

This ardent promise seemed, to Tom, a request that he consider her affection more seriously in the future. 'I'm sure of it, Audrey,' he said with a laugh.

Oscar presented Tom with a rolled up magazine. 'It's *Ally Sloper*,' he explained. 'It's very funny, we pass it about – me and the other newsboys. It's full of drunkenness and bad behaviour!' He seized Tom's hand and frowned. 'Remember, Tom, anyone who crosses you will have Oscar Limpkin as his enemy!'

Tom made the same oath, then left the Limpkins with a heavy heart to board his coach.

ON A SEPTEMBER MORNING, as a light rain fell, Tom left Vauxhall. His father escorted him on the train and arranged for their transfer to a public coach when they reached Millington. As they waited for their departure, Bedlam ordered a roasted chicken for himself and a small, cold meat pie for Tom. Since his father was unable to carry the trunk because of his wooden leg, it fell to Tom to help the driver hoist it up on the coach. Bedlam made many apologies for his infirmity but used it artfully to secure himself a window seat, as well as the right to first exit and entry when the coach stopped. His clothes had improved: he sported a clean linen shirt and a yellow waistcoat beneath his dark woollen coat. It occurred to Tom that he had made these purchases while they were shopping the other day.

'Did Mr Shears buy you those clothes?'

Bedlam laughed uneasily. 'Mr Shears wouldn't buy me a button!'

Considering his father's abashed smile, Tom felt his guess had been confirmed, and he concealed his dismay by looking out the window.

In spite of the buffeting along a rough road, Mr Bedlam fell asleep almost immediately. Tom tried to doze but was knocked awake by the coach's every lurch. He marvelled at the quiet of the countryside, the gentle pastures, blackberry bushes and beech trees that dominated the terrain. Though he looked for pavements, streetlamps, letter boxes, pillars and posts, for some time there wasn't a man-made object to be seen in any direction, and this concerned Tom, until he was reassured by the appearance of a stone bridge.

In a town composed of a crossroads, a tavern, and a small church whose mossy graveyard contained some ten stones, they left the coach and hired a man with a horse cart to take them the last few miles of the journey. Tom saw a farm with a straw-thatched house and a meadow with scattered sheep – the sort of place his mother might have imagined for their future. He cast Bedlam a glance, remembering the Bible and his father's assault on their savings.

Bedlam answered Tom's stare with raised eyebrows but no words.

At a fork in the road, the driver turned to the right and, at the bottom of a hill, slowed the cart to speak to a boy of eight, perched on a stile. One of the boy's eyes seemed loose and peered at the horses' hooves, while the other addressed the driver. He spoke in a slang Tom could barely understand. But his words must have been authoritative, because the driver turned the cart around in a pasture and went back to the fork, whereupon he took the other turn.

'Not far to go, lad, not far,' Bedlam remarked. The day had grown overcast, and the emerging terrain had become flat and treeless. A mile to the west, a wooded mountain lay shrouded in mist. When Bedlam repeated his previous assurance, Tom felt troubled. Though he was beyond reach of the billowing filth of Todderman's smokestacks, the blackened brick walls, the noisy streets, and the stench of the offal house, such things had the benefit of being familiar. He looked at his father again and wondered why he had accompanied him – they had shared very few words on the journey.

Bedlam must have sensed his son's lack of ease, for he spoke. 'Do you have a question, my boy?'

As Tom attempted to compose his query in a way that would not seem impertinent, his father ventured an answer. 'Never judge a man until you've borne his troubles on your shoulders, Tom.'

'I do not judge you, sir.'

Bedlam blew air through his lips sceptically. 'Whatever your mother told you was a lie. Let's begin there, shall we? The woman rarely spoke the truth.'

Tom's face flushed. 'You've no right to speak of the dead in that way,' he cried. 'How dare you?'

Bedlam turned in his seat and folded his arms, momentarily chastened. 'Oh, and how would *you* speak of her?' he inquired.

'She fed me, taught me to read, nursed me as a loving parent,' he replied.

Bedlam rolled his eyes. 'One day, my boy, if not now, you'll have dreams, ambitions, a calling, and when children appear, you'll understand what a sacrifice it is to care for 'em. You've no idea!'

'Neither have you!' Tom retorted.

Bedlam chewed his lip before composing a reply. 'I knew that Mrs Bedlam and I weren't ready for it. Too young, we were. Too innocent. Too foolish.'

'Well, that cannot justify murder.'

'Murder?' Bedlam looked offended. 'Who said anything about murder?'

'My brother,' Tom continued. 'Dead and buried at your hand.'

The driver edged away from Bedlam and cracked his whip at the horses.

Bedlam recoiled as if stung. 'She told you *that*? *That's* what she told you?' The man seemed sincerely disheartened by Tom's acknowledgment. 'All these years, she told you *that*?'

Tom related his mother's description of waking up to open windows and a chilled room, and the sight of Mr Bedlam dusting the snow from his boots.

His father fell silent, as if weighing two dark and burdensome choices. The driver cast him a glance, anxious to hear the result.

'Whatever else you think of me, Tom,' he said finally, 'I am no murderer. I'm sure your brother is alive and well. He was given up for adoption, with whom I do not know, but I left him in safe hands.'

For a moment, Tom was elated. The thought of such a possibility thrilled him. To have a confidant, a kindred spirit who shared his name, likeness, and perhaps even a similar perspective on his father's dubious character! Then, he reconsidered the messenger, and his smile faded.

Bedlam put his hand to his heart. 'I swear by St George's Fields, where I was raised a nameless whelp, that it is the truth. I am no murderer! Your brother was left in the care of an esteemed gentleman who promised to find him a good home.'

'Is he in London?'

'I believe so.'

Before Tom could ask another question, Bedlam gave a cry. 'Here we are!' he said. But when Tom turned, all he could see was a dark building almost concealed by a dense cluster of trees. In another moment or two, the cart's wheels struck pavement; the horses' steps echoed in a courtyard of flagstones.

'How long will I be at school?' asked Tom.

'It depends on you,' replied his father. 'Your grandfather will pay the bills.'

'I shall do my best for him,' said Tom.

Bedlam looked pained. 'Will you indeed? How sharper than a serpent's tooth it is to have a thankless child. *Who* deserves gratitude?' He jabbed himself with his forefinger. 'I brought you here, just as I brought you into the world. You bear *my* name, not the name of Horace Shears . . . Give a man his due!'

Chastened, Tom dutifully modified his statement. 'I shall do my best for you.'

'Of *course* you will,' said Bedlam indignantly. 'Goes without saying!'

IN WEATHERWORN GOLD SCRIPT, words on a warped board read: HAMMER HALL, DEDICATED TO THE EDUCATION OF YOUNG MEN. Below it, in script, was the motto VERITAS ET LABORUM. Tom puzzled over these words as the driver lowered the trunk and his father rapped on the door.

When the subsequent pause offered no sound of a latch being raised or hurrying footsteps, Bedlam paced the courtyard and assessed the building and its grounds. 'Where is everyone? I wonder,' he said.

'New term hasn't started,' said the driver.

'How inconvenient.' Bedlam frowned. 'Mr Shears was told that you were expected this week, or thereabouts.'

A linnet sang from a tree nearby. Mr Bedlam glared at it, then at his pocket watch, and turned his gaze back to the door, this time giving it an almighty pounding that, in Tom's estimation, would have stirred the dead from the little mossy graveyard they had passed a good hour back.

'Best try again another day,' said the driver, when Bedlam returned.

'Another day and the cost of a night's lodgings?' retorted Bedlam. 'We'll wait.'

He and the driver adjusted position to pass the time. Bedlam sat, arms folded, ready to present a formidable profile to anyone approaching the building. The driver, by contrast, adopted a rather insolent posture, feet spread beneath the golden letters, eyes closed, arms under his head. It was a pose that expected the arrival of no one.

Perched on his trunk with his knees pulled up to his face, Tom thought of his brother. If his father was to be believed, he might have passed the boy on the street somewhere in London. He would be older by a year, and probably bear Tom some resemblance, just as the Limpkins shared features.

Tom looked at his father. 'Did he have a name?'

'Who?' replied Bedlam.

'My brother.'

Bedlam shook his head. 'Somebody gave him a name, I'm sure.'

Tom was troubled by another aspect of his father's story, however. 'But there was a burial; you *told* my mother he was dead.'

Bedlam shook his head. 'The graveyard was full of babies who had died. I pointed to an unmarked grave. I wished to spare her the agony of imagining her son in the care of another woman.' He eyed Tom warily. 'I am not an *unkind* man. You understand that, don't you?'

Tom nodded, understanding merely that William Bedlam did not wish to be seen as unkind.

After an hour, the driver rose from his resting place, skirted Bedlam, and began a conversation with one of his horses. 'Well, Mrs Grey,' he said to the lumpy, ash-coloured mare, 'I don't fancy driving back along this road in the dark. Come back tomorrow is what I say, though it'll cost the customer twice the money.'

'I've no intention of paying *twice the money*, Mrs Grey,' snapped Bedlam, also addressing the mare, as if she might then negotiate with the driver.

The driver consoled the horse with an affectionate pat on the rump. 'We'd best leave now, Mrs Grey, the sun being where it is, unless we want to be wandering the night in the company of unsavoury folk.' By this, of course, he meant Tom's father.

'Oh, very well!' Bedlam replied.

The driver gestured for Tom to climb off the trunk in preparation for hoisting it back onto the cart.

'Not so fast,' said Mr Bedlam. 'Leave the trunk.'

'Yes, sir,' said the driver with relief.

Tom was about to climb back onto the cart when his father laid a hand on his shoulder. 'Here's the thing, Tom. Seeing as how I have brought you to the very door of your school – at considerable expense and effort – the best thing for me would be to get back to London.'

Before Tom could reply, Mr Bedlam continued: 'You've a sensible head. Now it seems to me that the housekeeper is on some errand. If she don't show up in five minutes, it'll be ten – if not ten, then no more than an hour. The sensible thing would be to wait for her. What do you say, lad?'

Tom didn't know what to say, but Bedlam took his silence as an assent. Within moments, the boy was perched on his trunk in the same way a sailor might be marooned on a rock at high tide while his vessel departed.

Mr Bedlam cried a farewell: 'Tom, I shall expect reports of your successes, and you shall, of course, hear of mine!'

BY EVENING, AN HOUR LATER, there was no sign of a soul, and Hammer Hall loomed over Tom Bedlam – dark, locked and silent.

As the last light faded, mist emerged and stole the clarity of what few shapes remained in his vision. He consoled himself by taking measure of his lot – he had an education promised to him, a life far from Todderman's furnaces and the squalor of the tenement. Yet, as he considered the locked building, the dark sky, his distance from London and all friends, the truth occurred to him that he had been abandoned.

Fear alone might not cause a fifteen-year-old boy to weep, but Tom was haunted by many other concerns: his father's breach of trust; the loss of his mother; his farewell to the Limpkins; the absence of all familiar streets and sounds. It seemed to him that he had only himself to blame, and no hope besides, and this provoked his tears.

How long he wept, he didn't know, but he was interrupted by a voice that was as harsh as it was sudden: '*Good heavens!* Cease that snivelling this instant before my ears shatter! Stop, desist, quit, I say!'

Tom opened his eyes and looked around with a start.

A figure in a woollen cloak and carrying an old leather satchel held up a lantern, revealing a face, furious, wrinkled, topped by a head of hair as sparse as the strands upon a coconut shell.

'What do you mean by such caterwauling? You're waking up the countryside!'

MR GRINDLE

'I'M ALL ALONE,' TOM REPLIED, WONDERING WHAT CREATURE HE MIGHT have disturbed.

'Incorrect!' snapped Tom's inquisitor. 'Clearly, you are speaking to me, which means that you are *not* alone, which based upon your premise, would be cause for silence! So, *stop*, I say, and explain your encampment on school grounds!'

'Well . . . Mister—'

'Sir will do.'

Tom gave his name and explained his father's logic in leaving him at the door.

'But there isn't any school for a week. It's the end of the summer holiday. What was the man thinking that he would leave a boy here?'

'My father was told that a housekeeper would be about.'

'But he did not find one, did he?'

It seemed that Mr Grindle had been teaching for such a long time that he led every dialogue as if he were leading a class.

To his credit, Tom adapted to the ritual quickly. 'No, sir.'

'Then your father's assumption was erroneous.'

'Erroneous?'

'Flawed, fallacious, faulty . . . *incorrect*!'

'Yes, sir.'

Mr Grindle unlocked the door and led the boy down a corridor to the school kitchen, where he removed from his leather satchel a loaf of bread, a bunch of radishes, six potatoes, a slab of bacon, a hunk of salt beef and six eggs wrapped in sacking. The walls were black with soot. A smell of rancid grease pervaded the chamber until the fire was lit and the comforting smell of burning wood, and its consequent glow, cheered the room. Mr Grindle placed his food into a tin cabinet, remarking with some dismay, 'This was to be a feast for a single man – my dinner for the next week. Apparently it shall now be *our* dinner, Tom Bedlam.'

'I couldn't eat your dinner, sir,' Tom replied.

'Then you shall starve, and I shall be responsible. Would you wish that upon me?'

'No, sir!'

In the severity of the man's eye, Tom recognized a shred of amusement. Mr Grindle served him a chunk of the cold beef, added several radishes, a dash of mustard in which to dip them, a pinch of salt, and a narrow slice of bread. As they ate, Grindle asked about Tom's circumstances, his life in Vauxhall, his mother, and his father's line of business. After the dishes were cleared away, he helped him carry his trunk to the top floor, which was an attic with a sloping ceiling on both sides and many cots running along both walls. Tom took one near the stairs and proceeded to make his bed while Mr Grindle waited with his lantern.

'A word of advice, Bedlam . . .'

'Sir?'

'You are entering a society no less harsh than the one you have come from. The factory and the farm are similar, my friend. The chicken that walks differently from its neighbours is pecked.'

'Sir?'

'Say nothing of your father's line of work, or your mother's. Your father is a crockery merchant, do you understand? Your mother tended you. You lived in a *house* in London, not a tenement building.'

'Yes, sir.'

'Very good,' said the master, who spun around and swiftly descended the stairs, taking the light with him.

As Tom released his grip on consciousness, he noted that Mr

Grindle, while lacking any gentility or kind words, had fed him, sheltered him, and settled his fears. While he felt an uncommon gratitude to a man he barely knew, he puzzled over it. Was it fair to weigh the kindness and generosity of the schoolmaster against that of his own father?

He decided to give it more thought tomorrow and promptly fell asleep.

IN DAYLIGHT, MR GRINDLE'S FACE was a weathered brown and his skin the texture of a walnut shell. It was impossible to tell his age, for his wrinkles vanished when he was in a good mood and multiplied when he wasn't. For three days, Mr Grindle kept a simple routine in Tom's company. They shared breakfast every morning: boiled egg, rasher of bacon with a slice of bread fried in the grease. Mr Grindle would retire to his books for several hours. They met again in the afternoon to take a walk in the hills above Hammer Hall, and on the way, Mr Grindle would slice a cold boiled potato, share it with Tom, and they would eat and talk of Tom's education, such as it was, and such as he wished it to be.

'What is it, then, that brings you here?' Mr Grindle asked.

'Why, to be educated and become a gentleman, sir.'

'A gentleman? Why, that is easily done, Tom Bedlam. Keep your word and you are a gentleman. Abide by your promises and never shirk your responsibilities. Can you do that?'

'I think so, sir.'

Mr Grindle spread his palms. 'Then you are a gentleman. Your mission is accomplished.' He narrowed his eyes at Tom. 'Satisfied?'

Tom was troubled. 'I don't know, sir. If it is so simple, why am I here?'

'Why indeed?' Amusement appeared in Grindle's wry features. 'My dear boy, you recall the pecking order I mentioned before?'

'Yes, sir.'

'Well, in adult society there is a pecking order too. Hammer Hall teaches its cockerels to strut!'

Though this made no more sense than Mr Grindle's last statement, Tom nodded because he feared the master's impatience.

'Tom Bedlam, you will not learn to be a gentleman here. Hammer

Hall will demand that you follow its rules. Mr Goodkind will punish you when you do not.'

'Mr Goodkind?'

'The headmaster.'

'Then *you* are not the headmaster?' Tom replied with disappointment.

'Good heavens, no!' Mr Grindle sniffed with disgust. 'I am a *teacher*! Now, where was I? Oh, yes, the *rules*. Your peers will expect you to break them. Occasionally, you will choose your own path in spite of the rules and the influence of your fellow pupils. This is what I call *learning*.'

'And if I can't find my own path?'

'Then you will be a dunce, and join all the other dunces out there in the world. You will find your future limited to two professions: your father's and the world of politics.'

ON THE LAST DAY BEFORE the pupils were to return, the school's cook appeared as Mr Grindle and Tom were having breakfast in the kitchen. Mrs Brasier's meaty face and small eyes took immediate offence at the sight of the schoolmaster and the boy seated in her domain. A breathless woman with pursed lips and yellow sweat stains around her collar, she ordered them out, threw a shovelful of coal on the fire, and announced that dinner would be served at six.

At that hour, Tom sat with Mr Grindle in the dining hall – a dim chamber of narrow benches and warped tables. The surfaces were carved with boys' initials and rough with the grime and spillage of many past meals. Tom tried to picture the room crowded with boys, but his imagination failed him. A cloud of white smoke poured from the kitchen, and Mrs Brasier emerged, panting and wheezing, her face shiny with sweat, carrying a tureen, from which she served a lumpy brown broth. The colour reminded Tom of the Thames, and the objects that bobbed in the turbid river after a long rain.

'Mrs Brasier,' said Mr Grindle as he sifted cautiously through the broth, 'I am always astounded by what comes out of your kitchen.'

The cook huffed and marched back to her domain.

The student and the master regarded their food hesitantly and looked at each other, acknowledging that the meals had been more palatable before the cook's arrival.

'Come, I believe I may have saved some beef for just such an outcome,' said Mr Grindle.

They shared the rest of Mr Grindle's beef as they walked the cart road that rose into the hills above Hammer Hall. It was a moody terrain. Mist lurked in the lower parts of the valley, and the only point of brilliance was the window of the school kitchen, where Mrs Brasier, even from half a mile away, could be seen engaged in open warfare with her fireplace. Flames swelled from the hearth while smoke billowed. Tom thought the small plume produced by Mrs Brasier was touchingly reminiscent of the output of Todderman's great smokestacks.

During the stroll, Mr Grindle brought up a matter of some concern. 'Tom Bedlam, one thing that has puzzled me is your name. Your father gave it to you?'

'It's the only thing he has ever given me, sir.'

'You know, of course, that it is the common name for a madman? What kind of father names his son after a madman?'

Tom explained his father's affection for *King Lear* and suggested that the name sprang into his mind for that reason.

'Tom Bedlam is not a *kind* name,' Mr Grindle replied. 'I advise you to change it when you've the opportunity.'

Tom thanked the schoolmaster and considered the virtues of Grindle as a surname.

The schoolmaster then reminded him that the other masters would return tomorrow and that Hammer Hall would be at full capacity by the evening. 'Bedlam, I cannot be the companion to you that I have been these past days, but I can promise you guidance when you require it. It will not be easy to act the gentleman in the company of *hooligans*, my boy. Do your very best,' he said.

THE FOLLOWING MORNING, Mrs Brasier proved herself as incapable of cooking breakfast as she was dinner. The porridge served to them had such a peculiar smell to it that Mr Grindle dispensed with veiled complaints.

'Mrs Brasier,' he said at the threshold of the kitchen (it was impossible to enter farther because of the pots, crates and litter of vegetables spread across the floor). 'I detected the odour of *tobacco* in the porridge. How in God's name is that possible?'

Tom peered over the master's shoulder to see that Mrs Brasier looked different: her jowled face was flushed, her nose blistered, and her eyelashes were missing. The fringe on her apron was burned brown, and her woollen dress bore scorch marks.

'Good gracious, Mr Grindle!' she cried. 'Don't I 'ave enough to cope with with 'undreds of mouths to feed and me alone, at the mercy of the fire and the elements?'

Unimpressed, Mr Grindle replied, 'Madam, unless I am mistaken, you cooked for three people this morning. Yet there was *tobacco* in the porridge.'

Mrs Brasier began to weep, threw a few lumps of coal onto the kitchen fire, and proceeded to pump the bellows, causing the fire to swell into an inferno, which licked at the fringe of her dress. She groaned. 'Ungrateful! That's what I call it, when I risk life and limb to feed the public!'

Exasperated, the schoolmaster gave up and coughed his way out of the room. He gave Tom a parting warning: 'Always sift through the broth for nails and other foreign items before eating, lad. The keys to the school were once found in Mrs Brasier's lamb stew, a sock in the mashed potatoes, and a baited mousetrap in the Christmas pudding!'

BY NOON, THREE COACHES had arrived bearing several schoolmasters and a few boys. No sooner had one left than another would pull up, followed by donkey carts, carriages and dogcarts, until a great dust rose in the courtyard.

The halls bustled with activity as a line of boys, punctuated by wooden crates and trunks, heaving and shoving, made their way up the winding stairs to the attic dormitory. Tom watched from his bed as the boys at the head of the line reached the summit, staked their claims, and argued over proximity to friends and foes. It seemed that his early arrival had saved him some trouble, since the arguments over beds came to blows.

Two fellows, Mansworth and Privot, seemed to be the poles about which the others clustered. Privot, a brutish fellow, took the bed farthest from the stairs, then tossed his belongings onto the four beds nearest him. 'Them's taken!' he roared in a gravelly voice as the other boys entered. He greeted his lieutenants by punching them in the chest and assigned beds in the same way, with belligerent humour and much shoving and slapping.

Mansworth, by contrast, acknowledged his acolytes with a glance. He ruled with folded arms and a brooding stare. His curly brown hair was parted in the centre and fell to his shoulders like a magistrate's horsehair wig. He never raised his voice, but exerted his authority with wry scorn. 'Lopping,' he warned one boy, 'if you hope to sleep peacefully, I advise you to take the one five beds down.'

By the end of the process, Privot commanded the row of cots on the north side of the room, while Mansworth had the south side, ending with Tom's, nearest the stairs. When only the cot opposite Tom's remained unoccupied, Mansworth ventured down the aisle and sat upon Tom's trunk.

'You're the new boy,' he said. 'Bedlam, is it?'

Tom admitted this, and Mansworth introduced himself.

'My father's a member of Parliament. What does your father do?'

Following Grindle's advice, Tom replied, 'A trade merchant.'

'London or elsewhere?'

'London,' Tom replied.

This seemed to be the right answer. Mansworth nodded. 'You're on my side of the room, Bedlam, so you'll be eating on my side too.'

'Side?' Tom replied.

Mansworth nodded. 'Privot's got the other side. You're better off with me.' After this remark, he introduced Tom to some of the other boys, each time exaggerating Tom's father's standing.

'Winesap, this is Bedlam. His father's a prominent merchant.'

'Perhaps you've heard of Bedlam's father, Cooper, he's a London tycoon.'

As each boy insisted to Mansworth that he knew of Tom's father, Tom realized the extent of his patron's influence. He also noted

Mansworth's eccentricities – flicking his hair aside but letting one lock fall across his face and wearing his Hammer Hall royal blue school jacket with the shirtsleeves turned out at his wrists. His features were soft, his mouth petulant. By contrast, Privot was all muscle, with a firm jaw and a shock of hair that stood on end. Privot's father, Tom learned, was from the north, a distiller, and most of the boys on Privot's side were northerners. Mansworth reminded everyone that his father had a dozen factories in London and 'a seat in Parliament', by which he meant the House of Commons. Hammer Hall was not a school for the offspring of peers. These boys were the sons of businessmen – the newly rich who wished their sons to speak like lords, even if they worked for a living.

Mansworth greeted his rival with an imperceptible nod. 'Evening, Privot. Good summer?'

'Can't complain. So, Bedlam's yours, then?'

'Yes. You'll have the next,' said Mansworth, indicating the cot facing Tom's.

BY SUPPER, THE HALL was full of boys. The sea of faces and the din stunned Tom. He briefly considered seeking solace in the kitchen when Mansworth called to him. 'Bedlam, over here!'

Tom complied, taking his place opposite Mansworth, who then introduced him around the table. 'This is Bedlam. His father has vast holdings overseas. You've heard of him, of course.'

Several boys nodded and eagerly shook Tom's hand, then quickly told him about their masters and the virtues of life at Hammer Hall. These young men, Tom thought, couldn't be the hooligans to whom Mr Grindle had referred.

The masters sat at a table at the head of the room. They might have been patients in an infirmary for the hacking coughs, bent backs, and accoutrements they carried – canes, spectacles, and ear trumpets. All were far beyond the prime of their lives. Ironically, Mr Grindle was the most youthful of the bunch. Tom met his guardian's eye, but the master merely raised his eyebrow in acknowledgment.

The headmaster, Mr Goodkind, gazed at his pupils with a robust smile. He was a tall man, soft-spoken, and when the room would not quieten for his opening remarks, his deputy, Mr Phibbs, a small, stout man with a black scowl and cheeks shiny with sweat, pounded his staff on the floor.

Reading his remarks from a piece of paper, Headmaster Goodkind welcomed the boys to the new term. Then he consulted the paper and addressed the new boys by name. 'You arrive here with an abundance of innocence, a youthful spirit – a blank slate unfettered by age, corruption or prejudice! But when you leave, my lads, you shall bear the stamp of Hammer Hall!'

The masters interrupted him with a coughing contest. Phibbs beat his staff against the floor for order again. From the kitchen, Mrs Brasier wheeled in an empty trolley and proceeded to clear away the plates from the faculty table, including Mr Goodkind's, yet untouched.

Determined to make a final point, Mr Goodkind raised his glass. 'To a fine new group of gentlemen!'

Mrs Brasier had removed all of the other men's drinks, so they looked at one another in puzzlement. Mr Goodkind downed the contents of his glass, his massive Adam's apple rising and falling.

When Mansworth rose from his bench, Privot shot up too. Both raised their cups. Implicit in this gesture was an acknowledgment of the power in the hall, with the sovereign on the masters' dais and the two houses represented by the northerners and the southerners. As cheers erupted, Tom caught Mr Grindle's eye – the master glanced at each boy, then tipped his head at Tom in warning.

A BLANK SLATE

TOM'S FAMILIARITY WITH THE BIBLE'S TEXT AND VOCABULARY PUT him ahead of many boys in his grammar class, but he found himself at a disadvantage in mathematics, geography and history, and pledged to catch up as quickly as possible.

One of the more elderly masters, Mr Trent, taught mathematics. His features were wrenched by gravity; dark bags hung below his eyes, jowls concealed his collars, and his chin wobbled over his top shirt button. No sadder face existed, and he had right cause for it, for the pupils were a constant disappointment to him.

Mansworth explained to Tom that there was a rule in Trent's class – the boys never answered a question correctly. Mansworth and Privot were taskmasters in this regard and set an example by offering the most pathetic replies.

'Will someone multiply twelve by three?'

'Thirty-seven, sir!'

'Wrong. Anybody else?'

'Thirty-five, sir?'

'Good heavens, doesn't *anybody* know?' cried Mr Trent.

Cooper, a small boy who clearly knew the answer, glanced back and forth between Mansworth and Mr Trent, like a terrier torn between duty and desire. Finally, his arm shot up out of sheer frustration.

'Cooper!' cried Trent, recognizing the spark in the boy's eyes. 'Please, enlighten us!'

But before Cooper spoke, Privot pressed the nib of his pen into the boy's spine. 'It's . . . thirty-two, sir?'

The shame on Cooper's face was matched by the despair on his master's. Trent rubbed his forehead, sank slowly to his desk and bitterly prescribed a set of ridiculously easy problems.

'But how are we to pass our exams?' asked Tom later.

'No one fails at Hammer Hall!' said Privot.

'Gentlemen pay good money to send their boys here, Bedlam,' added Mansworth. 'The masters could hardly justify their salaries by failing us.'

GEOGRAPHY WAS SIMILARLY CONTROLLED. Again, Mansworth led the way by insisting that the North and South Poles were a hundred miles apart. This provoked a diatribe from Mr Feeny that wasted a good thirty minutes of the lesson.

Tom noted that Lopping, a tall boy with a thin face, had written the precise distance between the North and South Poles in his notebook margin, but when he attempted to raise his hand, Mansworth slapped his head.

In short, Mansworth and Privot, through distraction and obstruction, ensured that lessons were brief and undemanding.

Mr Grindle's class was the exception. He taught Latin and began by hauling Privot and Mansworth to the front and addressing them: 'I know your game, sirs. If you fail to exert yourselves to the utmost during this term, I shall direct my correspondence to your fathers.'

Sober and chastened, Mansworth and Privot sat down. But one boy, Edgar Winesap, with a mop of ginger curls, raised his hand. He had a nasal voice and a sly air that seemed to defy both the fury of the master and the influence of Mansworth and Privot.

'Yes, Winesap?'

'Will you *certainmost* direct your correspondence to my father, sir?'

'*Certainmost* is not a word, Winesap, but yes, I will direct my comments to your father.'

Winesap nodded. 'Thank you muchly, sir.'

Reminding him that *muchly* was not a word either, Grindle approached the boy, alerted by the odd aspect of his question.

'How is your father's health, Winesap?'

'Consistent, sir.'

'Consistent with what, Winesap?'

The boy shifted uncomfortably in his seat. 'He had a bad spell, sir, but he's no longer in pain. I shall not hesitate to do my best work, sir, to spare him the *obligement* of correspondence.'

Grindle frowned. 'If you continue to use these idiotic expressions, I shall have to write to him. And, mark my words, I shall expect a reply!'

Winesap shrugged. 'My father's *muchly* a figure of *sanguinity* and *placitude*, sir; he rarely replies to anything.'

'I have no idea *what* you're saying, Winesap,' snapped Grindle. 'My letters always provoke a reply; I daresay they could raise the dead to respond!'

This remark caused Winesap to wince slightly.

Privot, his lips clamped to prevent a grin, raised his hand.

'What, Privot?'

'Sir, your letter *shall* have to raise the dead, because Mr Winesap passed away, sir, four years ago.'

ON FRIDAY EVENINGS, after dinner, the boys were permitted a few hours of free time. It was the first moment that Tom allowed himself a break from his studies. So he took out the comic that Oscar had given him as a farewell present – *Ally Sloper's Half Holiday*, the adventures of a drunken family man.

Tom had just made his way past the first page when Mansworth appeared beside him. 'What's that, Bedlam?'

Tom showed him the comic.

'Phibbs frowns on this sort of thing, Bedlam. I'll keep it for you. I hope you don't have any more of this stuff, because Phibbs will assuredly burn it.'

After Tom assured Mansworth that he had no more, Mansworth retired with the comic. In subsequent evenings, Tom noticed that Cooper,

Winesap and Lopping read his comic in quick succession. When Tom requested its return, he was told that each boy had *paid* for the right to read it. Lopping gave Mansworth two butterscotch sweets; Cooper, a farthing. Winesap had offered an essay on any subject – a dubious service, since his exotic vocabulary would give the author's true identity away in a moment.

Over the next month, Mansworth earned a considerable profit from Tom's comic. When he could contain himself no longer, Tom brought up the matter privately with him. 'You've made a right fortune off my property,' he said. 'And I haven't even *read* it!'

'Bedlam,' murmured Mansworth, 'has anyone been rude or unkind to you?'

'No,' Tom replied.

'Have you been ridiculed or maligned?'

'I don't think so.'

Mansworth nodded. 'Thanks to me, Bedlam, you have many friends. Thanks to me, you are in good standing, yet I've not received a single expression of thanks. Where is your gratitude?'

ON WEEKENDS THE BOYS of Hammer Hall were permitted rambles on the trails of Hammer Peak, which lay above the school, its gentle lower slopes often dotted with sheep. The summit rose sharply above the pastures in steep chalk cliffs, and the top plateau extended ten feet over the incline in both directions; this was the 'hammer' of Hammer Peak. Occasionally, a sheep would wander up, only to lose its footing and fall. Since the upper peak was often shrouded in mist, the stray was rarely discovered until severely decomposed.

'At first, they sound like babies bleating in the *meeze*,' said Winesap.

'*Meeze?*' repeated Tom.

'Misty breeze,' Winesap explained. 'Once I found a sheep in a *gravine*, all soggy and stiff and deadened like.'

'Gravine?'

Winesap sneered at Tom. 'Never heard of a *gravine*? It's a rock hole where they fall into.'

'There's no such thing,' said Tom.

'Certainmost is,' grumbled Winesap.

The element of danger on Hammer Peak freed the boys from their scholarly duties. Here they could wander and imagine themselves warriors in Sparta, or Marco Polo traversing the Silk Road, or elephant drivers crossing the Alps with Hannibal. In the gullies and on the paths, they were free from their work and free, also, from the overbearing influence of Mansworth and Privot.

MAIL WAS DISTRIBUTED once a week, and Tom was very excited when he received his first letter. It was from Sissy.

My dear Tom,

Thank you for your letter. I am well.

Your Sissy

Few words, but what words they were! From the simplicity of the message, Tom inferred Sissy's utter devotion. *Your Sissy.* He imagined her in his arms, her cheek against his, her petulant mouth upon his lips.

When Audrey's missives arrived, by contrast, he was so deluged with information that he missed the essence of her message, which had all the good intentions Sissy's note lacked.

Dearest Tom,

I do hope you are well and happy. We miss you here, and I cannot step out of my door without expecting to see you walking up the stairs patting the dust from your shoulders!

So much has happened since your departure. Oscar has become a reporter for the Vauxhall Gazette; *every evening he tells us stories about murderers on trial and the terrible things they have done. It quite puts Father off his food. Mother gets so upset that she keeps a chair against the door in the evenings for fear that half the murderers in London might come visiting as we sleep.*

I miss you, Tom. With Oscar working so hard, my days are spent keeping the girls from trouble and the Orfling from even worse a fate. I cannot leave the grocer's without finding something concealed in his squirrelly cheeks that should not be there. Thimbles, buttons, sweets, a sixpence! I fear that Oscar's awful stories of the Old Bailey may include the Orfling one day. And the dear little thing weeps so when I berate him. Perhaps all of our troubles are having an impression on him, for he refuses to grow older; I think he knows that nine months is the happiest age.

How are your studies? Have you made any friends? I do so miss you, and fear that you'll forget me, and I shall see you one day in London, dressed like a gentleman, and you'll not recognize Audrey Limpkin with all your learned respectability.

Please write soon,

Audrey

Tom wrote first to Sissy, but to her he expressed only his ardent affection. To Audrey, he poured out everything else. He told her about his father's revelation – that he had a brother somewhere in London, a year older than he – and admitted that this had compelled him to reconsider his father's villainy. Then he described his arrival at the school, Mr Grindle's care of him, Mr Goodkind's welcome, Mrs Brasier's habit of setting fire to herself, and wrote of Mansworth, and the fortunate manner in which Oscar's comic had paid for his popularity. Finally, he dismissed Audrey's concerns, vowing that he would never miss her on any street, and that he couldn't wait to see her again.

When Audrey replied, she promised to ask Oscar to send more comics and advised Tom to beware of Mansworth. 'I have the worst feeling about your self-appointed friend,' she warned him.

THE NEW BOY

THE CHRISTMAS HOLIDAYS LASTED TWO WEEKS, AND A NUMBER OF boys left to join their families, perhaps merely to avoid the dark dish Mrs Brasier called 'festive pudding' – a brown hash of pot scrapings sweetened with treacle that was served but eaten by only a few hardy souls. Of the boys who remained at Hammer Hall, many received packages from home. Mansworth and Privot distributed the boxes with mock generosity; the seals were broken, the contents ransacked.

'Winesap, only a pair of socks for you; Lopping, more handkerchiefs. *Use* them this time,' said Privot.

'Where's my Christmas toffee?' protested Cooper, as he turned his box upside down.

Mansworth patted his pocket. 'Delivery tax, Cooper.'

Tom received nothing from his father, but Mr Shears sent him a note enclosing two shillings. The money, of course, was missing when Mansworth handed him the opened letter. On New Year's Day, however, Mr Grindle presented Tom with a palm-size package wrapped in brown paper and sealed with string and red wax. 'It fell out of the masters' mail yesterday,' he explained.

Tom cut the string with one of Mrs Brasier's kitchen knives. Inside he found a lozenge tin with a note from Audrey. 'Dear Tom,' it read, 'Happy Christmas!' He kept the tin concealed in his pocket all day, and only when the lights were out in the attic, and his blankets covered him, did he open it and devour the crumbled lemon tart within.

IT WASN'T UNTIL A new pupil arrived that Tom realized how easy his entry to Hammer Hall had been. The boy was assigned the cot on Privot's side of the room, directly facing Tom's. He received his first punch – this was the way Privot greeted everybody – in the hall and promptly fell flat on his back.

Privot helped the boy up and dusted off his clothes, shaking him until he protested. 'Let go of me!' he shouted. 'I won't be touched!'

Challenged, Privot extended a finger provocatively and poked the boy in the eye. The newcomer slapped Privot's cheek, and Privot's boys gasped in anticipation of their chieftain's reaction. Privot shrank before the new boy in mock despair. 'I'm hurt, lads! Someb'dy get me to hospital!'

The ensuing laughter only made the new boy angry. 'Quiet!'

'Simmer down,' Privot laughed. 'What's your name then?'

'Arthur Pigeon!'

'Have you any sweets, Pigeon?'

'No!'

'Comics? Money?'

Since Pigeon's replies were disappointing, Privot went on his way, and Pigeon brushed himself down. Eventually he noticed Tom's fascination. Arthur Pigeon's skin was very white, and his face was disproportionately long, resembling that of a stained-glass apostle, or even one of Todderman's more pious figurines. His most distinctive feature was his hair, which bore a resemblance to Mansworth's in that it was long, and sprang from his temples like a cocker spaniel's ears. 'What do *you* want?' he snapped.

Tom said nothing and continued on his way, though he silently thanked Oscar Limpkin for the *Ally Sloper* comic.

IT TOOK THE OTHER boys only a day to size up Arthur Pigeon. In spite of a command from Privot to eat at his table, Arthur chose the farthest point from Mrs Brasier's kitchen (he had developed a cough from the smoke), by an open window.

In mathematics class, he compounded this error by answering three questions correctly.

Mr Trent was visibly moved. 'Pigeon,' he gasped, 'it appears that God has finally answered my prayers.'

To everyone's relief, Arthur offered no expertise in science. He did, however, give genuine attention to the lesson, which prompted Privot to distract him with a pinch and a twist of the sharp end of his pen in the boy's thigh.

'Pigeon,' Privot whispered, 'keep your mouth shut and stop looking *interested*!'

Although science was devoted to recitation of the amphibians, serious business was focused on slapping a chalk impression on the back of Mr Barby's waistcoat. The deaf old teacher endured many hearty slaps on the back as each boy attempted to place a perfect handprint between his shoulder blades.

'Please, sir, spiffing jacket you're wearing today!'

'Eh what? Continue with your work!'

'Just a compliment, sir,' the villain said with a smile, patting the old man with a fantail of dust.

Chalky rays of light streamed from the open windows as the game progressed. Mr Barby coughed. 'Why is it so dusty?'

Eventually, Mansworth left a perfect impression and, of course, nobody dared rival his achievement. Arthur, however, couldn't let the matter rest.

'Sir, I believe you've a smudge on your back!' he cried.

The old man, bewildered, attempted to examine himself, spinning in two full circles.

'Let *me*, sir!' said Arthur. He rose and gave Mr Barby a strong pat on the back, which removed the mark and provoked a thunderous glance from the dough-faced lad with the loose forelock. Though Arthur missed it, the other boys caught its meaning.

At supper they slid across the benches to fill any space when Arthur approached a table. When Mrs Brasier burst from her smoky haven to deliver the evening stew, young Pigeon was still wandering about the room like a lost puppy.

Mr Phibbs pounded the floor with his staff, causing Arthur to jump. 'Boy, find a seat!'

Wary of Mansworth and Privot now, Arthur strayed about the aisles until Tom – enlightened by Mr Grindle's stern glance – made room for him. By this time, Arthur was beyond gratitude; indignant and furious, he was silent for the meal, which provoked more whispering among the boys.

'What a cad! If Bedlam hadn't moved for him, he'd be sitting on the floor.'

'What do you *say* to your betters, Pigeon?'

'Swine' was Arthur's indignant reply. Then, closing his eyes, he repeated, 'All of you. *Swine!*'

Later Mansworth took Tom aside. 'Bedlam,' he said, 'I don't want *that one* at my table again.'

'He's got to sit somewhere,' Tom replied.

'He's on Privot's side,' replied Mansworth. 'He should be begging a seat from him.'

Tom nodded. 'Yes, but it doesn't seem like a very decent thing to turn him away. Privot's a brute.'

'If he sits on my side, you will lose *your* seat, Bedlam. You invited him without asking me. You're new too, remember.'

That evening one of Mansworth's boys gave Pigeon a forward thump that sent him stumbling down the stairs. This was accompanied by profuse apologies and the assistance of several of the perpetrators in carrying him back up the stairs with exaggerated fuss and concern. This mixture of kindness and torment would have driven any boy to hysterics. Arthur Pigeon, however, bore it with stoic detachment.

TOM WASN'T SURE what to think of him. It is hard to pity a boy so oblivious to his own abuse. Tom wrote to Audrey with his impressions. She replied quickly.

My dear Tom,

It is plain to me that you are bound to this boy in some way, and whatever comes of his mistreatment by the other boys will shadow you in the future.

Tom, I implore you to stand by him in spite of his difficult nature.

Prove yourself a reliable friend, Tom. Though boys can be so cruel, they recognize good and evil. If you stand by Arthur Pigeon, your kindness will earn him respect from others.

Outcasts do not reflect well upon any society.

Audrey

Emboldened by her advice, Tom tried in subsequent days to talk to Pigeon, but the boy merely squinted at him, as suspicious of kindness as he was of cruelty.

Breakfast was the one meal when the lines weren't drawn in the dining hall. The boys entered at intervals, taking their food from a table, where they could choose between porridge and a viscous, yellowish brown mixture that Mrs Brasier called 'cramblers', which seemed to be scrambled eggs mixed with leftovers from the previous evening, a generous variety of grease and other stray items. It was revolting to look at, but Tom had had enough porridge to last him another fifteen years; cramblers had flavour, and the stray items in it – a shoelace, a bone button – could be avoided if detected early.

When he saw Arthur sitting before a heaping dish of it, Tom took the opportunity to warn him about Mrs Brasier's knack for losing things.

'I'm not stupid, you know,' Arthur replied. 'I'm perfectly capable of looking after myself.'

'I'm only being friendly,' Tom replied.

'Yes, and I almost lost my teeth falling down the stairs thanks to someone being *friendly*!'

Tom lowered his voice. 'I'm not like the rest of them.'

At this Arthur's eyes seemed to darken. 'Every school is the same. This is my third.'

'If you make one friend then you're better off than you would be alone,' Tom replied.

Arthur seemed to acknowledge the wisdom in this by keeping pace with him in the hall later. He proceeded to dismiss Privot as a butcher, Mansworth as a royalist, and the other boys in his row by their weaknesses. 'Winesap's words are absurd. Cooper is an invertebrate. Lopping is pathetic.'

'Nobody meets your standards, then?' Tom interrupted.

After a pause, Arthur looked at him. 'Perhaps you do, Bedlam,' he replied. His breath smelled faintly of onions; Tom wondered if the odour was responsible for the other boys' hostility towards him.

He wrote to Audrey that Arthur was a snob. She replied with one sentence that confused him.

My dear Tom,

A person can dislike anyone, but you, of all people, know that a generous soul may recognize at least one good quality in the worst character.

Audrey

This remark contained a strange irony; Tom realized only later, as he lay in a light sleep, to whom Audrey had referred. Clutched in his hand was Sissy's first note. He had not received another, although he had written three times. If her silence indicated carelessness, forgetfulness or even indifference, it hadn't mattered to Tom until now. He had forgiven Sissy everything for the single virtue of her milkmaid's mouth.

IN SUBSEQUENT DAYS, WHEN Arthur Pigeon became an object of torment, Tom shadowed him. He caught the boy when he was tripped, and when he anticipated a prank, Tom warned away the villains. 'Or Phibbs will find out!' he hissed at Cooper.

'We're only having *funlike*,' Winesap retorted.

Audrey seemed to have been right; the ferocity of the attacks on Pigeon appeared to wane as Tom asserted his presence.

For all this, Arthur never thanked Tom. He seemed to think that Tom's efforts were the very least he could do.

One evening, Privot came walking down the aisle as Arthur stuck out his leg to tie a shoelace. Privot tripped, but Arthur said nothing, even when the boy glared menacingly at him.

Privot drew himself up. 'Pigeon, I've gone easy on you, your being new and all, but if I don't see some respect on your part, you'll suffer consequences.'

Arthur's lip curled. 'Don't strain your eyes,' he replied.

Privot rapped his knuckles on Arthur's head, but Arthur showed no pain, gave no quarter. Puzzled, Privot cocked his head but let him be.

News of Arthur's defiance travelled quickly, however; in Mr Trent's class, Cooper dared offer a correct answer. Then Lopping, in geography, located the Canary Islands. Disturbed by these acts of rebellion, Privot and Mansworth met that evening in a corner of the attic. Tom watched them confer and wondered what they would do.

THE NEXT MORNING, Arthur awoke screaming.

His head had been shaved close to the scalp; his long hair lay about his pillow. When he appeared in the dining hall, he was a frightening sight – his pale scalp exposed, with only wisps of hair still attached to it. There was a collective hush.

Nobody, however, was more shocked than Tom, for he saw something that caused him to reconsider Arthur's place in the world.

As he examined the boy's shorn scalp, the bloody nicks, and the patches of hair that made him resemble a hatchling fresh from an egg, he noticed a mark just below Arthur's left ear. First, he had to be sure that it was not a cut. And when he was certain, he smiled cautiously.

'What are *you* staring at?' asked Arthur bitterly.

'I never noticed before because of your hair, but you have a birthmark,' said Tom.

Arthur touched it. 'Yes,' he replied. 'What of it?'

Tom recalled his mother's delirium on the night of her death: *I'll know him. I'll find the poor abandoned creature!*

'Nothing,' he replied. But until he had evidence to the contrary, Tom resolved to remain Arthur Pigeon's keeper.

HAMMER PEAK

It was only now that Tom understood Mr Grindle's remark about hooligans. Arthur Pigeon was an example for all the boys – the pecked hen, the pariah, the lowest ranking member. In that regard, Tom had set himself a considerable challenge. He couldn't have picked a worse person to claim as a brother.

'Is the earth round or flat? Can no one tell me?' cried the exasperated Mr Barby.

Nobody dared offer any answer now.

Mansworth and Privot were not finished. Though Arthur was their whipping boy, he was hardly cooperative. A normal boy might have been driven to submission, but Arthur was not in this category. His discovery of the boot prints on his sheets the next evening prompted a typically flat statement: 'Swine. All of you.'

This stoic response reminded Tom of his mother's philosophy: Arthur was merely turning the other cheek. What could offer further proof that he was a Bedlam? Tom, however, was determined that Arthur repel his oppressors and sought a moment alone with the boy in the library – a pantry-size room filled with shelves of reference books and old novels. He took a seat opposite him, but he didn't know where to begin until Arthur eyed him suspiciously from above the book he held.

'Can you not leave me alone?' he murmured. 'I thought *this* would be the one place where everybody would leave me in peace.'

'But I'm on your side.'

'Why would *anybody* be on my side?' Arthur muttered. Then his eyes reflected suspicion. 'You're not one of *those*, are you?'

'What?' Tom replied.

'A master in the last school wouldn't keep his hands off me.'

Furious, Tom stood up and seized a book. 'I'll hit you with this to prove it. How's that? Maybe a bloody nose would make you feel better? Can you only believe people who want to hurt you?'

'What do you want?'

Tom eyed the spot on the other boy's neck. If Arthur was his brother, then the central riddle of his life would be solved. Was this the 'poor abandoned creature' of which his mother had spoken? Tom savoured the moment, preparing his question, anticipating its repetition in a triumphant story for Oscar and Audrey at some later date. 'Arthur,' he began, 'are your parents your *real* parents?'

Arthur seemed to puzzle over Tom's reason for asking such a question, but finally replied: 'Of course they are, aren't yours?'

'Yes.' Disheartened, Tom rose and left the room.

NOTING THE NEW predilection for torment among the older boys, Mr Grindle proposed an exercise regimen to the headmaster. Mr Goodkind agreed, since it required nothing of him, and made an announcement in the dinner hall.

'Your excess energy will be expended in the countryside,' he explained, 'beating the footpaths rather than each other, stalking wildlife rather than the weak among you, and ascending the lofty plateau of Hammer Peak rather than your own brutish hierarchy!'

It was left to Mr Phibbs to wake the students at sunrise for the new routine. On the first day, cursing, the stocky disciplinarian staggered up to the attic, struck his staff against the rafters to wake them, and cried in a grating tenor: 'Get a move on! Everybody up! Time for a run up Hammer Peak, lads. Even you, Mansworth, *and* you, Privot!'

—

THOUGH IT WAS not a treacherous run, the terrain demanded both exertion and caution. The path rounded a steep drop near the summit, and a mist that concealed this peril hung about Hammer Peak most mornings. The boys ran in clusters along the dark track, beating a rhythm through crackling twig and oozing mud, sometimes losing sight of their predecessors in the fog while they gasped resentment in billowing breaths that dissipated over the bracken. Swearing, wheezing, and whining, they spiralled up to the peak, hearts beating fast, noses red and runny, coughing and cursing, until they emerged upon a rocky summit and the sun enveloped them with its cool, pale glory. Here, squatting and breathless, the pimply group gathered its breath. They were guaranteed fifteen minutes' peace before Mr Phibbs, shrill and dripping with sweat, staggered up to the plateau and ordered them down.

During the lull, Privot showed off his excess of energy by doing press-ups while his followers kept count with respectful awe. Mansworth distinguished himself by adopting a languid pose, lying on the lofty ledge of Hammer Peak. He clasped his hands behind his head, forming a ponytail of his long hair, and closed his eyes.

When Privot finished his exercises, scarlet-faced, he pulled off his shirt and wrapped it around his head like an Arab sheikh, exposing the heavily pocked skin of his shoulders and strong biceps. A few boys fell to the ground to perform their own exercises while he did a circular boxer's dance, sweat flying, his ripe body odour provoking the sensitive among them to wince. Privot enjoyed mornings on the mountain: they were his opportunity to flaunt his omnipotence before his followers and, of course, before Mansworth. He ran on the spot, arms above his head, while sweat flew from his scarlet cheeks.

When Mansworth felt a stray drop, he made a show of removing a handkerchief from his back pocket and wiping the offending spot. 'Privot, we see now that you can gallop like a charger, but spare us your leavings, eh?'

When several boys smiled, Privot's colour faded. 'Where's Pigeon, then?' he said in an apparent attempt to change the subject.

Mansworth tipped his head to peer down the trail. 'Two minutes away, I'd imagine. Bedlam's making sure he doesn't fall off the mountain.'

Privot was feinting punches now. Mansworth flinched as more of his sweat struck his cheek. 'Honestly, Privot, go away! You smell like a plough horse!'

This time the laughter was less kind.

Privot adopted a smile to deflect the insult, but he lacked the necessary facial muscles to achieve much more than a pained sneer. Mansworth clamped his nostrils between thumb and forefinger, provoking more laughter.

Outraged that his physical prowess could make him the butt of a joke delivered by a physical inferior, Privot paced the overlook, then lay upon the rock, a few feet from Mansworth, and directed a small shot across the bow: 'He said you looked like a girl.'

Mansworth didn't stir.

'He said you *eat* like a girl,' Privot went on. 'And you *sound* like a girl.' He shrugged. 'That's what I heard.'

'And what are *you*? A parrot?' replied Mansworth, sitting up, looking not at Privot but at the expressions of the other boys.

'I wouldn't let him call *me* a girl,' challenged Privot, gazing innocently at the sky.

'I wouldn't let him call you a girl either,' Mansworth remarked, but his joke failed because the other boys were now considering Mansworth's long hair. The point was made, and Mansworth fell into a surly and petulant silence.

TOM HAD KEPT his distance from Arthur for a few days; they had not spoken since their discussion about Arthur's parents. But the run had brought them into proximity again, and Tom found himself slightly behind Arthur on the steepest part.

It was obvious that Arthur was no more comfortable with the physical world than with its society. His posture was comical: his feet splayed, his arms flailed, and he dodged bushes by either leaping over them or going ridiculously far out of his way to avoid them. He also had a habit of jerking his elbows outward as he navigated an upward step, and he poked more than one boy in the ribs as he passed by. Tom had an opportunity to overtake him, but he decided to keep his place behind him. To pass him would be an unnecessary betrayal.

They were still meandering through gorse, heather and tall pines, but the summit was near, so Tom paused to catch his breath and retie his shoes. Arthur lurched forward into the mist, and Tom heard voices ahead. Arthur was being greeted by several figures; Mansworth was easy to recognize because he kept shaking aside his long hair, but four other boys flanked him. Defiant words were exchanged. Tom let his laces be and ran to catch up. By the time he reached Mansworth, Arthur was gone, and two of Mansworth's disciples were pursuing him up the path.

'What's this?' said Tom.

'Nothing that concerns you,' Mansworth replied. 'Pigeon needs a lesson, and he's about to get it.'

'Mansworth,' said Tom, 'Privot bullies him because he's a brute, but why do *you*? He's harmless. What must you prove?'

Tom's question seemed to startle Mansworth; his eyes flickered at his two friends, who meandered down the trail a short distance away. 'The only one who can keep Privot under control is me. So when I make an example of Pigeon, I'm only keeping things fair for the rest of us. Do you honestly want a brute like Privot to run the school?'

Suddenly the boys who had followed Arthur returned, grinning from ear to ear, their task apparently accomplished.

'Choose your friends wisely, Bedlam!' whispered Mansworth, as he joined his acolytes.

When Tom found him, Arthur was lying between two large sandstone boulders. His hands were bound behind his back with long gorse stems, and his mouth was stuffed with heather. Tom untied him, and the boy spat out the heather, his eyes welling with tears.

'What did they want?' asked Tom, but Arthur's lips were so badly swollen that he couldn't form words. Even if he could have spoken, Tom guessed that pride would have restrained him.

When several boys came running along the path, they noted Arthur's condition and clustered around him.

'What happened, Bedlam?' they cried.

'Mansworth had him roughed up.'

'Why?'

'I don't know.'

'Privot told Mansworth that Pigeon called him a girl. That's the *bibletruth*,' said Winesap, who had returned from the summit. 'When you've got hair down *shoulderways*,' he added, 'it hurts your feelings, if you *have* feelings, I s'pose.'

Abandoning their obligation to reach the summit, the boys escorted Arthur down the path. It was an odd gesture of empathy with a pariah, Tom thought, though he suspected their compassion was mingled with the relief that Arthur's misery was an alternative to their own.

Mr Phibbs stood at the base of the mountain when the boys arrived. Tom and Winesap explained what had occurred. Phibbs examined Arthur with impatience. 'You're unhurt, aren't you?' he said impatiently. 'Nothing wrong, is there? You're in one piece, aren't you?'

Reminded of his father's habit of asking questions that permitted just one reply, Tom felt a surge of outrage. 'Perhaps we should speak to the headmaster, sir,' he said.

'I'll be the judge of that,' snapped Phibbs. 'Now, who hasn't been up the peak yet?'

But the boys stuck by Arthur until the disciplinarian gave up and ordered them back to the school.

WHEN PIGEON APPEARED at breakfast in the dining hall, he was a shock to behold. The scuffle in the woods had produced welts on his bare scalp, and his lips were bloated, bloody and misshapen. Tom, Winesap, Lopping and Cooper kept him company, and every boy who passed by couldn't help staring at his pale, vulnerable state.

Mr Grindle, eyes fixed on Arthur, directed a word into the ear of Mr Goodkind, who reacted as if his porridge had been purposely oversalted. Then he stepped down from the dais and approached Arthur's table.

'Stand up, Pigeon,' he said.

Arthur rose slowly. The headmaster kept his hands in his pockets as he stared at the boy's lips. The room quietened.

'An accident, Pigeon?'

'He was beaten, sir,' said Tom.

'He may answer for himself, Bedlam,' said the headmaster.

Arthur attempted to speak but was hindered by his inability to form certain consonants. ' 'Eaten, sir,' he replied.

'Speak up.'

Anger flickered in Arthur's dark eyes, but he tried again: 'I 'as 'eaten, sir, 'y two 'oys.'

Mr Goodkind frowned. 'Really, Pigeon, I cannot understand a word you're saying.'

'He was beaten by two boys, sir,' said Tom.

'Were you a witness, Bedlam?'

'No, sir.'

'Well, my boy' – Mr Goodkind smiled – 'you can hardly speak for him. If a boy wants to make accusations, he must do so for himself at Hammer Hall.'

A collective murmur acknowledged the headmaster's point. Tom noticed Mansworth and Privot rest easy in their seats. He wondered if any boy had ever before dared make such an accusation before the entire school.

Arthur, however, was struggling to form the consonants that had previously eluded him. As Goodkind turned to leave, he spoke.

'I . . . was *beaten by two boys*, sir!'

The headmaster turned. 'What were their names?'

'I don't know! I was pushed down!'

Mr Goodkind's features slackened. 'Then what am I to do?' he said. 'I cannot punish *everybody*.'

A murmur spread, and became a chuckle as it reached Mansworth's table.

Suddenly blood was flowing from Arthur's nose. Down his lips it dribbled, and fell upon his chin and shirt. The moment he saw it, Arthur fainted.

The room fell silent. The headmaster's next words contained a tinge of regret. 'Clean this boy. I'll see him in my study later.'

—

UNFORTUNATELY, MRS BRASIER's powers of healing were as dubious as her culinary skills. Tom found Arthur in the privy behind the kitchen. Though the nosebleed had stopped, and his lips had shrunk a little, he had developed diarrhoea from the dose of fish oil she had administered. 'I'm filthy,' he complained. 'Tom, could you get me some fresh clothes?'

'Of course,' Tom replied. He went to the attic and retrieved a clean set, although Arthur refused to put them on until he was sure his stomach had settled. 'She's a monster,' he said, nodding in the direction of Mrs Brasier's kitchen. 'She told me to let the blood pour out. Said it was *bad blood.* What an idiot! Wouldn't leave me alone until I told her I was going to shit her kitchen!'

'I've heard of letting out bad blood,' Tom admitted.

'My father's a *doctor*,' said Arthur, with a glare. 'I've had nosebleeds all my life. I have them when I'm upset.'

'I'm sorry,' said Tom.

Arthur stared uneasily at him. There was something else he wanted to say.

'Bedlam,' he began, 'there's something I said to you before that wasn't true. My parents adopted me, as you thought.'

'How old were you?'

'A newborn baby,' Arthur replied. 'I should have just admitted it, but I wasn't sure what you were up to. One can't trust anyone.'

'Arthur,' Tom began, 'I believe we may be brothers. I can't be positive, but my brother was adopted, and my mother told me once that he had a birthmark here, just as you do.'

Deep in the boy's hollow stare, Tom detected a look of surprise, then distress. Arthur Pigeon was completely unprepared for such a revelation – he was accustomed to being an outcast. The idea of *belonging* was too sweet to be believed, and perhaps in defence of being wounded again, his scepticism gave vent.

'I don't see how it is likely,' Arthur replied. 'We don't look a bit alike.'

'Haven't you known brothers who looked as different as strangers?' Tom replied.

'I have,' Arthur conceded thoughtfully. 'My father has often reminded me that I am adopted. When I misbehaved, he threatened to return me to my parents; he told me they were ruined, desperate folk and assured me that I would come to great harm in their company.'

Tom was quite dismayed by the element of truth in these words – what was his mother, if not ruined by abandonment and poverty? Was there a more desperate man than William Bedlam, who stole from his estranged wife and child?

'But you hardly seem the ruined, desperate sort,' Arthur added. 'I wondered why you protected me,' he said, 'because I didn't think anybody was, by nature, kind. A brother, though, is different – a best friend and a guardian – a trustworthy soul.' For a moment he pondered this idea. 'So, if indeed I was to *choose* a brother, you would be my first choice.'

Tom felt relief at this, for the evidence of their bond, however flimsy, was strengthened by Arthur's approval. He sincerely wished it to be fact, and Arthur seemed at least willing to consider it so.

Arthur extended his hand to Tom, who smiled with relief. They shook hands.

It was an odd scene: the smoky kitchen, the blackened walls and ceiling, Arthur's bloody collar and shirt, and the sober handshake. The fire in the hearth suddenly flared brightly and seemed to roar in celebration of their kinship.

Mrs Brasier approached, her face shiny with sweat, smelling of old potato peelings while sweat stains blossomed at her waist and armpits. 'What are you two so happy about all of a sudden?' she cried. They laughed while she stared at them, baffled.

'I'm a little better,' Arthur replied eventually.

She took a bottle of fish oil out of her apron pocket. 'It always does me a world of good. Will you take a little more?'

Arthur adamantly declared himself quite well, so Mrs Brasier replaced the bottle and sent him, with Tom as escort, to Mr Goodkind's study.

'What will you say to him?' Tom asked.

'I don't know,' Arthur replied. 'But I'll recommend the fish oil.'

At the headmaster's doorway, Arthur took a breath, knocked and entered. Tom stood alone in the corridor, smiling to himself. All at once he had an ally, a friend and a brother.

'YOU'RE IN FOR IT!' cried Privot. 'You should never have touched him. He's *mine*!'

Tom had walked into an argument between Mansworth and Privot in the attic. Privot was doing frantic knee bends on the floor while Mansworth lay upon his cot, arms folded, echoing Privot's vigorous gestures with casual disdain – yawning, for example, when the red-faced boy spat out his next caution: 'Mansworth, if he points the finger at *me*, I shall point it at you!'

'It's not as though *you* haven't tormented the fellow too!' replied Mansworth.

Suddenly, footsteps came up the winding staircase, and all eyes fell upon Arthur Pigeon as he entered, followed by Mr Phibbs. He walked to his bed and lay down.

'You wretched scoundrels,' began the little man as he surveyed the boys. 'Demons! Hooligans! You'll have your comeuppance!' From Phibbs's tirade, one might have thought that original sin was born in the faces before him. For their part, the boys stared downward with anything but contrition. They had heard all of this before.

Mansworth stood up, walked over to Phibbs, and murmured a private question. Phibbs shrugged. Mansworth placed a coin in the master's waistcoat pocket, which inspired him to depart.

He struck the rafters two times with his stick, cried out 'Hooligans!' and went down the stairs.

Arthur rested facedown upon his bed while Privot and Mansworth approached him. Tom rose to his feet to protect the boy, but Mansworth put a gentle hand on Arthur's shoulder, and Privot sat on the bed without offering threat or provocation.

'I'm sorry, Pigeon. It should not have happened,' said Mansworth.

'And it never will again. I'll make sure of that,' said Privot.

Arthur said nothing. Though his visitors waited, hoping for some intelligence on his meeting with the headmaster, he remained prone and silent.

'I suppose Mr Goodkind was upset,' said Mansworth.

'Furious, even,' offered Privot.

Arthur turned his head. He stared at his interlocutors but offered no word.

With each second of silence, Mansworth and Privot seemed to weaken. Eventually they withdrew to their cots. But Lopping, Winesap and Cooper were excited to see the pair vulnerable for once. Tom, however, was gazing at Arthur.

He was now convinced that Emily Bedlam's righteous stoicism had been reborn in Arthur Pigeon.

MR NEITHER/NOR

THE NEXT MORNING IN THE DINING HALL, MR GOODKIND DID NOT acknowledge Arthur, but at the conclusion of his meal, he shared a word with Mr Phibbs and left the room. Almost immediately, Mr Phibbs struck his staff upon the floor.

'Two boys shall report to the headmaster's study forthwith!'

Arthur's hillside assailants ducked under the table. Mr Phibbs marched right past them, however, surveyed the assembled boys, and with a nervous gulp said: 'Mansworth and Privot.'

Every boy was surprised, but the two addressed were the most surprised of all. They followed Mr Phibbs out, and the ensuing conversation in the hall took on an excited, joyous tone.

Winesap couldn't help but exclaim, 'Well, isn't that a *puzzlement*! Methinks they're in for an *upcommance*!'

Tom glanced at Mr Grindle, but the master's expression indicated neither surprise nor satisfaction. He turned to Arthur. 'What did you tell him?'

'What did you tell him?' echoed Lopping.

'I told him the truth,' replied Arthur.

'About what happened on the mountain?' said Tom.

'Why was Privot hauled up, then?' added Winesap.

'Mansworth said to me that he and Privot *run the school*,' said Arthur, 'so that was what I said.'

IN ANY INSTITUTION, especially one in which there is a vicious struggle for power, only the naïve think that the spoken truth can work like a thunderbolt from the heavens and mete out justice. Thus, the younger boys were sure that Mansworth and Privot would receive their deserved punishment and peace would result, while the older boys at Hammer Hall doubted this. They knew that Mr Goodkind wished for order, not justice.

More than an hour passed, and Mansworth and Privot were not released. During Latin class, however, Lopping pointed (through the grimy windows) at two figures – one with a red face, one with flowing hair – walking ahead of Mr Goodkind towards the stable.

'*Definitely* for the crop!' remarked one boy.

Winesap turned to Tom. 'Mr Goodkind has a nickname.'

'What's that?'

'Mr Neither/Nor.'

'Neither/Nor? Why?'

The boys all shared a knowing glance, and Lopping whispered, '*Neither* good, *nor* kind.'

A FEW MOMENTS LATER, the headmaster commenced the dispensation of justice in the stables. The harsh snap of the crop and the subsequent cry of pain echoed between the trees and across the courtyard. In the classrooms of Hammer Hall, the boys flinched with each blow; it was impossible to savour the ritual. Justice was one thing, but the sound of Privot and Mansworth begging for mercy was wrenching.

A CHANGE OF SUITS

After Mansworth and Privot had been punished, they did not linger on the summit of Hammer Peak any more; they shunned the other boys and each other, sharing not a word or glance. Each brooded upon his humiliation, the loss of his supporters and status.

One day Winesap joined Arthur and Tom on the run and asked when they would start enlisting.

'Enlisting?'

'*Side*,' said Winesap. 'Your side and Arthur's side.'

'No,' said Tom. 'No more sides.'

There were several inquiries like this – now that the boys were liberated, they seemed incapable of thinking in terms other than those of their recent oppression.

Arthur shook his head. 'The *first* thing they do after getting rid of tyrants is look for new ones,' he despaired. 'What's wrong with them?'

More attempts were made to split the boys into camps. Mansworth spread rumours of insults directed by Arthur against Tom, but Tom quashed them by announcing that he and Arthur were brothers. A new spirit of comity emerged. Mansworth found himself on the fringe again.

One day, as they ran up the peak, Arthur asked to know more about his past. He probed Tom for details about Emily Bedlam and Bill Bedlam's career and the circumstances of his birth. His own adoptive family consisted of an enormous array of uncles, aunts, nieces, nephews and cousins, so he was disappointed by the estranged nature of his family of origin. As for Bill Bedlam's decision to put him up for adoption, he was devastated. He asked plaintively, 'He told her I was dead? Did I mean *nothing* to him?'

'My father was afraid his career would be ruined.'

Arthur stopped running, as if his own value in the world had suddenly been reduced to some meaningless fraction. 'But I was a *baby*! I was helpless!'

'Aren't you better off,' said Tom, 'with parents who want you?'

Arthur, however, was shaken by the idea that he had been given away for any reason. He asked Tom more questions: 'Was I given a name? Where would I be now if I had not been given away?'

With his answers, Tom conveyed to Arthur a sense of Bill Bedlam's selfish pragmatism, the desperate piety of Emily Bedlam's existence, his own job feeding the furnaces of Todderman's factory, and the arrival of Mr Shears.

These revelations were shocking and changed Arthur's perspective on Tom. Sometimes Arthur would stare at him from his cot in a way that unnerved him, as if Arthur were weighing the value of Tom's life against his own, and the value of an adoptive family of caring relations over a natural family of estranged and eccentric persons.

'I am glad to have you as a brother, but I pity you, Tom,' Arthur remarked one day. 'You have so few friends.'

This amused Tom, for he felt the same about Arthur. 'But I *have* friends,' he replied. 'Haven't I told you about the Limpkins?'

Arthur shook his head, so Tom described his games with Oscar and Audrey, the lemon tarts, and the Orfling. When he next received a letter from Audrey, he read it aloud to Arthur to prove that he was not so alone.

The letter, however, brought shocking news:

My dearest Tom,

Forgive my silence, but much has happened; it is only now that I find myself free to write to you.

Father had been in worsened spirits after the new year, and by February, he had sunk very low. He walked with his hands in his pockets, eyes barely straying from the cobblestones directly ahead. He took to reciting his accounts as he walked, in the hopes of finding some solution to our debt.

When Mother announced that another baby was on the way, it was the final straw. 'But the Orfling was to be our last!' he cried. 'Wasn't his arrested condition a message to us?'

Indeed, the Orfling hasn't changed since you left, Tom. He's still the sweetest thing, though he remains a red-cheeked little darling, unable to walk or fend for himself.

I reminded Father that he would never be lonely with so many children in the house, but this only brought tears to his eyes. 'My dear,' he replied, 'I pray you keep such a good spirit in the face of adversity, for I am defeated!'

Father had never spoken so before, and we were all moved to silence. Even the Orfling curled up in my arms without a word. I began to walk Father to his offices, fearful that he might consider taking his life, but after a week, he was brighter. I imagined that the recitation of our accounts had presented him with a solution.

One Friday evening, Father didn't return from his office at the Mercantile Exchange, so I went to find him, but they told me he had left at the usual time, whistling as he stepped onto the street. I followed his path home, unable to find any sign of him. Then, on Sunday evening, Oscar went to the police station and learned that a man had been struck by horses on Chancery Lane. He was so badly injured that nobody could identify him. I went with Oscar to see him, but Oscar refused to let me see the body.

He had no doubt that it was Father.

Oscar took a collection from his friends at the paper to bury Father. We laid him to rest last week. But the matter of our survival weighed heavily upon me; Mother was due in six weeks, and Oscar couldn't support us with his job.

Seeing no alternative, I presented myself at Father's offices to replace him. They turned me away, declaring that a female could not possess the intelligence to count sums all day, and urged me to send my brother. That evening we wept – Mother, the twins, and even the Orfling seemed to grasp our dilemma. We Limpkins had always been wanting for money but wealthy in children. How ironic that we should now be wishing for another son.

After a sleepless night, I came upon the only possible solution: the following day I returned to the offices; but this time my hair was cut short (with Eloise and Elsie's help), and I dressed in Oscar's old clothes – shirt, waistcoat, tie, Father's shoes (two sizes larger than mine). I slumped my shoulders and kept my hands in my pockets as Oscar always does. And after I took their silly exam, I was declared competent to apprentice as a clerk!

I am now to begin my professional life in London as 'Edmund' Limpkin! I wear trousers, stockings and shoes, as befits a young 'man' of my station.

Audrey

'What fools not to let her work in the first place,' Arthur said.

'Well, of course,' said Tom, 'but she has been dishonest. Edmund Limpkin doesn't exist. You can't go about pretending to be somebody you're not.'

'William Bedlam makes a career of it,' rejoined Arthur, bitterly.

'Agreed,' said Tom. 'But he is a scoundrel.'

'Audrey, however, is supporting her siblings and her pregnant mother,' Arthur added. 'She may pass herself off as the Queen if it puts food on the table.'

'Don't you believe there's something wrong about having to pretend to be somebody you're not?'

Arthur's lips formed a smile. 'You've never told anyone else here that you worked in a factory, that our mother died, or that our father was an actor.'

TAKING ARTHUR'S PERSPECTIVE TO HEART, Tom wrote an answer to Audrey's letter:

Dear Audrey,

I think what you have done is courageous and admirable, but I hope that it is a short-lived circumstance. I miss you, and hope to see you soon.

Tom

'What about "affectionately", or "sincerely", or "fondly"?' added Arthur, reading over Tom's shoulder.

'I don't love her,' Tom replied.

'Oh,' Arthur sniffed. 'I must have been confusing her with the girl who *never* writes to you.'

'Is there anyone *you* love, Arthur?'

'No,' Arthur replied after some thought. 'But if one comes along, I shall expect you to be brutally candid.'

POLLY PECKAM

NOW THAT PRIVOT AND MANSWORTH HAD BEEN HUMILIATED INTO submission, Mr Trent was allowed to teach mathematics, and Cooper rose to the occasion, answering questions as frequently as possible. Mr Barby enjoyed a similar liberation and made progress with the boys on the subject of crustaceans.

Later in the week, Mr Trent was alarmed when eight boys solved their equations correctly; he visited Mrs Brasier, fearing that he was ill with a sustained delusion. The cook dispensed fish oil, and Mr Trent spent most of the night in the privy. The next day he returned to the classroom with an eager smile, though discomfort compelled him to teach standing up.

Mr Grindle, who was still in the habit of taking his morning walks in the countryside, was picking bramble thorns from his trousers when Tom greeted him.

'How are you, Bedlam?'

'Well, sir,' Tom replied. 'Particularly since Pigeon spoke to Mr Goodkind.'

Grindle nodded. 'Be careful, my boy,' he advised. 'The headmaster's solution is temporary. Those boys won't give up easily.'

Shortly after this exchange, Mrs Brasier succeeded in igniting herself during breakfast. A lick of flame crept up the back of her skirt as she spun in front of the kitchen fireplace and followed her into the dining hall. By the time she approached the masters' table, it was devouring her apron strings.

She ignored the boys' cries of warning until the fire engulfed her cotton cap. Then, clamping her hands over her ears, she cried, 'Oh, God save me, I'm ablaze!'

Mr Phibbs sprang to the rescue. Seizing his stick, he considered beating the flames off the woman's back but thought better of it and, instead, pulled Mrs Brasier's petticoats over her head to smother them.

One of the risks in having an unfortunate mishap in plain sight of scores of curious, fertile minds is its appropriation to school mythology. So inspired was Winesap that he composed a parody of Tennyson's 'Lady of Shalott':

There was a fire within a room,
That licked and sparked inside the gloom.
We all portended certain doom,
For the lady of Brasier.
One day it set her skirts aflame
And wrenched a cry from that poor dame,
Her backside was exposed (for shame!)
Poor old lady of Brasier.
When next you pass a fire, dear
Be sure to beat the embers clear
There's nothing worse than a burning rear
(Just ask the lady of Brasier).

Mrs Brasier, however, was more concerned with the loss of her hair than with the exposure of her person. Humiliated by her reflection, she marched up to Mr Goodkind's office and demanded an assistant. 'I slave in that kitchen at risk to life and limb. I must have help!' she cried.

'But, madam, there is nobody for miles who could fill such a position,' murmured the headmaster. 'What are the chances, with the available fees, that we might find someone worthy of you?'

Mrs Brasier, though prey to the elements, was no weak soul when she wanted something. 'I've a niece,' she replied, 'a girl of many talents. She could be brought from Boleford at a moment's notice.'

'Boleford?' Mr Goodkind frowned. 'To live at the *school*?'

'Of course,' said Mrs Brasier. 'She could sleep in the matron's chamber.'

'Of course!' the headmaster remarked. 'We've been in need of a matron ever since the last one passed away.'

'A matron?' Mrs Brasier scowled. 'She is to be my kitchen maid.'

'My dear woman, if she is to live under our roof, eat our food, she shall serve the school in every capacity possible. During meals, she shall assist you, and when she is not so employed, she shall care for the boys.'

'Care for the boys? Lord help them, she's a half-wit!' Mrs Brasier cried, forgetting that she had been singing the girl's praises.

Mr Goodkind interrupted her with the confidence of a man who has no doubt about the basic truths of men and women. 'She is of the *gentle* sex, Mrs Brasier, is she not? Surely she can administer aid if one of the boys falls ill?'

They negotiated a wage that Mrs Brasier was sure her niece would accept, and Mr Goodkind reduced that by a few farthings to please the board of trustees.

A WEEK LATER an apparition sailed across the moor towards Hammer Hall; Privot saw her first as he did his solitary exercises upon Hammer Peak. The folds of her woollen cloak billowed like a black spinnaker as she rode beside the driver on a cart. She was narrow-faced, with dark hair tied back in a bun.

'What does she look like?' the shortsighted boys asked as they squinted.

'She's a beauty,' declared Privot. Though his eyes were weak too, he saw an opportunity to assume authority and made the most of it. 'A natural beauty, she is!'

Like castaways watching a sail on the horizon, the boys spun their own fantasies from this first impression. As her features became more visible – a pale, slender face, sullen eyes and a minuscule pout of a mouth – Tom found himself yearning for Sissy, but the reverent silence around him suggested that the other boys were already smitten by the newcomer.

CLOSER SCRUTINY OF Mrs Brasier's niece took place at the evening meal. Plain-featured, with a nervous, bobbing chin, Polly displayed the awkwardness of a girl who had recently assumed adult proportions. Her elbows, fingers, knees and ankles conspired against her, jerking, bobbing and twitching. She was a sturdy girl: her waist wasn't narrow, and neither were her calves. For the evening she had braided her hair into pigtails, which swung jauntily and gave her a pretty grace that drew the attention of every boy.

When Mrs Brasier directed her to apportion the soup to the masters first, the girl seized a wooden ladle and, trembling, spilled most of its contents before reaching the first bowl. Terrified by the many eyes focused upon her, she became increasingly clumsy.

'Smaller amounts, Polly. Nobody will lick it off the table, my dear!' snapped her aunt, to which Polly would reply with a cascade of 'Oops, ma'am, forgive me, oh deary, sir, forgive us!'

Mr Phibbs received a generous serving of soup in his lap, and Mr Trent's waistcoat was sprayed with his helping. The other masters regarded the girl with a degree of fear as she approached. But Polly was determined to improve; she compensated by reducing the quantity she poured. By the time she had circled the table, the last master, Mr Grindle, received no more than a tablespoonful. He seemed gratified by this, however, and delicately removed the bone hairpin that lay adrift in it.

'Mrs Brasier,' he remarked, raising the item for the entire room to see. 'This, I believe, is yours!'

The cook snatched the hairpin without a word while Mr Grindle stared at her contemptuously.

As Polly served the boys, she encountered a more generous audience. Each lad forgave her when the soup was spilled, and all eyes followed her path around the tables.

To her credit, Polly *wanted* to do a good job; her lips were pressed so firmly together that they turned white as she ladled.

Lopping made the mistake of asking her name, which gave her such a shock that she emptied a ladleful onto his kneecaps. The boy bolted up from his seat with a scream, while Polly (torn between her roles as matron and ladler) spun about, spilling soup in an arc around her. Eventually she ran after Lopping (still brandishing the ladle), which convinced him to run out of the hall for fear of being burned again.

'I LIKE HER EYES,' said Cooper dreamily that evening when they were all in bed.

'How touching,' muttered Mansworth.

'Figuratively speaking,' ventured Winesap, 'she doesn't have much *bottomwise.* Mrs Brasier, on the other hand, has a solid figure.'

'So does a sack of potatoes,' countered Privot.

When Lopping entered, all eyes noted that his knees, bandaged with yards of gauze, were as bulbous as the joints of a flamingo. If Polly's affection could be measured in gauze, Lopping was now king of the hill.

Noting the others' jealous stares, he said, 'What?'

'Did it on purpose, didn't you?' said Mansworth with disgust.

'What?' Lopping repeated.

'You took advantage of her sympathies,' added Privot.

Perplexed by these accusations, Lopping winced down the aisle to his bed. Tom observed grimly that Mansworth and Privot had just claimed territory – not the classroom this time, but the devoutly desired affection of Polly Peckam.

ONE MORNING SNOW appeared over Hammer Peak. It iced the fields and sugared the fences and dappled the thatched roofs of the local shepherds' cottages. Tom surveyed this vista from the window at the head of his bed – in the attic, the windows ran along the floor, just below the eaves. He spotted a figure in the flurry. It was Mr Grindle, out for his morning stroll; the seat of his trousers was powdered with snow from where he must have rested to catch his breath, his wispy grey hair was in disarray, and his shirttails dangled from beneath his waistcoat. Tom wondered how it would be to teach, like Grindle, and see a pageant of boyhood pass while time aged him until his face was withered and his figure gnarled like an old tree.

Suddenly Tom smelled onions and felt Arthur crouching near him.

'How miserable must that fellow be?' whispered Arthur, pressing his nose to the glass.

Grindle paused by a patch of bulrushes topped with snow and burst into a coughing fit. For a moment, his hazy silhouette crouched and bobbed in the field as he hacked until his shirttails flapped and his head sank even lower to the ground.

'Should we help him?' Tom wondered.

Arthur narrowed his eyes. 'He's all right,' he said firmly. Indeed, within moments Grindle had recovered and resumed his slow pace through the snow. 'My father can tell at a glance what's wrong with a man on the outside. All he needs to do is listen to his chest and he knows what's wrong on the inside.'

Tom considered Bill Bedlam's virtues but could think only of a man on a tightrope, in a wedding dress, waving a parasol. 'Are you going to be a doctor?' he asked.

Arthur shuddered. 'Besides my terror of heights – that horrible run up the mountain makes me retch – I can't *stand* sick people. The sight of blood makes me faint. Anybody with an illness gives me the jitters. When Mr Barby had toothache, I couldn't go near him for a week.'

'But you can't catch toothache,' Tom countered.

Arthur's expression turned combative. 'When did *you* become a doctor?'

'I just *know*,' Tom answered, somewhat irritated by Arthur's disdain. 'Toothache is not like other diseases.'

'Many things that are wrong with people are transmitted,' Arthur replied. '*Communicable.* That's what they call it. Things we don't understand.' His stare lingered on Tom, as if to emphasize his authority in this regard.

'Not toothache,' Tom insisted.

'Cruelty, then,' Arthur continued, 'and greed. And *lust.* I don't know anything more catching among boys than those things.' He snapped his fingers before Tom's eyes. 'Just like that, they all become sick with it.'

'Perhaps cruelty is catching,' conceded Tom, remembering the round of assaults Arthur had received when he arrived. 'But I can't imagine *lust* being so.'

Arthur gave Tom a knowing glance.

'What?' replied Tom.

'If you're going to be a doctor, you must be *observant*.'

'I never said I was.'

'Then stop contradicting me,' Arthur glared. With that, he rose and walked away, taking the smell of onions with him.

There was an increasing number of scalding incidents. At the masters' table, smaller portions became the request (clearly an attempt at self-preservation). All of the masters had lost weight – the result of Polly's inability to convey any steaming substance from pot to bowl without risk of a burn or blister.

The inverse ratio was the case among the boys, who eagerly demanded second and third helpings merely for the privilege of gazing upon Polly's face and the sweet pleasure, if they were scalded, of forgiving her.

The Welsh laundress, Mrs Mollet, who washed the boys' clothes every two weeks, noted the enormous amounts of grey sludge that bubbled to the surface of her laundry tub. 'My word, how these lads spill over themselves. Like pigs at a trough!' she declared.

Of all the boys, Arthur was least enamoured of Polly, and he noted the others' adoration with scorn. 'Astonishing. You'd think she was doing them a favour by dripping all over them,' he remarked to Tom.

When Polly approached his place, Arthur withheld his bowl. 'Not for me,' he cried.

'Just a little?' Polly replied.

Arthur turned over his bowl to make his wish clear.

Polly seemed offended. 'You'll waste away to nothing,' she warned him.

'Better than having blisters on my hands and legs,' Arthur said.

Polly closed her eyes briefly. She seemed stung by his remark. Her ladling hand tipped, and Lopping received a piping hot dose of pea soup on his hand. He turned his yelp of pain into one of forgiveness. 'It's nothing, *really*,' he cried. 'I hardly felt it!'

But Polly gave him no smile. Arthur Pigeon's indifference to her had reined in her heartstrings. From then on, Polly begged him to eat, but Arthur spurned her.

'She likes you,' Tom whispered to Arthur when they were alone.

'It doesn't help her aim,' Arthur sniffed. 'She could kill someone with that ladle. Imagine my epitaph. *Death by ladle.*' Then he added, 'Have you noticed that she smells of onions?'

Tom tried a different tack. 'She watches you from across the room,' he said. 'She *adores* you, Arthur.'

COMPETITION FOR POLLY'S attention was becoming heated. After Mansworth gave the girl a pair of pink satin ribbons for her hair, Privot produced a black choker. Polly wore both gifts the next day and paused to display them to Arthur.

'Do you like them?' she asked, shaking her pigtails and touching her neck demurely.

'I neither like nor dislike them,' he replied.

Polly clamped her mouth shut and went about her duties, scalding many more boys at dinner than usual. It was clear that she was unhappy, so her admirers became all the more determined to win her heart. Ribbons, sweets sent from home and even scribbled portraits appeared on the dining tables, but they meant nothing to Polly because they were not from Arthur.

During an afternoon lesson, Tom noticed that a figure had been drawn upon one of the desks, carved with a penknife, then inlaid with black ink. It was Polly, with her solid frame and petulant features. Within a week, more of these images had appeared on desks, tabletops and even on the oak trees near the stables. When he pointed them out to Arthur, the boy nodded. 'See?' he said. 'Lust *is* catching.'

MANSWORTH'S REVENGE

IN APRIL, MRS BRASIER CAME UP WITH SOME INVENTIVE SOLUTIONS to the lack of beef at the market. One such dish was referred to as 'pigeon stew', though it was rumoured that almost anything from squirrel to vole might lurk in it.

Polly served all the boys at the table, saving Arthur for last. When she appeared before him, Arthur turned his bowl facedown.

'Pigeon stew?' she asked, trembling.

'Why on *earth* would I eat pigeon stew?'

'It would be *fowl* and *cannibalistic*,' intoned Winesap, 'for a *Pigeon* to eat pigeon stew.' Some boys laughed, but they were silenced by Polly's concern.

'I don't want you to waste away, Arthur,' she said. 'Please, let me find *something* for you!'

It was true: Arthur *was* wasting away. Tom noticed that the skin on the boy's wrists was drawn so tightly that he could see the throb of his pulse.

Polly whispered in Arthur's ear. 'Tell me what you would like to eat and I'll get it from the kitchen.'

Arthur whispered something to her, and she slipped away. To the other boys, however, it had looked like the most intimate kiss, and as if Arthur had scored another triumph.

—

LATER THAT EVENING, Arthur scrambled up the stairs to the attic with a bundle in his shirt. He spilled the contents into his cot and began to throw apples to the other boys.

'I have a dozen,' he declared, grinning. 'And they're delicious. Polly took them from Mrs Brasier's pantry. They're only for the masters, apparently.'

'I hope you're kind to her now,' said Tom.

Arthur threw his last apple to Mansworth, who caught it, staring at him with bitter derision. The apple in his hand might well have been a gauntlet.

AT BREAKFAST THE NEXT morning, Arthur inquired after Polly's health.

She looked startled. 'Beg pardon?'

'How are you, Polly?'

'I'm well, thank ye,' she replied, lower lip trembling. She reached into her apron and gave Arthur an orange.

He slipped it into his pocket. 'Very kind of you, Polly.'

Her forehead cleared, and she gasped, blinking, as if to savour this rare treat. As she went about serving the other boys, Tom noticed a new grace in her step.

Mansworth frowned as he observed this exchange from the far end of the bench.

'What are *you* looking at, Mansworth?' Winesap laughed.

'Lost love!' joked Cooper.

As the other boys echoed their amusement, Mansworth brooded over Polly through the dark curtain of his forelock.

AFTER THE INCIDENT in the dining room, Mansworth found another boy basking in his spot on Hammer Peak, in the same position, mocking his languid pose. And on the run down, a posse of boys made a habit of bumping him into the bracken. Each gesture inspired another to target the fallen leader.

Nobody bothered Privot. He was too strong, so he was left alone. He held Mansworth responsible for his fall, however, and appeared content to let his rival bear the abuse of the others.

Mansworth directed no attack on his tormentors; there were simply too many. Instead, he focused his fury on the boy he blamed for his troubles. He shadowed Arthur in the corridors and sat directly behind him in the dining hall, maintaining the proximity of a predator.

One Saturday afternoon, Hammer Hall was flooded with light. The boys tumbled out into the courtyard, where Mrs Mollet had hung the sheets for their half-yearly bleaching. The sun, a stunning blue sky, and the drone of bees on the meadow nearby signalled a new season, and the boys became giddy and silly. A game of tag erupted. Someone found chalk and started to scrawl pictures on the flagstones. Arthur seized a sheet from the washing line and spun it around his waist, then whirled across the courtyard chanting babble.

Mansworth, ruminating on his nemesis from a doorway, could contain himself no longer. 'Aren't you worried that you'll look like a girl, Pigeon?' he asked.

Arthur shrugged with careless abandon. 'It never occurred to me,' he replied. 'Do you worry about appearing to be a girl, Mansworth?'

Shaking aside his forelock, Mansworth growled, 'Give me that!' and seized the sheet so roughly that Arthur lost his balance and struck his head on the flagstones. In an instant, Mansworth was on him, pressing his right foot upon Arthur's neck until the boy was gasping for breath.

'Let him be, Mansworth!' cried Tom.

Mansworth eyed the others, daring them to join Tom in defending his victim. 'Who wants to help him? C'mon, let's see who all of his friends are!' Then he adjusted his heel to rest upon the boy's sternum.

Tom stepped forward, but before he reached Mansworth, Privot pushed him aside and, with a grin, shook Mansworth's hand.

Surprised, Mansworth acknowledged the gesture with a smile, but then Privot twisted Mansworth's fingers back and kicked his leg from Arthur's chest.

'Get off him, swine. Leave him alone.'

A chorus of jeers repeated this utterance, and Mansworth's gaze turned with dismay on his new critic.

'I'm not taking the crop again for you,' Privot warned him.

'Get on, you *bullyfrog*!' added Winesap.

As Mansworth recoiled, and Arthur got up, new footsteps echoed across the courtyard. It was Polly. She walked up to Mansworth. 'Leave him alone, you cur,' she said and spat in his face. She took Arthur's hand, and the pair walked out of the yard together – the leaden-footed girl and the gangly boy – swinging their arms.

A pang of jealousy struck Tom. How easily Arthur seemed to have fallen in with Polly. Tom's own desire for Sissy had cost him months of yearning, lust and cunning, and even the sacrifice of Audrey's lemon tarts. How had love come so easily to Arthur?

Tom noticed that he was not the only jealous soul. Every other schoolboy stared after them, no doubt estimating when his time would come and wondering if it would be as sweet.

Mansworth's expression differed, however: his lips were drawn tightly across his teeth in a ghastly smile; jealousy appeared to be the last thing on his mind.

The next morning, Tom was shaken into consciousness.

'Wake up, Tom,' whispered a voice. The Bible-size windows of the attic glowed blue in the darkness. Then the odour of onions filled his nostrils.

'I'm sleeping,' Tom muttered.

'You kept *me* up all night with your tossing and turning!' complained the voice. 'I need to talk to you.'

Tom groaned and opened his eyes. Arthur was kneeling beside his bed. 'Tom, there's something I must know. When is your birthday?'

'April twenty-ninth.'

'What year were you born?'

'Eighteen sixty-seven.'

Arthur sighed, and his head sank below Tom's pillow. When he reappeared, he looked upset. 'My birthday's in June of the same year. We cannot *possibly* be brothers.'

Tom put his hands behind his head and stared grimly at the dark rafters. 'I see,' he said, finally. 'It's quite impossible.'

'I thought I knew who I was,' Arthur muttered. 'And now it's a mystery. Can't you imagine what it's like to think you know who you are, then realize it's a riddle again? I'll spend my life passing strangers and wondering if they're my father, my mother—'

'—or brother,' Tom added glumly, but as he thought about Arthur's news, he couldn't help feeling that their bond remained intact. They were still friends – still allies. Regardless of whether they were brothers, they shared a mystery, and this was a strong kinship; but the anguish on Arthur's face was plain, and Tom suddenly felt sympathy for him. He needed consolation.

'Arthur,' he began, 'imagine the fuss here if we admit that we're *not* brothers. Winesap might start a rebellion. We should keep it to ourselves, if only for the sake of the school.'

Arthur looked relieved. 'Yes,' he said with a serious nod, 'you're quite right. No one shall know.'

Tom pulled up his blanket, but Arthur remained by his bed. 'Arthur,' he whispered, 'go back to sleep.'

'Tom, there's another problem. It's Polly,' Arthur whispered. 'It was a lark to hold her hand yesterday, but I was only joking. She's taken leave of her senses – if she had any to begin with. She's written "Mrs Polly Pigeon" all over the walls of her room. *Mrs Polly Pigeon!* It's enough to make one change one's name!'

'You're the envy of half the school,' said Tom sternly. 'However mad she may be, you can't tell *anybody* that. Everybody admires you.'

Arthur took this advice solemnly. 'But she's raving, Tom. What am I going to *do* with her? She'll drive me round the bend!'

Before Tom could reply, footsteps pounded up the stairs. Mr Phibbs struck his stick against the rafters. 'Come, hooligans – get dressed for your run!' On seeing Arthur by Tom's bed, Mr Phibbs's eyebrows rose. 'Dressed already, Pigeon? On your way!'

Arthur gave Tom a last imploring glance.

'We'll talk at the top of the peak,' Tom promised.

That morning a dense fog hung over the mountain as the boys made their ascent. Tom, last in a line of stragglers, rubbed sleep from his eyes as he dodged puddles and thornbushes. A stand of oaks marked the path leading to the peak; their trunks were twisted and grey, and reminded him of the lumps of decomposed meat lying on the street outside the offal house in Vauxhall.

He couldn't see more than a few yards, but he could hear boys talking in the mist about Polly being 'taken'. His thoughts turned to Arthur, and he wondered if his friend was simply repelled by affection of any sort, just as he had once rejected Tom's friendship. Perhaps Polly wasn't mad. Perhaps the shock of being wrenched as an infant from his mother's side had left Arthur unable to accept a kindred spirit.

Ahead, Tom could just discern the dense scrub where the path veered towards the summit of Hammer Peak, but trees stood in silhouette, with every open space portending a precipice. He slowed his pace, trying to recognize the turns of the path. A sudden spray of pebbles announced the descent of Mr Phibbs, who was pounding his gnarled stick on the path with muttered curses. 'On your way, lads!' The school disciplinarian's trembling cheeks shone as he paused before Tom, as if to sum up his progress, though he was merely catching his breath.

'Am I close to the top, sir?' said Tom.

'Not close enough, Bedlam. On your—' The master's feet slid on a patch of wet rock, and he righted himself with both arms flying out, jowls shaking.

Meanwhile, Privot was bounding down the trail. He panted behind Mr Phibbs. 'I'm out of breath, sir!' he said with an exaggerated gasp. In fact, he could barely stop himself leapfrogging the schoolmaster.

'Enough whining, Privot,' barked Phibbs. 'In my youth I walked *twice* this far every morning!'

'In an *avalanching* blizzard, with your father balanced on yer shoulders, I'll be bound, sir,' added Winesap.

'That's enough!' said the master, cuffing the boy's head.

Tom continued his ascent until their voices faded and even the heavy thump of Mr Phibbs's stick could no longer be heard. Then, rounding a corner where the fog rolled forward in the breeze of an unseen abyss, Tom heard a cry.

It was an awful sound – a long, guttural, helpless shriek.

Whether it was above or below him, Tom couldn't tell, but a chill crept up through his chest, and the muscles in his thighs went slack.

'Hallo!' he called.

There was no reply.

Spurred by his worst thought, Tom sprinted the last few yards to the summit. He saw nothing at first, just the awful whiteness of the drop. Then he recognized several boys peering over the southern edge, where Mansworth reclined on sunny mornings. Cooper turned to Tom with a wretched stare. He mouthed something quietly.

'What is it, Cooper?'

Cooper shook his head; his mouth was open, aghast.

'What has happened!' Tom cried.

'Somebody . . . somebody fell, I think,' said Cooper.

From behind them, Mansworth clambered up, gasping, his eyes bright and wild. There was no joy in his expression, though; the smug petulance of his mouth implied grotesque victory of some sort.

'Was that you?' asked Tom.

'What?'

'Who cried out?'

'It was,' Mansworth replied, meeting the glances of the other boys, who stared at him bleakly.

'I thought somebody fell,' said Tom.

'I almost did,' said Mansworth. He dusted off his hands. 'But as you can see, I'm unhurt.'

Tom noticed three scratches running down Mansworth's arm.

'What are those?'

'What do they look like?' Mansworth replied without looking at the marks.

His defiant reply seemed odd to Tom.

'Where's Arthur? Has anyone seen him?'

The other boys shook their heads.

'He must still be on his way up,' said Mansworth.

'He was *ahead* of me,' said Tom. 'Where could he be?'

'Probably back at school, where we all should be,' Mansworth replied, steering his eyes to the other boys. As if he exerted some new authority, the other boys retreated in single file down the path. Only Tom and Mansworth remained, their eyes locked.

'Where's Arthur?' Tom repeated.

Mansworth shivered; his eyes fell before Tom's direct stare, then returned, as if hoping the question would have evaporated in that short moment. But Tom wouldn't release him; his eyes bored into the fellow until Mansworth could bear it no longer. He composed a dismissive smirk, kicked the ground and stalked down the path.

Tom Bedlam trembled by the precipice. A fresh mist rolled forward. Arthur had been there; he could feel it in his churning stomach and the chill creeping over his skin. Somewhere deep in the chasm below, the boy lay. Tom's knees buckled. He told himself to breathe.

He had seen accidents on Procession Street, but there had been plenty of people to intercede. A huge crowd would gather, and remarks of outrage, compassion and doubt would be made; but here, on this cold peak, was a stark, palpable horror. He began to run down the path, oblivious to the sharp branches and bracing cold. His relief came only at the base of the mountain, where Mr Phibbs was standing by the grey oaks.

'Arthur Pigeon is missing, sir. I'm afraid he's fallen from the top of the mountain!'

'Fallen?' Phibbs was about to laugh.

'Yes, sir, I think so!'

The disciplinarian's smile faded. His expression turned to dread, then resolution. He told Tom to go to his classes while he went up the path to investigate.

All afternoon, the sun shone upon Hammer Hall, though the air remained chilly and damp. An unforgiving light spilled through the grubby windows, and the boys cringed. It searched the blackened walls of Mrs Brasier's kitchen and even penetrated the stuffy interior of Mr Goodkind's study until he closed his shutters. Polly was beside herself that afternoon. She asked Tom if he'd seen Arthur, confessing that she'd given him a lock of her hair the day before, tied with Mansworth's ribbon. Tom said he hadn't seen him all day.

When Mr Phibbs appeared at dinner, he took Tom aside and told him he had seen no sign of an accident. 'The constabulary has been alerted, but nobody has time to search the mountains for some hooligan dodging his lessons! Young Pigeon is probably having a good chuckle over this,' he added and promised that the harsher elements would drive Arthur home in a hungry and repentant state. 'Cheer up, Bedlam. No boy has *ever* died at Hammer Hall!'

When the lights were out and Arthur remained missing, some boys speculated that he had run away. Cooper and Lopping changed their stories. Tom suspected that Mansworth had threatened them, but it was possible that they too didn't want to believe the most horrific possibility. No boy had ever died at Hammer Hall. It was inconceivable and, therefore, impossible. Only by reminding himself of this did Tom fall asleep that night.

A WEEK PASSED, with much rain, fog and speculation. Polly went about her duties in a trance. She gazed accusingly at each boy until he shrank away and soon focused her attention on Mansworth, who defied her stare with patronizing humour. 'You're looking rather dour, Polly. Where's that pretty smile of yours?'

Tom's dreams kept taking him back to Hammer Peak; more often than not they concluded with that chilling cry. He would find himself sitting upright in his bed in a cold sweat, but by morning he had convinced himself that his nightmares were unfounded. *No boy had ever died at Hammer Hall.* His schoolmates concocted the most outlandish theories about Pigeon's disappearance: he had run away, been taken by smugglers, and was voyaging to Tahiti; he had stumbled upon highwaymen, lost an eye, but was now robbing travellers on the London road; he had been adopted by a baron who was grooming him to rule Bavaria. It was curious to Tom that the boys refused to entertain some tragic fate. Instead, Arthur was a figure of liberation.

'My money's on the army,' said Privot. 'They'll take you if you lie about your age.'

'Mine's on the circus,' replied Winesap. 'Maybe he's become a juggling sword swallower.'

'Well, either he's a sword juggler *or* a sword swallower. He can't be both!' said Mansworth.

This comment was answered with silence. Apparently Mansworth was not welcome to participate in such talk. Baking in their hostility, he exploded. 'You're all pathetic! Can't you talk about anything else? He's *gone*, and he'll never come back!'

Perhaps it was the air of authority, the grim conclusion or the bitterness in his voice, but everybody was cowed by this remark.

I'm sure he's in the circus, mouthed Winesap.

'Army,' whispered Privot.

SIX DAYS LATER, Lopping took Tom aside at breakfast. He told him he had seen Mr Grindle staggering through the fields followed by two shepherds. They were weathered, roughly dressed men, often seen wandering with their flocks on the steep rises of Hammer Peak. Lopping explained that one had been clad in an oily shearling coat, but the other had worn only his shirt in the mist. His coat was wrapped tightly around a large bundle carried over his shoulder.

Grindle didn't appear at breakfast. Cooper claimed to have seen him driving the shepherds and their burden in a cart towards the village.

'Probably found a *sheepling* or a *lambkin*,' said Winesap.

Tom, however, had to be sure, and approached Mr Phibbs as he finished his breakfast. 'Please, sir,' he began, phrasing his question with desperate optimism, 'they didn't find Arthur, did they?'

Perhaps the other masters had been dreading just such a question, for they suddenly frowned at their plates. The disciplinarian stiffened his lower lip and tilted his head to Tom without looking at him. 'Look here, Bedlam,' he said, then paused, sensing the glances of his colleagues. Suddenly, his reply became a protest. 'It's really none of your business!'

In an instant, Tom realized his worst fear. He withdrew with slow steps, as if the shepherd's burden now fell on his own shoulders. Every boy guessed from Tom's expression what Phibbs had refused to say. There would be no more talk about circuses and highwaymen. The fantasies were over. The hero had become a victim. It was the most wretched news.

In the hour before supper, as the dismal crew huddled in their cots – many of them silently contemplating the power of evil and the high price of rebellion – the thump of Mr Phibbs's stick called everyone to attention. Beads of sweat rolled down the master's cheeks as he staggered up the stairs and passed the cots, one by one. 'You think I don't know what's what, but I know. Hooligans! Savages!' He stopped, finally, at Mansworth's bed, his eyes boring into the boy with feverish intensity. Then he drew in his breath, whirled around, and shouted: 'Bedlam!'

'Sir?'

'To the headmaster's study!'

THE CHAIR OFFERED by Mr Goodkind came short of a normal seat by a good two inches, causing Tom's knees to rise above his waist and rendering the headmaster more imposing, and his desk all the more vast.

'You were friendly with young Pigeon?'

'Yes, sir.'

Goodkind circled the desk, folded his arms, and looked down at Tom. 'Pigeon was found,' he said. 'He must have fallen. You have been cautioned about the dangers of climbing, have you not?'

'We're sent up to the peak every morning,' Tom replied. 'There were no warnings.'

Disappointed by Tom's reply, Goodkind modified his tone. 'We must remember that accidents happen, Bedlam, especially to the careless. You've seen a young bird on the ground, have you not? A nestling, barely alive, fallen, through no one's fault, by the wayside?'

'Arthur was terrified of heights, sir. He would never have been careless.'

The headmaster stared at Tom coolly. 'Young Master Pigeon fell a great distance. This is an unfortunate *fact*. By the Grace of God, some prevail, and others perish.'

Grief is stealthy. Now it seized Tom unannounced, and in spite of the headmaster's stern gaze, he crumbled. If his friend was dead, then so too was he. His hope for Arthur's safety was dashed as assuredly as Arthur's body had been in that wretched, wind-torn chasm. Tom gripped the oaken rim of the master's desk, his eyes welled and sobs wrenched his chest.

Goodkind winced at the display before him. He stood, offering no gesture, waiting, simply, for it to subside. Tom, however, was in the grip of an anguish that had been pent up for many weeks, and had no control over himself.

Only when he finally gasped for air did the headmaster seize the moment. 'I need a sensible fellow like you, Bedlam, to speak to the constabulary. A witness to attest to this accident.'

Tom wiped his eyes. 'Yes, sir.'

'Good boy.'

The boy's eyes rose slowly to meet the headmaster's gaze. 'Except it was no accident, sir. It was Mansworth. He killed him.'

Goodkind skirted his desk and picked up his riding crop. 'Mansworth, you say?' He turned the crop through the air in a figure of eight. 'You saw him push Arthur? You saw a crime committed? You will swear to it?'

Tom regarded the crop. 'I did not see, but I know a crime was committed.'

'Either you saw something or you did not.' Goodkind scratched his cheek absently with the crop handle. It was a gesture rendered odd by its constant repetition. Tom began to feel as if he himself was the itch.

Closing his eyes, he pitted his conviction against the headmaster's threat. 'I *know* he followed Arthur up the hill, sir, and I *heard* Arthur's cry. Then I *saw* Mansworth climbing back after a struggle. I believe he was responsible.'

Putting the crop down, the man leaned forward, his face inches from the boy's. 'Well, Bedlam, the fact is that Mr Pigeon fell. Alone. From a great height. And only God knows how.'

'Mansworth had threatened him many times in the past—'

Goodkind picked up the crop and struck the desk with a hard snap. 'I must insist that you limit your remarks to the facts you have witnessed! *Have I your assurance?*'

Tom replied in the affirmative, but the headmaster gained no comfort from this, for the boy's eyes were still defiant.

A GREATER AUTHORITY

On June 11, two carriages made their way across the downs to Hammer Hall. The first arrived in the middle of a storm. Rain pelted down upon the three members of the party – Dr and Mrs Abraham Pigeon, and Sergeant Percy Ketch, of the Boleford Constabulary – as they alighted.

Tom scrambled up to the attic to watch while the other boys identified Arthur's parents in whispers. Mr Goodkind escorted the group across the muddy fields and up the path to Hammer Peak. Dr Pigeon followed the headmaster, while Sergeant Ketch offered his arm to the bobbing figure of Mrs Pigeon in her enormous grey skirts. From a distance, they appeared to float up the mountain and disappear near the misty summit.

A gnawing pain grew in Tom's stomach as he imagined himself to be Arthur, his bones broken, his body cold, lifeless, ascending in spirit, up, up, above the rocks, above the party of adults on the precipice, shining for a moment before hurtling towards the heavens.

When the party vanished, Tom went down to the dining hall. He found many boys clustered in small groups. Even the masters paced about the room, unsure what to do with themselves. All seemed aware that the future of the school hung in the balance. Mansworth lingered by a window, watching for signs of the party's return. An hour passed. Mrs

Brasier and Polly served lunch: cold pies with congealed suet and sodden pastry. Polly performed her rounds with a water jug, missing every cup with ghostly obliviousness.

When a cry came from the courtyard, followed by heavy hoofbeats and the attendant rattle of harness and carriage wheels, many faces flew to the windows to see what new visitor had come.

Tom spied two gentlemen disembarking from the vehicle. The first was a strikingly tall man with wiry black muttonchops in a silk morning coat and top hat. The second manipulated a crutch as he stepped down. William Bedlam smiled at something the fellow with muttonchops said and offered an eager nod in reply.

At that moment, the mountain party returned from their climb. Mr Goodkind seemed eager to quit the first party for the second and welcomed them heartily. 'Greetings, Mr Mansworth! And you must be Mr Bedlam! Welcome, welcome!'

Tom ventured into the courtyard; he was wondering whether Mr Goodkind had taken his charges to heart. Would Mansworth be accused? Perhaps the headmaster had more regard for justice than Tom had imagined.

'A pleasant journey, I hope, sir?' said Goodkind to Bronson Mansworth.

'The trains were efficient. The coach was slow, wretched and tiresome,' the man grumbled. 'But I had the pleasure of making a new acquaintance in Mr William Bedlam!'

'Yes indeed, sir,' replied Bill Bedlam, with a smile so broad that Tom feared his father's face might split down the middle. 'Aye, and we had a fine conversation!'

Goodkind nodded. 'It was my sincere hope that you gentlemen would cross paths, and avert an unnecessary scandal,' he added, glancing now in Tom's direction.

At this moment, Tom felt the group's attention bear down upon him.

Mr Mansworth spoke first: 'Young Tom Bedlam, I presume! Allow me to introduce myself. I am the father of Geoffrey Mansworth.'

'Sir,' said Tom, cautiously.

Mr Mansworth gave Tom's hand a sturdy shake and locked him in his glance. 'I understand that you are a friend of my son and the unfortunate deceased. Let me assure you that we intend to get to the bottom of this tragedy, my boy.'

'Yes, sir . . .' began Tom, but he didn't finish the sentence because of the sudden crippling pressure he felt when William Bedlam's fingers dug into his shoulder.

'Come, lad,' murmured Bedlam in Tom's ear. Lurching on his crutch, he hurriedly escorted his son into the building and down the hall. Tom saw Mr Mansworth smiling confidently at the headmaster – hardly the expression of a man with a condemned son.

'I bring the most unfortunate news, my boy.'

From his father's rigid frown, Tom half-expected to hear that Arthur's murderer had been identified as Tom Bedlam.

'Your grandfather Mr Shears has passed on. I'm told, from natural causes, though unexpected and grievous. Naturally,' his father continued, 'I inquired as to whether he had directed monies for your education or other sums, but I learned that, as he considered himself to be in good health, no provision was made. The destination of his fortune is now in the hands of the courts—'

Tom became deaf to his father's words. Mr Shears had been a good man – pugnacious, blunt, but generous. What now? His mother gone, his prospects doomed. All he had left was Bill Bedlam; it was a state of poverty indeed.

Tom nodded soberly. 'I see.'

'I'm sorry, lad, but the news came late to me, and so I bring it late to you. It puts your education in jeopardy.'

Tom nodded. '*That* is why you are here today?'

'Not exactly. I'm here at the invitation of Mr Mansworth.'

'Mr Mansworth?'

Bedlam nodded. 'For the price of a train and a carriage, yes. It's complicated, Tom, but you appear to wield some influence, so to speak.'

'Influence?'

The actor gave a wink that indicated the distant but expectant figure of Bronson Mansworth. 'His son may face criminal charges, Tom, and all because of you.'

'And his own actions,' Tom replied.

Bedlam winced, folded his arms, and brought his lips close to his son's ear. 'My boy, sometimes one finds oneself having to choose between one's beliefs and one's best interests. I know you hold young Mansworth responsible for the demise of this boy – Alfred.'

'*Arthur.*'

'But Mr Mansworth is a member of Parliament – highly placed, highly respected, much admired, with fat pockets and rows of factories at his disposal.'

'Arthur and I were friends,' replied Tom.

'And so I imagine him, up in heaven,' Bedlam interrupted, 'looking down, Tom, wishing the very best luck upon you!'

'I am the least of his concerns now,' Tom replied frankly.

'Tom,' said Bedlam, 'young Mansworth is in a fix, and his father desperately wants him out of it. You, my boy, are in need of an education. Mr Mansworth might offer it in return for your silence on the matter of his son's deeds.'

'My silence?'

Mr Bedlam nodded.

Tom swallowed. 'But I would be betraying a friend, more than a friend—'

Bedlam threw his arm over Tom's shoulders and shook him vigorously. 'The dead take care of themselves, my boy. Before you presume a murder, let the ghost come, as it did to young Hamlet. You're not a prince. You're just Tom Bedlam. Unless you return to school, you'll be warming your hands at Todderman's furnaces. Here's an opportunity! Please your father by taking it! Please your mother, God rest her, if not me.'

'Would it please her to hear me *lie*?'

Bedlam's wooden leg struck the floorboards, causing two rooks on the windowsill to take flight. He glared at Tom. 'You must *prevail*, Tom,' he said. '*Say* what Mr Mansworth tells you to say. *Say* it for your future and, if you haven't the sense to do that, by God, say it for *me*! *Say it!*'

Awed by his father's blunt words, Tom wondered if the man's cunning and duplicity had given way to some half-decent sentiment. Was it the first sign of fatherly concern for him?

'If I do as you say—'

'Mr Mansworth will show his gratitude, and you will have an *education*, lad.'

'But what about Arthur?'

'The dead rest in peace. The living must get on with their lives. You'll have done nothing wrong, lad. What's done is done! Didn't your mother always want an education for you? Didn't she say that?'

Tom noticed the rooks scatter above the trees over Hammer Hall. He remembered his mother's plans for him – life in the country, an education, a future.

He looked down and silently begged Arthur Pigeon's forgiveness.

A MIXED BLESSING

ALL TOM REMEMBERED FROM THE INQUEST WERE THE EXPRESSIONS of Dr and Mrs Pigeon – their grief and dismay – while Goodkind heaped words upon Arthur's memory to belittle his fate. 'An oddly unsocial boy, a wraith of a child, a bird sprung helplessly from the nest, an unavoidable tragedy.'

Tom longed to express his sympathy to them, but when he saw the disappointment in their faces after his testimony, he couldn't approach them. He was too ashamed.

He repeated his testimony in letters to Sissy and Audrey, as if, by repetition, the words would gain credibility. But as he posted these missives, he realized grimly that he had become his father's son; he now spoke words that were not his own, for the benefit of an audience's affection. But Tom was no actor; he could not pass himself off as a character alien to his own conscience.

Mr Mansworth kept his promise to make Tom's cooperation worthwhile. It was agreed that both Tom and young Mansworth would continue their education at other schools so that the taint of the incident would neither provoke nor burden them with second thoughts. Mr Mansworth recommended that Tom be sent to a Scottish school while the younger Mansworth attended a school in the south. Thus, the accused and the accuser would have a border between them.

Mr Goodkind was relieved to have survived the inquest and took steps to ensure that there would be no more accidents on Hammer Peak. He announced that exercise was a 'proven stupidity' and that from now on Hammer Hall would cultivate the character of its wards with the help of the riding crop. Since Mr Grindle had been responsible for sending the boys on their morning jaunts, he was taken to task and demoted to teaching younger boys. This demotion improved the character of every subsequent Hammer Hall pupil, as the master's influence on the younger lads produced a more disciplined and civilized lot.

ON HIS LAST DAY at Hammer Hall, Tom received a letter from Audrey that addressed the tragedy.

My dearest Tom,

Poor, poor Arthur. You described him as so stubborn, so strong-minded, and so cautious of danger that I can't quite believe his life could end so. Are you sure that boy Mansworth wasn't to blame? And what about Polly? What does she believe? The poor girl, I was so sure that they would be together. You must feel a terrible loss at Arthur's death. I wish we were able to meet on the landing, to talk about it, as we used to, with our legs dangling through the banisters. Do you remember? Has it been a year already?

They seem happy with my work at the office. I am so used to my place there, Oscar's clothes, the short haircut, and my 'name', which I answer to now without thinking. Mother seems gratified that I bring home a steady wage, pay the rent and buy food, but my short hair and clothing concern her. She would like her daughter to appear as a daughter. Frankly, Tom, I like trousers, and I don't miss having to brush my hair!

Oscar is deeply troubled by my situation. Although I pass across the bridge from Vauxhall to the City in a man's clothes, what has changed? I'm disguised for the benefit of those who fear change. I suspect I'm not the only female with this dilemma. Surely society will not come crashing down because a woman adds sums as well as a man. Oscar brought an article home explaining the research of a scientist who claims the female brain is smaller than a man's and therefore indisposed to man's work. But it seems to me that my capacities are no more inferior and my brain thus far more efficient!

What matters is that I am supporting the family. Mother's baby was stillborn, alas, but she has recovered; the twins are healthy; and the Orfling (though he steals) remains in his infant size, though he has the sweetest little heart and has learned a few words. He addresses me as Edmund and throws his arms around me when I arrive home in the evenings and promises that we shall be together always.

Audrey

Moved by this letter, Tom concluded that he and Audrey had been forced, under duress, to change something essential to their characters. He had sacrificed the truth; Audrey had sacrificed her femininity. Now she walked the streets of London in disguise, while Tom wandered the corridors of Hammer Hall as a false friend and brother who had allowed a scoundrel to go free.

An hour before he was to leave for his new school, he visited Polly to say farewell and to mourn Arthur with the one other person who had been touched by him.

Mrs Brasier, her cheeks war-painted with coal dust, knelt with the bellows to pamper the fire, then disappeared in an explosion of sparks, shrieking as flying embers pitted her petticoats with little black holes.

Tom found Polly sitting on the back step, oblivious to her employer's cries, peeling carrots with a vague smile on her lips, her eyes trained on some spot in the fields.

'Polly?'

'Master Bedlam.' Polly raised her skirt in a sitting curtsy and, wary of Mrs Brasier's cry, began to scrape at the carrots with a little more urgency.

'I came to say goodbye, Polly. I'm leaving for a new school today,' said Tom.

'I know'd that, Master Bedlam. Arthur said you'd come to say g'bye to me.'

Her answer was so matter-of-fact that Tom glanced at the field, expecting his friend to materialize. *'Arthur?'*

'Aye.'

'When?'

'Just now.' Then Polly shot a cautious glance at Mrs Brasier and quickly took up another carrot. 'She don't like me talking like that. Thinks I'm soft in the head,' she whispered. 'But it's true.'

'You've *spoken* to Arthur?'

Polly nodded. 'He's promised to stay with me always.' She smiled broadly. 'He's so worried about you, going off to another school. He wanted you to know that.'

'I feel terrible about Arthur, Polly,' Tom confessed.

'Everything will be all right, Tom,' she said. 'He don't blame *you* for what happened.' Her expression darkened. 'Mansworth will get what's coming. He will.'

At that moment she cut herself with the carrot knife. She paused to suck her thumb, and her eyes lingered on Tom. 'I swear he will.'

Tom could not help entertaining the notion that Polly had Arthur's confidence. 'I shall miss him,' he said.

'He'll always cherish you. Like a brother!' Polly replied.

'Like a brother?' Tom felt his eyes moisten. 'That's very nice, Polly.'

The girl showed him a ring drawn in ink around her finger. She explained that she and Arthur were married now and smiled – a vague, misbegotten smile, which assured Tom that Polly had, indeed, lost her mind.

TOM DRAGGED HIS TRUNK down from the attic and along the corridor with considerable effort until he arrived in the great doorway of Hammer Hall, where the board greeted newcomers: VERITAS ET LABORUM. Truth and toil. Two virtues. He noted that he was to leave Hammer Hall with only one to his credit.

He would travel to the new school in Aberdeen without his father. The prospect of a solitary journey to an unfamiliar school didn't worry him. What could be worse than Hammer Hall and its deadly summit?

As the coach entered the courtyard, Mr Grindle appeared, his hair in a dishevelled spray around his collar, knees bent. His normally fearsome scowl broke into a kindly smile.

'Ah, Master Bedlam, I understand you are moving on to bigger and better things!'

Suddenly Tom's grief and bitterness nearly overwhelmed him. He fought for control.

Mr Grindle put his hand gently on the boy's shoulder. 'It's a great pity about young Pigeon. Ugly business. Not a bad boy, and I've known some very bad boys.'

Tom whispered, 'I'm so ashamed of myself, sir.'

The schoolmaster nodded. 'Remember this, Tom. Power corrupts all those associated with it, not just the powerful. Redeem yourself with your next deeds and go on with your life. As for Mansworth, well, he has his conscience with which to wrestle, and his demons are fearsome indeed.'

'His father will arrange a good life for him, sir,' Tom replied.

Mr Grindle nodded. 'That is every father's responsibility.'

With that, the master shook Tom's hand, bade him good luck, and promised him a fine life ahead as long as he didn't devote it to the miserable task of teaching schoolboys.

KINDRED SPIRITS

THE SCHOOL WAS CALLED BRODIE, AND ITS PUPILS WERE KNOWN AS Brodie Boys. Depending on the speaker's affiliation, a Brodie Boy was either the intellectual cream of Aberdeen or an overcoddled scoundrel. Tom spent his two years as a Brodie Boy doing his best to avoid either appellation. In town, he never wore his hat with the Brodie crest; in school, he conducted himself cautiously, never taking sides, keeping his opinions to himself.

After having betrayed Arthur Pigeon, Tom considered himself a fraud, unworthy of anybody's friendship. He withdrew, seeming aloof in the company of his classmates, and his silence about his past was interpreted as haughtiness. Though he worked hard at his studies and earned good marks, he felt like an impostor, successful only because of Bronson Mansworth's influence. Mr Grindle had remarked that power corrupts all who are associated with it; young Tom Bedlam considered himself tainted, and the world around him in collusion.

All news from beyond his school gate reinforced this impression. Oscar Limpkin, for example, had kept Tom informed of events at home. At sixteen, he had been promoted to senior correspondent of the *Vauxhall Gazette.* Aggressive and resourceful, he was as tireless a reporter as he had been a boy enchanted by his own make-believe. He respected no secret, adored scandal, minded no locks and heeded no threats. He'd been to opium dens, confessionals, parliamentary corridors, and rat-infested prison cells in search of stories; had questioned lords, matrons, bishops and murderous robber kings. His affable grin had saved his skin many times – who couldn't admire his bravado? Though he never wasted time in learning to spell, he delivered the facts by deadline; and when he could not deliver the facts, he delivered marvellous fiction.

Through Oscar's letters, Tom learned about the devilry of despicable men, the saintliness of sweethearts, the sloth of landlords, the greed of bankers, the greatness of England and the diabolical villainy of her neighbours.

But Oscar's most damning exposé was on the subject of Sissy Grimes:

'Dear Tom,' he wrote.

Recent facts compel your loyal friend to expose the activities of a certain acquaintance of yours, Miss Sissy Grimes:

(1) The attractive young lady, an employee of Todderman & Sons Porcelain & Statuary, was observ'd in the close company of the nephew of the owner of same establishm't. (Note that Mr & Mrs Todderman were without issue, a side effect, no doubt, of seeing each other's faces in bed last thing at night and first thing in the morning.) Shortly thereafter Miss Grimes was promoted to the Accounts Dept., a post to which she was unsuited (accord'g to knowledgeable sources) as the young lady was unable to add the digits of her left hand to the digits of the right and get the same answer twice.

(2) Six months after said promot'n, Miss Grimes was observed to have gained weight (markedly more in the bellie than elsewhere). In such time, her addit'n had not improved, nor her subtract'g (though her fingers consistently remained five to a hand).

(3) Seven months after said promot'n, Joshua Todderman (bilious nephew and heir to the Todderman fortune) announced his engagem't to the comely Miss Grimes. Mr Henry Todderman, proprietor, was heard by this report'r remark'g that it was cheaper

for his nephew to marry Miss Grimes than keep her on the payroll, as she was costing a fortune in invoicing mistakes.

(4) One month later, the adorable Miss Grimes b'came the lawful wife of Mr Jos. Todderman, and promptly gave birth upon her wedding night. She also gave notice (to the relief of many in the account'g dept.).

(5) Seven months aft'r the birth of young Joshua Todderman, J. Todderman announced that his missus was pregn't again. (The account'g dept. was deeply gratified by this news, as their ledgers had been perfectly balanced since her departure.)

(6) Shortly after the birth of the Todderman triplets, Mrs Todderman was seen visit'g her husband at his place of business. The acc'ting dept. noted that Mrs Todderman was expecting again (observed by this reporter) and noted that she was now in grave danger of giving birth to more children than she could effectively count.

Your loyal servant begs your forgiveness for the intimate details described above, but attests to their veracity.

Oscar

Few documents could change a young man's sympathies so quickly. Sissy vanished from Tom's fantasies. Instead he began to entertain thoughts about Audrey. Her letters were frequent, her affection for him was constant and her character had ripened. Her last letter typified this new maturity, showing an awareness of city life that was a far cry from that of any other girl her age.

Dearest Tom,

Your last letter was very sweet. I imagine you now a very different boy from the one whose attentions I fought so hard to steer away from my brother. In fact I blush, thinking of my foolishness, and hope you have forgotten that silly girl.

I am not the same person I was, Tom, I know that. As I walk home in the evenings, Edmund feels less like a disguise than a second skin. I marvel at the freedom of men on the street. Men look where they wish, they carry themselves slowly, or meander, or sit without obligation to speak, or laze.

Women have no such freedom. A woman is suspect if she walks slowly or meanders, coy if she sits and ignores the greetings of passing men, provocative if she looks a man in the eye, and offensive if she reclines upon the street as a bricklayer or a sweep does, with his feet spread and his mouth half-open.

What freedom men enjoy! Is it fair? In my suit I can do these things; in my suit I can look a man in the eye and he thinks nothing of it; in my suit, I could go to sleep on a park bench and be left alone. But only a fallen woman dares sleep by herself in public!

I am a half-man, Tom. I straddle the line, gratified by this privilege, able to enjoy men on their terms. And women? Well, I look at women and count myself lucky to be one only part of the time.

Audrey

William Bedlam also sent letters – two a year – which evoked a consistent theme. To cite one such message would be to cite them all:

My Dear Tom,

I am on the verge of great prospects and expect to return to the stage imminently! It is merely a matter of time, for I have the talent, the wisdom, and the confidence!

Alas, circumstances and infirmities prevent me visiting or sending for you, but I hope to see you soon, with good news and renewed fortunes!

With high hopes,
Wm. Bedlam, Actor

Tom turned eighteen during his final term at school. He listened to his peers discussing their plans; many would apprentice themselves to their fathers, and others spoke of joining the army. Tom entertained the idea of becoming a doctor but doubted that the terms of his agreement with Mr Mansworth included the four years of training. His notes to his father went unanswered, and by his last week, he realized he hadn't even the train fare to return to London.

On the day before he left, however, a letter arrived enclosing a pound note. It was not written in his father's hand.

My dear boy,

On behalf of your father, I enclose a pittance, which should enable you to book train passage to London. I urge you to come as quickly as possible, as the planets are aligning above us, and all indications point to a flaming Apocalypse by late July!

May God preserve us,
Paddy Pendleton

There was no sign of the anticipated Armageddon as the train rolled past green meadows and the clutter of brick dwellings that marked the city's sprawling perimeter. It was a clear July day in 1885; the air was fresh, the sun generous and warm. Tom peered out of his window, looking for hints of his boyhood – a past that seemed distant, dark, and immutable now. But the call of the stationmaster was cheery, the mood in his carriage excited, and along the platform a parade of smiling strangers welcomed his fellow travellers.

All at once, Tom was reminded that he was a young man, ready to embark on a life that would challenge the successes and failures of his father. He vowed to be unhindered by the many corruptions of his youth.

LONDON

As TOM MADE HIS WAY FROM KING'S CROSS STATION, BAG IN HAND, wearing a school blazer and a low black hat, he cast a handsome shadow. His feet cut a long stride, his dark hair was trimmed short to the collar; he had his father's rigid nose, eyes of a pale and elusive blue, and one feature that belonged only to his mother.

It was a small, persevering smile – Emily Bedlam had married William Bedlam with it, greeted her first and second sons into the world with it, and bade farewell to the last patch of blue sky she saw with it. It wasn't much of a smile, but it was tenacious, enduring and uncynical. If she could have seen him now, she might have been relieved to see that it prevailed; for greater obstacles lay in store for him.

IN THE DISORIENTING CHAOS of the station, a man with muscles almost bursting out of a straw-coloured suit, sporting a riotous grin and a wide red moustache, gripped Tom with a firm embrace and a howl. 'Tom Bedlam!' he cried. 'Is it *you*?'

'It is,' Tom replied anxiously. 'Who are you?'

The man laughed. 'Do you not remember Oscar, Tom? Have you lost your *mind* in Scotland?'

'Oscar? Oscar Limpkin!'

Only in Oscar's wicked grin did Tom recognize his friend. The man who had once insisted on playing the hero and villain in every childhood game now led Tom from the terminus as he pointed out the notable figures in his city – as a journalist, Oscar was as proud of his knowledge as he was of his profession.

'See that fellow?' he said, waving genially to a bald-headed barber standing at the threshold of his shop. 'A wife killer, acquitted.'

Farther along the street he embraced a fat, bearded man named Mr Stickley and explained to Tom that the man had generously contributed hundreds of pounds to feed orphans in Sudan. Everyone seemed to like Oscar, even the woman with thick-lensed glasses and hair the texture of steel wool, who (Oscar explained) sold opium to brothel madams, ran a popular betting pool and slept on a mattress stuffed with pound notes.

'She told you such things?'

'Everybody loves to see his name in the paper,' Oscar assured him.

HE ESCORTED TOM to Tottenham Court Road, where they caught a horse tram. The afternoon crowd spilled alongside hansom cabs, coaches, and food carts. Sober-faced flower sellers with thick, bunched skirts offered small bouquets to passersby. A group of young nannies pushing perambulators in formation whispered behind their hands while people struggled to pass them. A beggar appealed for coins as he gestured to the grubby-faced tots tethered by a rope to his waist. A businessman sprang nimbly across the path of several clerks, who eyed him with tepid respect, and disappeared into a hansom cab. Oh, glorious London, thought Tom, for he had forgotten the city's human parade, its rhythm and thrill.

'Audrey wants to see you, of course, but she's working late,' explained Oscar. 'She's been promoted – a little more money, a lot more work. The price of success.' He wrote down an address and stuffed it into Tom's pocket.

'Has she really changed?' asked Tom. 'I know her hair is short and her clothing like a man's.'

Oscar paused, as if at a loss to explain Audrey. 'Well, she's a woman now, if that's what you mean – though you wouldn't know it to look at her. She still takes care of the baby while Mother works in the evenings.'

'Baby?' replied Tom.

Oscar nodded. 'The Orfling, Tom.'

'But he should be about eight by now,' said Tom.

'He *should* be,' Oscar replied, with a shrug, 'but he isn't. It's a marvel. We Limpkins were always a rather strange family, weren't we? Perhaps when you're a doctor you'll be able to make sense of us.'

'A doctor?' Tom replied, surprised.

'Of course. That's what Audrey thought you'd be.'

'Yes, I remember now,' Tom admitted.

Oscar issued Tom a warning: 'Remember, she's stubborn, well-intentioned but judgmental, and rather rigid, which is odd, considering she goes about pretending to be someone she isn't.'

'And supports her family by doing so.'

Oscar's blithe smile faded. 'She has my admiration for that, Lord knows. I will never be rich, but she takes this Edmund business rather too seriously. She *likes* wearing a man's clothes a little too much. What's wrong with being a woman?' Here, Oscar raised a finger, as if he'd finally found his point. '*That's* what it is, because I think being a woman is *marvellous*! I adore women!' Suddenly he seemed disheartened. 'Why wouldn't a woman *want* to be one? All my favourite people are women.' He paused. 'That includes Audrey – even when she's pretending to be a *man* – which doesn't make sense, does it?' he said, puzzled.

'No, it doesn't,' Tom replied.

They parted at Oxford Street. Oscar had to meet someone, so he directed Tom towards William Bedlam's residence.

'By the way,' he said, 'you'd better change your name if you're to become a doctor. No one in his right mind would seek treatment from Dr Bedlam!'

TOM WALKED SOUTH; he noticed the houses become smaller, the streets narrower and more crooked as they neared the river. William Bedlam's address was Number 23, Gilles Street. The building was slumped between the neighbouring houses like a drunk supported by two friends. Tom mounted the sunken front step, noting the cracked sills and shattered panes. The glass was pasted with stage bills, all featuring William Bedlam's face – the same picture that Mrs Bedlam had fixed with flour paste to the tenement wall in Vauxhall – so that, from Tom's perspective, his father appeared to stare at him from every window.

Upon Tom's first knock, a young man opened the door a crack. 'Yes?' he said, gazing at the visitor first with one eye, then the other.

'William Bedlam,' said Tom.

'Who wants him?'

'His son.'

The door shut abruptly. A few minutes later, there was a cry from behind the door, and William Bedlam staggered out. 'Tom, my boy! Come in, come in!' he bellowed. Then with a cautious eye to the street, he ushered Tom in, slammed the door, locked it and opened his arms. 'Tom, kiss your kind, old father, whose frank heart gave you all!'

Tom complied, and his father embraced him, tottering on his good leg, compelling Tom to hold him with equal vigour so that he didn't topple.

'Forgive the caution of my young friend here,' whispered Bedlam, 'but there's always somebody wanting money from me. Young Isaiah is very good at separating creditors from my friends.'

'That's easy enough,' murmured a deep voice. Tom recognized old Paddy Pendleton seated in the dim light of the kitchen. 'You haven't any friends but *me*!'

Bedlam asked Tom to pick up his fallen crutch and steered his son to the kitchen through a room stacked with newspapers, crates of bottles, scores of spades, pickaxes, rakes, hoes and two perambulators.

'Props for the next production,' said his father.

They looked more like the easily filched possessions of strangers than theatrical necessities. Tom spied a stuffed monkey in one perambulator, and a pumpkin wrapped in baby clothing in the other. At the entrance to the kitchen, he noticed that the floorboards had rotted to the earth below. A potbellied stove was smoking, a pan sizzling upon it. The young man was frying slices of bread in bacon grease while Paddy Pendleton sat, his enormous, majestic face perched above a small body clad in several woollen sweaters. He accepted a slice of fried bread from the young man and nodded to Tom. 'My boy, I trust my letter reached you.'

'Yes, sir. Thank you very much,' said Tom.

'*Somebody* had to bring you home,' said Paddy, eyeing Bill Bedlam.

'Tom,' began his father, 'I found myself short of cash.'

'As he *always* does,' added Pendleton. 'I took the liberty of sending you the money myself to ensure that it would *reach* you, instead of going to some *other purpose.*' Here, Paddy fired another glance at Bedlam, who turned to Tom for sympathy.

'He don't trust me. Me! His oldest friend, and he don't trust me. Rest assured, when my ship comes in, Paddy Pendleton will be the better for it!'

'I'm beginning to think your ship is the one upon which the Antichrist is embarked,' said Pendleton, rubbing his arms. He raised his head to the ceiling and nodded briefly – as if to acknowledge the Almighty's plans in this regard.

The young man paused from his work at the frying pan and gave the heavens a nod too. Then he offered Tom a slice of fried bread, which Tom accepted.

'Tom, this is my *protégé*, Isaiah Pound,' said Pendleton. 'Isaiah shares my concern for the salvation of humanity.'

The young man nodded to Tom. 'There are so many souls to save,' he murmured. He was very thin, with brown hair and a cowlick that sprang from the side of his head. He preened the sparse beard on his chin. Tom noticed that, although it was a warm evening, he had wrapped newspaper around his shins to cover the gaps between his socks and his trouser hems, likewise his wrists and jacket sleeves. The paper crinkled as he moved. When the fried bread was ready, he put a slice in Bedlam's hand, wiped his fingers clean on a rag, and sat down beside Pendleton.

'Have we any brandy?' murmured Pendleton.

'Not today,' said Isaiah.

'The Lord will provide,' said Pendleton. He and the young man gave the ceiling another respectful nod.

'And let us hope He is generous,' added Bedlam, winking at the rafters. He turned to Tom. 'So, my *learned* boy. Let us speak of your future. To what profession do you aspire?'

Tom considered the dirt floor, the crumbling plaster walls. 'It hardly matters,' he muttered. 'Mr Mansworth, I'm sure, is finished with my education.'

'God bless him,' said Bedlam. 'He paid for this here house.'

'God bless,' echoed Pendleton and Isaiah Pound, sharing another nod upwards.

'Why was that?' Tom asked.

'Terms of our agreement, Tom.' Bedlam sniffed. 'You was to get an education, while I received the funds to buy this house and staged a modest production of *Troilus and Cressida.* I've got the reviews somewhere here . . .'

So his father had profited from his testimony too. Tom's distaste for the man returned.

'Answer me, Tom, what do you wish to do?'

'I would study medicine, but—'

'A doctor!' Bedlam interrupted and looked to Pendleton and Isaiah with pride. 'A doctor!'

'Admirable,' said Pendleton.

'There is no hope of it,' said Tom. He looked at his father for a beat. 'Unless you'd sell your house to pay for my training.'

Bedlam put his finger wisely to his nose. 'Dr Tom Bedlam!'

'I'd use a different name,' said Tom, recalling the advice of Mr Grindle and Oscar. '*Bedlam* probably wouldn't inspire confidence in a patient.'

His father frowned. 'Bedlam's a good name. It's done me well. I chose it myself. I was brought up in St George's Fields Orphanage, and named myself after the hospital across the street. Nobody forgets such a name.'

Tom raised his eyebrow. 'Infamous, indeed,' he replied.

'Nobody expected much of me. I was motherless and nameless,' declared Bedlam proudly. 'So you see,' he said to Tom, 'you were fortunate as a youth in having a mother and . . . your father's name.'

Tom considered this. 'I am grateful for what I have,' he replied, 'yet I think it fair to say that there are more respectable names, just as there are more diligent fathers.'

Pendleton chortled.

Bedlam looked stung by Tom's remark, but for the sake of the company, he weathered it with a robust smile. 'Be assured, you have a diligent father now, my boy. But I understand that every professional name must inspire confidence in the public.' He narrowed his eyes. 'So what would you change it to, Tom?'

'Smith,' said Tom.

Here, Bedlam rose, insulted. 'Don't tease me, lad! If my son is to be a doctor and he changes his name, it should be one that I approve. When he marries, and when he has children, they're my grandchildren, are they not? And if they don't have *my* name, then I deserve some say in what name they have. So what's it going to be?'

Tom thought briefly. 'Chapel. Dr Chapel.'

'Chapel?'

'A good Christian name, I heartily approve,' said Pendleton. His protégé nodded in agreement.

'Very well,' said Tom's father to Pendleton. 'If Tom Chapel is what the young man wishes to be called, Tom Chapel it is. *Dr* Tom Chapel.'

Though Tom sensed a hint of scorn in this last expression of his name, he turned to his father and said, 'I thank you for your approval.'

Bedlam swallowed his son's bitter reply as if it were Mrs Brasier's medicine. 'Goes without saying. In that case, we shall visit the firm of Griff and Winshell tomorrow and make the necessary arrangements to secure your education as Dr Chapel.'

'My what?'

Bedlam tucked his thumbs under his lapels. 'Your *education*, my boy. The solicitors of Mr Shears – your deceased grandfather – found a provision in the man's will for his issue, and the issue of his issue, to receive funds for their education. I have spent the last three years in negotiation with them, to release the money.'

'Why so long?' Tom exclaimed.

Bedlam wilted. 'Well,' he said, 'as husband to your dear mother, I asserted my right to be a beneficiary – after all, I am a son-in-law! I petitioned for that right but was rebuffed. Thrice! The law is unkind, Tom, very unkind.'

Pendleton snorted.

'But I shall be able to go to a medical college?' said Tom.

'You shall, Tom. You shall become a doctor, and perhaps I shall be compensated at a later date.'

'Compensated for *what*?' asked Pendleton.

Bedlam's expression froze. 'Well,' he began, 'as Tom's father, I am entitled to *something* for my troubles, am I not?'

AFTER THE MEAL, Tom left to meet Audrey. He walked the streets, reconciling his memory with their twists and turns, noting the shops that no longer existed, and reading the signs that had meant nothing to a boy but had significance to a young man: army recruitment posters, shop fronts with signs that beckoned HELP WANTED, INQUIRE WITHIN. Had Bill Bedlam spoken the truth, or was there some catch? Tom hadn't forgotten the man's theft of Emily Bedlam's savings. His knees weakened. He had let a murderer go free for the sake of his education, and his father had gained a house from the same act. He was filled with fresh despair.

He strode towards the setting sun, hand shading his eyes, along the crowded streets, until he saw a public house called the Red Boar. A few drinkers sat at an oaken bar, huddled over their glasses like parishioners in their pews. In one corner, a party of six sang a song (with not a soul singing the same words). The smell of stale beer, grease and wet sawdust held Tom's attention until he saw a figure sitting in a corner in a white shirt, loose tie, trousers and black shoes.

Audrey had always been odd-looking, and slapdash in her dress – understandable for a sister minding her baby brother – but her recent letters to Tom had evoked a noble spirit with a sharp moral strength. It seemed to him now that her features had come to match this temperament. Her straw-coloured hair was cast back to reveal a slender if prominent nose, kindly blue eyes, full cheeks, and her mouth seemed poised to reveal some delightful truth. Though several inches shorter than Oscar (who was not a tall man), Audrey *seemed* tall. Perhaps it was her posture or her confidence. When Tom greeted her, she smiled as if *he* was the secret she had been nurturing.

'Tom Bedlam!' she said. He was about to embrace her, but she held his wrists to remind him of her disguise as *Edmund*. Grabbing her jacket, which she swung over her shoulder with casual ease, she led him outside.

On the street a lamplighter ignited a gas flame, closed the glass and climbed down his ladder, whistling. In this light, Tom tried to reconcile

Audrey's gentle features with the roughly shorn hair, the tie and jacket, and at once had no doubt that his dearest dream stood before him – the compassionate voice that had sustained him when he was alone at school without another soul for comfort. She had won his affection with her letters, her empathy, counsel and constancy.

Overcome, he seized her in an embrace. Audrey hung limp in his arms, her feet dangling off the ground.

A chorus of hoots and whistles erupted from a group of young men passing them.

'Come, Tom,' she said softly. 'We look like mollies to them.'

AUDREY AND THE ORFLING

THEY WALKED QUICKLY TOWARDS WESTMINSTER BRIDGE, THEIR conversation brief and breathless.

'Oscar told me you'd been promoted.'

'Yes! I have my father's job!' said Audrey. A crease of amusement appeared in her cheek. 'They say I'm a better behaved boy than all the others.' Her eyes danced at this irony.

'You must hate not being yourself.'

'Must I?' Audrey sounded surprised. 'It's rather fun. You should try it.'

Tom looked startled. 'Wear a dress?'

'Yes.' She laughed. 'Put a man in a woman's shoes, and you'd see society improve overnight.' She paused, as if startled by the despair in her own remark.

'Oscar seems troubled by the life you're living.'

'Oh, Oscar!' Audrey laughed again, and Tom wished he could listen to that laugh forever, because Audrey's humour was not careless, or foolish, or coy but the joyful expression of a warm spirit.

'He thinks you're afraid to be a woman,' Tom explained.

'Stuff and *nonsense*!'

They were crossing Westminster Bridge now, and rain was swirling around them – a confusion of droplets flying every which way that gave the lights a hazy glow. A sickly orange fog hung over the water – the product of coal fires, hemmed in by rain and London's peculiar topography.

'I think,' Audrey continued, 'that nothing is more terrifying to a man than a woman unafraid to act like one! And even worse, a man acting like a woman. People are stoned to death for *that*!'

'I wouldn't want you to be in any danger,' he replied.

'I'm safe, Tom,' she assured him. 'I make a good living – for an impostor.' She met his eye to emphasize her disgust at the necessity of her disguise. 'Nobody bothers with me,' she added softly.

Tom observed that Audrey received few glances from passersby. Women and men alike seemed to regard her as a slight young man; a few men of her physique passed by, and Tom wondered if they too were women passing themselves off as men.

The south bank of the Thames was enveloped in the same sulphurous mist. A red-faced old lady wearing a little candle on a strap around her forehead issued a catlike yelp that pierced the fog. 'Flowers here!' she cried, gesturing to the carnations in her basket. Audrey drew Tom's attention to the lady's oilskin sailor trousers. 'See, Tom? In Vauxhall, people don't care how anyone dresses!'

Audrey pulled her shirt free so that its crinkled tails hung to her knees, and her step changed; even her shoes sounded different on the cobblestones.

'What news of the Orfling?' asked Tom.

'Oh, as sweet as ever, though I have to keep an eye on him in shops because of his sticky fingers. Elsie and Eloise still squabble, mostly about boys. We can't imagine who would marry them.'

THE OLD TENEMENT BUILDING beside Todderman's factory seemed even shabbier than Tom remembered. The wet streets reflected the gaslight, and fine black soot wafted down past the streetlamps from Todderman's eternally smoking chimneys. On the walls, Tom noticed the accumulation of finger marks since his departure. He paused on the landing before the Limpkins' door and glanced towards his old room. The door was open a crack, and through it he saw a small face raise its eyebrows expectantly. Tom recognized its expression: the child was in a torment of neglect, waiting for a parent to pick it up and make it feel loved.

IN MANY WAYS time appeared to have frozen in the Limpkin household, except for the absence of the late Mr Limpkin. Mrs Limpkin greeted Tom warmly, and in her embrace he realized he equated maternal affection with her features – the pink, bloodshot eyes, the warm, buttery smell and the gentle pressure of her full breasts.

'Oh, dear me, Tom, sit down! Have something to eat. Oh, where are those girls? Elsie, bring us the gingerbread from the stove, dear!'

'I'm *Eloise*!' declared a tall girl, scowling and pulling strands of her hair between reddened fingers. Her sister became visible only after Tom made out a figure, beneath a sheet, seated on the floor.

'What on earth is Elsie doing?' cried Mrs Limpkin.

'Vapours, for her skin,' replied Eloise. 'She wants a rosy complexion.'

'Say hello to Tom, Elsie,' said her mother.

A high-pitched sneeze answered from the folds of the tent, and two pale knees shook, which caused the steaming bowl of water in her lap to spill. There was a shriek, the tent collapsed, and Elsie appeared, sweat rolling down pimpled cheeks. She gasped for air, eyes closed. 'How do I look?' she inquired.

'Like a boiled chicken!' her sister remarked.

Elsie fumed, threw the sheet back over her head, and shouted, 'Pig!'

'Sow,' countered Eloise.

'*Mama!*' moaned Elsie, a demand that Eloise be reprimanded.

Mrs Limpkin's nose wrinkled. She would not be drawn into the dispute. 'I'm late,' she cried. 'Audrey, will you please make them behave?'

Audrey murmured from the back room, and Mrs Limpkin gave Tom another bosomy embrace. 'Come again soon, Tom. You bring with you so many memories!' she said, with a melancholy sniff. Clutching two baskets of pastries, she disappeared through the front door.

'She still works?' inquired Tom.

Eloise nodded. 'Sells pastries to the night shift.'

Elsie's face came up for air; she narrowed her eyes at Eloise, cried, '*Baboon!*' and disappeared under the sheet.

'*Shrew!*' countered Eloise, but the tent did not respond.

'Where's the Orfling?' Tom inquired. Both girls pointed to the doorway, where Audrey held a baby who looked no more than nine months old with a big, drooling smile, a bald scalp and wide eyes, his head tottering on tiny shoulders.

'Here he is!' said Audrey, kissing his pudgy cheek. 'Here's my little dumpling!' The Orfling giggled with delight.

Tom's smile faded. He peered closely at the boy. 'He hasn't grown a bit since I left!'

This was apparently the wrong thing to say. The Orfling suddenly burst into sobs.

'Look what you've done!' said Eloise.

'Hurt his feelings,' said Elsie.

'He understands everything you say!'

'I'm so sorry,' said Tom, bewildered. 'You mean that, although he *looks* like a baby, he thinks like an eight-year-old?'

The baby let out a fresh bawl.

'Stop mentioning his *age*!' whispered Eloise.

'You're a wonderful baby,' said Tom hastily, but it was no good: the Orfling was wounded and indignant, and cast woeful glances at Tom as if he had been deeply maligned.

FOR AN HOUR the Orfling was inconsolable – his cry as sweet as it was pitiful, his little chest heaving, and tears pouring down his cheeks. When he had no breath to cry, he whimpered, and when he lost the energy to whimper, he burst into a fit of sneezes, then settled into a low wail.

They tried everything to comfort him. Audrey sang to him, the twins danced, told rhymes, and tickled his toes, but just when the Orfling seemed to forget his misery, he would steal a glance at Tom and begin to weep again.

When the girls had run out of ideas to cheer him, Tom pulled his lower lip over the upper, which seemed to startle the baby into silence.

Then the child emitted a deep gurgle of amusement. Gently, Audrey placed him on Tom's lap, and for the next ten minutes Tom talked with fish lips and rolled his eyes until the Orfling closed his eyes, and began to snore.

'He's forgiven you,' Audrey said.

Tom's shirt was flecked with spittle and stained with the Orfling's grubby finger marks; a pungent smell indicated the baby had wet himself.

An unfamiliar sense of peace overcame Tom as he sat in the muddled squalor of this family. He tried to commit it all to memory: the boxes stuffed beneath chairs and tables, every available surface covered with jars, bottles and used crockery, the linen hanging from the ceiling. It was chaos. It was precious. It was home.

'Mother thinks he's waiting for the right time to grow,' explained Audrey, 'and hasn't the *desire* to become older.'

It was agreed that the sleeping Orfling should remain in Tom's lap. Audrey turned down the gaslight and placed some cold pork on the table with a loaf of bread and a pat of butter. After she had sliced the bread and handed it around to Tom and the twins, she tried to make light of the Orfling's condition. 'You couldn't wish for a nicer baby.'

'Except when he steals,' remarked Elsie.

'He only steals the things he knows we need,' added Eloise.

'It's remarkable, Tom,' Audrey said. 'Once when we were about to be turned out on the street for the rent I found a pound note balled in his fist. It made up the difference, so you see, he *knew*, somehow.'

'That makes him remarkably intelligent,' Tom said.

'He's a blessing,' Audrey responded, 'and I know that one day he'll choose to grow up.'

'But how strange,' said Tom, 'for a baby to decide not to grow.'

'Strange?' huffed Elsie. 'Hardly! Look at us: one awful thing happens after another. We *never* know what's around the corner. The Orfling clings to the one good thing in his life: babyhood!'

'Come, Tom,' Audrey said. 'We'll put him to bed.'

Tom smiled, reminded of their pretend games long ago, when she had tried to make him kiss her.

He rose with the baby and followed her across the room to a chest standing beside a cast-iron stove. Audrey opened the bottom drawer to reveal some bedding and a small lace pillow that was yellow with age. Tom laid the sleeping baby in, and Audrey pushed the drawer in a little, leaving just a space for the Orfling's little pink face.

Kneeling a few inches from Audrey, Tom inhaled, breathing in her hair, admiring the glow of her cheek and the pale down above her lips. As he drew in her gentle essence, he realized that the sour milk smell was gone. In its place was something much more intense, primal and intoxicating. Tom was about to close his eyes and surrender to it when he became aware of Elsie's watchful eye. 'Are you leaving soon?' she asked sharply.

'Do you want me to?' he responded.

Elsie's gaze was direct. 'Audrey's perfectly fine, and so are we. We're happy *together.*' Her defiant tone surprised Tom. He never imagined that his affection for Audrey might be seen as a threat to the Limpkins' harmony.

'Don't take her away,' she warned him.

Audrey escorted Tom into the hall. 'Don't mind Elsie,' she said. 'Since Father's death, everything is a near calamity to her.'

'Perhaps she's entitled to be worried about me,' Tom replied.

'Nonsense.' Audrey kissed his cheek. 'You have a good heart, Tom.'

'I don't know if that's true. I've done some awful things,' he confessed.

Audrey shook her head. 'You'll make it all up raising your own loving family, Tom. I can see your life,' she whispered. 'Dr Tom. Like a picture before me.' She smiled. 'Do you remember how I used to bring you lemon tarts, and you would kiss me in return?'

Tom recalled that he had passed the tarts on to Sissy.

Audrey tugged at his coat lapel, drawing his face level with hers. He thought she was going to confess something, but her eyes indicated another purpose. She put her lips to his, as if she meant to remind herself of their youthful exchanges.

The pressure of her lips against his made Tom's heart start to pound. He wanted her and put his hands on her waist. The Limpkins' door creaked open.

'What's going on?' cried Elsie.

'Nothing!' Audrey replied. She pushed Tom towards the stairs.

At the bottom step he stopped and looked up. Audrey was gazing down at him anxiously. She blew him a kiss, and disappeared.

GRIFF & WINSHELL, SOLICITORS

THE ESTABLISHMENT WAS FILLED WITH HIGH DESKS, EACH WITH A clerk poised over his work, just as a jockey would ride his steed, scribbling across a sheaf of paper with his quill and tapping it periodically against his chair. Each man was working intently, his back crooked, quill trembling, eyes fixed on the paper, while the leaden smell of a dozen inkwells competed with the odour of parchment dust and pickled cabbage – one clerk's lunch. The floor was gritty with blotting sand and the ceiling blackened by a fireplace roaring even on this warm day, which made the room oppressively hot. The Bedlams were greeted by Samuel Winshell, a man with thick spectacles who stroked the desks with gaunt knuckles. His eyes settled on the fellow eating the pickled cabbage. 'That writ will be flawless, Duckworth, or you'll *swallow* it with your cabbage!'

Mr Winshell directed them to Mr Tobias Griff, who occupied an office at the rear. As they approached the door, a gentleman passed with the momentum of a tornado. He wore a shiny black top hat and a black morning coat. Wiry black muttonchops splayed from his cheeks like ravens' wings.

Mr Bedlam greeted him loudly. 'Sir, perhaps you remember me! I'm Bill Bedlam. I wonder if I might—'

But the gentleman strode past. His dark stare acknowledged Tom just long enough to remind him of their last meeting, at the inquest into

Arthur Pigeon's death. He threw open the door of a hansom cab and vanished into its dark interior. A moment later, Bronson Mansworth was no more than memory again.

Tobias Griff emerged from his office clutching a pair of brass tongs in one hand and a sheaf of papers in the other. Tom noticed that the tongs' handle was in the shape of a goat's head, with a tuft of hair on its chin that matched the grey curl on Mr Griff's. He threw the papers into the fireplace and poked at the curling ash with the tongs until the flakes separated and floated upwards into the flue.

'Few problems, Mr Bedlam, vanish as simply as that,' he said with solemn satisfaction. 'The affairs of many fine men in London are safe here. *Your* secrets are safe. No indiscretion has ever passed my lips.'

'Of course I know that, Mr Griff!' Bedlam winked, his eyes dancing over to Tom. 'This is my only son, Tom.'

'Your only son, Tom, eh?' Griff repeated. He looked at Tom with scrutiny, filing away his observations with the many secrets to which he had just referred.

Bedlam explained the need to enrol Tom in a college of medicine.

'A doctor?' Griff frowned. 'Why, young Mr Bedlam, you have my *sympathy.*'

'Why?' asked Tom.

'Because, sir, the lawyer and the doctor serve men at their own folly! I can only wish you a good night's sleep, for your conscience and convictions are doomed! Ours are *thankless* professions!'

Bill Bedlam made a remark at this point about Mr Griff's fee being hardly thankless, to which the lawyer replied scornfully, 'No man is satisfied with a lawyer's services unless his opponent is six feet under the ground. And no doctor's job is done until his client is in the same position! I speak of *gratitude,* sir! There is none to be had in either profession!'

'Gratitude?' replied Bedlam. 'You are paid. Is that not gratitude?'

Tom looked at his father, wondering if the man honestly believed that money was an earnest expression of gratitude.

'Not if gratitude is *respect.* Not if gratitude is *appreciation.* No sir.' Mr Griff sneered. 'Even after a fee is paid, I live with my decisions, through sleepless nights sometimes, Mr Bedlam.'

'Perhaps your conscience is a size too large, sir,' replied Bedlam. 'I sleep very well.'

Mr Griff raised one eyebrow. 'Then perhaps *your* conscience is a size too *small*, sir,' he countered.

After Tom had confided his interest in attending the Holyrood Surgical College in Edinburgh, Mr Griff offered to make inquiries.

'A good school, is it?' asked Bedlam.

Mr Griff raised an eyebrow. 'An excellent school.'

'Expensive, I'll wager.'

'Excellence is never cheap,' Griff replied. 'The boy will receive first-class training.'

'And what will I receive?' said Bedlam.

'There is no mention of you in the provisions of Mr Shears's will, sir,' said Griff. He smiled. 'At least you shall enjoy a good night's sleep.'

'But as the boy's father, how shall I visit him in Edinburgh? How shall I *sustain* the filial bond? Blood is thicker than water.' Bedlam looked anxious. 'I am a foolish, *fond* old man!' He placed his hand on Tom's shoulder. 'Surely some financial arrangement can be made?'

'Not so old, or so foolish, Mr Bedlam,' said Tobias Griff. 'The money goes solely to the boy's education. I'm bound by the dictates of the will. I shall make arrangements for the change of his name and inquire as to his enrolment at Holyrood, but your enterprises, sir, remain *your* enterprises.'

The lawyer then struck the floor with the tongs and declared the matter settled.

THAT EVENING, OSCAR TOOK Tom and Audrey on a tour of the sites of some dastardly murders he had covered as crime reporter for the *Vauxhall Gazette.* Audrey wore a dress, for the first time in years, Tom guessed, because she spread her knees wide as she sat in the tram, and Oscar had to remind her to sit like a lady.

Their first stop was at the north side of the Westminster Bridge.

'Here, beneath this bridge,' announced Oscar, 'a butcher named Emmanuel Connolly, after an argument with his wife about whether to serve goose or lamb for his birthday, cut her in half, dropped the legs into the Thames. The other half, he buried in Regent's Park.'

Tom's smile faded when he saw the look on Audrey's face.

'Oscar, that's a nasty story.'

'Some people *are* nasty,' countered her brother.

Audrey turned to Tom. 'I cannot stand it when he starts acting so blithe.' Oscar tried to speak, but she cut him off. 'Like all your reporter friends, you trade these stories as if they were jokes, as if it's funny that a woman is murdered.'

Oscar looked indignant. 'I certainly don't think murder is funny. But that was a story about marriage.'

'Marriage?' said Audrey. 'Because Mrs Connolly was treated like butcher's meat? Would it have been as amusing if *she* had cut *him* in half?'

Oscar looked to Tom for support, but Tom's sympathies were committed elsewhere. 'Really, Oscar,' he said, 'it's a grisly thing.'

'I will not be led around the city,' Audrey continued, 'while you describe the terrible things people do to their wives!' She started to walk away. Oscar went after her.

'Audrey, we were having such a good time. Let me show Tom one more place – no murder scenes, I promise!'

'Where?'

'Kensington.'

Audrey's features softened. 'Oh – very well,' she said.

They arrived at a vast and splendid house with enormous Tudor chimneys and elaborate brickwork surrounded by a garden filled with flowers. Oscar lingered at the gate but said nothing.

'What happened here?' asked Tom.

'Nothing.' Oscar gave a cryptic smile.

They remained at the gate while Oscar consulted his pocket watch every few minutes, keeping his eye trained on a dark window on the second storey. After a few minutes, Tom was ready to propose dinner when Audrey smiled. 'Aah, there she is, Oscar!'

A solemn young woman in a black silk dress, her brown hair in pretty ringlets, crossed the room and paused by the window to lift the sash. She sat down, adjusted the wick of her reading lamp, and raised a newspaper.

'Isn't she beautiful?' said Oscar.

'She's certainly pretty,' Tom agreed.

'*Pretty?* Is that all?' said Oscar.

'She's rather far away.'

'She's beautiful; absolutely, utterly beautiful,' Oscar gasped.

Tom looked at Audrey's face, lit by the soft light coming from the girl's window, and thought her more beautiful by far. The girl in the window was no match for her.

'Beautiful and unattainable,' murmured Oscar. 'I come here as often as I can, just to look.'

It was the first time Tom had ever known Oscar to accept a limit to his fantasies, and suddenly he felt sympathy for his old friend.

They returned to Vauxhall by way of the Thames. In the darkening evening, the boat traffic was illuminated by scores of lanterns flickering from the bows. It was a pretty sight, with reflections playing on the water, the sky still aglow above crouching houses, hovels and shacks interrupted by the spires of churches and the warm candlelight that spilled from public houses. When they stopped to ponder the city's charm, Tom remembered something that had happened earlier in the day.

'As I was walking into Griff and Winshell's, I saw a face I will never forget,' he said.

'I'm sure it was somebody up to no good,' said Oscar. 'Mr Griff serves a range of scoundrels.'

'It was the father of one of my classmates,' said Tom. 'Mansworth.'

All of a sudden, Oscar looked interested. 'Bronson Mansworth?'

'You know of him?'

'Of course!' Oscar replied. 'How would I *not* know of Bronson Mansworth?'

'He is not only a member of Parliament—' said Audrey.

'But a villain,' said Oscar. 'He's ruined the careers of his political rivals with false accusations. Cheated his workers, paid off his critics – and those he couldn't pay, he's ruined by exerting influence over their employers. He's the devil.'

'And,' said Audrey, giving Tom a knowing glance, 'the father of a very pretty daughter who resides in Kensington.'

'That girl?'

In answer to Tom's question, Oscar raised his palms to the heavens. 'It's the great paradox! A man of dark and nefarious villainy has produced a daughter so – so *pure*!'

'Well, I knew his son and—' Tom began, but he was interrupted by Oscar, who began a litany of Penelope Mansworth's finer points – her delicate hands, her exquisite face, her gossamer hair, and so on, until Audrey could bear it no longer.

'But you have no idea what kind of a heart she has!'

Oscar's joy became a sentimental appeal. 'But, Audrey, she teaches *little children*! She's as pure as the rain, as a sunny day—'

'—and utterly out of your class,' concluded Audrey.

THEY SHARED A MEAL in a raucous public house, where they tried to speak over the loud chatter, but it was impossible. Oscar, for his part, said barely a word; whether he was scheming or brooding, Tom didn't care, for he was content to stare at Audrey and imagine a life together with her.

Fog engulfed the far bank as they parted at Westminster Bridge. Tom asked to see Audrey the next evening, so she suggested they meet at her place of work at the end of the day.

'You must remember that I am Edmund,' she reminded him and, telling Oscar to turn his back, she kissed Tom hurriedly on the lips.

Tom walked home in a state of aroused confusion. The evening had certainly been an adventure. Good and evil had been defined in terms he understood. The malevolent villains responsible for Tom's corruption, Bronson Mansworth and son, had been painted in their true colours. Most of all, his feelings for Audrey had become profound. He was moved by her scent, her virtue, her spirit. He could not wait to see her again.

MR BEDLAM DID NOT answer when Tom knocked. The door was locked fast. Tom saw a light in the upstairs window, so he called, and eventually the door opened to reveal Paddy Pendleton's sphinxlike features.

As Pendleton ushered the boy inside, Tom inquired about Isaiah. Pendleton muttered that his protégé's animal impulses were provoked by the moon: 'By day he is pious, but by night . . .' Pendleton shuddered. 'The women he brings home. What awful creatures! I tell you, Bedlam, if women could see themselves from a man's point of view, society would change in a day.'

When Tom inquired after his father, Pendleton gave a dramatic shudder and led him upstairs. 'In body, your father is whole, but not in spirit, I fear.'

Pendleton led Tom into a room where Bedlam was seated in a tatty armchair, clutching a glass. There were two bottles beside him: one empty, one a third full, and he seemed intent on ridding the second of its burden.

'Father?'

With his chin buried in his chest, Bedlam acknowledged Tom bitterly.

'What's the matter?'

Bedlam attempted a reply, but his lips defied him. He scowled at the bottle, pressed his hands to his heart, as if to indicate the weight of his burden, then reached out to Pendleton.

'Your father would like me to explain that he has a number of concerns with regard to you,' Pendleton said, looking to Bedlam, who nodded approvingly at this interpretation.

'What is it, Father?' said Tom.

Bedlam pursed his lips and vigorously shook his head.

'Your father regrets that he is not in command of his, er, faculties, due mainly to your late arrival. If you had come home at six, he would have had no difficulty, but his faculties are compromised at this late hour,' said Pendleton.

'Mr Pendleton, would you please tell me what is wrong with him?' said Tom.

Pendleton took a gulp from his glass and drily remarked, 'I do not enjoy being the bearer of bad news. The day I was born, my mother was warned of this by the very nurse who brought me into the world. She said, "The way your baby cries, you'd think the world was coming to an end!" ' Pendleton raised his palms, as if he had no recourse but to blame the fates. 'Now I am obliged to warn mankind of its imminent destruction, but does it listen? The fools go about as if the fires of hell matter not. I am treated like a madman. But that is my lot. Those of us who see the truth must bear its flame against the howling gale of dissent and ridicule. This is life, is it not? Rack and ruin, then *out, out, brief candle*!'

At this point, Bedlam frowned and stamped his wooden leg against the floor.

Pendleton shot his friend a surly glance. 'Do you heckle me, sir? Be patient, I'm coming to the point.' He directed his gaze at Tom with suitable intensity. 'Your father is not pleased with you. First, you have changed your name.'

'We discussed this, I thought, to his satisfaction,' Tom replied. 'It is a professional necessity.'

'Perhaps,' said Pendleton. 'But what of your absence this evening? Surely a man is entitled to celebrate such an event with his son.'

'But if it displeased him,' Tom replied, 'why did he wish to celebrate it?'

'Hmph.' Pendleton too seemed puzzled and glanced back to Bedlam, who struck the floor again in frustration and wagged his finger, indicating several other grievances were to be addressed.

'Let me ask you this,' Pendleton continued. 'Are you ashamed of your given name?'

'It has served me well, sir,' replied Tom. 'But it is inappropriate to a doctor.'

'Are you ashamed of your father?'

'Why do you ask?' said Tom.

'Why do you not answer?' gurgled Bedlam, forgetting his mute status.

'I am *prepared* to answer,' Tom replied, 'but you will admit that it is a harsh question.'

Bedlam shrank back, as if the logic of Tom's reply had robbed him of the ability to speak.

'I believe it matters not to your father whether you are Dr Bedlam, or Dr Tom, Dick or Harry. But to celebrate in his absence, and come home at this late hour, is insulting. He is your father, your host, and your *benefactor*, and wonders why he receives no gratitude for this burden.'

Tom had kept his composure until now because of the absurdity of the situation, but this last question was the final straw. 'I am indebted to him for bringing me into the world. I am indebted to him *also* for deserting me, for abandoning and robbing my mother, and for leaving me at the door of my locked and empty school to wait in the darkness. Furthermore, I am indebted to him for the loss of my older brother!'

Pendleton gasped.

Though his voice was thick with emotion, Tom continued: 'I am indebted to him for coming to school to rectify a crisis that was not of my making, though he ordered me to resist my conscience, to *lie* and to accept the generosity of a man I believe to be a scoundrel. He *profited* by my perjury – buying himself this very *house*!'

Here, Pendleton turned back to Bedlam.

Still, Tom couldn't stop. All the bitterness he felt gushed forth: 'Today, I am further indebted to William Bedlam for attempting to take money that was left by my grandfather for my education. So, I ask my father: What gratitude does he wish of me? What do I owe him? Or, more to his liking, *what fee would he have?*'

A sound worked its way from William Bedlam's chest: it was a bottled roar. 'How dare you?' he cried. 'Are you fed? Are you clothed? You have been *taught*! If I have failed you in any way, show me the scars! You are in one piece, are you not?'

'Thank God I am,' Tom replied.

'Thank *me*, not God!' Bedlam shouted.

'I thank you for bringing me into the world!' said Tom.

'I deserve more than that,' cried his father. '*Much* more than that! I named you!'

'Indeed – after a *lunatic*, Tom o' Bedlam! An object of scorn and mockery! Please, don't ask me for *gratitude*,' Tom cried, quivering with rage.

'*Damn* your ingratitude! Leave my house!' shouted Bedlam.

'Gladly, sir,' replied Tom, picking up his jacket.

'Wait!' cried Pendleton. 'This is indecent! This is terrible! You cannot treat each other so!'

But Tom was walking down the stairs. He considered packing his bags but decided that to walk out now would be worth the loss of the few items he had left by his bed.

What a burden shed! As he stepped upon the shiny black street, he could hear Paddy Pendleton cry a protest from the window. He kept walking, feeling a sublime mix of relief and fear – the predicament of a young man liberated for the first time. The mist made his cheeks red, his heart pounded painfully; never had he felt so alive as he did now.

Tom walked London's wet streets, his fury burning in his chest, and he might have kept walking until he had circled the world if night had persisted. But eventually, the sun rose, the streets became busy. Tom lost his fire and, finally, his way. He decided to seek a voice of consolation.

PASSION

'I HAVE MET HER!' CRIED OSCAR.

Tom found him at the *Vauxhall Gazette,* where he was fussing over the final copy for the morning paper. A typesetter prepared the next page nearby, his thick fingers, filthy with ink, darting among the racks. He was a heavyset man, with a week's growth of stubble and a lachrymose pout. He wore a hat of newsprint; the sweat of his forehead darkened the paper in little mushroom shapes.

'You spelled *corrupt* incorrectly,' the typesetter noted woefully to Oscar, as if this were one more of life's many injustices.

'Then fix it,' replied Oscar, turning to Tom. 'Her name is Penelope, like the wife of Odysseus! And she has a voice so warm, so . . . rapturous!'

The typesetter sighed as his fingers slotted in the type. 'You shouldn't use words you can't spell, Oscar.'

'It doesn't matter how it's spelled; people know what I mean,' said Oscar. 'Tom, I went back to her gate last night and escorted her to school this morning. She's every bit as charming as I suspected. I am in ecstasy!' Oscar clutched his temples, as if this abundance of virtue threatened to blow his head to pieces.

'*Educated,* is she?' muttered the typesetter. 'What could you possibly have in common? I bet *she* knows *venal* doesn't have two *n*'s.'

'Our names were bound together in heaven,' said Oscar.

The typesetter snorted. 'I believe that those who cannot spell are dispatched to hell – at least, I *hope* so.' He waved Oscar's copy in the air with frustration.

'I spell *murderer* correctly,' replied Oscar.

'But you're no longer writing about crime,' noted the typesetter forlornly. 'You're in Parliament! *Murderer* simply isn't heard as often in the House of Commons as *corrupt*, *deception* and *travesty*, is it?' When Oscar didn't reply, the man turned to Tom for an opinion. '*Please* correct me if I'm wrong.'

'I shouldn't imagine it's heard nearly as often,' agreed Tom.

'I knew I would die if I couldn't meet her, so I waited outside her house, shivering, for hours,' Oscar continued.

'The next time you do that,' the typesetter said with a sigh, 'take a dictionary to pass the time.'

'She finally appeared, like Helen of Troy, her cheeks as pink as—'

'—undercooked pork?'

Oscar put his arm around Tom, as if to shield him from the typesetter's influence. 'I told her what I did for a living, and she'd read *all* of my articles!'

'Really?'

'Well,' conceded Oscar, with a shrug, 'the ones critical of her father.'

'And did she approve?' asked Tom.

'She said that I had sparked "much debate" in her household.' Oscar laughed. 'Oh, Tom, I will marry her. She's everything I've ever dreamed of in a woman!'

This seemed an appropriate time to make a confession of his own, so Tom told Oscar of his feelings for Audrey.

'You're the *perfect* fellow for her,' exclaimed his friend. 'Feet on the ground, a bit stuffy, solid and serious, you'll bring her down from her fantasies!'

Tom frowned. 'Stuffy?'

Oscar laughed. 'In my family, Tom, you're as stuffy as a meerschaum pipe! It's a compliment.'

'*Meerschaum.* I'll wager you can't spell that,' grunted the typesetter.

Tom wasn't so sure about the compliment, but he was glad of Oscar's endorsement and hoped it would be of some help to him when he proposed to Audrey. He then told Oscar about his argument with his father.

Oscar was stunned. 'Tom, you amaze me!' he cried. 'Perhaps you're not as stuffy as I thought.'

'I may need to ask your help in finding lodging.'

'Of course,' said Oscar. 'Naturally, I cannot put you up. My bed happens to be under here,' he explained, pointing to a bedroll under the typesetting table. 'But my mother will insist you stay with her. After all, you're practically her son-in-law!' Oscar gave Tom an appraising glance and grinned. 'Telling your father off is quite a reckless and foolish thing to do. I'm proud of you!' He chuckled. 'Audrey will be so upset.'

'Why?' Tom replied.

'She's a little old-fashioned.'

TOM APPEARED AT the Mercantile Exchange at precisely six o'clock and was directed to the basement. Though it was a spacious room, the desks were arranged like a labyrinth. Stacks of bound ledgers were heaped on every surface, and there were no signs, and no sense of order. Sunlight shimmered briefly on the ceiling – a passing reflection from a puddle on the street above. It reminded Tom of Plato's famous cave, for it was hard to imagine, in the dark confines of this gaslit chamber, what freedoms existed beyond its walls.

He asked for Edmund Limpkin half a dozen times before a pink-faced man with thick spectacles and a close-shaven head admitted that he knew the name. 'Follow me,' he said and led Tom between stacks and bookcases in a path that confounded Tom's sense of direction. 'Friend or relative?'

'Friend,' said Tom.

'Edmund keeps to himself. Secretive.' His guide looked back at Tom as if expecting an explanation.

'Works very hard, I'm sure,' Tom said.

'Yes, I suppose.' The man's stare, magnified by his lenses, offered no reassurance. It was cold and intimidating. 'Mr Murdick.'

'Mr Bedlam,' replied Tom.

A limp hand was offered. Tom shook it and left it hanging in the air. Murdick tipped his head at a stack of ledgers. 'He's here.'

'Edmund?' said Tom.

Audrey peered around the stack. She smiled but her face fell as Murdick came into view.

'Edmund, you have a friend,' said Murdick, as if this was a surprise to him.

Audrey closed her ledger. Murdick remained standing between them. 'Are you an old friend of Edmund's or a new one?' he asked.

'Old,' replied Tom.

'Ah. The best friends are old friends, eh?' Murdick said with a smile, his face inches from Tom's.

'Yes,' Tom replied.

'Of course, we *need* new friends too. Advancement. Progress. New friends. New ventures, eh?' Murdick's eyes danced. Then he nodded towards Audrey's desk. 'Tell Edmund so. He needs a friend to tell him that. One hand washes the other, eh?'

'I don't know what you're talking about,' Tom replied, but a glance from Audrey advised caution.

'Just passing the time of day,' Murdick said. 'No harm in that.' His tone was so bland that he almost sounded simple. His eyes, however, missed nothing in Tom's expression.

'No harm at all,' Tom agreed.

'I'll be going now,' Audrey said to Murdick.

'Have a pleasant evening, Edmund,' said Murdick, placing such odd emphasis on each word that it appeared he doubted it was evening, doubted it would be pleasant, and doubted that Edmund was Edmund.

He remained in place so that Audrey had to turn her back to him to slip past. As she did so, Tom noticed that Murdick bit his lower lip – it was either pain or exalted pleasure.

'I don't like him,' said Tom when they emerged from the building.

'None of the women like him,' said Audrey.

'Women? I thought women weren't employed here.'

Audrey sighed. 'Last year they hired a few women. Good news, I thought . . . until I discovered that a female clerk earned *half* of what I'm paid as a man – so, Tom, I'm still better off being Edmund Limpkin.' She frowned. 'Besides, Mr Murdick is not to be trusted around women. We lost a girl last week. She wouldn't say why she left, but she was very upset.'

'You must take care around him,' said Tom.

'I'm a *man*, Tom.' Audrey smiled. 'But the looks he gives women! Desire in a man's face can be repulsive, especially in one who dislikes women, and I suspect Mr Murdick *is* such a man.'

'Do *you* ever feel desire?' Tom asked, for his hopes and the subject seemed to have converged.

'Yes—' she replied, without meeting his eyes.

'For a man?'

'Sometimes I look at a woman as if I were actually a man, and desire her. Is it me? Or my clothes? Some women are so pretty, Tom, that I can't help myself. Perhaps it's the *power* of being dressed as a man, or perhaps it's something else.' Her words faded. She glanced nervously at him. 'I don't know what I really meant by that,' Audrey confessed, and lapsed into silence.

'Audrey,' Tom began, 'perhaps you should leave before Murdick guesses your secret.'

'I've a family to support, Tom, a duty to my mother *and* the children. Oscar's utterly unreliable; he disappears for days; he's reckless and impulsive, an absolute dreamer. I can't leave this job before the girls grow up, and the Orfling . . .'

Now Tom saw Audrey's situation as a form of imprisonment; she was trapped by her disguise, her duty and her sex. It inspired him to explain his new liberation from his father. He hoped, perhaps, to generate some kindred spark of rebellion in her. But after he recounted the scene she looked shocked. 'You see,' Tom concluded, 'he and I were bound to part ways eventually, and now I'm free of him. I owe him nothing. If I never see him again, I shall be eternally happy.'

'Oh, Tom,' Audrey sighed.

'Only one thing matters to me, Audrey – that we are together.'

She gave him a long, considered glance, and he felt himself judged quite thoroughly.

'I love you,' he said timidly.

'Of course you do, Tom!' she replied, squeezing his arm.

'The fact is,' he continued, 'both Oscar and I are hopelessly in love. He wants to marry that girl from Kensington, and I want to marry *you*!'

One can practise a confession of this sort many times, as Tom had, but no matter the confidence in his voice, or the conviction in his mind, he had never been able to picture Audrey's reply.

'I'm hungry,' she said with a smile, implying, Tom guessed, that a momentous decision should never be made on an empty stomach.

They stepped into a public house and ordered food and beer. The crowd was loud and boisterous. He waited for Audrey to answer his proposal. Her silence made him all the more anxious.

'My dearest Tom,' she said finally, her forehead creased. 'I am concerned about your father.'

'My father?' Tom replied. 'Why?'

'You can't banish him from your life any more than he can banish you. You're linked forever.'

'He deserted me and my brother.'

'Shamefully, yes; but you are obliged to be a good son to him and a better father to your own children.'

'Audrey,' Tom said, reaching for her hand, 'this is beside the point. I love you!'

She withdrew her hand, glancing around to see if anyone had noticed the gesture, but all the tables nearby were crowded with people singing and swaying together. It was a merry house on a Friday evening, and everybody seemed oblivious to them.

'I love you just as much,' she whispered.

Tom cloaked his reply between his hands. 'Is it foolish, then, to think that you would marry me?'

'No,' Audrey assured him.

Tom grinned.

But Audrey's expression became rueful. 'I'm afraid, though, that our lives cannot converge now.'

'Why not?'

'I must support my family. Were you to marry me, you would assume that burden and abandon your studies. I cannot allow it.'

Tom's joy faded. 'I don't believe you. Is there someone else?'

'How dare you?' she replied. 'I am not cruel, and I wouldn't taunt you with such a deception. I love you and wish you to succeed, Tom. But this world takes advantage of those who don't value their own worth. To me, you have *always* been a doctor. For you to pass that up, even for my benefit, would be a tragedy.'

Tom brooded for a moment. 'I must be with you,' he said. 'Come with me to Edinburgh, or I shall stay here with you.'

Audrey shook her head. 'Oh, you silly boy, be reasonable. You must apologize to your father and devote yourself to becoming a doctor.'

'Oh, Audrey,' he groaned. 'Every reasonable thing I have done has broken my heart. Don't ask me to be reasonable. Don't torture me!'

He seized her hands, a gesture that caught the hawkish eye of the elderly barmaid who had been collecting glasses on a tray as she meandered through the tables. She drew nearer. Using her hip to bump Audrey's chair, she interrupted their conversation to remove the full mugs of ale on their table.

'We've not finished,' said Tom.

'Oh, yes you have, luv,' she replied sharply. 'You and your friend should find yourself a mollyhouse, because your sort don't belong here.'

'My sort!'

'Come, Tom,' murmured Audrey.

They made their way to the door while the patrons, seeing two young men cast out in disgrace, began a jeering contest that escalated to pushing and shoving. Tom and Audrey found themselves cuffed and battered as they tried to run the gauntlet of drunken and abusive hecklers. As they struggled through, one face in the crowd turned away so as not to be recognized: a pink face, clean-shaven head, with thick spectacles that reflected the gas lamp sconces on the walls. Pleased with his reconnaissance, Mr Murdick smiled and downed the contents of his mug.

Audrey wiped spit from her cheek as Tom sheltered her with his arm; they staggered into the street but kept walking until the scrutiny of passersby became indifferent. Eventually, they stopped while Tom investigated Audrey's bruises; she was unhurt but in tears.

'I'm sorry,' he said. 'I forgot who you were, where we were—'

Audrey looked at him with forgiveness, but it was not the expression he wished to see. From it, he drew his own conclusion. 'I'm not fit to love you.'

'Of course you are,' she said. 'But I have a duty to my family, and you have an opportunity to better yourself.'

To better himself? At once, Tom wondered if Audrey was comparing him with Bill Bedlam. Was there any worse example of a faithful husband or a supportive father? And if Arthur Pigeon were to weigh in, he might remind her that Tom had betrayed him at his inquest. In short, it seemed to Tom that Audrey needed no reason to doubt his decency – the evidence against him was ample. Though she took his hand and held it close to her cheek, Tom had already concluded that she was rejecting him.

'This is not the end of happiness, Tom. We are not mayflies; love endures; we live far beyond one careless summer. I dearly love you, but if my love can't last beyond a temporary hardship, I would seriously doubt its strength. The Orfling will grow, the twins will become independent young women. Wait for me,' she said.

Grimly, he replied, 'How long?'

'However long it takes. I don't know what obstacles I face, but I love you in spite of them.'

What obstacles? he wondered bitterly. His own defects? How long would she wait to see him prove himself a more reliable man than his father? And if he failed?

They parted on the Westminster Bridge, with the boats passing underneath – little packets of light dancing on the water. It was a beautiful evening in London. Audrey might have kissed his cheek; he couldn't remember. Though the fog had lifted, he was blinded by sorrow; and though her words of consolation were sweet, Tom heard nothing but the echo of her rejection. He lingered on the bridge, watching his hopes, his life imagined, his comfort and sense of belonging vanish in the dark oblivion of the river.

HEARTBROKEN

'I BELIEVE I OWE YOU AN APOLOGY.'

Tom had found Paddy Pendleton and Bill Bedlam seated at dinner. Because there was no other chair at the table, he remained standing in the doorway.

'I am very sorry,' he added.

Stunned, Bedlam looked to his friend to verify his son's contrition.

'What's that, Master Bedlam?' said Pendleton.

With his mind on Audrey, Tom proceeded to say exactly what she had advised. And, perhaps because he had suffered a greater indignity in the pursuit of love, the words came easily. Tom's shame at having to apologize was considerably diminished by the astonishment apparent on his father's face.

'I'm deeply sorry for whatever pain and disappointment I may have caused you, Father. I hope you will forgive such ungrateful behaviour.'

Pendleton murmured, 'Hallelujah' and began to sob into his napkin. Taking his cue from the colporteur, Bedlam rose unsteadily from his chair and extended his arms to Tom, as though he were onstage for the homecoming scene. He clasped him to his breast, determined to outdo Pendleton's emotional display.

'Oh, my boy, my boy! All is assuredly forgiven! Nothing could *ever* break the ties that bind! It's only natural for a son to rebel, but you have the decency and wisdom to know when you are *wrong*! I heard from Mr Griff today; you have been enrolled at Holyrood. You shall go to Edinburgh, become a doctor, and I shall be proud! We have only each other, and in the years ahead we know that blood *is* thicker than water, and that which binds us, no man can tear asunder!'

Once again, Tom felt a mixed sense of accomplishment. Once again, he had done the reasonable thing – reconciled with his father – but now, in the man's firm and hearty embrace, he felt cold. The stifling affection of Bill Bedlam was no balm for Audrey's rejection. Without her, he was an empty vessel.

OSCAR INSISTED, HOWEVER, that Tom visit one last time for the sake of his mother. 'She adores you, Tom, and will be heartbroken if you do not come!'

Tom didn't want to see Audrey again, but since the Limpkins were the family he wished he had, he went. Outside the building he stood as darkness fell, holding a bunch of yellow roses for Mrs Limpkin, trying to will his broken heart into repair for one more evening.

Finally, emboldened by a remark of the late Mr Limpkin's – *Silence is as scarce in the Limpkin household as solvency!* – Tom entered the tenement.

Audrey was first to appear at the door when he arrived, and before he could speak she closed the door behind her so that they were alone in the hallway.

'I ask one favour of you, Tom,' she said.

'What could I possibly do for you?' he replied bleakly.

'That letters be exchanged between us, as they always have, and that we never lose touch, for though you are injured—'

Tom tried to deny it, but Audrey placed her trembling forefinger on his lips. 'I know you better than you know yourself.'

'You do not,' he replied.

But she looked at him with such compassion that his heart sank. 'I can't stay, I can't bear it,' he said, buttoning his coat.

'I love you,' she whispered, 'but I won't see you abandon your future; I must stay for my family's sake.'

'Marry me anyway,' he pleaded, 'before I go.'

She considered this. 'Become your wife in one minute and say goodbye to you in the next? My heart would break, Tom.'

Yet it was obvious to Tom that *his* heart would break if she did not. There lay the dilemma, and before the sides could further their pleas, a noise came from below – the thunderous footsteps of Oscar, jubilant and oblivious to this tender scene. 'I must be applauded!' he cried. 'Do you hear me, this minute!'

As he reached the landing, Oscar seized Tom's and Audrey's hands. 'I have obtained information concerning a gentleman known as Bronson Mansworth! Information from a secret source which *proves* that our friend in Parliament is up to no good!'

'Oh, Oscar,' replied Audrey sceptically. 'It'll hardly help your standing with his daughter.'

'You'll see,' promised her brother cryptically. With typical fanfare, he threw open the door, greeted his family, and changed the emotional weather with the subtlety of a hurricane.

The rest of the evening was spent in the clamour of the Limpkin household, with Oscar alluding to but never revealing his secret, Mrs Limpkin fussing over Tom and his prospects as a doctor, and the Orfling wailing piteously until he was permitted to sit on Tom's lap, where he happily dribbled and squirmed. Throughout, Tom did his best not to look at Audrey or reveal his unhappiness.

When it was time to go, Mrs Limpkin gave Tom one of her enveloping squeezes, and the Orfling daubed his cheek with a smooch of drool. Tom felt his pain recede. Elsie gave him a hug and kissed him rather determinedly on the lips before her twin sister protested with outrage and, probably, envy. Then Audrey led Tom to the door with anxious eyes and trembling lips.

He could barely look at her. In her face he thought he saw her resolution break and silently hoped she might change her mind now, at this last moment, as they were inches from parting.

'Tom?' she said.

'Yes, Audrey?'

'I – I shall need your address when you arrive in Edinburgh.'

He lowered his eyes. 'You shall have it,' he replied.

Audrey kissed her finger and put it to his cheek, as if any gesture more intimate than this might damage him. Tom would have cracked into pieces there and then if Oscar had not thrown his arm around him and walked him down the stairs. 'Never mind about Audrey, Tom,' he said, dismissing his friend's agony with a shrug. 'When next we meet, I shall be married!'

'To Penelope Mansworth?'

'The same.'

'And what else?' said Tom miserably, turning away from the figure on the banister above. 'I can see you have plans.'

Oscar's face widened into a jaw-breaking grin, and he tucked his thumbs in the crooks of his arms. 'I plan to be a member of Parliament, Tom. And Mr Mansworth, if he knows what's good for him, will help me!'

'You're a scoundrel, Oscar.'

'Not yet, Tom' – Oscar laughed – 'but I hope to be!'

A SOFT, BARELY VISIBLE rain enveloped Tom as he left Procession Street. He paused at the corner and glanced back at the towering factory, its chimneys boring into the night sky; a fiery glow turned the raindrops to vapour at the top. The tenement leaned against Todderman's building, its cracked windows twisted into imploring sockets. Tom vowed that he would never return to this spot, for if the tenement did not collapse, he surely would upon sight of it.

TOM CHAPEL

IN THE AUTUMN OF 1885, TOM BEGAN HIS TERM AT HOLYROOD Surgical College in Edinburgh. Most of his classes were in the Gramley Building, a large eyesore of granite and limestone. The building had a lighthouse turret, flying buttresses, Norman windows, Roman doorways, alternating Ionic and Doric columns, and floors of hexagonal, pentagonal and octagonal tile – the total effect of which induced nausea in its visitors.

The structure was based on the final thesis of an architectural student who had left the university in disgrace when his design was rejected. Fifteen years later, he returned – as a self-made millionaire from Chicago – having transformed a cough medicine into a popular remedy for sexual impotence. His name was Francis Gramley, and his elixir was called Gramley's Bull Tonic. Determined to make it a success in Britain too, Gramley wanted to stage a publicity event and offered to build his alma mater a new lecture building, to be named after him, of course. His only stipulation was that it had to incorporate his rejected design.

In spite of the faculty's protests, the trustees knew a bargain when they saw one. The building was erected and had been an object of derision ever since.

The most respected member of the medical school faculty at that time was Professor Henry Harding. He taught anatomy in Gramley's immense lecture theatre. In those days, more time was spent on anatomy than on any other class in medical school. Harding wore wire-framed glasses and had a bristle moustache. His tongue was as sharp as his scalpel, and it was said that his students often emerged from his classes in more pieces than his cadavers. Entering the theatre wearing a rubber apron and starched shirt with rolled up sleeves, Harding would whip the sheet off the lesson's cadaver with a flourish and order his students to gather around the examination table.

'I'm sure you were all up last night preparing for this class, so let's get on with it. We shall be examining the liver. Who can tell me where it is?'

A simple question. They all knew the answer. But a direct stare from Harding could make any student forget his name.

'Have I walked into the wrong room?' asked the professor. 'This *is* anatomy, is it not? Do you aspire to be doctors or coal miners?'

Tom raised his hand. Harding reminded him of Mr Grindle – another figure of unassailable veracity. Both men, Tom realized, were substitutes for his father.

'Not you this time,' replied the professor. 'You *always* answer. Let's have this fellow, here—'

He had selected Cornell, an overweight young man with a prominent nose and wispy ginger hair. Nervously, Cornell indicated a spot below the cadaver's navel. 'Um, in the groin, sir?'

'Highly improbable,' said Harding, using perhaps his most strident condemnation. He turned to Isaac Dorfman, a student with dark eyes and a miserable frown. '*You!* Where's the liver?'

'Left hypochondriac region, sir!'

'Correct – if I had asked for the *spleen*! Must we spend all day looking for the liver? Are you sure *you* have a liver?'

Harding turned to his assistant, Niles Beechcroft, a tall, elegant fourth-year student with a black beard and pince-nez spectacles. 'Beechcroft, please, tell us the function of the liver while we wait!'

Beechcroft fingered his lapels and spoke with the lazy confidence of a graduate. 'The largest gland, sir, secretes bile, removes toxic material from the blood. In classic mythology Prometheus was tied to a rock where his liver would be eaten out every day—'

'Yes, yes, yes, that'll do, Beechcroft. Now, have any of you miners *found* it yet?'

All eyes, however, were focused on Beechcroft. First, Harding had acknowledged him by name, a sure sign that he was blessed by the master. Second, Beechcroft's bushy beard added years to his babyish face. Every student in that room stopped shaving after seeing the assistant in the good graces of Professor Harding.

OF COURSE, TOM GREW a beard too. Beyond the inspiration of Beechcroft, a beard had practical uses. It was a cheap protection against Edinburgh's damp cold and offered the illusion of maturity to the youngest face – a student pursuing his midwifery requirement had to attend twenty labours; nothing seemed more humiliating to an inexperienced young man than the thought of having his authority questioned by a woman delivering her fourth or fifth child. The likelihood was that she would know more than he did. All the medical students put their razors away and walked the city resembling anarchists. In Edinburgh's tea shops, they sat for hours, five at a table, nursing cups of Darjeeling and slicing a single pastry into more helpings than the biblical loaves and fishes.

A barber near the High School Yards performed the same haircut on hundreds of young men for a keen price and ten minutes in the chair. Tom encouraged the man to give him a more extreme version – temples shaven and a thick swath of hair that tumbled over his forehead like a cockerel's comb. Studious, serious and self-involved, Tom faced the often bitter wind that tore between the old buildings of Infirmary Street with his teeth clenched and his brows furrowed at the crest of his nose.

Young men trying to get over love will do the most foolish things. Tom took to walking in the rain without umbrella or coat, clutching his books raw-knuckled and shivering, only the lee side of his body dry, as if he could erase his affection for Audrey by suffering. He struck most residents of that Scottish city as a quixotic figure. What fool endures such weather without a coat? Wallis Cornell dubbed Tom 'Cortez the Killer' for his intense frown and absurdly pointed beard. Cornell was the son of a rich London doctor. Thanks to a substantial remittance from his father, he usually paid for tea, cake and, on occasional evenings, beer. His beaky nose tilted a few degrees when he spoke.

'You see, Cortez, my future is settled,' he explained. 'My father has a fine practice, which I shall join' – he shuddered – 'if I get past those wretched anatomy classes with Harding. In London my practice will be waiting for me: fat, old people ravaged by wealth, good living, infidelity, sloth, vanity and self-importance.' Cornell's nose tilted slyly. 'And I shall soon resemble one of them.'

Tom admitted that his own plans were modest. 'I've no doctors in my family,' he said. 'When I have my degree, every step I take will be a first one.' He confided to Cornell that he had adopted a new name.

'Cortez suits you far better than Chapel,' Cornell replied. 'Are you sure you won't change your mind? Women love a foreign name.'

Cornell talked about women a lot, but he was cowed in their presence. During the occasional social event held by the department, the heavyset student would merge with the wallpaper, a stricken smile pasted to his face. He feared small talk, blushed in a woman's presence, and lost his voice when spoken to.

By contrast, Tom's brooding profile drew interest from the opposite sex, but he made a point of ignoring women, especially those attractive to him – as if, by treating them as invisible, he were scoring some victory against the one woman who had rejected him. He had written to Audrey just once in his first year; a terse note, giving his address only. She replied quickly, forgiving him his bitterness.

Dear Tom,

I know you are in pain, and that I am the cause of it. Know that I love you dearly. Please know also, that if you ever come to regret your silence to me, as I fear you will, nothing should prevent you asking my help or advice.

Audrey

Tom, of course, resented the kindness of her letter as much as he had resented her rejection. Every angry young man recognizes a perverse happiness in misery. Self-pity is the love affair of the solitary soul.

Isaac Dorfman would join Tom and Cornell after Harding's lectures to compare wounds. He would produce a complete surgical kit from his jacket pocket, remove a scalpel, and expertly slice a tart into three identical sections. Dorfman had many talents: he was a pianist and could play a serviceable Moonlight Sonata. He had considered a career as a classical pianist, but he suffered from stage fright. 'I fear humiliation,' he confessed grimly, 'and Professor Harding rekindles my fear at every opportunity.' Some friends are attracted by mutual admiration, but Tom, Cornell and Dorfman seemed united by their shortcomings.

One evening Dorfman produced a set of worn Tarot cards.

'Oh, for heaven's sake!' cried Cornell.

Dorfman replied, 'This is an ancient art. Older than anything you're learning here.'

'No science in it,' remarked Tom.

'Science and faith are natural antagonists,' said Dorfman. 'But who has ever died,' he said, 'from an overdose of Tarot?'

'What nonsense,' sneered Cornell.

Dorfman placed the deck before Tom. 'Cut the cards,' he said, 'and take the top one.'

Tom did as he was asked.

'The Queen of Pentacles. Interesting,' said Dorfman.

Cornell chuckled. Dorfman glared at him, shuffled the cards again, and presented them to Tom. Again, the Queen of Pentacles appeared. 'Interesting,' said Dorfman again. 'This nurturing mother figure keeps reappearing.' He shuffled the cards, and the same card came up.

'Should I do it again?' asked Tom.

'Why bother?' muttered Dorfman. 'What are you looking for, Chapel? Your mother? A wife?'

'Cortez hates women,' Cornell chuckled.

AT THE NEXT ANATOMY class, Tom offered a few answers that seemed to catch the professor's attention. After the lecture, Harding took him aside. 'You, what's your name?'

'Chapel, sir. Tom Chapel.'

'Well, Chapel, I'm holding a soirée for my daughter. She plays the piano. On Thursday evening.'

'How nice, sir,' Tom replied.

'You must come, Chapel.' The professor folded his apron. 'Eight o'clock?'

Tom nodded, giddy at having been addressed by name.

THE HARDING DAUGHTERS

TOM POLISHED HIS SHOES, RETIED HIS SCHOOL TIE THREE TIMES, and as an extra precaution, consulted his anatomy books for fear that the small talk at the party might involve a discussion of the lymphatic system or perhaps the digestive organs. Was he nervous? Of course. He was entering his professor's home, a new realm.

Harding lived in a small Georgian terraced house on Blackwell Terrace, which marked the eastern edge of Edinburgh. The Salisbury Crags rose behind the house. Tom paced up and down, intimidated by the ordered, genteel calm of the neighbourhood. When he finally stepped up to the door, it opened to reveal one of his friends.

'Cornell?' said Tom, surprised.

'I thought you'd never come in,' replied Cornell with amusement. 'Welcome to the Harding mansion. Wipe your feet and keep your hands to yourself.'

'Am I late?'

'No, just less early than I was. We're ahead of Niles Beechcroft.'

It was a modest house. The parlour was tidy without being fancy. The wallpaper was striped, of colours faded and hard to identify in the tint of the gaslight chandelier – the purple flowers might have been green, and the pink stripes might have been yellow. The curtains were old burgundy velvet with an aged yellow lining. An upright piano stood by the window, partnered by an empty stool. At the far end of the room stood a table covered with a lace cloth, a punch bowl, a plate of biscuits, and a basket of fruit – a meagre offering for a party. Across from the piano a desk was crowded with brass-framed photographs of a wedding couple, a mother holding a baby with a little girl on her knee, and several photographs of two little girls on a sun-drenched veranda – somewhere hot, India perhaps. A central staircase rose to the next floor. In comparison with William Bedlam's cluttered abode or the Limpkins' domestic jumble, the room seemed sadly empty.

'WELCOME!' CRIED THE PROFESSOR, emerging from the kitchen with glasses on a tray; he set the tray down with a clatter and offered his hand to Tom. 'Now' – he squinted – 'you're . . .'

'Chapel, sir.'

'Good of you to come, Chapel.' He hesitated. 'Student? Teacher?'

'Student, sir.'

'Hard to tell with the beard,' muttered the professor. 'Everybody looks the same.' He looked at Cornell. 'Have we met?'

'I was the first to arrive, sir,' replied Cornell.

'Of course, Walters!' the professor said with a laugh.

'Cornell.'

Harding nodded emphatically. 'You must keep reminding me. I invited everyone I could think of. Too few in a concert audience makes for a *catastrophe.* I hope you can help us bring out chairs and tidy up, of course!'

'Of course,' his students replied.

'Give Eve a hand, won't you!' He nodded towards the kitchen. Tom and Cornell exchanged a glance and set about making themselves useful while the professor took stock of the table. 'Let's see: punch, biscuits, fruit.'

When Cornell picked at a grape, Harding admonished him. 'Don't eat too much, eh, Walters? You'll make me seem ungenerous.'

When a female voice called from upstairs, Professor Harding excused himself and hurried away.

'Well,' whispered Cornell indignantly, 'not only does he not have a clue who we are but we've been recruited as servants. Shall we leave?'

A rustling in the kitchen, however, quelled the impulse. A young woman appeared in the doorway. Though her features were simple – brown eyes, shiny black hair parted in the centre and sealed in a bun – she went about her task with a grace that transcended their austerity. 'Hello, I'm Eve,' she said warmly. 'You must be Father's first victims! What sports you are! You'll love Lizzy. My sister plays so very well once she has overcome her fright.'

'I can't wait to hear . . .' began Cornell. His voice failed him and his face turned a deep crimson.

Eve offered him a glass of water, which he swallowed gratefully. She asked him about his studies, his childhood in London, and coaxed back his confidence. Tom, however, reverted to brooding in the corner of the kitchen, his usual manner with women, and wondered how an abrasive man like Harding could have produced such a charming daughter.

When Cornell answered the doorbell, Tom found himself alone with Eve. 'You're not like your father,' he muttered.

'I'm told I take after my mother,' Eve replied. 'She died in Burma. Lizzy and I were born there,' she explained. 'My father encouraged us to bring ourselves up, so we did.'

At that moment, feet stamped down the stairs. Harding followed his second daughter, Lizzy, a slender young woman with wire-framed spectacles. She was tall but drew her shoulders together as if she wished to appear smaller. Her face was freckled, like her father's, and she was in a state. 'Where's my music? What time is it? I've forgotten *everything*!'

'Haven't you committed it to memory?' Her father squinted in the withering manner he reserved for his students.

'You know *nothing* about performance!' his daughter spluttered, causing the professor to flinch.

'Your music is on the piano,' Eve assured her sister.

Lizzy tore past Tom. Cornell attempted a greeting but lost his voice again. When the doorbell rang, he fled to answer it. In moments, the parlour was crowded, and the offerings on the table had swelled with wine, whisky, cake and other treats.

'Do you often have such gatherings?' Tom asked Lizzy, who peered from the kitchen in dread at the excitement.

'Oh, no.' The girl cringed. 'It was Father's idea. He's doing it to show off Eve!'

'Shouldn't you be out there too?' Tom asked.

Lizzy's eyes widened with fear. 'No. Eve has all the charm.'

Lizzy tore off her spectacles, breathed on them, and rubbed the lenses fiercely with a fold of her dress. 'I didn't have a wink of sleep last night. Perhaps if I left now, I might take a tram to the docks and board a ship.'

Tom nodded. 'I can see you sailing the North Sea, concertina in hand, playing shanties for the sailors.'

Lizzy turned to him with fresh interest. 'Did you tell me your name? If you did, I've forgotten it. All Father's students look the same to me.'

'Tom,' he replied.

Suddenly the professor called to her from the parlour, and Lizzy ventured in. The guests steered her to the piano stool though she tried everything to avoid it. Tom was now interested to see whether she would survive the ordeal.

She fussed with the stool, cleared her throat, threw back her hair, pulled it forward over her shoulders and adjusted her spectacles once more. All at once everybody was quiet. She closed her eyes, placed her hands on her knees, then took a breath and began to play.

It was a Brahms intermezzo, and the melody quickly silenced the coughs, rustles and whispers. As Lizzy coaxed wistfulness out of the piece, the expressions of Harding's students changed. They stopped staring at the girl's fingers and sank into their own thoughts, seduced by a mood of regret and reconciliation.

Rarely does a performance transcend its surroundings and carry an audience to some intangible realm. Tom had never experienced such a thing before. He started to think of Audrey and was ashamed. His year of self-pity began to seem foolish. He had asked her to commit herself to him, and what had he offered her? His bitterness was unjustified, his disgust with women unfair, his scholarly isolation grandiose thoughtlessness.

The music continued, and a new passage seemed to forgive these indulgences, or so he imagined. Tom stepped forward, to the kitchen doorway, and saw his own melancholy etched on other faces. Then he felt Eve beside him, willing her sister on with a subtle nudge of her chin.

After the last note had faded, Lizzy's audience remained still, immersed in the mood she had evoked – a tender grief. Only after Cornell started to clap thunderously did everyone stir into applause. 'Well done,' he cried. 'Brava!'

The sisters shared a glance across the room. Eve pressed her shoulder against Tom just enough to acknowledge his presence. 'She's so talented,' she murmured. 'I envy her so. Father is convinced she'll bowl over some young man with her gift.'

'Isn't she a wonder?' cried Harding as people returned to their drinks and conversation. He came up to Tom and Eve, shook Tom's hand vigorously, then meandered past his other students, insulting each one by introducing himself again.

'Poor thing,' said Eve, staring after her father. 'He's afraid his daughters are almost too old to marry. He'd thought he'd be rid of us by now.' She smiled faintly.

THOUGH PROFESSOR HARDING had forgotten his students' names by their next class, the Harding sisters had not: Tom and Cornell were invited to a New Year's party during the first rainy week in January.

It was a merry gathering. The sisters' aunts – two craggy dowagers from their mother's side – plied everybody with food and wasted no time in assessing Cornell's pedigree, then Tom's. One had seen William Bedlam perform his *King Lear;* the other owned a piece of Todderman's pottery. 'A shepherdess,' she sighed, 'with the sweetest smile.'

'Which one do you like?' whispered Cornell, as they made their way home after the party.

'The aunts?'

'The sisters!'

'Both are pleasant enough,' Tom replied. 'Why?'

'Well, Lizzy's mine,' Cornell declared.

'Very well, Cornell,' Tom responded drily.

His companion chuckled. 'Good thing for me you hate women, Cortez.'

About a week later, Tom encountered the Harding sisters on the street. They waved to him and fell into a breathless sibling banter in which one completed the other's thought: 'Lizzy gives piano lessons to the children of Father's colleagues,' explained Eve.

'Eve works for the Head of School,' explained Lizzy. 'We've been thinking about your friend, Cornell—'

'We think he deserves a nickname,' said Eve. 'You, for example, *look* like a Cortez—'

'Yes, I can definitely see an ambitious conquistador in your profile,' agreed Lizzy.

'And a touch of dishonesty in your eyes,' added Eve.

'Handsome, though,' said Lizzy.

Eve smiled to her sister. 'Of course he's handsome – but angry and hostile to women.'

'You don't know me well enough to mock me,' Tom said.

'We know your *sort*,' Lizzy replied, 'don't we, Eve?'

'Oh yes. You need to be brought out of that hard shell,' Eve continued.

'Oh, Eve,' cried Lizzy excitedly, 'what shall we call Mr Cornell?'

'Dodo suits him perfectly,' said Eve.

'He won't like that,' Tom told her.

'Of course he will,' said Lizzy, confidently. 'He'll be *charmed*.'

THEY KNEW CORNELL'S sort too. He accepted his nickname gladly. Isaac Dorfman warned his friends that they had been bewitched, and that it would come to tragedy in the end. 'I'd be happy to read your cards, Cornell,' he said, 'to be reassured you're not barking up the wrong tree.'

'Nonsense!' Cornell laughed.

'As for you, Cortez' – Dorfman frowned – 'I haven't forgotten about the Queen of Pentacles.'

BY HIS SECOND YEAR, Tom Chapel's shell had cracked. He liked his patients at Holyrood's clinic and drew satisfaction from a successful treatment. Though he still enjoyed marching through the rain, he accepted from the Harding sisters a used grey raincoat – rescued from a parish poor box. It comforted him, for it proved that somebody cared about him; and of course, the sight of him clad handsomely, striding through

Edinburgh's wet streets, assured the sisters that Tom was not resistant to improvement. It wasn't long before he exchanged gifts with them at holidays. Other traditions were established – walks along the Salisbury Crags, tea with the aunts, and every now and then the professor would sit Tom down in his study to advise him on his courses.

'Chapel,' he said, 'you have good judgment and a grasp of procedure. You're ambitious too. You remind me of myself. You'll make a great doctor and, I imagine, a poor husband.'

Tom didn't notice the irony in the compliment: his consummate wish was to follow in his mentor's path. What else mattered? He was still running from the furnaces of Todderman's factory, driven to forget his painful losses. That Professor Harding considered him a poor prospect as a husband seemed irrelevant.

It was not irrelevant to Eve, though; during Tom's third year she steered him to the best professors and wrote letters on his behalf, inquiring about positions at the better hospitals. She undertook a mission to improve his appearance and gave him scarves, mittens, and other items that softened the profile of the conquistador marching into the wind on Infirmary Street.

EVE'S INVESTMENT IN HIM became evident one evening in the summer, when the family invited Tom to celebrate the late Mrs Harding's birthday. They lit a candle, said a prayer and passed around a picture of her. Suddenly, the professor embarked on a sermon about ambition.

'Great men, Tom, make terrible husbands. The greater achievements of humanity are made by the selfish: the obsessed and the hungry. But a satisfied man makes not a dent in the world. Be a bachelor, Tom, that's my advice.'

'Don't be silly, Papa,' said Eve.

'I speak for myself,' Harding replied. 'I was a hardworking doctor; I shaped a fine hospital out of grass huts, suffering and misery. But I killed my wife working such long hours. My distraction. My folly.'

'Dysentery killed Mama,' explained his daughter. 'It wasn't your fault.'

Harding removed his glasses. 'Burma killed her, and we were there so that I could run a hospital in Rangoon.' He paused. 'I made my name there, built a reputation. Despite Burma,' he said, pressing his finger against the table, 'and of all my notable achievements, of which there are many' – his voice faltered – 'I am ashamed to have been such a poor husband!' The professor rose abruptly, slipping his wife's image into his pocket, and left the room.

Lizzy stared after him. 'Poor Papa,' she said.

IF PROFESSOR HARDING treated Tom as his protégé, he conferred the complementary title upon Cornell. 'What a good husband you'd make for Lizzy, Dodo,' he said, adopting the sisters' nickname. 'You're similar in temperament and colouring. I can just see my grandchildren, all with red hair and—'

'Yes, Papa,' Lizzy groaned, 'I've heard this a *hundred* times.'

Cornell basked in these remarks. Lizzy's protests amused him; he believed she would abide by her father's wishes, just as he would follow the expectations of his father.

Tom, however, knew otherwise, for a more subtle seduction was continuing during his moments with the Harding sisters. He often found himself invited an hour earlier than his friend or asked to linger after Cornell had left. His affection for both women grew, and each sister expressed hers for him out of sight of the other. Lizzy would give him a sideways nudge with her hip when she wished to share something with him. Eve would face him squarely, her head tilted forward, and whisper so softly that he would have to press his ear to her lips. These small gestures became an advancing competition for Tom's heart. And, since he responded with passivity, the stakes were raised with every gesture.

A LETTER HELPED to clarify Tom's feelings about his future:

Dear Tom,

I have not heard from you in a year. I fear that you would prefer to forget Audrey Limpkin altogether. I am writing to assure you that my affection endures, and perhaps, when my circumstances improve, our relations will improve too.

The fortunes of the Limpkins have been dark this year. Mother has been sick, and unable to do her rounds, though the girls have been helping. The Orfling is well, though we cannot understand why he still does not grow as he has the appetite of a child three times his size.

Mr Murdick has been promoted and now depends on me more than ever. He is a most wretched human being, Tom. He stares at me from behind those spectacles as if I were some riddle. This is still preferable to the slack-jawed leer he reserves for the female clerks. I thank my stars I am not a woman here.

The worst news is about Oscar. Oh, Oscar!

You may recall that he had secured some important information about Bronson Mansworth. The father of your young acquaintance at Hammer Hall was selling munitions at inflated prices to the British Army in Khartoum. This while serving as an elected member of Parliament! After Oscar published this information, Mansworth suffered considerable injury in the press, though he remains in his seat, without public apology or official redress.

Oscar, of course, was hoping to marry his daughter, Penelope. He waited nine months before approaching him again for his daughter's hand.

Mansworth agreed to the marriage, but his terms were harsh. Oscar had to abandon journalism entirely; only upon his tenth year with Penelope would he receive her dowry.

Well, Oscar agreed to it. The lovelorn fool! He has left the newspaper, his pride and joy, and is going to write biographies while Penelope continues to teach. She is a sweet girl, but we Limpkins find ourselves no better off now than we were without a millionairess in the family!

Such is the price of love.

Audrey

The Limpkins, formerly his adoptive family, were in fortune's ebb, and this made it easier for Tom to look at the Hardings with fresh admiration.

Tenement life was a distant memory, and the genteel life of the Hardings was more familiar, more appealing, and prompted Tom to shed his ambivalence. It helped, of course, that Eve wasted no time when she wanted something.

TOM'S ROOM WAS in the cellar of one of the college houses. He liked it because of its private entrance to the street. The boiler was next door, and thanks to the pipes laid across the ceiling, it was always warm – though otherwise dark, shabby and charmless. Eve might never have visited him but for its privacy, for it would have been unseemly for a young woman to be seen alone with him. She always brought a parcel of some sort – clothing, flowers, food, shaving soap – so that her visits appeared charitable. At first, this wasn't far from the truth: she cleaned his room, found an old wooden chest for his clothes, and promised that she would not visit if he failed to keep the place tidy. Tom trimmed his beard and picked up his things, so the visits continued. The room became a more pleasant place for them to talk, and one afternoon, when a January wind whistled through Tom's window, Eve rocked on her heels before him.

'Cortez?' she said. 'Do you find me attractive?'

Tom admitted that he did.

'Why have you not said so?'

'I once confessed my love to a girl, and it led to catastrophe.'

This amused her. 'Well, I've burned my tongue on a roast potato, Tom, but I could hardly refuse dinner. It's time you had some practice in confessing love to a girl.'

Eve sat upon his bed wearing a thick cardigan and woollen skirt, arms folded. It was cold in the room, but she was the picture of warmth; her cheeks glowed, and when she smoothed her hands across her skirt, Tom's pulse raced. 'I'd like to kiss you,' he said.

'Not so fast, Tom,' she said. 'Am I pretty?'

'Yes,' he replied.

Eve pursed her lips in reproach. 'How like a doctor! A woman needs to know her best points, Tom. *Flatter me.* Begin at my feet, and don't stop until I say you may.'

When Tom had described her beauty to her satisfaction, she coached him on the virtues of her nature. Finally, she told him he might have a kiss.

Some men would have lost patience during such coaching, but Tom had found it strangely arousing. Eve told him where to put his hands, and when she uttered her first sigh of pleasure, he felt pleased. This was Eve – a bit like Sissy – whose terms Tom had understood very well.

WHEN LIZZY NEXT SAW Tom, she recognized her sister's modifications. He was in a tea shop, scratching his diminished beard and frowning at a textbook. Lizzy's slender figure was bowed by the baskets of groceries she was carrying. She put them down and placed her hand upon his knee as she greeted him – perhaps farther up his knee than might have been considered polite.

'There you are,' she said. 'But where is the rest of your beard?'

'Eve thought it was too much,' he replied.

'Please grow it back, Cortez.'

After severe entreaties, he agreed.

He accompanied Lizzy on the walk up the street to her house. 'I've met Dodo's father,' she explained. 'He reminded me of a roast goose I saw once in a shopwindow: all browned and shiny, well-preserved but not much to say for himself. Happily rich, I thought.'

Tom laughed, but her eyes regarded him anxiously. 'What shall I *do* with him, Tom?'

'Is there nothing you like about him?'

Lizzy looked disappointed by the question, which implied that she *should* see something in Cornell. 'Yes, but I can't imagine myself having his children or growing old with him, or curled up with him on a cold evening, or sharing a joke—'

'He hasn't asked you to marry him, has he?'

Lizzy frowned. 'No, Tom. He's *counting* on it.'

THEY WERE TOGETHER one evening – Tom, Cornell, Lizzy and Eve – sitting by the fire in the Hardings' house, when Lizzy happened to notice Eve's toe resting on Tom's shoe. Later, when the professor complained of feeling cold, Lizzy asked Tom to help her fetch another blanket from the high shelf in the linen closet. As he reached for the blanket, Lizzy rested her cheek upon his shoulder.

'Lizzy?'

'I just wondered what it would be like to sleep beside you,' she sighed. 'To wake up with your face on the pillow beside mine. Do *you* ever think of such things?'

In truth, he had imagined this and more.

'No, I have not,' he replied, knowing better than to admit such a dangerous thing. He was acutely aware of the rivalry between the Harding sisters. There was no apparent solution, he thought, except to deny that he felt anything for her.

But Lizzy eyed him with contempt. 'No? And not with Eve either? *Liar.*' She pressed her finger to his lips to prevent him speaking. '*Of course, Lizzy,*' she said, mocking his tone, then scratching an imaginary beard, '*you must remember that you're practically engaged to Dodo.*'

She took the blanket from Tom and slipped it over her shoulders. 'I am a chattel,' she remarked. Then she added fiercely, 'If you marry her, I shall hate you forever.'

Lizzy always mixed her jokes with the truth – a way of protecting herself, Tom supposed. The funnier she was, the more likely that some revelation was on the way. 'In fact,' she continued, 'it's easier to imagine myself with lots of little Chapels running around the garden than lots of little Dodos. So you'd better decide on one of us soon, or we shall *both* hate you!'

Tom leaned forward and kissed her. They had shared many kisses of the polite sort – quick, tight-lipped, brushing kisses – but this one was an apology. Or it began that way, except that Lizzy kept her lips against his in soft supplication, as if this was her chance, perhaps the *last*, to make her feelings known. And Tom felt himself spinning, bound to her, better judgment cast aside, and utterly smitten.

Cornell's voice boomed from downstairs. 'Lizzy, I must have a word with you!'

When they returned to the parlour, Cornell had accepted a cigar from the professor and had forgotten why he had summoned her. It was Eve who glanced back and forth between Tom and Lizzy. She knew something had happened, just as her sister had intuited some change before.

Tom realized then that he had to make a decision he didn't wish to make and betray someone he didn't wish to hurt.

As they walked back to Holyrood that evening, Cornell talked incessantly, but Tom remained mute and troubled.

Eventually, Cornell glared at him. 'Well, Cortez?'

'What?' said Tom.

Impatiently, Cornell repeated: 'Lizzy seemed at sixes and sevens this evening.'

'You noticed?'

'Of course!' Cornell retorted. 'What the devil was it about? Was it *me*? I hope you put in a word—'

'We talk about you all the time,' Tom replied, with a hardened glance.

'Really?'

'Really,' he snapped. 'Chasing the little Dodos across the garden, while you sip port and fall asleep, ravaged by wealth, good living, infidelity, sloth, vanity and self-importance. Yes, Cornell, we've talked about *everything*.'

Cornell's smile faded. 'I *knew* she was fond of you, Cortez, but I didn't imagine you cared for her.' He looked wounded. Then he drew himself up before Tom. 'Poor Eve! What a damned wretch you are, Cortez!'

Explosive rage in a normally gentle man can look comical. Cornell secured his coat but misaligned his buttons and twisted the belt so that the pin wouldn't fit. He tied it up in a knot, cursed silently, and turned to face Tom. 'Look here, Chapel,' he said, 'I . . . I've left my umbrella behind.'

'You may have mine,' Tom offered, but his rival waved away the attempt at conciliation and began to walk back to the Hardings' house, his coat bunched, the belt askew.

FOR THE NEXT TWO days Tom locked himself in his room. He had exams to study for, but there was a more pressing reason for his interment – his thoughts were in a muddle, and he was afraid to show his face.

Thinking about the Harding sisters distracted him from his work, yet when he tried to sum up his feelings, he shrank back to the sanctuary of his studies.

He began to attend interviews for a position at a local hospital. But how, he wondered, could he make decisions in a hospital if he was incapable of choosing between Eve and Lizzy? How could he assume a position of trust when he had lied for Bronson Mansworth? Furthermore, if Audrey couldn't rely on him as a husband, why would a hospital entrust to him its patients? At one interview he threw himself into convincing the hospital governors that he was wrong for the post, and won it with his candour.

THE FOLLOWING MONDAY there was a knock on the door. When Eve entered, she drew back at the sight of him. Tom was unshaven, unwashed and melancholy. Her manner became clipped and formal.

'Cortez, would you mind explaining what happened to Dodo? He came to our house after you had left and demanded that Lizzy have dinner with him the next day.'

'I may have upset him,' Tom said cautiously.

'Upset him? He proposed to Lizzy,' said Eve, 'and she refused, which upset us all. Papa told her she was foolish, as did I.' She waited for Tom's concurrence. 'You agree, I'm sure.'

Tom hesitated. 'Why did she turn him down?'

Eve frowned. 'She claims to love *you*!'

Again, she waited for Tom to clarify his feelings, but all he said was 'Poor Lizzy.'

Eve stiffened. '*Poor Dodo*,' she replied. 'He thinks you've confused Lizzy and that she would have accepted him if you hadn't led her astray. Those were his words.'

'I haven't misled her.'

'No?' Eve's voice was brittle. 'Then is it I you have misled? Because if that's so, you're a scoundrel and the most careless man I've ever met!'

Her cold fury was magnificent, and Tom offered the most foolish reply in his defence. 'Perhaps I am, but I have a dilemma, Eve. I love two women.'

Her eyes glittered. 'You *fool*, Cortez,' she whispered. 'You *fool*!' She drew out a handkerchief and wiped her eyes. 'Before you ruin both our lives, you'd better come to your senses!'

The door slammed behind her, and Tom heard Eve's footsteps fall like truncheons on the pavement.

How could he choose one without hurting the other? And what reasonable woman forgives a man for betraying her sister? Should he exile himself from both? Those questions dogged him as he walked to college, oblivious to everything but his dilemma. He found himself, as bad luck would have it, sitting beside Cornell at the morning lecture.

'I'm sorry for any harm I have caused you, Dodo,' he whispered.

Cornell answered, with a glassy smile, 'Listen, you swine, I've been generous to you since the day we met. You've repaid me in the shabbiest way. I hope you go to hell.'

Pompous fool, Tom thought. Cornell had taken Lizzy for granted. She was gentle, sweet and sensitive, and he had ignored her and courted her father instead.

Tom decided to appeal to his mentor for advice. Professor Harding was in his study at the college. When Tom knocked at the door, he didn't seem surprised, or even sorry to see him. In fact, he looked relieved. 'Ah, Chapel, there you are! Let's have a drink together, lad!'

They exchanged pleasantries on the way, ambling through a current of fresh students – young men with downy cheeks. *Boys.* How different Tom felt from them now. Such *children.* How simple their lives were compared with his. What few cares they had! Now he understood the Orfling's impulse to remain a baby.

At the pub, the two men sat in silence, nursing their pints in the gloom. After drinking an inch from his beer, Harding wiped foam from his moustache. 'Look, Tom,' he said, 'I understand how things can get out of hand, especially with women. Dodo has appealed to me . . .'

Tom was about to say that Dodo's concerns were of the least importance to him, but the professor continued. 'You must understand, Tom, that my daughters' futures require my careful consideration.'

'Of course,' Tom replied.

'A woman makes an investment in a husband. She must assess his good character, and the life he can offer her.'

Tom nodded.

'I always thought you would go far, Tom. I've made inquiries on your behalf with a former colleague at St Ambrose Hospital. You've heard of it? A fine group of doctors there and the most modern equipment. They agreed to take you – and it will be a good start, Tom. You'll do well there.'

Tom was about to thank him when his mentor raised his hand; he hadn't finished.

'Tom, I *want* Lizzy to marry Cornell. I see no future for her here. She's an odd girl; clever but awkward, and too tall for most men, but he won't hold that against her. She has looks but no dignity, pride but none of her sister's charm. Eve, on the other hand, will go far. She has grace, tact and the resources to find herself a successful man.'

'Certainly,' Tom agreed.

'But Lizzy might remain a spinster, giving piano lessons for the rest of her days. Now, Cornell adores her. She'll never want for money or attention. And when she sees no alternative, she'll recognize his virtues.'

Harding might have appraised his daughter's prospects accurately, but his conclusion struck Tom as a betrayal. *I am a chattel*, Lizzy had remarked. No wonder Audrey Limpkin clung to her disguise.

As the professor paused to clean his glasses, Tom felt a flash of revulsion. Clearly, the man was baiting him with this offer. But what of the sacrifice? He tried to clear his thoughts. Did he pity Lizzy or love her? If he merely pitied her for the prospect of a life with Cornell, then it was her matter to settle. Conversely, he imagined a successful life with Eve, but would it be happy?

'I put it to you like this, Tom,' Harding continued. 'Become a fine doctor, and let Eve and Lizzy carry on with their lives.'

'Eve *and* Lizzy?'

'As I said before, you'll make a poor husband, Tom. I see your ambition, your hunger. In the right position you'll do great things, but I have no desire to see either of my daughters with an absent husband. I *was* such a man, Tom.'

'I've no desire to *be* such a man,' Tom replied.

Harding blinked as if he had been poked in the eye; he had cast Tom in his own image, and now the young man had contradicted him.

'Tom, I feel the same affection for you that I would for a son, so I speak as much for your own good as for my daughters'—'

Tom put his head in his hands. 'Have you told them?' he asked.

Harding paused. 'I will tonight, and they will understand.' He took a few coins from his pocket and placed them on the table. Then he put on his hat and coat and nodded. 'Drink up, Tom, you have a great life ahead of you.'

AN ETERNITY AWAY

DORFMAN LEFT COLLEGE JUST BEFORE THE START OF HIS FOURTH year. There was a rumour that he had failed his exams, but Tom knew the truth. Shortly before his disappearance, his friend had made a pithy observation: 'Have you ever wondered what the difference is between a doctor and a mystic, Cortez? Think about it. They both deal in the well-being of men; they claim to know more than they really do; they consider their discipline superior to all others.

'Here's the difference. Doctors expect their patients to be believers. Mystics, however, face sceptics every day. How can your philosophy be credible if you do not face your sceptics?'

Without Dorfman, Tom suffered; his last year was bitterly lonely. He had written notes to the Harding sisters, but no replies came. He worked in a hospital near Granton, north of the city, and lived in constant expectation of a chance meeting with them. He prepared for it, rehearsed his greetings, apologies and peacemaking gestures, all for naught.

It is one thing to be separated by a continent or a river, but Tom suffered the torture of proximity. Lizzy and Eve shared a city with him, breathed the same air, heard the same thunder on stormy days, and might turn the same corner and come face-to-face with him at any moment. In short, although he accepted his banishment, he could not erase them from his thoughts.

In despair, he decided that the only solution to his misery was to go somewhere so far from them that they would slip from his mind. He wrote to hospitals in India, Australia and Africa; when a position was finally offered to him, he spent most of a night tossing and turning until, at three o'clock in the morning, he rose to compose a letter to Professor Harding.

Sir,

In spite of your generous offer to use your influence to secure my residency locally at St Ambrose, I could no more appreciate it than enjoy the absence of Eve and Lizzy in my life. In short, my life is a misery.

Therefore, I am taking a position at Port Elizabeth Hospital in Southern Africa. They require a surgeon with modern training, and I look forward to many challenges in a place far from you and your daughters.

Make no mistake, I leave with gratitude for all that you have taught me, but I am a better man than you think me.

Yours sincerely,
Tom Chapel

Tom's bags were packed, his trunk stuffed with clothing for a new climate. He spent a sunny Saturday giving away his furniture to the other students in his lodgings. And when his possessions were stowed at the railway station, he walked for an hour around the castle, past the graveyards, the gardens, the grand Georgian houses and the little brick dwellings. He felt no sentiment, no affection for the streets. He was glad to leave.

There was a tea shop near the platform, and in it a tall woman, with auburn hair and wire-rimmed spectacles, sat, shoulders hunched, at a table stirring her tea.

'Lizzy?'

She started when he spoke, and her teacup spilled across the table.

Lizzy's smile was frail. 'They told me you were leaving, and I wanted to say goodbye,' she said and covered her mouth – the very act of saying it had been more painful than she'd expected. Tears rolled down her cheeks, and Tom reached out to take her hand. 'I've missed you so,' he said.

'What *happened* to you, Tom?'

'Didn't your father explain?'

'He said you didn't wish to see either of us again.'

'That is not so, and I've missed you terribly.'

Lizzy's voice failed her, but she mouthed the same words. He was still holding her hand when they paid for the tea and walked away together. She gave him news of her piano students, and all the while, their fingers remained entwined. Finally, Lizzy proposed that she pay him a visit.

'That would be difficult, Lizzy. I'm going to Africa.'

'Africa?' She looked shocked. She spoke suddenly in a torrent of words, perhaps to stop her tears. 'Of course! Well, I might run away too,' she added. 'I acquired a suitcase a few months ago in case Dodo proposed again. Do you think a convent in the French Alps might take me? If not the Alps, perhaps Shanghai or Burma. Papa always complained about Burma, but it must be better than listening to Dodo chortle as I become fat and wretched in old age.'

As Tom listened, Lizzy's bitterness and frustration resonated in his heart. Here we are, he thought, two souls wishing for flight. How absurd it seemed for them to rush away in different directions.

'Come with me, Lizzy,' he said.

In a moment they had walked to her home. Tom waited on the step while Lizzy slipped inside for her bag and some clothing. A plume of smoke rose from the station where the train was waiting. It was foolishness, Tom thought. Africa was an eternity away. The professor would be devastated; and Eve – Eve would never forgive him.

When Lizzy emerged, she had a small suitcase in one hand and some volumes of music fastened with string. She was breathless, her cheeks bright with colour, eyes wide and anxious. She looked around wildly for Tom – he was not on the step.

'Cortez?'

He stood up from the kerb and tilted his head. 'Lizzy,' he said, 'are you *sure* you should accompany me?'

She lowered her suitcase. 'Would you rather I remained here?'

'Of course not,' he replied. Tom cast a glance across the city skyline, at the castle, the steeples, the houses backed up like biscuits, and far in the distance, the absurd glass turret of the Gramley Building. A whistle sounded from the station.

'Come,' he said, holding out his hand.

She took it, and they ran down the street as passengers for the London train lined up with their tickets.

AUDREY'S STORY

THE LETTER ARRIVED FOR TOM AT HOLYROOD, BUT HE WAS already on a steamship bound for Port Elizabeth with his new wife. It wouldn't find him for six months. In those days the mail was carried by ship, and a letter might visit several continents before it found its recipient. The return address was simply 'Newgate Prison'. The pages were written in the precise, delicate cursive one might find in an accountant's ledger.

Dear Tom,

I hope this letter finds you safe and healthy. I can assure you that I remain in the same capacity, though that is as much good news as you can expect from this letter.

The worst fortune has struck, Tom, and I ask your forgiveness in sending such a tale of woe, but I must keep myself busy, above all things, and to lay the recent events of my life on paper will afford me some brief peace of mind.

You may remember Mr Murdick. Perhaps you recall that several young women in the offices had left his employment rather suddenly.

In the last year Mr Murdick had come to depend upon me for my accuracy and competence. In fact, I believe I was responsible for his rise through the company. He hired men who were submissive and humble; those who defied him were abused and dismissed. He preyed upon the women he hired, keeping them in such fear of dismissal that they would suffer anything. There was a file room near his office that they nicknamed 'Finger Alley' because of his habit of pouncing on them there. I heard that one poor woman was raped by him; ironically, her husband begged her to keep the job. Murdick dismissed her after she appeared at work missing two fingers from a kitchen accident (now I wonder if this was a desperate attempt to free herself from his employment).

After hearing these stories, I supposed, foolishly, that I must be too valuable to Mr Murdick to be a victim of his abuse. Recently, however, he was awarded a post in Hamburg. We all breathed easier at this news. We would have a new manager, and Mr Murdick would be forgotten.

What I didn't know was that he had guessed my secret and, indeed, had been aware of it for years. A week before he was to leave, he would linger by my desk, asking questions about my family, and about you, Tom. Then he told me that he had followed us that evening into the public house and later observed us part ways on Westminster Bridge.

'Why would a girl as pretty as you pass herself off as a man?' he asked. 'What's wrong with you?'

'Nothing,' I replied.

He accused me of lying to him. I reminded him that my father had been a loyal employee, and that I was his daughter, and no harm had been done. I begged him to let me stay, Tom, for my mother, the baby, and the twins. I said I'd change my clothes if he preferred, but he told me to remain as I was, that he wouldn't be made a fool of upon the eve of his promotion.

That night I remained to finish my work. Murdick came back later, after his dinner, and told me to take out a ledger I'd just finished, and as I turned, he came up behind me and placed his hands upon my breasts. When I wrenched myself away, he pulled my shirt cuffs back, clenching them together with one hand while he unfastened my belt. He told me that I was going to 'make up' for my deceit. With my hands pinned behind my back, he eased me onto the floor and slid my trousers down to my ankles so that my feet were bound too.

Tom, he was so strong – it was frightening how strong he was for one not much bigger than I. Then he threw his weight upon my hips to stop me struggling, and I felt a bone crack and the most awful pain shoot down my leg. I couldn't move. He tore away my shirt, vest, and underclothes, and tightened my belt around my ankles. I kept telling him I was sorry because I couldn't think of what else to say, and I cursed myself, Tom, because you warned me, and you weren't the only one, and I was so foolish for believing myself safe. Then he rolled me over and parted my legs, and my hip felt like fire.

I wept for the pain. He told me to lie still like the other girls. Oh, my conceit! I had been as vulnerable as any other female in the office, Tom, and my insulation from their suffering was unforgivable. I had done nothing to help them, and here was my reward: Murdick whispering in my ear to be quiet when, oh, God, I had been so selfishly quiet for years!

He said that he had always loved me. Then he unbuttoned his trousers and tried to take me.

The pain in my hip was all I could feel. My mind became simple. I felt myself become very small, shrinking into insignificance, to nothing. Suddenly, whatever he was doing wasn't happening to me, but to somebody else, there on the floor.

I remembered our games as children. Do you recall the sword fights? I thought of a battle I had fought with Oscar. You cheered me on, Tom, but it was impossible for me to pierce his heart because he wore a pan lid over his chest. I thought he was invincible. Then you whispered that I could pierce Oscar's heart from the side, under his arm.

Suddenly, I awoke beneath Murdick again. He was cursing and kissing me; his breath was hot and poisonous. I felt about the floor. My hand grasped the brass invoice spike from my desk.

I held it and waited. Murdick shifted on top of me, and I felt a fresh burst of pain as he tried to take me again. Then he began to talk, and that was when I took the spike and pushed it hard through his armpit, deep into his chest.

I thought the ceiling would collapse from the sound coming out of his mouth. Then he stopped moving, and there was an awful smell. I knew he was dead, but I couldn't move him off me. I was trapped beneath him.

For hours I lay there, Tom. Sometimes I woke, then I passed out again. I saw flashes of light on the walls and ceiling, like sticklebacks swimming in a jar, shiny, glittering in the air all around me, and I thought I was dead.

I woke up in a hospital with two policemen at the door. They spoke harshly; I was called a murderess. I fainted from the pain in my hip. They revived me, but refused to give me anything for the pain until I had answered their questions, so I told them what had happened, and they accused me of tempting Murdick to his death.

I was charged with murder. They put stories about me in the newspapers. A Temptress in Trousers. As soon as I could walk, I was sent from the hospital to Newgate.

Oscar found me a lawyer, but warned me that the circumstances of the case were too bizarre for reasonable folk to understand. A woman passing herself off as a man, found half-naked with her victim lying on top of her – it looked terrible, Tom. The prosecutor spent most of his time describing Murdick's fine character, his hard work and recent rise in standing. I was portrayed as a base and lowly parasite. My reward for supporting my family and defending myself against a predator was twenty-eight years in prison.

I'm learning to walk again. I share a cell with ten other women. We sleep on mats on the floor, which is painful, but during the day I can sit and weave. The wardswoman killed a man too; but she has a bed instead of a mat. She promised me that good behaviour will earn me a bed.

Perhaps there is good in this. The Orfling is growing. He comes to visit me with Mama. He's bright. Perhaps, without me there, he realized it was time. Eloise and Elsie look like young women. They work in a brush factory.

Oscar thinks I'll get time off for good behaviour, and if I show regret for my actions, my term might be reduced.

Regret? I don't know if I can show something I don't feel. The judge told me my term was compensation for twenty-eight years stolen from the life of Mr Murdick. So be it, I say. I shall relish each stolen minute, Tom, on behalf of every woman who shall not have to fear that man.

In the meantime, I take my days as they come, sustained only by the one precious blessing born of my misfortune.

Your Audrey

PART TWO

THE IMMIGRANTS

IN 1889, DR TOM CHAPEL BEGAN A NEW LIFE IN PORT ELIZABETH Hospital as its resident surgeon. Little Margaret was born the next year. Tom sent a photograph to Edinburgh of the baby – a beatific face with a little shock of hair pricking up from her scalp like a halo.

It was hard for Tom to reconcile his good fortune with Audrey's tragedy. He had a loving wife, a daughter, and a house overlooking Algoa Bay. Life was precious. Like a tightrope artist preparing for his first step, Tom checked his moorings every morning – first Lizzy, sleeping beside him, then Margaret, snoring in the crib at the foot of his bed – only then did he feel ready to face the world.

When Iris appeared two years later, they sent another photograph; this one showed a baby wrapped tightly in soft flannel, eyes open and alert, her Buddha lips poised to utter her first remark on the condition of the world before her.

When no answer arrived from Edinburgh, Lizzy was disappointed but not surprised. 'Father doesn't forgive easily,' she explained. 'I once buffed his brogues with red shoe polish. He spent weeks trying to get out the colour. For years he talked about those shoes.' She sighed. 'As for Eve,' she said, 'well, she loved you, Tom. I doubt I could have forgiven *her* if she had taken you from me.'

'But you're *sisters*,' Tom said, recalling Audrey's devotion to the twins.

'There are all kinds of sisters,' Lizzy reminded him.

Charity was born three years after Iris, in 1895. She developed an early passion for lace – she insisted on white socks fringed with lace and wore an enormous lace-edged bonnet that framed her solemn, pudgy face the way paper frills garnish a lamb chop. She would follow her mother around the house, thumb in her mouth, fingers clutching a fold of Lizzy's skirt.

It would be fair to say that Tom and Lizzy leaped headlong into family life. The ship's captain who had married them had issued a cryptic admonition before sealing their vow: 'A hasty departure yields an ill-equipped voyage.' The Chapels' marriage, however, was founded on affection and respect. Thus 'equipped', they appeared quite prepared for the challenges of parenthood. Though a nurse present at Margaret's birth warned them that 'children are quite capable of ruining a perfectly good marriage,' Tom and Lizzy enjoyed their children, and considered the attendant chaos and emotional upheaval a blessing and an adventure. It was only when Tom declined an offer to become head doctor that Lizzy wondered if he would one day regret the demands of his family.

'Eve would have insisted that you take such a position,' she said.

'That's why I married you, my dear,' he replied. 'The head doctor must spend three of his evenings at meetings in the hospital. Three nights a week away from my family? That would be like skipping three in seven instalments of *The Pickwick Papers*. I'd miss so much.'

For that reason, Tom and Lizzy were not seen among Port Elizabeth's polite society. They missed dinners to admire sunsets, skipped balls to play Igloo with the sofa cushions, and spent afternoons dressing the children in togas and war paint instead of attending teas. Tom saved his money and bought Lizzy a Bechstein piano for her birthday. Babies, music, and domestic bliss – that was the life they chose.

THE CHAPEL GIRLS were spoiled; not with extravagant clothes and playthings but with the approval of their parents. Tom and Lizzy believed this to be the best sort of spoiling – it formed their daughters' characters, which were strong and unapologetic.

Margaret, at nine, was as long-limbed as her mother and imitated Lizzy's drawn shoulders when she begged for tea at the breakfast table. She wished to be as beautiful, and as wise, as her mother – she certainly possessed her mother's high cheekbones, freckles and auburn curls – and helped to care for her younger siblings. Margaret was vain, to be sure, but it was in worship of her mother, which was probably why Lizzy forgave it. Margaret prided herself on her maturity. She raced through *Pride and Prejudice* and carried the book with her for many weeks afterwards as a badge of her achievement.

Iris, by then seven, had limp blond hair and a small frame. Envious of Margaret's role as caretaker, Iris often challenged her sister with fast wit and mockery. She loved a rhyme and a grand show. When a production of *The Mikado* came to Port Elizabeth, she rocked in her seat, mouth agape at the glorious pageantry of the costumes.

In 1899, when the Anglo-Boer War broke out, Tom could not ignore the headlines; the British expatriates in the south were building forces to take on the two Boer provinces. All of Tom's professional acquaintances joined the British Army – it was the required thing to do – and when he was invited to serve as a surgeon lieutenant, he was assured that he would never be called to duty. His weekends, however, were dominated by drilling and tactical training. Lizzy tried to compensate for this break in the family routine by taking the children to see their father marching in his uniform.

Iris loved to watch the soldiers on parade, adored the khaki uniforms, their accoutrements, the glittering grandeur of the commanding officer's polished brass medals, and the unintelligible cries of the sergeant. To her it was theatre.

'What's happening, Mama?' she asked.

'The privates are being inspected, darling.'

Shortly afterwards, Tom saw his daughter march naked through the house with two of his belts strung bandolier-style across her chest. She came to a halt and dropped a hand mirror upon the floor.

'Good heavens, Iris, what are you doing!' cried her father.

Iris squatted over the mirror and announced in a gravelly voice, 'Just inspecting my privates, Papa!'

WHEN TOM WAS PROMOTED to surgeon captain in the Prince Alfred's Guard regiment, he was ordered to the northern Cape to serve under General Roberts.

Little Charity peppered her father with increasingly anxious questions. 'Will you fight? Will you be shot? Will you die?'

'I shall be quite safe,' Tom assured her. 'Doctors don't die in wars, my sweet. Their job is to tend the wounded soldiers.'

'But what if a *doctor* is sick? Who heals *him*?' Charity asked with an intense stare.

At a loss for an explanation, Tom replied, 'The doctors take care of the soldiers, and *God* takes care of the doctors!'

Lizzy urged Tom to send notes with little pictures home to Charity, assuring her of his safety. The little girl adored them and counted the days to the arrival of each one. She was the only one who took to saying prayers at bedtime.

AT ABOUT THIS TIME Tom lost his faith in God. It happened in Koepsburg, shortly after he joined the staff of the army hospital.

For a brief period, the war had made everything simple. The British fought like gentlemen, costumed in orderly rows upon the battlefield, while the Boers wore civilian clothes and conducted midnight raids and ambushes in small parties without a front line. Generals Kitchener and Roberts adapted to this brand of warfare by ordering a scorch-and-burn policy, destroying Boer homesteads with their crops and livestock to prevent them supplying aid and support to their fighters. The families of the Boer soldiers were then interned, having lost their farms and livelihood.

When Tom's duties were expanded to care of the sick women and children at the Koepsburg internment camp, he was glad that his family remained in Port Elizabeth. His first sight of the place was a grid of dusty tents in a green valley, like a grand picnic, but as he drew nearer he saw the harshly weathered faces of children and women, old and young, eight to ten in each tent. The stink of overflowing sewage invited vast columns of flies and mosquitoes to hover, bearing disease in clouds more toxic than Todderman's smokestacks. In the frigid evenings when frost graced the canvas tents like icing sugar, there was the stench from the refugees' fires, which they fed with spare clothing, shoes and excrement. Tom found himself caring for five hundred women and children, all undernourished and ill. What God could permit such misery? he wondered. Certainly not a God he could believe in.

Tom learned his most bitter lesson from a twelve-year-old Boer boy with open sores across his face. 'Have you a pet?' he inquired, trying to distract the child while he dressed his inflamed cheek.

'General Kitchener killed my dog,' replied the boy. Then, without condemnation or irony, he added, 'General Kitchener burned my father's farm, took our sheep and pigs, and sent me and my sisters here to rot in shit.'

'Where's your mother?'

The boy indicated a figure wrapped in a blanket on a wagon; flies spun in a column over the body.

The boy lasted two months before he came down with tuberculosis. Tom spoke at his funeral. Only one sister was well enough to attend, a girl of eighteen: her body had the emaciated proportions of a starving eleven-year-old.

Tom lost 10 per cent of his patients to disease in the first year. By the time his son was born, his moral outrage had overwhelmed his sense of allegiance.

A fellow doctor argued the case for Kitchener. 'These men don't fight by the rules. They hide, raid the innocent! They don't behave like *proper soldiers*!'

'If this was your land, how would *you* defend it?' argued another. 'They're killing thousands of our soldiers by fighting this way. War is war. The entire notion of morality in warfare is absurd!'

When his requests for more doctors, nurses, supplies and improved conditions were ignored, Tom fell sick of a disease common to those with a thankless task – despair.

To heal the doctor, his commanding officer agreed to bring Tom's family to Koepsburg to be near him. The Chapels were given a house in the centre of town on a green where a military brass band gave concerts under a pretty white pavilion. This merely enhanced Tom's doubts about the war's legitimacy. He would sway with his fretful newborn son on the veranda as the band played 'The British Grenadiers'. The local residents resented the British occupation, and there was constant tension between the townspeople and the army personnel. Tom's daughters were taunted by the children of one Boer family.

'You should speak to their mother,' Lizzy demanded.

'And say what?' said Tom. ' "Be polite to us, even though our soldiers have slaughtered your relatives"?'

One evening during dinner, the Chapels' front window was broken. A cobblestone had been tossed through the glass. A delicate cabinet that had been sent by Lizzy's aunts from Edinburgh as a wedding present was ruined.

Tom's neighbour, Captain Shaunnessy, offered to 'grab a few soldiers and hunt down the hooligans'.

Tom declined the offer with a weak smile.

'What can be so damned funny, Chapel?'

'Just that word, *hooligans*.'

He imagined Mr Phibbs, pounding his stick upon the rafters and addressing a contingent of British and Boer soldiers as he had the boys of Hammer Hall.

IT TOOK THE CHAPELS months to choose a name for their fourth child.

'Why not Tom?' said Lizzy.

'No, Lizzy, I'm not proud enough of my accomplishments to let my child bear that name.'

'Well, I named Margaret, Iris and Charity, so this one shall be your choice, darling.'

That evening Tom paced the veranda with his sleeping son in his arms. He asked himself what he expected of fatherhood and immediately thought of William Bedlam.

'Very well,' he said to the infant. 'Let us be clear on this. I don't expect your *gratitude.* It is a dubious privilege to be brought into a world like this one.'

He remembered Mr Limpkin and Audrey's efforts to take his place. 'Be loyal to your family,' he added, 'but allow yourself the right to live your own life.'

Then the spectre of Bronson Mansworth and his son, Geoffrey, came to mind, and Tom made one final request of his son. 'Be a decent fellow,' he said, then corrected himself: 'At least *try* to be a decent fellow.'

It was dark now, and the houses flickered with the orange light of their paraffin lamps. The distant skirl of bagpipes sounded from the barracks across the green.

The baby woke and stared up at his father. It was an expression of astonishing clarity – neither judgmental nor demanding. *Here,* he seemed to say to Tom, *we begin with a clean slate, as equals.* Suddenly Tom realized there was only one possible choice for a name. Rather than setting the boy a challenge, he decided to set himself a mission as his father. The name would acknowledge the brother Tom had lost and serve as a vow to raise his son with all the love, generosity and selflessness denied him by William Bedlam.

'All right, then,' he said. 'You'll be Arthur,' he whispered. 'Arthur Chapel.'

This said, the baby closed his eyes, satisfied for now with the terms of this covenant. Across the green, the bagpipes were playing 'Mist Covered Mountains', and the crickets' chatter seemed to swell with applause.

DR AND MADAME WARDOUR

BY THE BRITISH VICTORY IN 1902, TOM WAS HAPPY TO PUT HIS uniform in mothballs. War had changed everything, however. When he inquired about his old position, Tom was gently advised by his former colleagues not to return. It appeared that his post had been filled by a doctor who not only had secure allies at the hospital but gladly attended evening meetings. So Tom chose to move to the Johannesburg suburbs and establish a practice of his own.

In Gantrytown, he found a house for his family on an acre of land. There was a stable, a coach house, and a shack suitable for a consulting room. Now he faced the delicate ritual of introducing himself to the community. A doctor had to be accessible, generous, but not desperate. Through acquaintances in the army and colleagues in Port Elizabeth, he gained introductions to a few prominent folk in Gantrytown who promised to pass his name along.

Dr Chapel made house calls in a dogcart – a small lacquered carriage that had room for two seats in the front and two in the back. He wore a bowler hat, a black jacket and grey striped trousers. A beautiful black gelding drew him past the rows of imported weeping willows that graced Gantrytown's suburban streets.

The property magnate Harris Gantry had founded the suburb in 1880 and built his own mansion in the more affluent neighbourhood of

Belgravia. It was in the Victorian style, with magnificent floors of broad-planked Oregon pine and verandas edged in cast-iron shipped from a Glasgow foundry. He donated a park to Gantrytown and commissioned a statue of himself to stand at its entrance; displeased by the likeness (he declared it 'diminutive, fat and uncharismatic'), Gantry dismissed the artist and commissioned a new statue of a tall, slim, commanding figure that bore little resemblance to him but satisfied his opinion of himself.

In the shade of the statue, Tom would examine the lunch Lizzy had prepared for him – usually an odd mix of items: dried and salted meat, or biltong; an avocado pear; and some pancakes from breakfast, which quickly congealed into a doughy wad. He would cast the pancakes into a rhododendron and watch a bird dive in the greenery to retrieve them. Nothing was wasted: ants scuttled away with the scraps of biltong that landed between his shoes, and a lizard lapped at the avocado pear, which had been softened into a pulp by the fierce heat.

In the park, Tom saw the black women in their white head scarves who tended his neighbours' children. And with too much time on his hands, he lamented his small practice and the expenses incurred by a family of six.

By 1903 Gantrytown was a thriving suburb of middle- and working-class families. Horses pulled the trams, and paraffin lamps were the lighting of choice – though there was much envious talk of the electric lighting in Harris Gantry's mansion. Every backyard had an outdoor water closet; under the seat a pail with a trapdoor opened into the sanitary lane. At night, Africans manning carts replaced the full pails with empty ones. Tom often passed these foul-smelling carts when he attended a late-night birth. Coal fired the stoves on frosty mornings. Ice was delivered to those who could afford it, and laundry was collected by muscular 'washboys', as the Zulu men were known: each balanced his burden upon a white-turbaned head, steadying it with a stick in one hand.

Did the European families consider the vast disparity between their means and those of the washboys? Rarely. The class divisions of England were replicated by race in Gantrytown. Harris Gantry thought no more about the emancipation of his black butler or cook than a rich Londoner did about his white one. Tom, however, could afford neither a cook nor a butler.

Two fine educational institutions served the community: St Peter's School for Boys and St Ruth's Collegiate School for Girls. When Margaret started attending St Ruth's, the cost was twelve shillings and sixpence a month. Tom insisted that his children receive the best schooling he could afford – an echo of Emily Bedlam's constant refrain.

Friends had assured Tom and Lizzy that Gantrytown needed another doctor and a piano teacher, but the suburb already had one of each. Dr and Madame Wardour were an elderly couple who resided in another stately Victorian house perched on a raised spit of land overlooking the town; they served the community's needs with a brand of old-fashioned severity.

Old Dr Wardour spoke from the corner of his mouth – the result of a stroke suffered a few years before. The curl of his lips gave him a curmudgeonly snarl. His French wife was strict. Although Madame Wardour frequently dismissed her students, nobody *ever* dismissed Madame Wardour. Everyone was terrified of the woman. She wore black exclusively and anchored her hair with a multitude of hairpins to show off her long neck, narrow face and bayonet-like blue eyes. Lizzy pointed out her beauty to Margaret when they saw her at a fête. 'Beauty, Margaret, is a matter of having a good opinion of oneself,' she said. She pointed out that Madame Wardour behaved like a beautiful woman and, thus, *was.*

A Masonic temple and three churches – Catholic, Presbyterian and Dutch Reformed – catered to the community's spiritual and communal needs. When actors or noted musicians performed in town, the Masons lent their temple.

Tom attempted to make friends with the old doctor at the annual Gantrytown Freemasons' Ball. 'My name's Chapel, Dr Wardour,' he began, 'and I believe I have the honour of serving with you in the community.'

Wardour reacted to this greeting as if he'd been goosed with a pike. 'Sharing what? Who the devil are you?' The old man brandished his trowel and, with his shock of white hair and distorted squint, resembled nothing if not Blackbeard's onboard surgeon.

'Chapel. Dr Tom Chapel.'

'Oh, *Dr* Chapel, is it?' murmured the doctor. 'What kind of a practice have you?'

'A general practice, sir,' said Tom.

'Well, good luck to you, Chapel!' said Wardour scornfully. 'We must all begin somewhere, eh?'

Tom's smile faded. 'I'm hardly a beginner, sir. I was a surgeon for nine years in Port Elizabeth Hospital, three in the war.'

'Indeed? If any of my patients care to risk their lives with a *youngster*, I'll send them along!'

The pitch and tone of the man's voice marked the Chapels as pariahs in front of their neighbours. Having drawn first blood, Dr Wardour tucked his trowel into his apron and stalked away.

Although the residents of Gantrytown were loyal to the cantankerous doctor, they preferred their children to be taught music with sweetness and kind words. Lizzy gathered two students in the first week and three more in the next.

'You're *much* nicer than Madame Wardour,' confessed one child to Lizzy, but it was a small consolation to Tom that his wife robbed the Frenchwoman of a few pupils.

THE BUTCHER-BIRD

THERE WERE DAYS WHEN TOM SAW NO PATIENTS AND WOULD SIT IN his consulting room, pondering his shortcomings, afraid to show his family that he had nothing to do. Sometimes he would pull a chair to the window and listen to the children as they played on the lawn while Lizzy was with a pupil.

A stiflingly hot breeze caused an eruption of jacaranda blossoms as Arthur circled his sisters on one such afternoon. It required the efforts of all of them to amuse the three-year-old; when they grew tired and collapsed on the grass with flushed cheeks, they fanned themselves with the hems of their dresses.

A clumsy, halting melody floated from the parlour window – 'The British Grenadiers', played on the piano, accompanied by Lizzy's claps. The musician picked up speed until it had become a robust marching song.

The children listened to their mother's cheers with silent envy. Bored, Arthur begged his sisters to chase him around the garden. '*Pleathe* chathe me. *Pleathe!*' he cried.

'I'm too tired, Arthur,' Margaret replied, her small nose and freckled chin flushed red. 'But if you sit down, I'll tell you a story!'

The boy turned to Iris. 'Will *you* chathe me, Irith?' he squeaked.

'Only if you say my name properly,' Iris warned him.

'Irith.'

'No, Arthur. Repeat: Iris. Iris. Iris.'

'Irith, Irith, Irith.'

She shook her head. 'That simply won't *do*, Arthur.' He began to cry.

'Iris, you *know* he can't say your name,' Margaret scolded. 'It's hardly fair!'

'If he can say Margaret,' Iris replied, 'he can say *Iris*.'

'You're being very unkind, Iris.'

'I prefer my name spoken correctly,' Iris haughtily replied.

Desperate, the little boy pressed wet lips to her ear: *'Irith, Irith, Irith . . .'*

'Arthur, that's disgusting!' Iris cried, shaking her golden hair free from him to reveal a high forehead and cheekbones, and her aunt Eve's perfect little mouth. People often remarked that Iris was the prettiest of the Chapel girls. Such a pity, they agreed, that her tongue had the sting of a wasp.

Now, Arthur cautiously approached his third sister, who lay with her eyes closed, clutching a family of clothes-peg dolls. Charity had never recovered from Arthur's arrival. He'd claimed her crib, inherited her toys, and worst of all, stolen that which was most dear to her – the glorious doting expression on her mother's face and the welcoming lap of her father, both of which had once assured her that she was worth more than the earth, the moon and the stars combined.

When Arthur usurped her position, Charity vowed never to forgive him. Perhaps that was why she clutched her own little 'family' so tightly: two parental figures with knobbed wooden heads, and three children – girls, of course – each with a small enamelled smile and dotted eyes, drawn by Margaret, and a dress of silk and linen scraps, stitched by Iris. Their faces were worn and brown from years of affection.

Suddenly little Arthur noticed something about the family. 'Mama, Papa, Margaret, Irith, Charity . . . Whereth *Arthur*?' he inquired.

'*My* family doesn't *have* an Arthur.' Charity glared. 'My Arthur *died*.'

As the full import of his sister's remark struck, the boy's eyes brimmed with tears. With his pink belly heaving with emotion, he blurted, 'Arthur died? *Arthur died!*'

Their baby brother's weeping became more than the elder girls could bear.

'There, there! I'll make you an Arthur doll!' Margaret sprang up from her place on the grass.

Margaret looked for a clothes peg beneath the washing line. Iris clad it with a piece of cotton and drew two pencil-point eyes on its little round head with the knob of pencil she kept behind her ear – she was always scribbling verses on scraps of paper. She had read one to Tom that morning at the breakfast table:

Young Miss Finger liked to linger
By the shoulder of a soldier,
Sang a tune, began to swoon,
Fell in his lap!
Lucky chap!
No longer single,
She's Mrs Dingle.

Charity wandered towards the house, clutching her ideal family to her breast. At the veranda she stopped. A canary cage hung from the eaves, its wire door swinging open in the breeze.

'There we are, Arthur!' cried Margaret. 'He's *just* like you!'

Iris finished by drawing a smile on the clothes peg. A flash of delight crossed Arthur's face, but then he wept with more calculated purpose. 'But,' he sobbed, 'I want a *whole* family – like Charity's!'

'Of course you do,' gushed Margaret. 'We'll find more pegs.' Like starlings after a shower, the two sisters darted and pecked in the long grass. All the while, Charity watched them. She would have loved to join in, but she was cast as Arthur's tormentor. She turned her back on them, fixing her eyes on the canary cage, where clues to an unspeakable atrocity now caught her attention.

'That makes six pegs, Arthur. We've a whole family now!' cried Margaret.

Charity let out a shriek, her finger pointing to where a butcher-bird stood with its long beak clamped around the fluffy yellow head of the family canary. The decapitated remainder of the bird lay on the floor of the cage. 'The canary's dead!'

Margaret groaned. 'Again?'

'How could it be dead *again*?' remarked Iris, emerging from the house with her mother's sewing box.

'Another bird bit his head off!' sobbed Charity, tottering from one foot to the other in a motion similar to that of the winged assassin on the roof.

Margaret had Arthur in her lap as she held up the pegs. 'Iris, would you *please* go to her?'

'I'm busy,' replied Iris. 'Besides, that canary never sang *or* talked,' she added, as if this was clear justification for murder. But Charity kept wailing, and after a second glance from Margaret, Iris stamped over to Charity and embraced her. 'Really, Charity, it's only a butcher-bird. You *know* what they do!'

TOM ROSE FROM HIS chair, preparing to attend to the matter, when he heard Lizzy call from the veranda. She had finished the lesson and was summoning the children inside. In a moment, she had assessed the crisis, caught Charity in her arms, and sat down with the other children gathered around.

By the time Tom emerged from his consulting room, Charity's tears had dried, and Lizzy was singing to her in a sweet soprano, her white linen dress spread across the grass. Arthur was in Margaret's lap, clutching his newly fashioned family. The domestic scene was so inviting, so idyllic, and Lizzy so pretty that Tom became inspired with a solution to his problems.

'You'd make a fine nurse, Lizzy,' he said. 'Sometimes I think that's what people really want to see when I pass by. They look at me as if I were an undertaker rather than a doctor.'

'I could certainly help you on your rounds,' suggested Lizzy, 'though I shall have to be at home for my pupils.'

'Oh, Mama, you'd make *such* a pretty nurse!' cried Margaret.

'Oh, Mama, you'd make *such* a pretty nurse!' mimicked Iris.

'Silence, Iris!' replied Margaret in her most mature voice.

AT THE DINNER TABLE, the strong character of the Chapel children was on full display as a fresh struggle began for Tom's attention.

'Papa, the canary's head was chopped off by a butcher-bird!' wailed Charity.

'Quiet, Charity!' cried Margaret.

'*Quiet, Charity!*' echoed Iris, mocking her sister.

Tom struck the table with his hand. There was silence, until Charity burst into tears.

'Oh, Charity,' cried Lizzy, hoisting her onto her lap again. Tom picked up Arthur, while Iris and Margaret glared at each other.

'Don't you think Mama would make a very pretty nurse?' asked Tom.

'Oh, *yeth*!' cried Arthur.

'So do I!' said Margaret, for she knew she resembled her mother and wished to be just like her.

'It's a wonderful idea, Papa!' Iris said, not to be outdone. 'Mama, you should sing when you ride with him. You have such a beautiful voice, and I'm sure people will *flock* to be cured.'

Now Arthur waved his clothes-peg family in his father's face urgently.

'Good heavens.' Tom smiled. 'What's *this*, Arthur?'

'My fambly,' said Arthur. 'Mama, Papa, Margaret, Irith, Charity, and Arthur.'

Tom looked at the clothes pegs: one was draped like a bride in yellowed lace and reminded him of his father's tightrope act.

'Boys don't play with dolls, do they, Arthur?' he said.

Arthur clasped the clothes-peg family tightly to his chest. 'I love my fambly,' he insisted.

The children were dispatched to bed with breathless efficiency. Margaret read *Through the Looking-Glass* to Iris and Charity: the Tweedledum and Tweedledee chapter, which Iris knew by heart and insisted on reciting as her sister read it out loud. Papa told nursery rhymes to Arthur. Mama played a lullaby on the piano, and the lamps were turned down.

Margaret was permitted to stay up a little later; in gratitude she made cups of tea for her parents as they sat on the veranda. She tiptoed between the bougainvilleas, then sank to the ground, folding her legs under her. 'I'm so happy tonight, I don't know why,' she said. 'Might I be in love?'

'*Is* there someone you love?' Tom replied cautiously, for Margaret was about the same age as Audrey had been when she had exchanged lemon tarts for his kisses.

Margaret took a deep breath, as if to inhale the joy about her, then stood up and pirouetted to the door. 'No,' she answered, 'but I feel as though I'm going to meet him very soon!'

'A lucky boy, I'm sure,' said Tom.

'But what will I *do* when it happens?' said Margaret, her eyes dancing with anticipation.

Here, Tom glanced nervously at his wife.

'When the time comes, I'll tell you *exactly* what to do,' Lizzy promised.

Margaret smiled, retreated inside, then darted out to kiss her father's temple, her mother's cheek, and disappeared.

'Poor Margaret,' Tom remarked.

'Why?'

'Suppose she pins her hopes on someone who cannot return her love?'

'I shall be her guide,' Lizzy assured him.

Tom looked at his wife with relief. 'I will rely on you.'

Lizzy took this remark as licence to offer advice. 'Tom,' she began, 'Charity needs to be reminded that you love her. She's jealous of Arthur. She counts *every* glance you spare him and tallies it against her own score.'

'She *baffles* me,' Tom admitted. 'Whenever I'm near her, she seems to be either crying or furiously angry.'

'You always greet Arthur first when you come home, my darling. It's rather hard on her. She'd cry less if *you* held her once in a while.'

Tom acknowledged this, and agreed to make more of an effort. As the evening breeze subsided, the night jasmine became especially pungent.

Lizzy added up the week's receipts in a little accounts book; it was she who had the clearest idea of their finances. She was not the insecure and fretful young woman Tom had taken from Edinburgh; he could never have predicted her hardiness, her flexibility or her willingness to do anything to ensure their survival.

'Well,' she concluded, 'we can pay for school this month, with a little to spare. But I'm worried about next month.'

Tom had been watching her. 'Lizzy, do you ever imagine being a rich doctor's wife in London?'

She closed her accounts book. 'Married to Dodo?' She looked amused. 'I haven't thought about him in years. And what about you? Eve would have made you a wonderfully successful doctor.'

Tom shook his head.

Her forehead creased. 'Not a satisfactory answer, darling. Either you have regrets about Eve or you do not.'

'I have none whatsoever,' he declared.

She leaned forward and looked into his eyes. 'Tell me why it was destined for us to run away together.'

He frowned. 'Well, for one thing, Eve couldn't play the piano.'

'Neither can I any longer. I'm so out of practice.'

'But you are a fine teacher,' murmured Tom, 'an exceptional mother, an excellent nurse, a best companion, a brilliant and superlative wife, not to mention my harshest critic and least cooperative patient.'

Lizzy's eyebrows rose with amusement. 'Because I ask questions? Because I question your judgment?'

'I *am* a doctor.'

'Well, *I* am a doctor's daughter,' she sniffed. 'I probably know my anatomy better than you do.'

Tom frowned again. This, he knew, was probably true. 'I thought I was supposed to pay *you* compliments,' he said. 'You seem to have taken it upon yourself to do so.'

Lizzy sighed. 'I wonder whether Eve would have been a better wife for you. She was ambitious. You would have been highly placed by now. She would have moulded you into a pillar of society.'

'I didn't want to be moulded.'

'We are *all* moulded, darling, whether we like it or not.'

'My father never moulded me.'

'He certainly did. The minute you were born he set you on a course by giving you a name and walking out of the door.'

A dog began to bark in the distance; this caused the parrot next door to echo it. It was an irksome bird; when Indian street vendors walked from house to house offering potatoes, cabbages, lettuce or bananas, it would take up their cries and repeat them for hours, infuriating the women who would emerge from their houses expecting to buy vegetables or fruit.

Lizzy's expression became melancholy. 'Are we happy, Tom?'

'With children, there isn't time to think about it,' he admitted. 'I suppose that means we *must* be.'

'I'd hate you to feel you had taken a wrong turn. Eve will certainly have made a success of her husband by now.'

Tom took his wife's hand. 'Lizzy, my life might seem a failure by Eve's standards, but I declare myself a happy man.'

He cast his eyes to the shrinking red sunset. 'There's always more work for me when it rains. I shouldn't wish for accidents, but . . .'

'Farmers pray for rain, so why shouldn't we?' said Lizzy.

The couple looked at the horizon but kept their wishes silent.

THE NEXT TWO WEEKS brought no rain to Gantrytown. But the nurse who appeared on Dr Chapel's dogcart in white linens created a storm of her own. Perhaps people *did* like to see a nurse beside a doctor, or perhaps it was the songs she sang. Lizzy passed the time singing everything from Gilbert and Sullivan to psalms and nursery rhymes. It had never occurred to Tom that people listened to passing traffic, but Lizzy's singing drew everybody – children, the elderly folk, nursemaids and gardeners – from their houses without hesitation. Tom became busier than he had ever been. With Lizzy in attendance, tea was always offered, questions were frequent, and new patients appeared every day. Soon the doctor found himself with a healthy practice while his wife had to turn away prospective pupils.

Dr Chapel, now known as the Doctor with the Singing Wife, found that his fame had spread as far as the neighbourhood of Belgravia. Harris Gantry's wife drove up one morning in her grey Berliet limousine. The Chapel children climbed about the wondrous machine, Margaret admiring her reflection in the car's shiny brass fittings while Arthur bounced on the red leather upholstery.

One man from Doorfontein who arrived with an ear infection was quite upset when he heard that Lizzy was too busy teaching to attend his treatment by the doctor. 'I *must* insist on meeting the singing nurse!' he cried and refused to leave until Dr Chapel took him into the house to hear his wife coaching one of her young pianists. The man was sated only when Lizzy sang 'Twinkle, Twinkle' with the two-fingered accompaniment of her pupil.

AUDREY'S SON

HER LETTERS ARRIVED MONTHS, SOMETIMES YEARS AFTER THEY were sent, as if the winds mixed them up, sending some round Cape Horn while others came direct. A few were lost. Tom wrote back to Audrey but suspected that his replies followed a similarly confused route. It took years to establish the events of her internment.

Lizzy was curious about Audrey's effect on her husband; Tom always read her letters aloud, as if to show that he had nothing to hide. This assured Lizzy that Audrey was not a rival, but she observed Tom's bitterness, or perhaps it was disappointment, whenever they discussed Audrey and sensed that he was still at the mercy of his feelings.

Dear Tom and Lizzy,

I hope I may include Lizzy in this letter; I am sure it was she who sent me the charming picture of your children. A photograph permits one such a blessed illusion of intimacy. I regret I shall never know them as children, so please forgive the following interpretations: Margaret strikes me as responsible and eager to grow up. Iris, standing beside M. with her heels raised, appears to be trying to eclipse her sister, while Charity seems more concerned with the position of her brother in her father's lap. Lizzy, you are quite beautiful, and I imagine that Tom never says so, though he believes it in his heart. It always takes Tom an eternity to express in words what is very obvious on his face.

I have no pictures of my son, Jonah. He remains the blessing left to me after my attack. His birth, here in Newgate, was quick and sweet and came shortly after my trial. I might have lost my mind without my dear little boy. He marked time for me, learning to walk, to speak and to comfort me. He broke the tedium of these walls, the minutes, hours, days and months.

Several women in Newgate have children that they raised in their cells. It is not as bad as it seems – they would be in orphanages if they were not with their mothers. The problem comes when they reach the age of eight, for then they must leave the prison. The authorities don't want them to be influenced beyond that age by the so-called criminals in here.

Jonah left me five years ago. He is now in Elsie's care. She took him to Australia with her husband and children. I try to imagine the sunsets he sees, instead of the dim half-light through my barred cell window.

It is best for him, I remind myself. Yet I hear from Elsie that he is an angry child. He has been arrested for theft. I'm sure he is angry with me. Oh, Tom, do your children as good a turn as you can. Nothing upsets me more than the thought that I've placed such a troubled soul into the world's care.

I am a wardswoman now. Though I am entitled to a bed instead of a rope mat, I can't say that sleeping is any easier. My hip always aches in damp weather, and my walk will always be clumsy. I teach reading to my wards; the Bible is our only text. While I am not very good at explaining the actions of a brutal and vengeful God, I assure them that to read and write will be of great use in the outside world.

My love to you all,
Audrey

'The poor woman!' Lizzy remarked after Tom finished reading.

Tom didn't reply. He sat in his chair with his fingers pressed together, his eyes fixed on the window. The children were leapfrogging across the lawn.

'You must miss her,' Lizzy said provocatively.

'Not really.'

'But what a hard life she leads. You must pity her at least?'

Tom nodded. 'I regret that she suffers.' He paused, then added, 'At least she doesn't suffer from anything I have done.'

As he rose from his seat and stepped to the window to cheer on his children, Lizzy pondered his last words. 'How did she let you down, dearest?'

Tom shrugged. 'I asked her to marry me, and she wisely refused. I was impulsive and unreliable. I was my father.' He turned back to the children so that Lizzy couldn't see his emotion. 'She has an insight into me that makes me ashamed,' he said. 'A man has the right to forget the bad things he has done. He has the right to change.'

Lizzy nodded. 'I'm sure she has forgiven you, darling.' She joined him at the window. 'It would probably do you good to forgive her.'

Tom sighed, keeping his eyes fixed on the children.

ARTHUR

WHEN THE SMALLPOX EPIDEMIC OF 1904 BROKE OUT, TOM WAS commissioned by the Gantrytown Board of Health to administer inoculations. People arrived by the dozens to receive them, and many became regular patients. His practice had never been busier. On the days when Lizzy was with her pupils, Tom enlisted the help of his children. It was an alarming process. The doctor used a sharp trident to perforate the skin in three places on the patient's arm – a triangle of three spots of blood. Through a glass tube he would then blow lymph onto each piercing. The patients would return in a week so that Tom could examine the scars and satisfy himself that the inoculation had 'taken'.

Many patients fainted during the process, so he needed someone to distract the nervous ones. Margaret, however, proved to be rather insensitive. She entertained one woman by telling her the story of a little boy who had blown off his hand while playing with a detonator he'd found hidden in a weapons cache left over from the war. At mention of the amputation, the woman's eyes rolled up and Tom banished his oldest daughter from the surgery.

Iris was next. She told limericks to the patients. Her favourite owed a debt to 'You Are Old, Father William':

You are bold, Dame Matilda, the young girl said,
With a body as big as a beadle.
Please hold still and don't scream
While I poke through your spleen,
With the very sharp tip of this needle!

Dismayed that Iris had inherited William Bedlam's penchant for verse, Tom replaced her with Charity, who made a point of telling each patient that the pain he or she was feeling was beneficial.

When she recognized a nun from St Ruth's Collegiate School for Girls, Charity said, 'It's painful, but it's nothing compared with the eternal fires of hell, don't you think, Sister?'

Arthur, however, had a calming effect on the patients. 'I've got three *thithterth*,' he would explain. 'How many *thithterth* have *you* got?' Between his endearing lisp and a genuine need to know something about each person, he became the favourite.

At five, he was less demanding and more eager to please his sisters, obliging them by performing in their games dressed up as a baby, a poodle, Jesus and the Sleeping Beauty. He quickly grew weary of lying in a straw manger so that Charity could be Mary, but Iris could persuade him to do almost anything, so entranced was he by her cleverness and fertile imagination. She would take him for a walk around the garden, pretending to be a duchess to his duke, then abruptly change the game. 'Oh, bother, Baby!' she would exclaim. 'I've got a smudge on my knee, and it's all *your* fault!'

Arthur would oblige her with a reply. 'Goo goo!'

'Just for that,' Iris continued, 'I'm going to turn you into a piglet!' She removed his clothes, drew a circle on the ground around him, and muttered an incantation. Then she led him next door to sell him to the neighbours' children as a piglet.

The Horvath boys had no imagination. This was obvious to Iris because they had never given their parrot a name or taught it anything interesting to say. It was no wonder that it imitated the Indian fruit vendors – the bird was utterly neglected. So it required considerable effort to convince them to accept Arthur as a piglet.

'He's a little boy,' they cried, 'not a piglet.'

'Piglets are pink, are they not?' replied Iris.

'Yes, but—'

'They squeal and run on four legs, do they not?'

'Well, yes—'

Iris set Arthur down and cried, 'Run, piglet, run!'

Arthur tore across the lawn on all fours, screaming at the top of his lungs until his entire body was a brilliant pink. The Horvath children conceded that he *was* a very convincing pig and rewarded Iris with one of their mother's toffee apples in exchange for Arthur.

Lizzy had to fetch him at dinnertime. 'Honestly, Arthur,' she said after finding her son in the Horvaths' washtub, where he had been nestled in a bed of hay, 'you shouldn't let Iris sell you to the neighbours.'

'But I was a piglet. I couldn't talk.'

'Nonsense! You have a voice, you have words.'

But Arthur liked the idea of slipping into a different skin. He enjoyed the drama, the surprise at the end when he became himself again, and especially, the fuss made by his mother.

Tom recognized his son's gentle spirit and even thought he had the makings of a doctor. He gave the boy an old stethoscope, complaining to Lizzy that Arthur should look more like a boy. His hair, a pale, lustrous ginger, fell to his shoulders. Lizzy couldn't bear to cut it. Also, he still carried around his clothes-peg family.

Lizzy advised her husband not to be too strict with his son, but Tom couldn't help it. He was casting Arthur in his own image with a wary eye to the alternatives – Audrey's wayward son and, of course, the Mansworths and Privots of the world. The mere utterance of his son's name was a constant reminder of his responsibility to the boy and his inability to reconcile Arthur Pigeon's death and Mansworth's acquittal with the relatively placid and happy life he now enjoyed.

FALLING IN LINE

TOM GAVE ARTHUR A SET OF LEADEN SOLDIERS FOR HIS SIXTH birthday. Smartly dressed in red tunics, and carrying muskets and satchels, they lay side by side in a box, preserved like sardines or cigars. Arthur stood them on the shelf by his bed, their dark metallic faces fixed at attention. But he continued to play with the clothes-peg family, whose cheery, warm features (painted and repainted with fresh smiles) remained his constant companions. He slept with them tucked under the covers. During Iris and Margaret's frequent arguments, Arthur preached conciliation to their wooden counterparts.

Margaret had taken a new interest in the boys at St Peter's. On the way home from school, she would stop at the playing fields to watch the older boys at cricket. One player, Peter Carnahan, would leave the game to flirt with her for a few minutes. Iris was still young enough to consider boys an alien breed, and she took to spying on Margaret and Peter, fascinated by the preening glances and joking that served their courtship.

Each rendezvous lured Iris closer, until she believed that she understood the terms of the ritual. Then, one afternoon, she boldly sauntered across the field towards Peter, and curling a blond pigtail around her grubby finger, fixed the boy with a sultry glance. 'Peter? I've made up a limerick, would you like to hear it?'

Margaret arrived in time to exclaim, 'Iris! What are you doing? *Go away!*'

'There once was a boy named Dick, who was known for the size of his—'

'Oh, pay no attention to her, she's only thirteen,' Margaret interrupted quickly. 'Iris, go *home*!'

This dismissal pierced Iris's pride; she stalked home in a fury, preparing her retribution for the dinner table.

'I'VE COMPOSED A NEW limerick,' Iris announced. 'Would you like to hear it, Papa?'

Tom regarded the spark in his daughter's eye. Those infernal limericks, he thought, recalling his father's rhymes again. 'Not now, Iris,' he replied.

'I can play "The British Grenadiers" far better than fat Julian,' interrupted Charity.

'Charity, you are not to speak of my pupils in such a disparaging way,' replied Lizzy.

'You're both interrupting,' said Iris. 'Would *you* like to hear my limerick, Mama? It's about Margaret.'

'Of course, Iris,' replied Lizzy, before Tom could protest.

'But I don't want to hear it,' said Margaret.

'Why can't *I* have piano lessons?' Charity asked.

'*I'd like piano lethonth too*,' murmured Arthur.

'Of course!' Charity sneered at her brother. 'You *always* want what I have!'

'It's a wonderful idea, Charity,' said Lizzy. 'Arthur, perhaps you could learn to play the violin instead of the piano.'

'It goes like this,' continued Iris:

There once was a girl who would greet,
Every boy that she passed on the street,
When they said to her, 'Miss,
Would you give us a kiss,'
She'd say—

'That's *enough*!' cried Margaret.

'But I'm not finished,' said Iris. 'She'd say thanks, but I've already—'

'It's nasty and rude, and absolutely *false*!' cried Margaret, tears bursting from her eyes. 'Mama, Papa, how *can* you let her say such terrible things about me!'

Serenely, Iris replied, 'But you don't know what I'm going to say.'

'I don't *need* to,' wept Margaret.

'I want to hear the end,' cried Charity, pounding the table.

'Stop it!' cried Margaret.

'She'd say thanks, but I've already kissed – Ow!'

Margaret had seized Iris's hair, and her sister fell backwards onto the floor.

'Margaret, that's enough!' shouted Tom.

Iris knew the advantage of a rapt audience; even as Margaret was dragging her across the dining-room floor, she repeated the limerick, ending it with 'She'd say thanks, but I've already kissed Pete!'

At this, Margaret slapped Iris across the face, which stunned her sister into silence. Margaret, now trembling with shame, slowly knelt before her mother, head bent in an attempt at contrition. 'Oh, Mama, I'm so, *so* sorry!'

In the silence, Iris seized the opportunity to sweeten her vengeance. 'I've another limerick about Margaret that's even better: There once was a tart named Meg—'

Before she could continue, Tom took his second daughter to the consulting room, where her mouth was filled with water and surgical soap, a smell Iris would associate with punishment long into her adult life. It did nothing for the sharpness of her tongue, but it did cement the antipathy she felt for Margaret.

After the children were put to bed that evening, there lingered a fog of bitterness in the Chapel house. The strong characters of the children, fostered and encouraged, were getting out of hand.

'Have we failed them?' Lizzy whispered in bed.

Tom sighed. 'Margaret should be encouraged to enjoy her youth,' he said. 'She's in too much of a hurry to become a woman.'

'I was as bad as she was at this age – vain, selfish, hated my father.'

Lizzy glanced at Tom. 'Boys are, at least, a distraction from such feelings.'

'But it's our duty to protect her from the things she doesn't understand. She's not *ready* for them,' Tom declared, meaning that *he* wasn't ready for Margaret to be ready for boys. 'As for Iris, her tongue is guaranteed to make her more enemies than friends. And Charity needs her own pastime.'

Lizzy agreed with him, but she voiced one further concern: 'We must encourage them to respect one another, even when they differ,' she said. 'I fear that when we are gone, they might become estranged.' She paused. 'Nothing would be worse than that.'

THUS MOTIVATED BY a desire to steer their children into happier relations with friends and family, Tom and Lizzy formed a plan. At the breakfast table it was announced that each day Margaret and Iris were to walk home from school together. This would tighten the bond between the girls and repel the advances of Peter Carnahan.

Upon hearing this, Margaret assumed the grief of a martyr. She sat staring at her lap, hands folded. It was a wrenching experience for her parents to see this normally effusive creature so stifled.

Iris was forbidden to mock her sisters at the dinner table, her incendiary limericks were banned, and her access to Lewis Carroll, Hilaire Belloc and Guy Wetmore Carryl was reduced.

'From now on, you will read the Bible only,' said Tom.

'My dear,' warned Lizzy, 'the Old Testament is full of the most wretched behaviour. Couldn't we give her the collected works of Shakespeare?'

'Shakespeare it is,' Tom replied. He was tempted to ban *King Lear* too but decided the likelihood of his second daughter taking to *that* play was quite slim.

Iris punished her parents by vowing to reply to them in the way that Echo had been doomed to repeat the words of her lover, Narcissus.

'You understand why we must do this, my love,' said Lizzy.

'*Love!*' echoed her daughter.

'It's for your own good,' added Tom.

'*Good?*' Iris huffed, burying herself beneath the couch cushions.

As for Charity, she would begin piano lessons with her mother. This granted her the distinction of having a precious hour alone with Lizzy every week.

WHEN LIZZY CHAPEL held the annual Yuletide recital for her pupils, the parents patiently endured even the most ham-fisted performer because they looked forward to the teacher's concluding performance. Lizzy's playing, in spite of her misgivings, was as popular as her singing. This Christmas, however, she chose not to overshadow her daughter, so everyone learned instead how far an acorn might fall from the tree. When Charity struck that keyboard, she proved that a girl with a tin ear could throttle anyone's holiday spirit. Tone-deaf and insensitive to tempo, dynamics and melody, Charity drove away her audience with one consoling notion: if Mrs Chapel could give birth to a musical failure, anybody else was as likely to produce a prodigy.

ONE AFTERNOON, IN his consulting room, Tom heard Charity and Arthur having a bitter argument. Their shrill voices echoed across the garden, distracting him from his notes. He found Arthur playing beneath the dining table while Charity pounded away on the Bechstein, shaking the crockery and glassware. A new yellow canary hopped back and forth across its cage in sonic agitation. When Charity struck a wrong note, Arthur whistled the correct one, provoking a scream of outrage.

'He's *torturing* me!' cried Charity, as she kicked the piano pedals.

'Arthur, I'm trying to work; you must stop whatever you're doing . . . What *are* you doing?' said his father.

'Nothing,' murmured Arthur glumly, his ginger hair fanned upon the floor.

Tom knelt beneath the table. The clothes-peg family was arranged before the boy. The father was wearing a white apron to administer tonic to one of the daughters, while the smallest one was playing a matchbox piano, makeshift keys painted on the rim with chalk and charcoal. A clothes-peg boy lay under a matchbox table, his little wire arms clutching the sides of his head.

'Where are your grenadiers, Arthur?'

'In my room.'

'You'd have a lot more fun with them. Why don't you get them out?'

Arthur did not move – it was the most defiant gesture he could muster. Suddenly the clothes pegs were scooped up. A moment later his father returned with the grenadiers and propped them in a row, their bright red uniforms reflecting on the waxed floor as the Queen's own guards must have appeared on a rainy morning at Buckingham Palace. The doctor's gesture seemed well-intentioned and kindly, but although the boy wanted his family back, he hadn't the will to contradict his father.

Charity resumed her assault on a Bach prelude while Arthur repositioned the grenadiers so that the sergeant major could administer tonic to one of his men, while a private played a minuet on the matchbox piano; six more writhed beneath the table.

Tom watched his son play on the floor. Suddenly, he saw pale Arthur Pigeon kneeling at his bedside at Hammer Hall on the morning that he had promised to meet Tom on the peak – the morning he had disappeared.

Grimacing, Tom took the clothes-peg figures and threw them into the incineration pail that stood by the door of his consulting room. Immediately feeling a pang of shame, he wondered whether to fish them out. Poor Arthur, he was only *playing*. But then Tom recalled Arthur Pigeon, shaved to the scalp, taunted and ridiculed, and couldn't shut out the image of a body ravaged by a violent fall.

Tom's jaw flexed as he wondered about his son's future at school. Arthur *must* fit in – we must all fit in, or we do not survive, Tom reminded himself. To stand out is to be betrayed by friends and enemies alike.

Bitterly, Tom seized the incineration pail and tossed its contents onto the embers of the morning fire.

ABOUT A WEEK LATER, Tom received a visit from his son in the consulting room. The little boy's hands hung by his sides; he bit his lower lip as he fixed his gaze upon his father's polished shoes. 'Papa,' he said, 'I want my old dolls back.'

Tom paused to admire his son's courage, but he was not about to relent. 'You're a big boy, Arthur,' he replied, 'too big for dolls.'

Arthur's mouth went slack. 'Where *are* they?' he gasped.

'Lost,' his father replied, and turned his back to his son, surprised by his own cowardice. He had uttered a lie as wretched as Bedlam's nonsense about lemon tarts.

WHEN THE NEW SCHOOL term began and Arthur's sisters climbed aboard the tram to St Ruth's, excited, talkative, each wearing a new dress to begin the year, he wept. 'I'm all alone,' he told his mother.

Though Lizzy offered to read to him, then proposed games and walks, nothing seemed to break his melancholy. When she brought out the box of soldiers, Arthur took one glance at them and began to weep.

'Oh, Arthur,' Lizzy sighed. Casting a glance at the consulting room, where Tom was busy with a patient, she fetched her sewing box.

Later in the afternoon, Tom saw Arthur playing with the grenadiers. Pleased, he knelt beside him and listened to the murmur of a child immersed in make-believe. But it was not soldier talk he heard: 'There, there, little one, you can have your *own* piano lessons if you want . . . Thank you, Mother . . . Quiet now, it's time to eat your brussels sprouts. There once was a sprout named Jill, who made the entire family ill . . .'

Tom drew nearer and saw that the grenadiers were wearing new uniforms. One had a skirt of yellowed muslin, another a red velvet gown. Two more were draped from collar to boots in flowing garments of cotton gauze.

'Arthur? What's going on?'

'Nothing,' replied the boy. 'That's the mama, and those are the daughters.'

'Arthur, you can't have girl soldiers.'

A voice piped up from the cushions of the sofa. 'Joan of Arc was a soldier.'

Tom addressed the cushions directly. 'Iris, she *always* wore a suit of armour.'

The lump of cushions shifted. 'She must have worn dresses *some*times.'

Tom lowered his voice in an attempt to confine the conversation to the ears of his son. 'Anyway, grenadiers shouldn't wear dresses.'

'Yes, Papa,' came the earnest response.

'What about the Mongol hordes?' said Iris. '*They* wore skirts.'

'The Mongols were not heroes,' snapped her father.

'They were to other Mongols,' Iris replied.

'That's *enough*, Iris!'

In deference to his father's fury, Arthur solemnly removed the soldiers' new clothes. But the difference he observed in his parents' sympathies fuelled his growing conviction that he had no choice but to assume one character in his father's presence and another in his mother's, just as he had once pleased Charity as the baby Jesus and the Horvaths as a piglet.

MARGARET'S EYES

In the African rainy season, when the downpours were swift and violent, the residents of Gantrytown emerged from their houses to find the geography altered. Islands of silt appeared in the middle of a thoroughfare. Streets were jammed by the detritus of a torrential rain – branches, huts, henhouses and heaps of sodden vegetation. Landmark trees were wrenched from the earth, and houses were flattened like cards.

The wetter months also brought malarial fever. The anopheles mosquito had only recently been identified as the carrier, and it flourished in such weather. Children were the most susceptible. The Chapels draped their beds in netting and tried to keep their children inside on those days when the air was still and sunless – the hardest time to keep a child in the stuffy confines of a house. The symptoms were familiar enough: lethargy, headaches and recurring fever. In serious cases, delirium was the last stage before death. There was no effective treatment.

A February rain brought the worst floods in ten years, but the topography of the Chapels' world was changed in an entirely unexpected way. Ever since the limerick incident, Iris had regarded her older sister with equal portions of envy and scorn. She witnessed every glance her sister received from the boys and, as she shared a bedroom with her, gave Margaret's physical development equal scrutiny. Watching Margaret dress one morning, Iris couldn't contain her surprise. 'Gosh, Margaret, your breasts are *huge*!'

'Oh, be quiet,' muttered her sister.

'But, it's true. No wonder the boys stare at you. Do you think I'll get ones like yours?'

Margaret didn't grant Iris the satisfaction of a reply. Now that she was sixteen, her face had her mother's high cheekbones and small mouth. It was reminiscent of one of the saints featured in the chapel at St Ruth's. The nuns even asked her to play Mary in the Christmas Nativity play. Thus blessed with a saintly face and a sinner's body, Margaret presented every boy on St Peter's playing field with something new to dream about.

Her bosom eclipsed her mother's by two sizes in late 1906, and her parents became concerned. They began to discuss their daughter's breasts as though they were a separate entity, with their own history and ambitions.

'I don't understand where they *came* from,' said Lizzy. 'Nobody in my family—'

'Perhaps on my father's side,' Tom suggested.

'You don't think they'll grow any *bigger*, do you?'

'If they do, they'll have to pay rent,' the doctor replied. 'Next they'll be wanting their own education.'

'Shame, Tom,' chided his wife. 'She's so self-conscious about them. I wish you wouldn't stare at them so.'

'I don't!' protested the doctor. '*They* stare at *me*. She should train them to look in different directions.'

His wife frowned.

Tom was hardly laughing. He remembered his fantasies about Sissy; and while he could forgive the boys of St Peter's (after all, they were boys), he spent most of the Christmas play wondering if the staff and half of the audience were wishing they were in the place of the Jesus statuette that Margaret held close to her breast.

It was different for Iris; small and flat-chested at fourteen, she fully hoped to wake up one morning blessed with her sister's proportions. In the meantime, she watched the effect of Margaret's figure on the opposite sex with fascination. Peter Carnahan caught a cricket ball right between the eyes because he had been staring at Margaret's breasts during a game. The lump on his forehead swelled to the size and colour of a plum and remained for a week. This inspired Iris to compose a poem. Since she wasn't allowed to recite it at home, she submitted it to the school periodical, *St Ruth's Weekender:*

Pete Carnahan got struck in the head today,
Serves him right, for the boy was so cocky!
It wasn't the batter that led him astray,
But the sight of my sister at hockey,
Some are as tiny as thimbles,
But my sister's are bigger than cymbals.

Even though Iris had protected herself by titling the poem 'Margaret's Eyes', everybody knew what it was about. The girls recited it at hockey matches. St Ruth's had the lowest place in the league, but when Margaret's breasts became the unofficial school mascot, boys from St Peter's began to turn up at the games. Soon both faculty and parents showed up to see what all the fuss was about.

They were not disappointed. As cheers erupted whenever Margaret bounced up the field, the team began to play more aggressively, and in 1907 they reached the semifinals.

Iris liked to think that her poem was responsible for more than a surge of morale at St Ruth's. The St Peter's boys' choir grew threefold simply for the privilege of being invited to St Ruth's to sing Handel's 'Hallelujah Chorus'. As all male eyes rested on Margaret, Father Johannesson remarked that he'd never seen such sublime exaltation on the faces of those young lads. Then the annual Shakespeare production was announced, and fistfights among prospective Romeos erupted when it was announced that Margaret would play Juliet.

Lizzy wrote of these events to her sister. She hoped they might remind Eve of their own school days in Edinburgh and perhaps affirm their bond. 'I'm not surprised by the boys,' she wrote, 'but the sight of all of these openmouthed fathers with their eyes glued on Margaret is appalling!'

Lizzy took her daughter aside to discuss her 'gift'. 'My sweet, boys and men may be counted on to behave like fools in the presence of a well-endowed woman. Believe little of what they say and none of what they promise.'

If anyone was guilty of overestimating the power of Margaret's breasts, it was probably Margaret herself. She believed they were a barometer of lust, and if a boy's eyes strayed below her collar, she immediately judged him shallow. A more cunning girl might have exacted favours or tortured her admirers, but Margaret was looking for love; unfortunately, her breasts only hindered her capacity to trust any friendly boy.

In time, the boys learned to moderate their stares. Some gathered in a contingent by the lamppost outside the Chapels' house in the evenings. They serenaded Margaret with sweet voices and three-part harmonies.

Tom couldn't stand them. He refused to allow them to cross the no-man's-land between the garden fence and the house. Like Rapunzel, Margaret was compelled to accept tribute from a distance of sixty feet. She looked forward to the serenade, but wouldn't associate with the boys in person.

'What the devil is wrong with them?' said Tom, watching from the curtains. 'Have they nothing else to do?'

'They're only boys,' said Lizzy to her husband.

'*Boys*,' Iris echoed wistfully. She was beginning to feel differently about them now.

A round of applause sounded as Margaret slipped outside to hear a rendition of the St Peter's rugby song.

This drew little Arthur to the window. He watched his sister sigh and shake her hair over her shoulders so that the moonlight could properly outline her figure. Each boy strutted, preened, and pecked at his friends with insults and broad gestures in an attempt to show Margaret that he was the fittest among them.

Although he was only seven, Arthur recognized actors in a pantomime of desire. The last act of this nightly performance always brought Tom to the veranda, whereupon father and daughter argued until Margaret was banished to bed. Tom would remain where he was, hands on his hips, while Margaret's admirers dispersed in languid and unwilling steps.

It was then that the Horvaths' bored parrot chose to repeat for Tom's sole benefit the rhyme it had heard all evening:

Some are as tiny as thimbles,
But my sister's are bigger than cymbals!

LETTER FROM HOLLOWAY

AUDREY'S LETTERS ALWAYS CONTAINED A RAY OF HOPE. TOM ADMIRED her spirit, for she was now in her seventeenth year of incarceration. Newgate had been closed down and razed. Her last five years had been spent in a new prison near London, named Holloway.

Dear Tom,

I have had good news from Elsie; my son, Jonah, has joined the Australian Army. It is my dearest hope that he will find some sense of satisfaction as a soldier, more so, at least, than getting into scrapes for petty crime.

Oscar has published a biography of General Kitchener, which, I understand, is selling well. It has been featured in the Weekly Standard, *in serial form – the first time Oscar has been published in a newspaper in almost ten years. Perhaps you may even find a copy in Gantrytown.*

Poor Oscar! He visited me last week. He walked into the visitors' room, and was as startled by the inmates on either side of us as he was by his fallen sister.

He and his wife make a reasonable living; they have a son now, but it is expensive in London. Most of all, he misses the urgency of writing for a newspaper and confesses that his biographies are sterile portraits of their subjects. His publisher demanded that he remove any mention of Kitchener's scorched-earth policy and all references to the Boer concentration camps, claiming that although people will happily read about scoundrels in the newspapers, they refuse to purchase bound volumes on the same subject.

Bronson Mansworth died last month. His son, Geoffrey, claimed the first four pews at Westminster Abbey for his soldier friends, dignitaries and his father's industrialist peers, while his closest relations, Penelope and Oscar, were placed far back in the cathedral, with the press, ironically.

It seems that your old friend from Hammer Hall has not changed, Tom: Geoffrey is determined to claim his legacy, political and otherwise. He has contested his father's will, putting Penelope's inheritance in jeopardy.

He claims that Oscar and Penelope have violated the terms of Bronson Mansworth's marriage agreement. You may recall that Oscar agreed to refrain from journalism to marry Penelope. Now, ten years after they received their dowry (with which they bought their house in Bloomsbury), Geoffrey claims that because Oscar's book was published in the pages of a newspaper, Penelope's right to a share of her father's fortune is forfeit.

It seems, Tom, that the Limpkin name is a curse to all who bear it.

At times like these, I count myself fortunate to be a ward of the state.

Audrey

ARTHUR'S GIFT

'ARTHUR, IT IS TIME YOUR HAIR WAS CUT SHORT.'

'Why?'

'So you will resemble the other boys.'

'I like my hair.'

'The others will make fun of you,' his father warned.

'I don't care,' the boy declared – a tacit acknowledgment that he had, in fact, been the butt of pranks. 'If you mean the other boys to be more comfortable with *me*, I suppose I should cut my hair, but it won't do *me* any good. I'm different from them,' he said.

'*Of course* you're different,' his father replied. 'We're all different! But don't you wish to be accepted as a friend, at least?'

'Not really.'

Tom threw up his hands and turned to his wife.

'Arthur, there's nothing wrong with being different,' said Lizzy, 'but it's nice to have a friend with whom you can share your thoughts.'

'I have Iris and you, Margaret and Charity,' Arthur replied.

At the dinner table, Arthur passed his time staging romances between his knife and fork or vendettas between the salt and pepper shakers. He sculpted the Alps with his mashed potatoes and the moon's surface on a slice of cheese. He talked to himself as he wrote in class, uttered muffled replies to rhetorical questions at the school's Friday mass, and seemed to cherish his solitude. Tom feared that the boy was becoming as eccentric as his namesake.

ARTHUR'S FIRST REAL BULLY, however, was not a Mansworth or a Privot but a teacher – Mr Willard Bench, the grammar and sports master at St Peter's. Bench believed idleness and contemplation to be the devil's playground – a busy boy was a clean boy. If the pupils weren't running, kicking or exercising, they were probably up to no good.

'Turn around, Chapel,' he shouted one afternoon at cricket. 'You can't hit a ball like that.'

'I'm left-handed,' Arthur replied.

'Nonsense. Only criminals are left-handed. We don't educate criminals here at St Peter's.'

When Bench noticed that the boy wrote with his left hand too, he issued a predictable directive: 'Note Mr Chapel's way of writing, boys,' he said. 'Is this the *correct* way to write?'

As a resounding *no* filled Arthur's ears, Bench patted his shoulder, confident that social humiliation would remedy the matter.

A day later, when Arthur was still writing with his left hand, Bench decided that he was stupid. The master considered anybody who couldn't drop-kick a ball stupid; this included the majority of the faculty, intellectuals, writers, composers, poets and musicians. Even the boy who could extemporize on Caesar's conquest of Gaul was no match, in his opinion, for a consummate football player. *Mind and body together* was one of his favourite phrases.

'Go home, Arthur, and don't come back until you can write with the other hand!' he ordered.

THE NEXT DAY, Tom noticed his son sitting about the house. 'What are you doing here?'

'I'm a criminal,' Arthur replied. He explained Mr Bench's philosophy to his father and received, in return, a diatribe on the cruelty of schoolmasters. Tom told Arthur about Hammer Hall, Mr Goodkind, and his riding crop. Then, provoked by these memories, he left Arthur in order to fire off a letter to the teacher.

Dear Sir,

Although darkness has been conquered by the electric light and we are blessed with inventions from the typewriter to the tea bag, some ignorant souls choose to live in the past.

As a doctor, I consider left-handedness to be a natural facility and suggest you indulge in such superstitions at home rather than during working hours.

Arthur shall continue to write with his left hand.

T. Chapel (Dr)

This letter accompanied Arthur to school but never reached the master. Consumed with anxiety about the trouble it would cause, Arthur chewed up his father's riposte and blew the wad of pulp into a bed of rhododendrons. He had decided that his life was his alone and required no amendment.

From that day forward, Arthur wrote with his right hand in Mr Bench's class, not to please the man but to prove, again, that he could be any*thing* to any*one*.

Thus, Mr Bench claimed another victory for the right-handed world, while Tom claimed it by virtue of Mr Bench's silence on the matter. At one of the football matches, Arthur observed his father's handshake with Mr Bench: each man smiled with triumph at the other while the boy took silent tally of his deception.

A month later, however, Arthur was in trouble again. His parents had received a letter:

Dear Dr and Mrs Chapel,

Arthur was caught playing the school's piano. This is strictly forbidden. It seems that the boy's rebellious streak is deeper than we had surmised. I must urge you to correct his trespasses.

W. Bench

The boy sat before his parents, his face buried in his hands. 'You don't understand, I *have* to play it,' he explained, wiping tears from his eyes.

'I had no idea that you liked to play the piano, my sweet,' said Lizzy.

'Charity won't let me play at home.'

'What do you mean, she won't *let* you?'

'She'd murder me if I did' was the simple reply.

'Please play something for me now, Arthur,' said Lizzy.

Arthur sat at the piano and was about to play when the front door burst open. Charity and Iris had raced each other home. But the sight of Arthur at the piano, with their mother as audience, caused Charity's smile to vanish. '*What's Arthur doing at the piano?*' she cried. 'He can't play anything!'

'I can,' the boy replied. 'I play at school.'

Charity raised her eyebrows. 'You don't have lessons.'

'I'd like to hear him play, Charity,' said Lizzy.

'Very well,' said Charity, flopping beside her mother on the sofa. '*I'd* like to hear him too.'

'Go on, Arthur,' said Iris.

'Yes, give us a *treat*, Arthur,' Charity added venomously.

Nervously watching his sister, Arthur performed Minuet in G. It was a halting, studied performance that ended with the wrong chord. Charity laughed at his clumsiness and went into the kitchen. Lizzy, however, looked puzzled.

'Do you remember Charity's Minuet in G?' she asked Tom.

'Vaguely. It wasn't very good,' Tom whispered.

Most of Charity's pieces were hammered indelibly into the family's collective memory. 'Charity always misses the last chord too,' Lizzy remarked. 'Arthur, how did you learn to play the piece?'

'Copying Charity,' he replied cautiously.

'Very good. I'm impressed,' said his mother faintly. In fact, she was shocked; now she wondered if she had been teaching the wrong child to play the piano.

'It wasn't very good,' protested Iris. 'He's *much* better than that, aren't you, Piglet? Go on, play something else you've heard.'

Arthur played 'Für Elise'. He had heard a boy perform it at school recently. He replicated it now with gentle ease.

His parents shared a glance.

'Would you like lessons, Arthur?' said Lizzy.

Arthur nodded but qualified his reply by looking at his mother. 'But not with you.' He looked towards the kitchen. '*She'd* make it impossible.'

'Very well,' said Lizzy. 'I know of another teacher.'

LIZZY WOULD HAVE taken Arthur to meet Madame Wardour, but she woke with a fever. It had been bothering her for weeks, rising and falling, and that morning she didn't have the energy to get out of bed. Before he left, she spoke to the boy softly, urging him to do his best. 'I'm sorry, Arthur,' she added.

'Sorry? Why?' he replied.

'For not recognizing your talent. I should have been paying more attention to you,' she said.

Arthur forgave her with a kiss on her hot cheek.

TOM TOOK ARTHUR to the Wardours' house with its commanding view of Gantrytown. It had a conical slate roof with a copper weather vane of the moon in a quarter phase. Tom surveyed the Wardours' broad veranda with its cast-iron filigree. 'It's the nicest house in town,' he murmured. 'Pity your mother's ill. She'd love to see it.'

A gaunt, white-haired man appeared through the stained-glass window; the robust Freemason who had humiliated Tom years before was almost as faded as a ghost now.

'Yes?' said the man, recoiling slightly from the morning light. His hollow cheeks were white with stubble, and his eyebrows flared wildly off gaunt temples.

'I'm Dr Chapel. My son is here to meet Madame Wardour.'

This time the old doctor showed no contempt; he led them from a dark hall lined with small framed sepia photographs into a sitting room. The house evoked a well-worn affluence – cracked Balinese carvings, an elephant's foot wastepaper basket, a ship sculpted from a yellowed ivory tusk and a mirror scarred by curled silvering.

Arthur, however, saw only magnificence. An ancient Siamese cat darted between his feet as he took three steps into the piano room, which was filled with sprays of cherry branches and Moorish tiles, and had a glass ceiling that suffused the space with a perpetually pink twilight. Where was the sultan? he wondered, for he truly expected to find a man topped in an immense turban smoking a hookah and flanked by concubines. Instead, the figure who emerged from behind a beaded curtain was a woman with cold blue eyes, an aquiline nose and high cheekbones. Her grey hair was pinned up so tightly that her face seemed pulled awry. She folded her arms like an enormous hawk in repose.

The doctor introduced himself and was rebuffed.

'*Je sais qui vous êtes,*' she murmured. 'The *other* doctor.'

Tom tipped his head. 'This is my son, Arthur.'

The hawk turned to Arthur. 'And you want to play the piano?'

The boy nodded.

Her eyebrows rose. 'When I ask a question, Arthur, I expect an answer.'

'*Yes*, Madame.'

She directed him to sit at the piano and issued her next remark without looking at Tom. 'I expected to see your wife.'

'Unfortunately she's unwell. She teaches too.'

'I know she does.' Madame Wardour sniffed. 'Many of my less capable students have become *hers.*'

The barbed authority of his prospective teacher reminded Arthur of Mr Bench; instinctively, he tucked his left hand safely out of her sight.

'Dr Chapel, your wife may accept every pupil who walks through her door, but I haven't the patience. If he or she has no talent, it's hardly worth the time, is it? Incidentally, I should make it clear that I shall charge for this lesson, whether or not I accept your son.'

She sat Arthur before the piano while Tom took a seat and checked his watch, ready to whisk the boy out of the place as soon as the hour was over.

'Now, Arthur,' murmured Madame Wardour, 'have you had any lessons?'

'No,' Arthur replied.

'Can you read music?'

'No.'

She turned to Tom, but he fixed his eyes on the old cat, which pressed itself against his leg in a desperate plea for affection.

'Very well,' she sighed. 'Play the best thing you know.'

Arthur chose one of Bach's preludes. It was a piece Charity had struggled with for months.

As the boy started to play, Tom recognized it. To his dismay, Arthur played it with the same wrong notes and uneven tempo.

Arthur might as well have struck Madame Wardour with a hammer. She recoiled. 'Who taught you this?'

'Nobody. I copied my sister. That's how she plays it.'

'There is a special place in the afterworld for a composer, Arthur,' said Madame Wardour. 'It is a place where he is forced to hear the most wretched interpretations of his music. So, let us try to ease poor Monsieur Bach's pain, shall we? Play it again for me,' she asked, and issued a directive. Arthur was to play the piece as if it were a conversation between two voices.

As Arthur played, Tom closed his eyes to listen. He was struck by how sad the melody became. If the voices were in the boy's head, then his spirit was melancholy indeed. He had glimpsed his son's loneliness.

When he opened his eyes, Madame Wardour was standing by his chair.

'I will see him twice a week,' she said.

'Twice?'

'He must learn to read music, and he has habits that must be broken.'

'*Twice* a week? Is that essential?'

'*Imperative,*' Madame Wardour replied. 'He shows ability, but he can only play what he hears – a talented cripple. Of course, if you prefer that he play as badly as his sister, let him be. Waste his talent,' she sniffed. 'It's up to you.'

THE FEVER

ON THE TRAM RIDE HOME, ARTHUR LOOKED EARNESTLY AT HIS father. 'Did I play well?'

Tom nodded. 'Splendidly.'

'Thank you, Papa.'

His son's reply struck Tom to the heart. It made him feel unworthy. The child carried such dark sorrow within himself. How was it possible, in such a short, sheltered life, that Arthur could conjure such sadness out of the ether? What folly, then, are a parent's attempts to ensure a happy life for his child?

Observing his father in a silent trance, Arthur wondered how a man could have so many things to think about on such a lovely evening. An overpowering scent of jasmine wafted into the tram car from one of the grander houses on Alderton Street. Palms and jacaranda trees floated past him. There was a languid mood among the passengers; the working week was over, and the sway of the vehicle acted like a narcotic.

Against a golden mackerel sky, Tom and his son walked the quarter mile up their road, immersed in their own thoughts until they saw the girls standing in a row on the veranda. They stood stiffly – like Charity's old clothes-peg dolls – with clasped hands and immobile stares.

When he saw their faces, Arthur fell behind his father.

'Papa!' cried Margaret. 'Her fever's worse, and she's delirious.'

Leaving Arthur with the girls, Tom went into the house.

'What's wrong with Mama?' the boy asked.

Iris and Charity deferred to Margaret.

'Nothing!' Her smile was lopsided and taut. 'It's all right!'

Charity suddenly burst into tears. As Margaret tried to console her, Arthur sought the truth from Iris.

'She's very sick, Piglet,' said his sister, 'with a fierce fever.'

Only when he was alone with his wife did Tom let his panic show. Lizzy's hand felt as hot as the emanation from Todderman's furnace doors – an unnatural heat matched by eyes that showed no recognition, though they were open and animated. He feared that it was cerebral malaria, rare at such a high elevation as Gantrytown, but there had been a few cases.

When he kissed her cheek, she spoke: 'Such news, my love! Eve is here!'

'What?'

She spoke without looking at him. 'I knew my letters were reaching her. Eve has *come*, Tom. She has *forgiven* me. She is in the spare room, putting her things away!'

'Eve?' repeated Tom.

'You must have seen her. She's wearing a beautiful green velvet dress, and she has not a single grey hair. Imagine! After all this time!'

Tom squeezed her hand. 'Lizzy. I took Arthur to his lesson. He played terribly well. The teacher has—'

'Ah, there she is!' cried Lizzy, as a figure appeared at the door. 'Eve!'

Tom turned from his wife's feverish smile to the slender figure silhouetted in the doorway.

'Eve!' cried Lizzy again.

Margaret was about to correct her, but Tom raised his hand, advising silence.

'Do you remember when we used to go shopping in the high street, Eve?' Lizzy cried.

Margaret wilted, but her father nodded with a smile. 'Do you remember, Eve?' he said, looking at her.

'Yes,' replied Margaret. 'Of course.'

Smiling, Lizzy closed her eyes and sank into her pillow. 'I must sleep now. So tired. Forgive me.'

Tom drew up his wife's covers, and Margaret left the room.

A SOMBRE SILENCE settled over the household. Lizzy mistook Charity for one of her own childhood friends and Iris for her first piano teacher; each delusion seemed to reach further into her childhood and distance her more from her children.

'She always thinks I'm her sister now,' Margaret lamented at dinner.

'It will pass, Margaret,' Tom explained. 'You are doing her a kindness by accepting it.'

Iris looked disgusted. 'By *lying*?'

'It is not lying, Iris, to reassure your sick mother.'

Arthur looked at his father. 'She *will* get better, won't she?'

They all turned to Tom. 'Yes, Arthur, I believe she'll be fine,' he replied.

Charity pushed aside her plate and pressed her hands together. 'Shall we pray for her?'

In other circumstances, such a demand would have provoked irritation in her sisters; the Chapels were not fervent believers, but now they were desperate. Tom put his hands together, as did Iris, Margaret and Arthur.

There was an uncommon silence at the table, and then, their faces cleared a little.

Tom removed his untouched plate and, after scraping it in the kitchen, steadied himself by gripping the window frame. He wasn't sure if it had been kind to offer false hope to his children, but he felt empty of resource, powerless and bereft.

THAT SATURDAY MORNING Lizzy died. Tom broke the news to his children one by one as they woke. Charity spent the day weeping; Iris was stoic but couldn't go nearer than the doorway of the bedroom where her mother lay. After she had shed some tears, Margaret pulled herself together and assured each sibling that Lizzy had gone to heaven and was looking down upon them at that moment; she reminded them to be brave and cheerful. To Tom's astonishment, this seemed to calm them.

Only by the evening, after he had put Arthur to bed and the girls had retired, could Tom permit himself to grieve. He hid on the veranda in the dark and sobbed in anguished gasps. The night cooled; he saw his breaths billow before him and recalled the frost on the windows of his Vauxhall tenement and his mother's last moments. She had been in a hallucination of her own, speaking to him of her lost baby and cradling his bundled coat. He began to weep for her, for lost babies and parents, lost friends and lovers. What had his life been, after all, but a parade of lost loved ones?

After a fresh bout of tears, Tom became aware that he was observed. He turned to see Iris standing at the door. She was an extraordinary sight – cheeks rouged, chalk white face, a garish smile, toreador's hat and a brilliant scarlet robe emblazoned with a serpentine dragon and fringed with gold tassels, a gift from a Chinese patient. The robe dwarfed Iris, the hem curling in a shiny red puddle of silk at her feet.

'Good heavens, Iris!' he gasped.

'I mean to look shocking,' she said, approaching him. 'I once read a story about a man who wanted to frighten death away from his house so he wore the loudest, most ridiculous clothing.' She gestured to her costume with a dramatic sweep. 'Will this do?'

'I believe so,' Tom replied.

'Good,' she said. She smiled, kissed his cheek, turned with an elegant flourish and walked back to her room.

THE WAKE

There was a rootless aspect at the gathering of Lizzy's former pupils, their parents and the many patients who had been entranced by her singing in the early days of Tom's practice. Searching for evidence of the vivacious woman they knew, relative strangers wandered through the house, fingering the picture frames, the yellow Provence earthenware for which Lizzy had bartered piano lessons, the photographs of an Edinburgh schoolgirl, the dog-eared music, the collection of pencil stubs on the piano, the wide-brimmed straw hat with the black ribbon she'd worn on hot afternoons beneath the scorching African sun, and the white nurse's uniform. They pawed the odd objects she had collected on the kitchen shelf – seashells from Port Elizabeth, three shoe polish tins containing locks of her daughters' hair, a piece of dried moss from the Isle of Skye. But her verve, sense of humour, and straightforward manner couldn't be summed up by her possessions. So when Charity announced that she was going to perform one of her mother's favourite pieces, a Schubert impromptu, everybody gathered in the sitting room.

Visitors took their seats with smiles and nods. It would be a fitting memorial to Lizzy, the passing on of her talent. Some spoke in hushed voices; it was almost like a séance – perhaps Lizzy would come back from the grave and infuse her daughter with her spirit.

Tom knew what was coming and tried to spare his daughter what could only be a humiliating experience. 'Charity,' he whispered, as she sat down at the piano, 'perhaps instead we could sing one of her favourite songs. Perhaps *that* would be a fitting way to remember her?'

His daughter looked wounded. 'Please, Papa, it would mean so much to me,' she said.

Tom nodded. Funerals are for the living, he reminded himself and took a seat, hoping for the best.

From the first bars, however, her audience was wincing. Charity's leaden fingers set the punch bowl swaying and the candles tumbling. One by one, the little children began to stray and bleat; then a few elderly folk hobbled away.

Margaret disappeared into the kitchen and closed the door.

Shortly afterwards, Iris lurched out of the house and disappeared between the bougainvillea and hibiscus blossoms. She dug into her pocket and opened a tin box containing hand-rolled cigarettes and some matches. In the sunlight, Iris's hair was blond, though indoors it appeared brown. At all times it was limp and thin, and something of a disappointment. She rarely dwelled on such shortcomings, just as she had resisted wearing the wire-rimmed spectacles her parents bought for her, believing that she could fool anyone into thinking she had normal sight. She also lifted her heels during conversation, to appear taller, and memorized quotations to appear erudite. Now, however, it seemed the time to give up such pretenses. She put on the spectacles and noticed a bee circling the hibiscus – her mother's favourite flower – and realized that she would be motherless forever. Shortsighted forever. Small forever. Glancing warily at the house, she lit her cigarette and pondered her unhappiness as the smoke curled around the sweet peas and sunflowers.

Arthur noticed his father slipping out of the room, but he remained in his seat. In spite of Charity's clumsy performance, he lapsed into a reverie; he recalled his mother playing this piece in the evenings, and remembered its longing, the sweet regret and consolation in its melody; he would never forget the way she had played it.

Tom skirted the house, ducked beneath the washing line and peered through a window to see how many visitors lingered. The music seemed to have driven most of them away.

Suddenly, Charity burst out of the kitchen door, eyes red.

'Thank you, Charity,' he began, 'for playing.'

'Almost everybody's *gone*!' She frowned. 'You'd think, for Mama's sake, they would listen. Did they leave because of my playing?'

Tom put his arm around his daughter's shoulder. 'It doesn't matter why they went.'

She wasn't mollified. 'Arthur is better, isn't he? I'm fifteen, Papa. You can tell me the truth.'

'If you like to play, you should play,' he replied. 'It's not a competitive sport.'

The girl frowned again. 'But I played for *her*. I tried so hard. I wanted to be good for her.' Her voice faltered. 'Whatever shall I do now?' she said.

Tom had no reply. The question might have been his own or, indeed, that of any of the Chapels.

The Horvaths did not attend the wake. Though their house was fifty feet from the Chapels', they behaved as if such a distance was an unbreachable chasm. It was a surprise to them when their bored parrot began to repeat Charity's words.

'*Whatever shall I do now?*' it lamented, in the middle of their dinner. And later, in the early hours of the morning, its words echoed through the house in a weary existential cry: *Whatever shall I do now?*

SEVERAL MORNINGS LATER, Tom found Margaret up early. She had rearranged the kitchen cupboards. 'Papa,' she said, 'I shall need more sugar and mealie meal, and to know what Mama did for you in the surgery.'

'Margaret, I don't expect you to do *everything* your mother did.'

His daughter was insulted. 'Of course I shall,' she replied. 'How will we manage if I do not?'

Margaret sincerely *wanted* to fill her mother's shoes, and for the rest of the day, she performed with selfless dedication. She took Arthur to school, shopped, brought him home, and after assigning tasks to the other girls, discussed Lizzy's death with him.

'You see, Arthur, although Mama has gone to heaven, she is still here. You will feel her presence watching over us. She will never desert you.'

This idea puzzled the boy. Although at ten he was old enough to grapple with its spiritual meaning, his heart compelled him to seek some literal embodiment of his mother.

During his next piano lesson, Arthur gave his teacher a penetrating glance. He searched for his mother's fingers when Madame Wardour demonstrated a finger placement, sought his mother's breasts in the haughty grey figure, even peered at her hem in the hope of finding his mother's legs. Unnerved, Madame Wardour remarked, '*Mon Dieu*, Arthur, do not stare at me as if I were an apparition!'

'She died,' he said. 'My mother.'

'When?'

'Last week,' he replied.

She looked at him – eyes cold and magnificent. 'You must be strong, Arthur. You're a big boy, now. Make me proud of you.'

Though Margaret would still baby him, Madame Wardour's remark gave Arthur his direction. Just as his father had adopted Mrs Limpkin, Arthur chose Madame Wardour to fill the maternal role. He worked hard for her, resisted his gift for mimicry and learned to read music. As he proved himself a passionate pianist, he learned two languages – that of Bach, Chopin, Mozart and Schubert, and Madame Wardour's, French, peppered as it was with Breton.

The more pressing matter, as far as Tom was concerned, was what would become of the Chapel girls. He sat alone one evening realizing just how much he had depended on Lizzy for perspective on his children. Now he alone would have to console them, encourage them and direct their futures. In the early hours of the morning, he wrote to Audrey, confessing his panic, his ignorance, and his loss. He ended his letter as follows:

> *Audrey, perhaps my most prominent flaw is a failure to forgive. I still hold my father accountable for deserting me and, alas, you for*

rejecting my hand in marriage. Now I find myself accountable to four children – I can only hope they have more generosity of spirit than I.

You once told me that we are not mayflies and that love endures. What a fool I was not to believe you.

Tom

FITTING IN

WHEN CHARITY ACCOMPANIED THE ST RUTH'S CHOIR, IT WAS THE first time the singers had to be instructed to drown out the accompanist. The music teacher, Mrs Sweet, redirected Charity's musical aspirations by introducing her to the organ.

'It will complement your *gifts*, Charity,' she said tactfully, 'in the sense that you will be free to indulge in melody without the necessity of force or delicacy.'

'But I've not played one before.'

Mrs Sweet had never been so desperate to get a girl out of her department. 'Hardly an impediment, my dear. The organ is the piano's simpler cousin! The Presbyterians, my dear, have an excellent pipe organ. *They* could put your talents to good use.'

As it happened, the organist at St Andrew's was rather too fond of drink. One weekend when his wife asked Tom to treat the man's indisposition, Tom prescribed bed rest and offered his daughter's services to the minister.

Perhaps she was seduced by the stops above the keyboard that could give any note the gravitas and splendour of a thousand angels, or perhaps it was the sheer volume that playing in such a space achieved, but Charity thought she had found her niche. She loved playing in a church, she loved the service, and her piety found release.

To the minister's despair, however, she also demonstrated an alarming knack for interpreting even the most joyous psalm in a dark, foreboding manner. After the first Sunday, he offered plaintive comment. 'Remember, this is a house of *joy*, Charity!'

How could she feel joy? She had lost her mother, and pined for her. Furthermore, as she turned sixteen, her body betrayed her. Charity would have been happy to assume Iris's proportions, but instead she grew breasts almost as large as Margaret's while her height remained at five foot two. Then, one day, she found herself unable to read her music. Tom took her into town for spectacles – with fashionable tortoiseshell frames. But her improved vision only complicated her troubles, for when she saw herself clearly in the mirror – bespectacled, diminutive, with a high waist and cleavage, Charity was horrified. 'Dear God,' she prayed, one morning, 'why have you given me this body?'

She became painfully shy. Unable to find clothes that flattered her, she used Lizzy's sewing machine to make dark dresses with lace collars that played down her bosom but gave her figure a curvaceous grace. One afternoon, Tom found her sewing furiously, tears rolling down her cheeks.

'I've been dismissed,' she explained.

'By the minister?'

Charity nodded. 'My playing is too angry or melancholy or something!'

How could it be too melancholy for Presbyterians? Tom wondered. 'What about the Lutherans?' he suggested.

Charity's stint with the Lutherans lasted about a month before they too asked her to leave. It was the same with the Catholics, the Dutch Reformed and the Methodists.

'Charity,' Tom promised, 'there *is* a place for you somewhere.'

IF PEOPLE THOUGHT CHARITY strange, they found Iris downright shocking. One of Tom's lady patients had spotted her wearing her father's trousers on the veranda. Tom didn't mind this; he admired Iris's spirit, but he warned her that she couldn't wear his trousers any farther than the edge of his property.

She continued to publish her poetry in *St Ruth's Weekender*. It was satirical but carefully disguised. She mocked the school's music teacher, a bewhiskered gentleman who devoured his lunch while lecturing the class, with a poem titled 'Ode to a Walrus':

The Walrus is a bulging beauty,
His slothful greed is so acute, he
Gobbles herring, mashes guppies,
(Hardly noticing his puppies).

Only a few parents and a couple of her teachers appreciated Iris's subversive ditties. Everyone else considered her eccentric, Bohemian, and feared her reckless spirit.

Tom was encouraged by his patients to make plans for Iris. She was in her last year at St Ruth's, a time when many girls entertained the prospect of marriage; but boys were afraid of Iris: her jokes were too bawdy, she was outspoken and had opinions on too many subjects.

Mrs Gantry suggested that Iris would make a good teacher. 'Teachers can be peculiar, and nobody minds,' she said. 'It's a safe, reliable career for such an odd girl.'

Tom discussed the idea with Iris.

'I'd *love* to teach, Papa!' she replied.

'Good. I'll make inquiries at St Ruth's,' he said.

'Unless you object, Papa,' Iris said, 'I'd rather teach at St Peter's. Boys are so much more fun than girls.'

Tom made good use of his connections and secured his daughter a position in the English department at St Peter's for the following year.

In the meantime, Iris wanted one thing from her final month at St Ruth's: to go to the leavers' dance. To be in Margaret's place, desired, resplendent, and happy – but no invitation arrived. Finally, Reggie Plimpton invited her; he was an athlete, charmless in character but a strong physical specimen. *Strapping* was the word Iris preferred. Margaret had introduced Reggie to Iris, and he would do anything to earn Margaret's favour. Iris was so thrilled to be going to the dance that she revised a poem she had written about Peter Carnahan as she raced home to tell her father the news.

Reggie Plimpton
You're my victor,
Lips of Byron
Strength of Hector!

Might of Atlas
Heart's desire,
Reggie darling,
I'm on fire!

Like an oak tree,
Strong and limber
Oh, to touch your
Sturdy timber!

Carnahan, of course, had been smitten by Margaret ever since she provoked his cricket injury; he was her constant companion, though his Byronic lips and sturdy timber earned him little more than a peck on the cheek. Margaret wanted to feel love first, like the breath of angels, before she would indulge in any groping. Carnahan clung to her with earnest good humour, hopeful that one day she would surrender her affections to him. Because Margaret was going with Peter Carnahan as a chaperone for the St Ruth's event, Iris assumed Reggie would appreciate her own attractions once they were alone together.

The Chapel girls threw all their energies into preparing Iris for the dance: Margaret set curlers in her sister's limp blond hair; Charity sewed her a rustling pale pink frock. Iris practised gliding in it for hours, determined to master this role just as she had once dressed to frighten Death from her door. She imagined herself as Juliet, Hero, and Titania.

When Reggie arrived in a white jacket and black trousers, Tom took an instant dislike to him. The boy did not meet his eye and answered his questions by addressing the ceiling.

'Iris,' whispered her father just before she got into Reggie's polished two-seater carriage, 'what *on earth* do you see in the fellow?'

'Oh, Papa,' she replied, 'it's just for the evening.'

Reggie drove her to the dance at breakneck speed, offering barely a nod when Iris tried to make conversation. Then, as they entered the dance hall, he took her aside in the foyer, where a forest of coats and jackets muted their voices. 'Look here, Iris,' he murmured, 'understand that I will do the talking. You're to nod when I speak to you. You need not be funny or clever, because that's not what I expect from a girl. You're to be pretty, which you should be able to do with your mouth closed. Is that clear?'

'In other words,' she replied, 'I must hang from your arm like a trained monkey.'

'Now, Iris, don't insult yourself. You're quite a good-looking girl – when you aren't talking.'

Iris's spectacles fogged. 'Thank you,' she said. 'And you're better looking than a monkey too.'

'We want to have fun, don't we?' Reggie frowned. 'So be a good girl.'

Iris had looked forward to the dance for weeks. It was the first time she had ever been with a boy to a social event. So she agreed to Reggie's terms and clung to his arm as he led her into the hall. A small orchestra played popular tunes at the edge of a freshly polished floor. The girls looked pretty and happy, and the boys were handsome in their white jackets. While Reggie greeted his friends, Iris was mute, doing her best to smile as her soul collapsed. She observed the glowing faces of the other girls and chided herself for failing to enjoy the evening.

When she saw Margaret and Peter Carnahan standing at the buffet table talking to friends, Iris realized her predicament: clutching Reggie's arm, having agreed not to speak, she had relinquished her wit and intelligence, the very qualities that distinguished her from her sister. And for what? She felt tears rolling down her cheeks.

Reggie presented her with a glass of punch. 'Iris,' he said, 'I'm going to dance. Stay here, and I'll collect you in a few moments.'

'I'd like to dance,' said Iris.

Reggie gave her a warning glance and told her to wait. Iris felt her cheeks burning. This couldn't be happening. She'd never anticipated such humiliation. It was to have been a romantic evening. Was it possible that other girls felt as she did? She surveyed the dancers, the smiling couples, and the chatting clusters of her classmates. But the weight of her own disappointment isolated her. The first moment of her joyous adulthood had been stolen. Her cheeks were sticky with tears, her spectacles hopelessly fogged.

Iris rose slowly, wiped her spectacles, dabbed her cheeks with a napkin, and edged her way timidly along the periphery until she arrived beside Margaret.

'Iris, you look flushed!'

'I'm— No, I've – twisted my ankle. Could I borrow Peter? I want to go home.'

'Will Reggie not take you?'

'He told me to sit down and keep quiet.'

Margaret apologized on Reggie's behalf, but Iris saw a hint of amusement in her sister's face. It was clear that Margaret was to blame for her suffering.

Margaret dispatched Peter Carnahan, and within moments, he and Iris were bumping along together in his open carriage through the tree-lined streets of Gantrytown.

CARNAHAN WORE HIS FATHER'S tie and white jacket and looked very smart. He drove his horse at a confident clip as Iris clung to him, silently comparing his bronzed face and sweeping blond hair with Reggie's weak chin and bulbous eyes.

'What's that wonderful smell?' Iris asked softly. 'Is it your hair, Peter?'

Carnahan smiled. 'Lily of the valley,' he explained. 'It's Truefitt and Hill, the best, I think,' he said, neglecting to mention that it was his father's, and the only hair cream he'd ever used.

Iris leaned against his shoulder. 'It's delicious.' As they rounded the incline to her street, she clutched his arm a little more tightly than was necessary. Carnahan didn't resist, which surprised her.

'I'm sorry to have dragged you away from the fun,' she said.

'Not at all,' he replied. 'How is your ankle?'

'Better,' she said. 'Margaret's so lucky to have a friend like you.'

'I wish you'd tell her that.' Carnahan grinned. 'Lately she's hardly noticed me.'

'I'm sure she adores you,' Iris replied.

'Really?' Carnahan checked his surprise. 'She's a wonderful girl, Iris, no doubt about it.'

They turned along a bumpy road draped with willows. The carriage tilted, and Iris tightened her grip on her escort's arm. 'Poor Peter,' she murmured. 'Margaret should pay you more attention.'

He glanced at her, fearing her famous mockery, but her expression was innocent. 'You deserve someone who appreciates you, Peter.'

Iris removed her spectacles. A new idea had entered her head. As she sensed the slight incline towards her house, she asked Carnahan to stop before they were in view of the windows. Tom had hung a lantern from the veranda for the girls' return, and she could see it through the trees, but she wanted a moment alone with the boy.

'I should walk from here. I don't want to wake my father,' she explained. Smoothing her dress, she drew a stray lock of hair behind one ear and raised her eyes to meet his. 'You're very handsome and gallant, Peter. Any girl can see that,' she said, though he was a blur before her. 'Margaret certainly should.'

Carnahan thanked her for the compliment. He sprang down, circled the carriage, and helped Iris from her seat. She held on to his hand for a moment longer than necessary, then reached up and stroked his hair.

'Lily of the valley . . .'

She smoothed her narrow waist with both hands, directing his gaze to her figure.

'Iris, you're sweet too,' he conceded.

'Oh, Peter,' she cooed.

Suddenly Carnahan took her in his arms and kissed her. Perhaps it was a kiss meant for Margaret, but Iris returned it longingly. His body was muscular and taut. She felt his ribs as she put one hand against his chest in feigned resistance. 'Oh, Peter,' she sighed.

'I'm sorry,' he blurted.

Iris lowered her head meekly, as if she were ashamed. 'You had probably saved that kiss for Margaret. I shouldn't have provoked you.'

Carnahan shook his head. 'Iris—'

'I envy Margaret,' she said. 'I'll never be as pretty as she is, but—'

'Iris?' he declared, 'you're a fine girl! A damned fine girl!'

Iris leaned forward, planted her own kiss on his lips, and, with a demure smile, turned towards the house.

Carnahan called after her, 'Iris, what about your ankle?'

'Oh.' She smiled. 'Cured!'

'Iris, I'll see you again soon!'

With a snap of the reins, he was clattering down the driveway. Iris quickly put her spectacles back on and hurried up to the house. Tom was sitting on the veranda with Arthur at his side.

'You're early. Is everything all right?'

'Oh, yes,' she replied, '. . . blissful.'

WAR

It started in August 1914, and everybody expected it to be over by Christmas. Once the British Expeditionary Force began to march, there was no doubt that the colonies would join it, which brought the war to the Chapels' doorstep.

Tom hadn't forgotten his experience in the Anglo-Boer War, and viewed the daily headlines with dread. He observed, however, that as his children wrestled with the issues at the breakfast table, their opinions of the war were framed by personal experience.

Iris, who had now taught grammar to the boys at St Peter's for several years, dismissed the war as a school yard fight between bullies. 'The assassination of the Archduke, for example,' she explained, 'was no different from the fight in the dining hall just the other day! One braggart lobbed his football boot across the room and struck another boy in the eye. Half a minute later every other ruffian was punching his worst enemy in the face!'

Iris's affection for the teaching life was tempered by such observations. She still loved literature and cherished producing the annual Shakespeare performance, but she considered the other teachers a stuffy bunch and the boys savages. Her one consolation was the affair she had provoked with Peter Carnahan; he made monthly visits to Margaret, but

Iris seized each opportunity to make some small impression on him. She would dust his shoulder, or adjust his tie, or ask him to examine a speck that had fallen into her eye. Eventually, Carnahan appeared at the Chapel house, knowing that Margaret would not be there, and Iris seized the opportunity to seduce him in the Horvaths' apple orchard. Once she had laid claim to his lips and sturdy timber, the visits to Margaret ceased.

This probably explained Margaret's opinion on the war. When the Germans advanced upon Brussels, all she could think about was her sister's theft of Peter Carnahan. 'None of this would have happened if people respected *borders*!' she argued. 'The Germans had no right to invade Belgium. They must be stopped, and driven back!'

She was twenty-four when the war was declared, and the sting of losing Carnahan was an open wound. He would call to see Iris, his blond hair thrown back carelessly, his skin glowing, and Margaret would stare at him with saintly longing. Carnahan, she realized, was probably the only man worth marrying in Gantrytown. She still considered herself the sole match for him, but Iris, with her bawdy jokes, her silly rhymes, her dramatic gestures and deceptions, had taken him for good. Margaret was trapped at home – the doctor's nurse, accountant, housekeeper and cook. Filling her mother's shoes hadn't been the joy she had expected.

The war made the most profound impact on Charity. She pored over the newspaper every morning, consumed not by the politics but by the spiritual ramifications of the conflict. 'Thousands of people are dying, nations are at war, and the world is falling to pieces,' she lamented. 'The signs are everywhere. Even a blind man could tell that the day of reckoning is upon us!'

Tom became alarmed by her remarks. His mother had spoken of such things. 'I don't believe this is the final battle, Charity,' he replied.

'Well, the *Pendletons* think so!'

'Who?'

She held out a pamphlet that had arrived in the post. She had been keeping it in her Bible. It was a little worn, but the message was clear:

Friend—

DO YOU SEE HUMAN DISGRACE IN THE NEWSPAPER
AND WONDER WHAT WILL BECOME OF OUR WORLD?
DO YOU FEEL THAT THE GREAT MACHINE
WE CALL 'PROGRESS'
IS RUNNING FULL THROTTLE WITHOUT A DRIVER?
YOU ARE NOT ALONE!
JOIN US IN AN EVENING OF EPIPHANY! REVELATION! JOY!

—The Pendletons

'What a gloomy evening it must be,' remarked Iris.

'I went last week, and I've never felt such happiness!' insisted Charity. 'They gather in a big tent, and there's music, and people speak, and it *all makes sense*!'

'What does?' asked Tom.

'Well, this is part of God's plan for the end of the world. The streets will be washed of sin, the evil will be swallowed into the earth, and the meek shall rise to heaven.'

'I see,' Tom said. 'You mean that the end of the world is a good thing?'

'The streets being washed of sin must appeal to you, darling,' said Iris to Charity. 'You were always a tidy child.'

'And you've found some good friends?' asked Margaret.

Charity might have taken offence at her sisters' condescension if she had not been so happy.

'And, of course, you're playing the organ,' offered Margaret. 'You were having *such* a difficult time with the churches.'

'They love my music,' Charity claimed. 'I'm playing tonight. You should come.'

'No, thank you,' said Iris breezily.

Margaret, however, was looking at the pamphlet with interest. 'Well,' she mused, 'I do wonder what's to become of the world, but I'm not sure about the religious side.'

At that moment, the doorbell rang, and Margaret rose to answer it.

'Hello, Margaret!'

Peter Carnahan grinned. He was wearing a khaki serge uniform with brass buttons and puttees.

'Oh, Peter, you've enlisted,' she cried.

He beamed. 'How do I look?'

Margaret's smile faded. There couldn't have been a more handsome soldier. But he was *Iris's* soldier.

Iris howled when she saw Carnahan in his uniform. She steered him out of the house, and as their feet crunched across the gravel in the direction of the Horvaths' orchard, she commanded, 'Peter, you *must* make love to me in your uniform!'

Margaret stared after them, dismayed. Tom wanted to assuage her misery. 'Margaret—' he began.

'How is it,' she interrupted, 'that Iris has Peter Carnahan, and I . . . have *you*?' With that, she disappeared into the kitchen.

AMID THE APPLE and pear trees, Iris fell backwards on to the lush grass and issued Carnahan a sultry glance. 'Take me!'

He stood before her gingerly. 'Well, Iris.' He hesitated. 'I don't want to spoil my uniform. After all, it belongs to the army.'

'But I want to be debauched by a *soldier*!' she pouted.

'But it's *me*, Iris,' he said.

'Oh, Peter,' she replied, 'I'll imagine I'm being ravished by Achilles or Cedric the Saxon.'

'Who?' He frowned.

'The heroes of the ages!'

Because Iris was his first love, Carnahan assumed that all girls had such fantasies, giggled during climax, and sang 'March of the Toreadors' afterwards. He agreed to keep his tunic on but hung his trousers and puttees on a branch.

This time, after Iris had uttered a delicious wail, Carnahan fussed over the grass stains on his tunic. She jumped up, blouse dishevelled, and tried on his trousers. Then she danced across the orchard.

'Iris!' he cried. 'I came to ask you a question!'

'Very well, Cedric.' She laughed.

'Will you marry me when I come back?'

Iris wrinkled her nose. 'Gosh! *That's* an awfully serious question.' Her expression implied that he had broken some rule.

'I know,' he said. 'But if I don't ask now, who knows what will happen? I'd like to think, when I'm in battle, that I'll have something to look forward to when I come back.'

Iris fell against him wearily, as if his sentiment had sapped the life from her small frame. 'Of *course*, Peter.'

'You'll marry me then?' Carnahan replied.

Iris removed her spectacles and gave him her most earnest smile. 'Of course we'll be married.' She slipped out of the trousers, handed them to him with a theatrical flourish. *'I would not deny you; but by this good day, I yield upon great persuasion; and partly to save your life.'*

Baffled, Carnahan grinned. 'Oh, Iris,' he exclaimed, 'you're a fine girl!'

THE CHAPELS GAVE Carnahan an enthusiastic send-off on his last day. The doctor took a photograph of him, in uniform, with Iris, and promised to send it to him. Arthur chased Carnahan's carriage while Tom, Margaret and Iris watched the dust rise from the road in clouds.

'Do you think he'll come through safely?' asked Iris.

'I hope so,' Tom said with a frown. 'War is madness.'

'It is, isn't it?' she sighed.

This provoked Margaret, who had been dabbing her eyes with a handkerchief, to issue a bitter judgment: 'Really, Iris,' she spluttered. 'You're so cruel. If you loved him, why didn't you marry him before he left?'

Iris looked at her sister. 'If *you* loved him, why didn't you marry him years ago? He'd been pining for you forever. All I did was fill a void, Margaret. He was yours for the taking!'

Leaving her sister to nurse her regrets, Iris strode back to the house.

—

'WHERE'S ARTHUR?' ASKED TOM, suddenly. The boy was nowhere to be seen, and the awful thought that he was riding away with Carnahan crossed his father's mind.

As the dust cleared, Arthur appeared, marching home with a stick perched like a rifle on his shoulder, his lower lip pushed out in a stern imitation of an infantryman.

'Arthur!' cried Tom. 'Stop that!'

The boy dropped the stick and began to kick stones, watching his father from the corner of his eye like a chastened hound.

THE RALLY

Beneath a broad white tent, the Pendletons welcomed visitors with gentle smiles and open arms. They all wore black suits, with purple piping along the lapels and sleeves. The men had single lines of piping that ran down the outsides of their trouser legs. The women wore skirts hemmed four inches below the knee. Charity modified her uniform: she narrowed the waist, added lace to the rims of her shoes, and pleated the skirt so that she could manipulate the organ pedals.

Tom sent Margaret to investigate. 'Perhaps then you will be able to reassure me that these people are *sensible*,' he said. Margaret was glad to get out of the house; she couldn't bear to be alone with Iris these days.

Charity introduced Margaret to a few friends, then hurried over to the orchestra. A small tin pipe organ stood at the centre of the stage.

'First time?' inquired one of the young women.

'Yes,' admitted Margaret.

'You're lucky, then,' said a man. 'Isaiah Pound, our founder, is with us tonight. He's come from England. He's brilliant. You'll see!'

'Quite brilliant,' echoed another man.

'There are Pendletons on every continent now,' explained the young woman.

These weren't her sort of people, Margaret decided. They were pleasant enough, but she didn't like the uniforms and wondered why such a church group lacked a cross or a single picture of Jesus. In fact, the one picture visible was a poster of Isaiah Pound – a narrow, humourless face with a probing stare.

Although spare seats were everywhere, Margaret was encouraged to fill one at the front. Suddenly, the lights went down, and the organ began Bach's Toccata in D Minor. A man appeared onstage, his face illuminated by the podium light. His voice was tinny, but had a strangely compelling monotony.

> If part of you is missing a loved one, a family member, a wife, a husband, then you are my friend.
>
> If you see human folly on the front page of the newspaper and wonder what is to become of mankind, you are my friend.
>
> If you wonder whether the great machine we call 'progress' is going full throttle without a driver, you are my friend!

Attired in a black suit and a purple clerical collar, Isaiah Pound addressed his small audience as if it were a multitude. Margaret felt herself shaken by his appeal. She thought of Peter Carnahan and felt sorry for herself. She *had* lost someone, someone very dear.

> We have one another, my friends. We are not alone. We don't wander through the Valley of the Shadow of Death unassisted. God is with us. He has a plan for us all!

Isaiah Pound's thin black hair was shaven in a fringe that left an inch of bare scalp around his ears.

Voices cried out in agreement, and Pound extended his hands in appeal.

> Welcome, friends. Tonight we share a common roof, we share the love of our fellow man, the respect for the vast unknown, and a deep, abiding awe of our Almighty Creator.
>
> Perhaps He has spoken to you. He speaks to me, friends, all the time. And He asks, 'What has become of man?' He asks, 'Why do

the weak suffer, the innocent perish, and the sinful prevail?' And He says, 'Something must be done!'

The preacher leaned forward on his lectern and smiled.

Here is the good news, friends. He has told me that the end is near. He wants you, friend. The prophets are returning. A beautiful day is at hand. A day of cleansing – an end to smoky skies, filthy streets, the sinful, the callous, and the apostates who take His name in vain. We are invited into His shining kingdom, my friends, the undiscovered country, the kingdom of heaven. Join me, friends!

His hands reached out, and scores answered his appeal from the seats below. Suddenly Charity's ominous music filled the hall, accompanied by a chorus of heavenly voices – like angels preparing for the final conflict. Heaven was ripping apart, the trumpets sounded, and the end was a glorious, horrific, rapturous cacophony. Isaiah Pound turned to watch Charity play, clearly impressed by her performance.

Finally, he delivered his appeal:

Join us! Prepare for the end, and rejoice!

THE SHEER EMOTIONAL FORCE of the event had everyone in tears. They held hands, swayed and wept together. Margaret, however, felt marooned by her own scepticism. Her sister had obviously found something special here, among these people, but Margaret was a solitary holdout, unmoved, isolated, consumed only by envy. When, she wondered, would *she* experience such joy?

'I'm so glad you came with me, Margaret,' Charity began, 'I wanted someone else to see—'

'It's certainly exciting,' her sister interrupted.

'Oh, yes' – Charity smiled – 'and ever since Mama died I've felt this empty spot inside me. I never understood quite what it *was* until I heard Isaiah Pound speak tonight. Margaret? I'm *joining* them. They like my playing; they want me to tour with them. I'm going to do it. There's nothing for me here,' said Charity. 'What do you think Father will say?'

'I can't imagine,' Margaret gasped.

LATER, HOWEVER, MARGARET TOLD her father about Charity's intentions and described the Pendletons to him. 'They're even more emphatic than Catholics,' she said. 'The *hell and damnation* theme seems particularly important to them.'

'Should I let her join them?' he asked.

Margaret was incensed by the very idea. 'Absolutely not!'

But Charity pleaded her cause to her father with wrenching urgency. 'They understand me,' she said. 'They appreciate my music. I'm accepted by them. I fit in.' She added that she would never find such satisfaction in Gantrytown. 'This is a chance for me to help save humanity, Papa!'

'What if you fail?' Tom replied. 'What if humanity is a hopeless cause?'

'They need me,' she explained, 'and I need them.'

'Are these people reputable? Trustworthy?'

'They read the Bible every day.'

Tom was tempted to challenge her reply, but he knew doing so would only fire his daughter's obstinacy. He hadn't been able to talk her out of playing at her mother's wake, and he doubted she could be talked out of performing for an appreciative audience. He wished for Lizzy's wisdom on the matter. She would have known what to do. Finally, he made a modest request: 'Will you write? Promise me that?'

'Of course, Papa!'

Charity would have promised him anything to be allowed to pack her bags. So, as she packed, he stood, hands in pockets, asking questions, trying to reconcile himself, for his own peace of mind, to his daughter's departure.

'They believe the end of the world is coming on November eleventh, nineteen eighteen,' Charity explained. 'Armageddon. It is vital to prepare for that day, to save as many souls as possible, so that they may gain entry to heaven.'

'And you *believe* this?'

'Of course!'

Tom frowned. 'Charity, I had an old friend who used to predict Doomsday. It never came, but he would advance the date along the calendar convinced that it was fast approaching. I know that I *cannot* – and I will not – prevent you from doing what you believe is right, but I wonder about the wisdom of this campaign. My friend's name was Pendleton. Perhaps it is a coincidence, or perhaps not . . .'

'Father, I hardly think every old figure from your childhood has relevance to my life.'

Tom gave his youngest daughter a helpless smile. 'I hope that is not the case too. How can I stop you? You are nineteen, a grown woman.'

Charity hugged him, not realizing that his remark was meant as an appeal rather than a concession.

THE NEXT MORNING TOM drove Charity to the fairgrounds. There was frost on the grass. The trucks and caravans were lined up ready to leave.

Before Charity hopped into the Pendletons' battered bus, Tom gave his daughter a copy of Masterson's *Simple Cures to Common Ailments.*

'What's this?' she asked.

'Oh, just a little common sense,' he replied. 'I put a pound note in every chapter,' he explained, hoping this would be an incentive for her to leaf through it at least once.

She hugged him and boarded the bus, and Tom studied his footprints in the frosty grass. He expected to feel lighter of step with Charity on her way in the world, but this was not so. His burden felt heavier.

Audrey had explained this sensation in one of her recent letters about Jonah.

> *The daily vigilance I felt for my son was not relieved when he became old enough to avoid skinning his knees or having his pennies stolen by bullies. Once he could earn his own living, my day-to-day concern for his welfare advanced to concern for the world at large. I became invested in the larger forces that would govern his life – the honesty*

of people, the virtue of authority, the generosity of society towards the weak and unfortunate, and peace between nations.

You see, Tom, once we assume the parental burden, we become helplessly invested in the justice of the playground and, by extension, the justice of the world at large.

A BRIGHT BOY

When Willard Bench became headmaster of St Peter's, Tom decided that the school was doomed. He transferred Arthur to King Henry IV School in Ballydorp.

King Henry's was a more serious school than St Peter's. While the boys of St Peter's entered their fathers' businesses in the Johannesburg suburbs, those at King Henry's were expected to go to college in England. King Henry's link to the mother country was never so obvious as when South Africa announced her entry into the war: seven schoolmasters volunteered. When news came that two had perished while serving on the Western Front, the war lost its abstract quality, even for a fifteen-year-old boy.

Memorial services were held in the great assembly hall – a vaulted room that would have pleased Cedric the Saxon. Each service brought a cry for more men to enlist. It was made clear that King Henry's contribution to the fighting forces, and the peace of the world, was essential.

The boy who had the best command of the facts was Wally Hill, who kept an updated list of all the South African soldiers who had been killed in France, Africa and the Balkan Peninsula. Wally had a missing front tooth, and his surrounding teeth were splayed so that, when he closed his mouth, they rested on his lower lip like tablets. When there was an argument about war statistics, everybody went to Wally to clear the matter up.

By his fifteenth year Arthur was fluent in French, thanks to Madame Wardour. He spoke to her only in French and surprised his teacher at King Henry's with his easy command of the language. No boy at King Henry's was permitted to have an easy time at any subject, however, so Arthur was delivered to Mr Boyle's Latin class, to be humbled by a dead language. Andrew Boyle was a handsome fellow with a thin, drooping moustache and a sophisticated air. He taught a university-level Latin class and inspired many of his boys to become classics scholars, to the dismay of their parents. He was quick to point out that brilliant writers deserved to be read in their own languages. Cicero should be read in Latin, Cervantes in Spanish, Dante in Italian, and Milton in English.

Arthur, however, seemed to trouble Mr Boyle from the start. Within a month or two, the teacher asked for a private meeting with Tom.

'Your son, Mr Chapel,' said Boyle, 'has an extraordinary grasp of language. He understands the rules – declensions, syntax, vocabulary – but he insists on making up everything else.'

'What do you mean?'

'Well' – Boyle paused – 'he invents his own nouns and verbs. They *sound* like Latin, and they conjugate logically, but they are not Latin. It's remarkable.'

'You mean,' Tom replied, 'he is making it up?'

'Yes,' said Boyle. 'I've seen plenty of boys dodge their way through my classes – idiots, many of them, and a few bright ones who are simply too lazy to do the work. But Arthur is no fool. He's not lazy, either. He understands Latin very well. But . . .' Boyle pushed a paper across his desk for the doctor to see. Tom squinted: the words below his son's signature *looked* like Latin.

'Those words don't exist,' said Boyle. 'They make good sense, in a way, and Arthur seems to have invented his own language – which is all very well, brilliant, perhaps, but I can't give him good marks for mastering a tongue I don't understand.'

'What do you propose?'

'He's a bright lad – but solitary. I think he needs a friend.'

Tom admitted that he had been concerned about this for years. Boyle offered to introduce Arthur to other boys.

That was how Arthur met Wally Hill. Wally was personable and sensed Arthur's unusual intelligence. He showed Arthur a code he had put together to foil the enemy. Arthur revealed his secret language. In short, the war became Arthur's social icebreaker.

Arthur pored through the newspapers for war news that Wally would appreciate. When a South African fighter pilot and cricket hero, George McCubbin, shot down the famous German ace Max Immelmann in an air battle over Flanders, Arthur spotted the article in the paper and took it directly to Wally Hill.

'Well done, Chapel. I could use a bright boy like you,' Wally said and engaged him as his deputy. He showed Arthur his 'war room' – a garden shed that had been wallpapered with maps, aeroplane charts, and news clippings about prominent battles. He lent Arthur his dog-eared copy of *The First Hundred Thousand*, by Ian Hay, which Arthur devoured hungrily. It was a funny, rousing description of soldier life under General Kitchener at the beginning of the war.

After his air victory, McCubbin had been given permission to visit the country of his birth. When Arthur discovered plans for the man's visit to Johannesburg in the newspaper, he danced around the house.

Tom protested this: 'Arthur, will you please sit down? I hardly think a victory celebration is appropriate.'

'Why, Papa? He beat the German pilot.'

'What's wrong with supporting our side?' Margaret asked, frowning.

'A war is not a football match,' snapped the doctor. 'When people are dying at the hands of others, only one thing is worth celebrating. The war's end!'

Downcast, Arthur sank into a chair.

Margaret, however, would not let Tom have the last word. Charity's departure had been the final straw for her; although she had never expressed the desire to leave home, she felt that, as the eldest, she should have received the first offer. She frequently sent him out of the house for infractions such as smoking a cigar or pouring himself one too many glasses of sherry. Today, she vented her scorn for his politics. 'Any defeat of the Germans is worth celebrating! Our own neighbours' lives are at stake.'

'Our neighbours?' The doctor balked. 'The other day a patient told me that Immelmann was a relative of hers. She was heartbroken about his death.'

Porridge bowl in hand, the doctor stalked into the garden. His family watched him scatter the oats across the lawn while the birds flocked down.

Iris studied the newspaper. 'It says here that Max Immelmann had studied to be a doctor. How ironic,' she mused.

'Ironic?' said Margaret.

Iris gave her sister a patronizing smile. 'Surely you, as a nurse, know the Hippocratic oath, darling: *First, do no harm.*'

LETTER FROM ABROAD

TOM RECEIVED A LETTER FROM CHARITY THAT WAS JOYFUL AND detailed, describing the camaraderie of her flock, the singing of psalms, the joy of the mission, and the exotic cities she was visiting as the Pendletons toured South America – Buenos Aires, Montevideo, São Paulo, Rio de Janeiro, Caracas. 'I send my love to you, Margaret, Iris and Arthur,' she wrote, with more emotion than she had ever expressed at home. It occurred to Tom that perhaps the Pendletons had, indeed, liberated his daughter. She was seeing places and people who might change her philosophy and her sense of herself. He hoped her exposure to so much of the world might disabuse her of the conviction that Armageddon was the only solution to its ills.

Carnahan's letters to Iris were all the same: a mundane description of drills, brief moments of fighting, and an expression of undying love. When she read them, Iris felt ashamed that she did not love him. The letters began to gather, unopened, on the sideboard. A visitor changed that. Peter Carnahan's mother, looking as if the wind had blown her to the Chapels' door, appeared clutching a yellow telegram. Her eyes were red with fury. 'I've been informed of Peter's death on August seventeenth, nineteen fifteen,' Mrs Carnahan said, her voice cracking bitterly. 'But I'm sure it's wrong.'

Carnahan's mother had badgered the cricket umpires during his games; Peter could do no wrong and, apparently, that included dying. She held up the telegram between thumb and forefinger.

'Place of birth: Parkhurst,' she read. 'Well, *that's* wrong. He was born in Parktown.' She settled on another line. 'Age twenty-one. Well, he's twenty-five, so *that's* wrong *too*! I ask you, Iris, how am I to know whether this Peter Carnahan is *mine* or some other luckless mother's boy?'

Iris had met the woman only once before, when she had visited Peter's house to be greeted frostily: 'How is Margaret? Such a pretty girl.' Iris recalled the many photographs of Peter on every mantelpiece and table – the woman lived for her son.

'Mrs Carnahan,' began Iris, 'I'm sure I have a letter more recent than August the seventeenth.' As she said it, however, she began to panic: as long as the letters had arrived, she had assured herself that Peter was alive and well. As she sifted through the envelopes, Carnahan's mother stood at the threshold, tall, glassy-eyed, and furious.

'Here it is,' Iris remarked with relief, when she found it. The letter was addressed to her in Carnahan's clumsy script – he was a graceful athlete, but his writing was almost illegible.

'Look,' she said, showing the date to Mrs Carnahan, hoping that would satisfy the woman.

'Read it to me,' the mother commanded, lowering her broad frame into an armchair.

Iris opened the letter, read the first line, and caught her breath.

'Read it,' Mrs Carnahan repeated.

'*Dearest Iris*,' she read.

As I write this, my feet rest in six inches of mud. I think I must have a slight fever because the evening actually seems less dismal than usual. A very light rain falls about us, and tiny droplets linger on our uniforms. We look as if we are sheathed in silver. We'd be magnificent if we weren't so miserable. At nightfall we're to attack a machine gun position. It's the third try in as many days, and I've been out twice before to bring back the wounded from earlier assaults. It feels like a matter of luck, Iris, and I can only hope for the best.

My captain has given up trying to read my scrawl and simply stamps my letters 'censored' as a formality, which is why I dare say the following: Iris, it's awful here. Haven't had a bath in weeks. Nobody knows what's going on. Two boys doing reconnaissance this morning were shot down by friendly fire. I worry less about being killed by a German than by someone on my side.

I'm giving this note to a fine fellow next to me named Harry Dill. If you receive it, I'm afraid my luck has run out.

Iris lowered the letter. There must be some mistake, she thought. Nobody of her age had ever died. At least, nobody she knew well. Then she wondered if she and Mrs Carnahan had at least one thing in common: both had believed it impossible for Peter to be dead. Impossible.

'Is there any more?' asked Mrs Carnahan.

Iris was never normally at a loss for words, but now she didn't know what to say. She felt the pressure of a hand on her shoulder. Mrs Carnahan's lips trembled by her ear. 'Is there more in the letter, dear?'

'Yes,' gasped Iris.

'Please—' It was a plea. 'Read it.'

Iris focused her eyes on the words.

Here's a funny thing: I have named our trench Horvaths' Orchard in your honour, dear Iris, because that was the last happy moment I can remember. When my knees start to wobble, I just imagine you marching through the apple trees half-naked in my trousers, and it still makes me laugh. Thank you, Iris, for all the good memories. I will love you always, Peter.

Iris dropped the letter.

Mrs Carnahan rose from her chair. 'Would you show me the orchard?'

'What?' said Iris.

'I want to see the orchard he mentioned.'

Iris wiped away her tears with the palms of her hands. 'It's a long way . . .' she said, tipping her head in the direction.

'Please,' said Mrs Carnahan. '*Please,* Iris.'

So they made their way down the path behind the Horvaths' property, up past a row of white stinkwood trees, along a stone wall, and entered a grove of apple trees. The grass was soft and thick. As Mrs Carnahan surveyed the scene of her son's last carnal experience, Iris felt a creeping sense of humiliation.

'How pretty.' Mrs Carnahan sighed, turning from the trees to Iris. 'How often did you come here?'

Iris blanched. Did the woman really need to know how often she had *slept* with her son?

'Oh, Mrs Carnahan,' Iris gasped. 'I don't know. What does it matter now?' The strength drained from her legs, and she sank to the grass, overcome with remorse. Poor Peter, with his tender pledges, his innocent affection, his pride, and his last words: *I will love you always.*

'I'm sorry,' Iris wept, 'I'm so sorry—'

Mrs Carnahan knelt beside her. 'I'm sorry too.'

Iris shook her head and sobbed. 'He was such a nice, sweet boy. I should have told him not to go!'

The look on Mrs Carnahan's face, however, was not reproachful. 'Well, my dear, at least you turned him into a man. The army did nothing but turn him into a corpse.'

MRS CARNAHAN REQUESTED that Iris stand beside her at Peter's memorial service. She sent a black dress for her to wear; it was a gorgeous, elaborate thing of black lace, with many layers and ruffles. Even Margaret admired its quality. Iris took one look in the mirror and realized with horror that it was, in effect, a wedding dress.

When Mr and Mrs Carnahan arrived to escort Iris to the church, Tom sent Arthur outside to chat with them while he searched the house for her.

He found her buried under the sofa cushions – her favourite spot as a child.

'Don't tell them I'm here, Papa,' Iris begged.

'Iris, it's a memorial service. Poor Carnahan.'

'But they're treating me like his *wife*,' said Iris. 'I didn't deserve to be his wife. I certainly don't deserve to be *treated* like his wife.'

Tom smiled at his daughter. 'You make a very pretty widow,' he admitted.

'Poor Peter,' Iris fretted. 'He was so simple. I'm an absolute spider! I'm a monster, Papa, a *monster*! Margaret will be looking at me with that serves-you-bloody-right expression on her face. I can't do it!'

'You were always so good at make-believe, Iris. I remember listening to you in the afternoons from my office.'

Iris looked at her father. 'Make-believe?'

'Just for today,' said Tom. 'The service can't last *forever*, can it?'

'I suppose not,' she said.

So, as the Carnahans' voices echoed in the hall, Iris clambered out of her hiding place while Tom shook out the beautiful black dress and hoped his assurances would be confirmed.

IT WAS A SUCCESSFUL memorial service – if such events can be successful. Kind words were spoken about Carnahan's character; he was remembered as a brilliant athlete and a good fellow. His life had been so short – there wasn't much to say, so faith was pledged in the armed forces, the Allies, and all the courageous boys doing their bit for the war effort.

The young clergyman who delivered the sermon was new, sent from a seminary in Cape Town. Tall, nervous and awkward, John Bonney had a large, shiny face and receding temples. His eyes searched the mourners for approval and finally settled on Margaret, whose slender figure, full bosom, and saintly face startled him. By the end of the sermon, his eyes addressed her only. Margaret was perplexed; she had never suffered such scrutiny without feeling angry, but his demeanour was sincere and appealing.

In subsequent weeks Iris found herself adopted by Mrs Carnahan. She was invited to join her in church on Sundays, pressed to attend birthday celebrations, and summoned for the burial of Bumsy, one of the family's three Yorkshire terriers. Mrs Carnahan even confided her most private feelings to Iris about their first encounter. 'I thought you were one of those girls who turn an honest, brave boy into a craven sensualist,' she said, 'but Peter was brave to the end.'

'Oh, I *am* awful,' Iris admitted, hoping this would exempt her from the next pet burial.

'Oh, no, Iris. Peter always said you were a fine girl, and I agree.'

Those words haunted Iris. The last thing she wanted was to be a *fine girl.* 'God help me, Papa,' she complained. 'What man in Gantrytown will come near me now? I might as well have been buried with him. I'm doomed – *doomed*!'

KINGS AND CHARISMATICS

TOM UNDERSTOOD IRIS'S BURDEN AND GUESSED THAT SHE WOULDN'T have any peace until she left Gantrytown. He was not about to suggest that she go, however. He still missed Charity, for she had tempered Margaret's rage. Without Charity to help at mealtimes, Margaret threw food upon the table and often withdrew plates before the family had finished eating. She clearly hated housekeeping and her role as her father's assistant but refused Tom's offers to hire a nurse. She couldn't allow a stranger to replace her mother.

Charity's next communication would be her last. Instead of a letter, it was a postcard, with the Pendletons' oddly cheerful motto: 'PREPARE FOR THE END – REJOICE!'

'In this mission,' Charity wrote, 'we must all act as one, cast aside our doubts, our differences, our conceits.' The tone of her message was far less exuberant than that of the last; in fact, Charity seemed to be describing an internal struggle. She said that the Pendletons were returning to England to focus on their 'most urgent mission'.

Her last words troubled Tom. 'Don't be alarmed if you do not hear from me for a while.'

'Well, no news is good news,' said Iris, thinking of Peter Carnahan's last letter.

'She's probably in love, Papa.' Margaret was convinced that her sister was enjoying the very pleasures she was denied.

As the war swept up recruits across the Southern Hemisphere, the Pendletons gathered converts in increasing numbers. New Zealanders, Australians and South Africans all harkened to the possibility that the Great War was, in fact, God's rallying call. Never before had millions died in a conflict. Perhaps the end *was* near.

WHEN JOHN BONNEY paid the Chapel family a social visit, it stretched into a four-hour marathon. Tom and Arthur were confused. They couldn't understand Margaret's suddenly buoyant mood, or the vicar's lack of purpose. Margaret would not let him leave. She peppered him with questions and served him, to Arthur's count, six cups of tea. Lovers in the first stages of attraction speak in harmonic dissonance – echoing and remarking on things that make no sense to anyone else but their intended. The rest of the family looked on, baffled by the tone of conversation, and astonished at the capacity of the man's bladder.

Iris was first to pick up on the courtship. She caught the vicar stealing a glance at Margaret's figure as she left the room to boil the kettle and surmised a courtship.

'So, Mr Bonney,' she said, with calculated innocence, 'are you single? Any prospects?'

'None,' stuttered the vicar.

'Ah, a free man,' intoned Iris. 'Perhaps you don't *wish* to be so.'

This caused Margaret to stamp back into the dining room. 'That was hardly an appropriate remark to a clergyman, Iris! You should be ashamed of yourself.'

'I was only making conversation,' Iris chirped.

Margaret glared at her sister, then smiled for the vicar's benefit. 'Biscuits?' she inquired, laying a plate before him.

'Margaret's biscuits are the best,' said Iris, with a saucy wink. 'In fact, I composed a limerick about—'

'*God spare us*, Iris!' cried Margaret.

'I like limericks—' began the vicar.

'Not my sister's—'

'But surely—'

'No!'

Iris watched the exchange between Margaret and the vicar with amusement. 'You two make quite a couple. You won't let each other finish a sentence, just like two old ladies who've been living together half their lives.'

Here, Margaret turned crimson, the vicar stared at his cup, and Tom realized what was happening. It was clearly a painful ordeal for such an angry young woman to feel tenderness. He decided that she deserved the right to proceed without interference; Iris must leave before she said something to shatter the delicate courtship.

'Iris, there's a production of *King Lear* this evening. I think you should go. Take Arthur!' Tom ordered.

'I'll stay at home,' said Iris breezily. 'I prefer a good domestic drama.'

'I'll pay,' insisted her father.

THE POSTER SAID, 'Straight from London's West End', but the reviews were all at least two years old. The travelling company, the Barber Street Players, claimed to have played *King Lear* on 'three continents' in its mission to bring the Bard to Britannia's farthest outposts. Since Gantrytown had no theatres, the production was staged at the Masonic temple.

'What's it about?' asked Arthur as they took their seats.

'The king's gone mad,' explained Iris. 'He decides to split his kingdom between his daughters, with the best share going to the daughter who praises him most. The dishonest sisters claim to love him more than life itself, while the honest one admits that part of her heart will always belong to her husband. The king, of course, splits his kingdom between the lying daughters, and the honest daughter gets nothing.'

Arthur smiled vaguely, realizing why it appealed to his outspoken sister. 'What happens to the king?' he asked.

'He rants and raves while his fool says, "I told you so." '

'What's the point?' replied Arthur, who had learned from Iris always to expect a point to any story.

'The point?' She frowned. 'There *must* be a point, mustn't there?' She thought for a moment and finally came to a conclusion. 'In order to proceed in life,' she began, 'one must *act*, as Lear does, but a rash judgment can result in tragedy. It's quite terrifying how the most careless action can lead to such trouble.' She thought of her own travails with the Carnahan family. Her spectacles began to turn foggy, so she removed them and gave the lenses a furious rub.

Arthur put his arm around his sister. At sixteen, he was now several inches taller than she. 'Are you all right, Iris?' he inquired.

'Oh, bugger it all, Piglet, I don't know what's wrong with me!' she wept. 'My eyes are waterworks these days. It's a good thing it's dark in here.'

She locked her arm in his and rubbed her lenses on Arthur's shirtsleeve.

'Does anybody die in this play?' he asked.

'Lots of people. It's a tragedy.'

'Excellent,' Arthur replied.

When the houselights were dimmed, the entire cast appeared onstage to express a few words of condolence for 'our fallen heroes'; then after a rendition of 'God Save the King', the play began.

Almost as soon as King Lear appeared, Iris felt an all-consuming relief to be burdened only by the troubles of a mad king and his misunderstood daughter. When Tom had first told her that his father had played Lear, Iris had set about learning the play in much the same way that someone might memorize cricket statistics or the values of obscure stamps.

The production was uneven but moving. The actor playing Lear portrayed a grand, vain, bombastic and childish man. When his daughters betrayed him, the audience became vocally sympathetic, and some people even hissed at Edmund when he betrayed his stepbrother. But it was in the final scenes that something went wrong.

The problem was clear: Cordelia was weak and petulant when she should have been ardent and dedicated. Iris became so exasperated with the actress's intonation that she corrected the woman from her seat; during one monologue, the audience was listening to Iris rather than to the Cordelia onstage.

In the final scene, when Lear was expected to enter carrying his dead daughter, the actor playing the king merely gestured to her in the wings because the actress was fifty pounds heavier than he was. At that moment, Iris issued a contemptuous sigh.

Nevertheless, the house gave the cast a hearty standing ovation for honouring such a distant colonial outpost with the Bard. Iris, however, reserved her praise for the actor playing Lear.

When people filed out, Arthur felt himself tugged towards the stage. 'We're going to say hello,' Iris explained.

'Iris, they'll be furious!'

Nevertheless, Iris led him onto the stage and meandered through the wings in search of the cast.

Lear sat on a stool, his white hair and beard putting him, in Arthur's view, on the old side of seventy.

Iris took a gallant step forward, and a torrent of praise spilled out of her. 'I loved everything you did!' she gushed. *'Thank you!'*

Arthur was baffled by his sister's gratitude, but the actor took it happily. He removed his beard with a slight wince to reveal a man on the younger side of fifty.

'*Everything?*' echoed Lear. He wiped his face with a towel, removing wrinkles that had been drawn on and the grease that had hollowed his cheeks. Then he reached behind his head and removed the white wig to reveal a mop of shaggy brown hair and a face no older than thirty-five.

'Well, *almost* everything,' Iris conceded. 'Cordelia was a bit off, wasn't she?'

The man replied archly, 'A bit *off*, you say?'

'Actually a *terrible* disappointment,' Iris amended. 'I mean, she's supposed to be the voice of reason, isn't she? Not a *twit*!'

The actor seemed torn between loyalty to his troupe, and amusement at Iris's nerve. Finally, he chuckled. 'You could do it better, I suppose?'

Iris promptly quoted Cordelia's pivotal words, the words that had lost her her share of Lear's kingdom: 'That lord whose hand must take my plight shall carry half my love with him, half my care and duty: Sure, I shall never marry like my sisters, to love my father all.'

Arthur watched his sister turn into Cordelia for a few moments and was quite impressed.

Apparently the actor agreed, because he asked her to repeat the lines, which she did. He looked her up and down, inquired about her weight, then invited her to say the same few lines to the stage manager, a bald fellow named Mr Spalding, who was upbraiding his two assistants a few yards away.

'Spalding! I'd like you to hear something,' said the actor.

The stage manager cursed. Fingers pressed to his temples, he approached and listened to Iris speak her lines. Arthur observed that the actor, whose name on the bill was Gregory Limpkin, now removed his nose, which was made of rubber. He had an odd face, which lacked any defining lines. His age became perplexing, for in his features, he resembled a baby with full pink cheeks and a button nose. The comparison, however, ended at the neck, for he had a small man's frame.

Upon hearing Iris speak, the stage manager and Mr Limpkin shared a few words. Then Mr Spalding asked her how well she knew the play.

'By heart,' Iris replied, and to prove it she delivered Edmund's 'excellent foppery of the world' lines.

Arthur, meanwhile, became distracted by the chaos of the backstage area. The actors were shedding their costumes and turning into normal people, the scenery was being dismantled, and the lighting along the stage extinguished, leaving little wisps of smoke to trail after the footsteps of the crew.

On the tram home, Iris linked an arm around her brother's. She waited until they had reached halfway before she confessed a secret. 'Guess what, Piglet! They've invited me to be their Cordelia.'

'What? You mean, join the theatre?'

'Well – the company. They go from town to town performing in schools, theatres, churches, and wherever they can find a stage.'

'What fun,' said Arthur, thinking of them running around in their costumes and the pageantry of Lear's court. It all seemed to merge in his head.

'Oh, Piglet, it's an awful life,' she sighed. 'Lots of travelling. No money. They share lodgings. It's a shabby existence. Certainly no life for a respectable schoolteacher.'

Arthur saw the thrill in his sister's eyes, and his heart sank. He knew he was about to lose her.

THE MISSION

THE CHANGE IN IRIS'S MOOD SIGNALLED TO HER FATHER THAT something had happened. He learned more from Arthur and telephoned Dr Wardour to find out about the Barber Street Players. They were a small, dedicated company that had performed at the Gantrytown Masonic temple several years before. Their production of *Lear* was booked in three cities in Australia and two in New Zealand. The cast was paid a small but regular salary. William Bedlam would have been envious.

Secretly Tom attended the play. He was surprised and moved to see Iris as Cordelia. She seemed to hold the audience from the moment she walked onstage, and when Lear dismissed her, there were murmurs of disappointment from the seats. Tom fled before the lights went up, but Iris seemed to know that he had been there.

At breakfast, she told him of her plans.

He replied soberly: 'One daughter takes to the Bible like her grandmother; another to the theatre like her grandfather. Please tell me what mistake I made in your upbringing.'

'Papa, actors *can* be honourable,' Iris replied.

'They all disgust me!' cried the doctor.

'Are there not dishonourable doctors?' she replied.

'How dare you?' her father said in despair.

Iris removed her spectacles. 'Papa, I don't want to hurt you, but I can't stay here. I need to find something to do with my life that is satisfying, not merely *appropriate.* I'm damned if I'll stay at St Peter's. I'll die of boredom!'

Tom looked stricken. 'And what if you fail, Iris?'

'Oh, Papa' – she smiled – 'I'm young. I can bear a few slings and arrows.'

'Iris—' He held his breath.

'Oh, God, Papa, please don't cry,' she said.

Tom buried his head in his hands. As Iris packed her books and clothes, he considered Audrey's advice and realized that, as his personal burden was lifted, his investment in the decency of the outside world was now doubled.

Tom was hiding amid the hibicus when Iris came to say that she was ready to leave. Tom stood and looked at her. 'What'll I do without you, Iris? Without your wit, your limericks, your troublemaking?' he asked.

She smiled. 'You'll have Arthur to worry about.'

At the train station, Tom presented her with a copy of Masterson's *Simple Cures to Common Ailments.* 'There's money between the pages,' he said.

'I've found it already,' Iris said with a smile.

'Have fun, Iris,' he said. 'And if you're not having fun, please come home.'

She disappeared into the train, her suitcase trailing clothing, for she had packed quickly.

Tom walked along the platform, chiding Arthur as they went. 'Didn't you try to dissuade her?'

'Yes,' said Arthur, and then remembered something: 'But, Papa, *you* suggested she see the play.'

Tom frowned. 'As usual, I have only myself to blame.'

Suddenly, a window opened, and Iris's head appeared. Her spectacles were foggy, but she smiled and waved. In the next window beside her, another face appeared: a man, with a babyish smile. He nodded pleasantly and gave Tom a brief nod.

'Good heavens,' Tom said. 'The *Orfling*!'

'The what?' cried Arthur.

'The Orfling!' Tom shouted.

The man in the window grinned, and the train shunted forward as Tom pondered the strange convergence of his past with the lives of his children – first the Pendletons, and now *Lear*, with the face of the Orfling.

KING HENRY'S

ONE MORNING, GAZING INTO THE MIRROR, ARTHUR RECOGNIZED TOM'S features. It was a moment of pride and despair, for though he considered his father a handsome man, Arthur had imagined springing into manhood self-made and unique. Now he realized the curse of procreation – his peers' faces were assuming their parents' aspect. Ernest Wiggers had inherited his father's potato-shaped nose; Wally Hill had become gaunt, and when Arthur met his mother, he could barely tell them apart. Across the dinner table, he stole glances at Tom, tallying his father's best qualities against his weaker ones. He decided he wouldn't mind his father's jawline, but the furtive eyes were to be avoided. It would be satisfying to have a beard like Dr Tom's, but Arthur didn't like the wiry hairs at his ears.

'What is it?' his father inquired, his fork in midair.

'Did you look like *your* father?' Arthur asked.

'Unfortunately, yes,' Tom replied and shot Arthur a sympathetic glance.

'Is he alive?'

Tom frowned at his plate. 'I don't know. We were at odds.'

'Why?'

'Arthur,' Tom replied, 'I hope you don't have the same contempt for your father that I had for mine, but I fear it is inevitable.'

'Oh, no,' Arthur promised. 'I never shall.'

Margaret, who had been listening without comment, now stole a glance at her brother.

'It is inevitable – ask your sister,' Tom told him.

WHEN ARTHUR WASN'T IMPRISONED in a classroom with his knees bobbing helplessly beneath the table, he was marking charts with the advances of the Allied forces. Madame Wardour took to slapping his knee with a ruler when his leg bobbed too much during piano lessons. 'I cannot wait for you to grow up,' she remarked after one lesson. 'There is nothing more irritating than the restlessness of an adolescent!'

'I'm seventeen,' Arthur replied. 'It's almost over.'

'Hardly,' she rejoined. 'You have ten years of stupidity ahead of you.'

A boy in Arthur's grammar class, Crockett by name, became popular for passing around a set of racy photographs. They had come from his cousin who lived across the ocean in a wondrous place known as Coney Island where, apparently, American women walked around wearing practically nothing but skintight black swimwear. He charged twopence to boys who wanted to take the grimy, dog-eared photos home for the night and made a substantial fortune. Arthur, however, had seen his sisters in various states of undress, as well as naked women in his father's medical books, and was unimpressed. He cut out some of the more arousing medical pictures, mounted them on cards, and offered them for the same price. Within a day, he was hauled before his headmaster, Mr Poole. Tom was called to the school and argued with Mr Poole, in front of Arthur, about the pictures.

'They are medical photographs. What is the matter?'

The headmaster was incredulous. 'Isn't it obvious?' he said. 'They are indecent pictures, especially for boys who are easily aroused and sure to be confused by their significance.'

'Aroused? Confused?' Tom laughed. 'Good heavens, if they don't start being confused and aroused now, they'll never catch up with the rest of us!'

'I'm sure I need not remind you that they are young men,' Poole replied. 'We are trying to cultivate loftier sentiments here.'

'Loftier sentiments? Such as crushing the enemy on a hockey field?'

'Now, Doctor, you can hardly compare lust with the merit of sport.'

Tom sighed. 'Quite right. We each owe our *existence* to lust. What can we attribute to hockey, aside from relieving a few lads of their front teeth?'

Cornered, the headmaster smiled. 'We can argue about degree, Doctor, but your son should not be selling photographs of naked women at King Henry's. The board of trustees expects me to expel him; instead, I am willing to give him another chance.'

Tom prepared to leave, his hand on his son's shoulder, when a thought struck him and he whirled around. 'What about the other fellow, Crockett? I don't see *his* father here.'

'His pictures were of clothed women.'

'Aah,' Tom sniffed. 'Neither arousing nor confusing, then?'

During the tram ride home, Arthur waited for his father to reprimand him, but Tom simmered in silence. Finally, the boy could bear it no longer. 'I'm sorry, Papa,' he said.

The doctor winced. 'How much did you make from the pictures?'

'Only about sixpence. Then Crockett saw them, and that's when I was sent to the head's office.'

Now Tom smiled. 'Crockett, eh? I expect he reported you because he was afraid you might drive him out of business.' The tram came to a halt at their stop, and Tom looked at his son with amusement. 'Forget about this,' he said. 'There are far worse things you could do.'

Margaret and Mr Bonney were waiting at the house when they returned. Tom sensed fresh tension and halted with Arthur at the doorstep, wondering what new crisis might greet him.

MARGARET AND BONNEY

'THE THING IS, WE HAVE BEEN TALKING, AND FEEL—' BEGAN BONNEY.

'*Together*, for we are in agreement,' interrupted Margaret.

'That the time has come to make our wishes—'

'What are you talking about?' asked Tom.

'Marriage?' ventured Bonney, looking cautiously at Margaret.

'Of course!' she cried.

'And we seek it with your blessing, sir.'

'My blessing?' replied Tom. He wondered how Margaret and Bonney could possibly endure together. His daughter seemed to bully the vicar at every visit. She ended his sentences, corrected his remarks, even directed his eating habits – reduced the sugar in his tea, urged him to eat his vegetables. *Was that love?* All this time, Tom had pitied the man for his infatuation. It hardly seemed a romantic match; Margaret offered not the slightest gesture of physical affection. Tom had expected her to fall for a man whose temperament echoed hers – an angry chef, perhaps, who banged pans and wrenched half-eaten meals from beneath the noses of his guests.

Should he set this gentle fellow free by denying him his daughter? Tom stood up and buried his hands in his trouser pockets.

'Father,' said Margaret, impatiently, 'does he have your blessing or not?'

Tom frowned at his daughter. 'Don't badger me, Margaret. I would like a private word with him, if you don't mind.'

Bonney rose, and Tom took his prospective son-in-law into the garden, behind the hibiscus bushes.

'*Of course* you have my permission, Bonney,' he whispered, 'but before you do something you may regret, let me ask you this: Where will be the fun in it? She does nothing but finish your sentences and criticize you. Please don't misunderstand me, I love her dearly and wish to see her happy, but you must understand why I worry about the equality of this enterprise. What is in it for *you* – if I may ask?'

The vicar seemed amused by his appeal. 'Sir,' he began, 'Margaret seeks *certainty*. She derives more pleasure from *ending* my sentences than I achieve from *beginning* them. In short, I do not mind that.

'In my work, I must view two sides to most matters, sir,' he continued. 'I've counselled unhappy husbands and wives, bitter parties, estranged relatives. It is my job to be impartial, sometimes to a fault. I am always available, I do not turn anyone away. Margaret, however, is judgmental. She fills this void in my nature. She is my advocate when I strive to please too many people at once. She insulates me, bolts the door at the end of the day, puts an end to my ruminations before they consume me.'

'And you grant her this authority?' asked Tom.

'I do, sir.'

'And she doesn't bully you as she bullies me?' asked her father. 'Because I have breakfast in the garden out of terror of her moods.'

'Never, sir,' said Bonney.

'Very well.' Tom sighed, adopting the compassionate expression he reserved for the incurably afflicted. 'It's not a marriage I understand, I'll admit that, but I'm willing to permit it.'

They returned from the garden to find Margaret and Arthur seated at dinner. Then Bonney reached for Margaret's hand, clasped it, and assured her that all was settled. Tom kissed his daughter's cheek and felt, in her sway, a softening of the fury that had risen between them. Perhaps, he thought, this was simply Margaret's way of leaving home.

'The wedding shall be on November eleventh, next year,' she said. 'That will give us time to plan everything perfectly.'

'Very prudent,' said Tom. 'I'm happy for you both.'

'November eleventh, nineteen eighteen?' said Arthur. 'Isn't that the day the Pendletons predicted the end of the world?'

'Yes,' said Margaret, 'but nobody believes it will happen!'

Tom turned to Bonney. 'Well, John? Do we agree that the world will not end on that day?'

'It is my ardent belief that it will not, sir!' said Bonney, and he embraced Margaret, who tolerated this for a moment, then dusted his jacket and wiped the shine off his forehead with her handkerchief.

AS THE WEATHER GREW sultry, the dark-panelled corridors of King Henry's stank with the odour of ripening adolescents. The masters were used to it, but the younger boys often hurried down the hall holding their noses. As scores of them worked out their frustration on the football pitch, others fed the burning fuse of this wild age with smutty verses scrawled in the bathroom cubicles, angry tirades about God and country, and jokes played upon boys whose voices were slow to change, or who hadn't grown pubic hair. Some were ridiculed by their mothers' names: Wally Hill suffered the indignity of being known as Fiona for most of his senior year. Ernest Wiggers kept a little red book in which he awarded stars to local girls depending on their willingness to kiss, grope or indulge in other racy activities. The masters periodically confiscated it – though mainly to satisfy their own curiosity. Wiggers named his tome *The Book of Virgins*, which wasn't entirely accurate since he awarded four stars (the highest rating) to two girls whose actions, by definition, disqualified their inclusion on the list. When Mr Poole's daughter earned a four-star rating, Wiggers's parents were summoned, the boy was suspended and the book vanished. The legend lived on, however; an enterprising Greek teacher spread a rumour that the book's pages were scattered among the classics in the library, which inspired a run on Aeschylus, Herodotus and the dustiest Homeric texts.

Though a few King Henry's boys might have been seen riding the Gantrytown trams arm in arm with two-star virgins on a Saturday night, the majority, Arthur included, were terrified by sexual attraction and turned their interests to that other vessel of passion – the war.

It was in the newspapers every day; it was *good* versus *evil* and *us* versus *them;* it made men of boys and heroes of clay. It shattered families, created orphans, robbed parents, and widowed spouses. It was a seduction, a distraction, an entertainment and an addiction. At King Henry's, the boys marvelled at the technological advances that separated this war from all other wars: mustard gas, phosgene, U-boats, depth charges, hydrophones, machine guns, tanks, biplanes, zeppelins. It was the war of the future.

Andrew Boyle, the debonair Latin master, considered it a war as old as time. He drew upon the writings of Julius Caesar and Marcus Aurelius to put the novelty of battle into perspective. Eventually, he came under scrutiny by some parents when he sent his pupils home with a remark by Cicero: 'An unjust peace is better than a just war.'

A letter was published in the *King Henry's Gazette* that said, 'The master who chooses to undermine our brave fighters would do well to reconsider his influence on young minds.'

Boyle's orderly classes were interrupted by pupils wishing to take issue with his pacifism. They left cards with the words *coward* and *traitor* in his books and jacket pockets and heckled him during lessons.

'When are *you* going to war, sir?'

'Would you rather fight for the Allies or the Germans, sir?'

'What did Cicero say about the *Huns,* sir?'

In 1917, a single man in his twenties could not live in Gantrytown without being asked about his contribution to the war effort. Andrew Boyle faced twice that pressure because of the rumours that erupted from the *Gazette* letter and the hostility engendered by his remarks. One day, to the surprise of many, he announced his enlistment in the officers' corps.

Almost immediately, twenty boys committed themselves to follow him onto the battlefield after they had left school.

Tom, who considered Boyle the institution's last bastion of common sense, asked him if he'd lost his mind.

'My mind? Not yet,' he replied. 'But I feel the ground slipping beneath my feet. Who am I to preach about war? I've seen nothing of it with my own eyes.'

'What is to become of any generation if it refuses to learn from history?' Tom asked.

'Didn't you serve in the South African war?' Boyle asked him.

'I did, but I regretted it.'

'Well, I must confess, Doctor, that I, too, value hindsight over ignorance,' Boyle replied.

AT THE END of term, Wally Hill made a present of his maps and newspaper articles to Arthur. 'I don't need these any more,' he said.

'Oh,' said his friend. 'Have you found a girl?'

'No.' Wally laughed. 'I've enlisted.'

He hardly seemed the type; he was so thin and skittish. Although he was an expert on troop movements, the thought of him thrusting a bayonet at anyone was laughable.

Wally had been inspired by Andrew Boyle's announcement of his enlistment: it had instantly reclassified the 'soldier type' as urbane, scholarly and dashingly handsome. Quite a few lads who might have lived long, sedate and scholarly lives would die on Flanders fields for following Boyle's example.

'I want to go to the Western Front,' said Wally, 'earn a few medals, and come back here to teach, just like Boyle.'

'But you're not old enough,' said Arthur, who knew that the enlistment age was eighteen and a half. Wally had just turned eighteen.

'I got into a conversation with the recruiting officer about the Battle of the Somme,' Wally explained. 'I knew tons more about it than he did! He let me through without even looking at my papers! If you're eighteen, you can probably pass, as long as you don't have flat feet or bad eyes.'

Arthur's subsequent conversations with Wally rarely veered from his enlistment plans. Wally's family was having a big party for him before he left.

It was another big adventure, and Arthur could barely keep envy at bay. He played the piano with the school orchestra at the farewell assembly, which Dr Chapel attended with Margaret and John Bonney.

On the stage, the debonair Andrew Boyle appeared in uniform and was given an enthusiastic send-off. All the boys who had enlisted were asked to walk up for a round of applause. Their jubilation was in sharp contrast to the ambivalence of their parents. Never had Tom seen a group of more anxious faces. The masters were grim – five of their peers had been killed in the war; now another two were missing in action. As prayers were said for the fallen, the older folk stifled tears while the young applauded the handsome boys before them. Suddenly Tom noticed that his son was enthralled by those gallant figures. A grin split Arthur's face as he played the first notes of 'Onward, Christian Soldiers'. The doctor felt an urge to seal the boy's eyes and ears from this madness and carry him home, but it was too late.

AFTERWARDS, JOHN BONNEY accompanied Tom back to the house. The crickets chirped, and the scent of sweet peas from the gardens they passed enriched the night air.

'What a moving occasion,' declared Bonney.

'What a *waste* of time,' replied Tom.

Bonney's smile faded.

'If I had known I was to be subjected to a recruitment rally,' said Tom, 'I'd have stayed at home and removed a few tonsils!'

At this moment Margaret and Arthur caught up with them. 'Since when have you been removing tonsils in the evening, Papa?' she remarked.

'If patriotism could be removed as easily as tonsils, I'd work night and day, believe me,' said the doctor.

Bonney laughed nervously. 'Surely we must acknowledge the war effort.'

'Then let us acknowledge *foolishness* too,' replied Tom. 'And folly and *stupidity*. When millions of men die for no good reason . . .'

'It is a shame,' Bonney agreed. 'But we cannot abrogate our responsibilities. Once a war is begun, we should be dedicated to its end!'

Tom frowned at the young man. 'And if everybody were to walk off the battlefield – that would be an ending, would it not?'

'Well, of course, but—'

'I've heard stories of soldiers calling a truce to remove their dead and wounded from the battlefield,' said the doctor. 'If a truce can last a few hours, why can it not be extended ad infinitum?'

'I've heard those stories too' – Bonney smiled – 'but privates cannot run the war, can they? Surely we must have faith in our leadership.'

'It failed us when war was declared,' Tom replied. 'War is the subjugation of reason by might. Thanks to our leaders, we are *all* savages again.'

'Sometimes it's necessary for people to die for a principle,' interrupted Margaret, 'or the principle is not worth defending.'

'What principle?' Tom replied. 'A series of border disputes between nations?'

'Well, sir,' Bonney asserted, 'I believe God is on our side.'

'Oh yes.' Tom nodded. 'And on the side of each dead Englishman, and each dead German. I just hope he's not on *my* side – I may not have long to live!'

Margaret put her hand up to her fiancé's shoulder to buttress him against the doctor's sarcasm. 'Shall we talk about something else?' she said.

Arthur saw an opportunity. 'I'll be eighteen in ten months' time!'

'What are you going to do when you leave school, Arthur?' inquired Bonney, equally anxious to change the subject.

'He'll work with me in the surgery,' replied the doctor. 'He can't come to any harm there.'

'Yes, Arthur will replace me,' said Margaret. 'Then Papa will see what a hard job it is – for *anyone*.'

'I want to go to war,' said Arthur.

'Out of the question,' replied Tom.

'*Everybody's* going to war!'

'And when they return with missing arms and legs, *you'll* be here to sew them back together,' answered the doctor.

'I want to fight!' said Arthur.

Tom felt his heart race. 'Look, Arthur, if you enlist, you'll find no glory, no pride, no happiness, no honour. At best, you'll witness humanity's disaster; at worst, you'll suffer mutilation or death. *I forbid it.* Do you understand?' he shouted.

Arthur stormed past his father into the house.

'How can you speak to him like that?' said Margaret.

'Easily,' Tom told her. 'I don't want Arthur to fall for this foolishness. It *is* foolishness – soldiers, uniforms, valour, patriotism. It's seduction of the young by the old.'

'Foolishness?' repeated Margaret. 'Who told him that boys didn't play with dolls but with toy soldiers? Who told him he must *fit in*? Who is to blame for that? You brought it all on yourself!'

Shaken by her words, Tom changed his tone. 'Margaret, you have no idea how cruel boys can be. I was trying to save him from isolation, from being an *outcast* like—'

'Who sent him to King Henry's?' Margaret continued. 'A school where half of the teachers are enlisted?'

'I did, of course, but—'

'Then what do you expect? *You* turned him into a soldier!'

ON THAT CLEAR, moonless night, the sky seemed to pulse with incredible intensity; each star was a point of brilliance; its power to steer destiny might have caused any sceptic to think twice on such an evening. Father and son couldn't help pondering their fates.

Arthur wished himself in Wally Hill's brand-new army boots and wondered why he was cursed with a father who blocked his way while his fellow classmates were applauded for their willingness to serve.

Tom stood in his garden, horrified by his mistake. All he had meant to do was protect Arthur from the Mansworths and Privots of the world. Margaret was right. He had himself to blame.

He sat down in the grass as the evening clamour of crickets swelled. In his pocket, he felt the impression of a letter he had saved from the mail that morning.

Dearest Tom,

I hope this letter finds you well.

You may remember that my son, Jonah, had been in the Australian Army. The last I heard he was on a ship to Gallipoli.

Within these four walls, I have struggled to instil in my wards a desire to reform, along with the conviction that the outside world is a place of opportunity, hope and second chances.

Oh, Tom, what is wrong with the world? Have they all gone mad?

Audrey

As the stars glittered above him, the doctor emerged from the garden, spent but miserably defiant. Audrey was right, he decided, the world had gone mad. And he was damned if he'd surrender Arthur to such madness.

THE RECRUIT

'How old are you?'

'Eighteen and a half, sir.'

The officer's magnificent moustache was waxed into two perfect semicircles. His eyes were a startling blue, and his tie was perfectly set between a khaki collar and polished brass buttons. Now he put down his fountain pen and stared at the boy with formidable intensity. 'What was the date of your eighteenth birthday?'

'Second of September, sir, nineteen seventeen' came the reply.

The officer's gaze remained fixed on Arthur. It was an interminable moment.

Arthur had memorized the date on the tram ride; it was six months before his actual birthday – today. If they sent him away, he would be disappointed, but he was determined to enlist now, for he suspected that his father would keep a much closer eye on him once he reached his official recruitment age, in six months.

'Very good,' the officer said. He noted the date and directed Arthur along the hall for a medical examination.

Arthur passed everything without difficulty until he came into a small room for his vision test. 'Cover your left eye,' said the doctor, 'and read down the chart.'

Arthur hesitated. Ever since Mr Bench's ultimatum, he had had difficulty distinguishing his left from his right. But now he remembered that his left eye was weaker. Slowly he read out the letters, trying to commit them to memory in preparation for the other eye, but the doctor rapped the table with his pencil. 'I've got a line of men waiting behind you, sonny. Can you read the letters or not?'

Arthur finished quickly. 'Cover your right eye,' said the doctor. At that moment, the nurse called him away. Arthur quickly scanned the three smallest lines, then covered his right eye again.

'Get on with it,' said the doctor, returning.

Arthur recited the lines and waited.

'Good,' snapped the doctor. 'Down the hall, second left.'

An officer presented Arthur with his reporting papers and a railway warrant. 'Next Monday you're to report to Fort Wynyard, Green Point, Cape Town.'

TOM KNEW WHAT HIS son was planning. It was one of the reasons he had employed Arthur in the surgery even before the boy had finished his studies at King Henry's. He trained Arthur to clean wounds, set broken bones, and deliver anaesthesia. One evening he called his son in from the house to help him cauterize the leg of a man whose foot had been crushed under a tractor wheel. Margaret chided her father for exposing the boy to such a horrible sight, but Tom wanted to prepare him for the things he would see at war.

If he couldn't talk him out of enlisting, he planned to recommend Arthur for a position in the medical corps. At least he could ensure his son's safety in one of the mobile hospitals.

But Arthur mentioned none of his medical training to the recruiting officer – he was afraid the man would call his father for confirmation, then send him home.

IN THE WEEK THAT Arthur was to report for duty, Tom went to Pretoria to attend a conference. Arthur left a note for Margaret, went to Johannesburg Station with one of the Horvath boys, and boarded a train bound for Cape Town – eight hundred miles south of the only place he knew in the world.

In the Cape Garrison Artillery, he was taught to roll his puttees, polish his buttons and boots, salute and march. The second week he was trained to load the naval guns at Fort Wynyard, slamming hundred-pound shells into the open gun breeches. The guns were six inches in diameter, and the shells were rammed into position with handspikes. As Arthur staggered under the weight of one, a couple of burly regulars from the garrison striding by laughed at him; each of them had two shells balanced on his shoulders.

After a month of drills, Arthur received his orders to board ship with about seventy other men from the South African Heavy Artillery. The *Walmer Castle* was a commercial steamer that had been turned into a troopship. Another two thousand men came aboard before she left her berth and anchored in the middle of Table Bay, where she waited for a convoy of eight ships to assemble, then sailed north.

The convoy stopped in Sierra Leone, where the cruiser HMS *Britannia* left them in the care of the *King Alfred.* They sailed for twenty-eight days across tropical waters that glittered with phosphorescence as bright as the stars above. One evening a soldier let out a cry when he saw the glowing white tracks of what appeared to be torpedoes heading towards the *Walmer Castle.*

'Those are dolphins, you fool!' replied a more seasoned hand. 'They stir up the phosphorescent algae in the water.'

Portholes were blacked out at night, and no smoking was allowed above decks. Nine ships kept formation in the darkness; not a single light was exposed for fear of giving away their presence to prowling German submarines. But Arthur was oblivious to such dangers, consumed with the thrill of being at sea for the first time, headed for lands he couldn't imagine.

MRS MANSWORTH

'ANY INTERESTING CASES, TODAY, DOCTOR?'

Tom's gloom seemed to have reduced his hearing and vision. Bonney put the question to him again, and Tom tried to muster enough concentration to reply. 'No.'

Though he administered to his patients without difficulty, he found himself walking blindly from the consulting room to the house, oblivious to the fragrances in the garden, the cries of the Horvaths' lonely old parrot, and the greetings of his future son-in-law, whom Margaret invited to dinner every evening. She let her father drink in peace, but there was always a moment during the meal when she turned to him with a patronizing air, as if *he* were the child of the house. 'Not hungry, Papa?' she asked.

'No,' Tom replied. Of course he had no appetite. He hadn't felt hungry for months. Wine and water tasted the same to him, and Margaret had never been much of a cook. She could boil the flavour out of horseradish.

'Surely, sir, you must ponder the incurable cases as philosophers ponder life's paradoxes?' said Bonney.

'Here's a paradox,' Tom snapped. 'A man doesn't know how wealthy he is until he has lost everything – or everyone.'

Margaret's reply was quick: 'Everybody will come back, Papa, I'm sure. They *have* to come back for our wedding, don't they?'

Tom gave his daughter a hard stare. 'We'll ask the Germans and the Turks to suspend hostilities, shall we, so that Arthur can be here? Perhaps a letter to Lord Kitchener will do the trick!'

'Papa, please!' said Margaret.

'Actually,' murmured Bonney, 'Kitchener hasn't been minister of war for two years. He died on the HMS *Hampshire* off the Orkneys . . .'

'I know that,' muttered Tom, though, in truth, he had forgotten. 'Good riddance! He was a butcher. I treated his victims – hundreds of Boer women and children. Their crops burned, livestock slaughtered, wiped out by malnutrition, typhoid, malaria, hundreds, thousands—'

'As you've told us many times . . .' Margaret replied.

Tom's rant was stifled by the condescension in her tone. He glanced at his son-in-law hoping for sympathy, but Bonney was busy aligning his silverware. Tom nursed his embarrassment. Had it come to this? Was he to be cast as the elderly lunatic of the household? Would Margaret be Goneril to his Lear? Without Iris and Charity in the house, his eldest daughter, he decided, was a monster.

Bonney broke the long silence. 'What's the new fellow's name? The new minister?' He looked to Margaret. 'Mansworthy?'

'His name is *Mansworth*,' corrected Margaret.

Tom lowered his glass. 'Mansworth? *Geoffrey Mansworth?*'

Margaret paused. 'Yes. That's it.'

'I went to school with him.'

'Really?'

'I did,' insisted Tom. 'He was a monster.'

'You knew . . . this Mansworth fellow?' said Bonney.

'He murdered my best friend,' Tom replied.

With a glance, Margaret warned Bonney not to encourage him. It had to be nonsense. Her father had never referred to Mansworth before. She was beginning to think Arthur's departure had unhinged him.

'Well,' replied Bonney, with astonishment, 'there must be some mistake. Murderers do not become ministers of war!'

Tom shook his head. 'No. I'm sure it takes years of training.'

He rose from the table, picked up his mail from the desk, and retreated to the garden. Amid the delphinium, larkspur, foxgloves and hollyhocks, he heard the subsequent murmur between his daughter and her fiancé. The words spoken were familiar: *'impossible,' 'bitter,' 'miserable,'* and then *'out of his mind.'*

He sifted through the letters – there was nothing from Arthur. His son's last news had been that he had become an assistant bombardier, which was better than being in the infantry but not as safe as the medical corps. Tom surmised that Arthur had kept his medical experience to himself. Tom had searched his files for any patient who might have had influence with the army, but even Mrs Gantry admitted she had none with the South African war machine. Tom's stomach churned. If only he could do something, *anything* – it seemed so wrong that a parent could devote himself to raising a boy, only to see him sacrifice his life at the first opportunity.

There were two items: a postcard and a letter. The postcard bore a photograph of an ocean liner. Iris's large, emphatic print was unmistakable:

Dearest Papa,

Finished with Lear*! New production is a war protest revue!!! Smashing response in Melbourne!!! Lots of controversy, esp. from politicians saying we're aiding enemy!!! Full house for last six performances!!! Leaving Austral. for Liverpool to do more damage. Love to Piglet, Marg. and the Right Reverend!!!!*

Iris

The stamp on the letter caught his eye. King George's bearded profile was flanked by caducei. It was not a colonial stamp or an armed forces stamp; this missive was from England. The handwriting was vaguely familiar, but it was neither Arthur's nor Audrey's. Tom tore it open as he circled the hibiscus.

My dear Tom,

Why do I choose to write now, after so many years? Not for lack of trying, I assure you. How could I forgive my sister for stealing the man I loved? And how could I forgive you for stealing my dear sister?

With the news of Lizzy's passing, I felt the most acute grief, and the guilt that my own envy was in some way complicit in her illness. I realize now that I need to reconcile such matters. Tom, I am so sad for you and your family. I miss Lizzy more than ever.

I have a family of my own, Tom. A husband whom I love and a daughter on whom I dote. I also realize that I owe my dear sister a debt, as aunt to my nieces and nephew, just as I hope you will honour your role as uncle to my daughter, Josephine. Please forgive my silence, send me news of them and their dear father, and permit me a role in their life, as any loving aunt deserves.

Eve Harding
(Mrs Geoffrey
Mansworth)

Margaret and Bonney observed the doctor from the window. As still as a fence post, he stood amid the purple blossoms. A yellow butterfly alighted on his shoulder and slowly batted its wings; Tom tipped his head slowly to one side, almost as if the butterfly were whispering into his ear. The letter in his hand fell into a spray of Shasta daisies.

Finally, he turned and walked back towards the house. 'I shall book passage to London!' he said.

'Why?' asked his daughter.

'I'm going to bring your brother home,' he explained. 'I've just learned that the minister of war is also my brother-in-law. If I cannot appeal to the War Ministry, I will appeal to the minister himself.'

'But, Papa, Arthur's probably on his way to France!'

The doctor paused. 'France?' Suddenly, a thought struck him, and he smiled. 'He's still underage. I'll write to London. That should delay him for a few months, and allow me time to find a doctor to run things here.'

'Why not write to the minister?' suggested Margaret.

'Some favours are best asked in person.'

'And if Arthur doesn't *want* your help?' asked Bonney.

The doctor paled. Then he said, 'He'll come to his senses. I know he will.'

A TASTE OF IT

'I AM SERGEANT FANNING, AND THIS IS A SPECIALIST CLASS FOR observers. The guns you will be trained on will not be the same as those used in the field as every one has been dispatched to the fronts. We shall be using muzzle-loaded guns, without wheels.'

A soldier with half an unlit cigarette in the corner of his mouth glanced at Arthur, tipping the butt in derision; the sergeant seemed to anticipate this reaction.

'Some of you men are probably wondering what the point of learning to operate "antiques" is. The answer should be clear. No gun is the same as any other, but the same principles apply. Breech, dial sight, elevation wheel – each gun has them but in a different place. If you remember these principles, whether you are dealing with a muzzle loader, a howitzer, a rifle, a pistol, or even a ruddy popgun, you may save your life or the lives of your fellow soldiers. The burden rests upon you to use the intelligence God blessed you with to *adapt* on the field. If you cannot adapt, God help you, and God help your fellow soldiers. Is that clear?'

A murmur of grudging humility circulated among the boys, and the lesson proceeded.

Afterwards, the soldier with the cigarette introduced himself to Arthur. 'Georgie Goode,' he said. 'I'm with the Lancashire Fusiliers, over there.' He pointed to a series of white bungalows and remarked, with considerable pride: 'We have the biggest crop of potatoes in Scotton Camp.'

Arthur had to smile.

'Once you've tried the slop in the canteen,' said Georgie, 'you'll be planting away, boyo, mark my words!' He seemed to know everything about Scotton Camp. 'Forty thousand men, regiments from Scotland to Australia,' he said. He also knew his gardening and encouraged Arthur to help with his plot.

Georgie couldn't have been much older than Arthur. He was slight, but his narrow moustache and perpetual smirk gave him a randy leer. Arthur suspected that Georgie was all pretence, but they became firm friends nevertheless.

On days off, they rode bicycles out of Catterick and across the countryside. Once, when they passed an attractive young woman walking along the road, Georgie stopped to ask her for a light. A conversation led them to the public house where the girl worked. The soldiers spent an hour chatting with her before going on their way. It was the only time that Arthur saw any practical purpose to his companion's cigarette. When he tried to keep a soggy half cigarette in his mouth for an hour, he realized what a skill Georgie had mastered.

'I'm going to America when this is over,' Georgie explained on the ride back that evening.

'New York?' Arthur replied.

'Yes.' Georgie grinned. 'I'm going to be a millionaire.' He kept a stack of postcards sent him by a cousin: the St Louis World's Fair, the brilliant lights at Coney Island's Luna Park and the Statue of Liberty. There was also a picture of a man, in a double-breasted pin-striped suit, having his shoes polished at Grand Central Terminal. Georgie cherished that one; he would examine it every night and practise the careless, worldly expression of the dapper man with the cigarette projecting over his lower lip.

Early one morning a chorus of bugles sounded across the camp. Georgie burst into Arthur's tent and ordered everybody to get dressed. 'Fall in on the parade grounds! There's an air attack!'

Quickly, Arthur joined thousands of sleepy young men as they lined up by regiment in the misty darkness. They were warned not even to strike a match. After half an hour of waiting in the damp half-light, a rumour circulated that a zeppelin raid was in full swing.

Everyone scanned the horizon, more in excitement than fear. Suddenly, they heard a muffled burst of explosions, and Arthur's heart pounded.

'Good gosh!' one of his tent mates said with a laugh. 'Has anyone ever *seen* a zeppelin?'

'Not me,' replied Arthur.

A flash in the sky lit up his neighbour's grin. 'Crikey!'

The horizon settled into darkness, and somebody called that the zeppelins had moved on. There were giddy cheers and a spattering of applause, as if the men had scored some victory by shivering in the darkness. As his fellows walked back to the tent, Arthur hesitated, wondering why his heart was still thumping. Was it terror at the earthshaking power of man? Or the camaraderie of thousands assembled at dawn? Or even the idea of the carnage that now lay at the site of those flashes? Perhaps the combination of these sensations had set his heart into a gallop. All he knew was that he wanted more of it.

The next day Arthur was called to the office of his commanding officer. 'Gunner Chapel,' he said, 'I've a letter here from your father. He says you're two months below enlistment age.'

'I'm ready to fight now, sir,' Arthur replied.

'Anything wrong with your hearing, Chapel?'

'No, sir,' said Arthur.

'You shall remain at camp until you are of regulation age. Is that understood?'

Georgie Goode and Arthur had a farewell drink together before Georgie departed for the front. He gave Arthur three tomatoes and half a dozen small potatoes – the bounty of his vegetable plot. 'We'll meet in New York,' he promised. 'I'm fighting for the sake of my reputation. A businessman needs one, and medals are the fastest way a fellow can earn one.'

Over the next two months, Arthur repeated his drills and classes with a new company of enlisted men. His pleasure in being at Scotton evaporated. The last child in his family to leave the nest, he now feared he would be the last man sent off to war.

A FISH IN THE WRONG CURRENT

Although Mrs Mansworth's letter offered a ray of hope to Tom, many other factors would prevent his departure for England. Ships were overbooked, convoys were delayed, and it was September 1918 before he gained passage on a steamer. The *Allerton Castle* had been refitted to carry troops and armaments. Several thousand soldiers were berthed on the lower decks – South Africans headed for the Western Front. When Tom left his porthole open for the little air it allowed into his cramped cabin, he heard the incessant chatter of the recruits and imagined Arthur having much the same conversations.

During the days, the doctor took strolls along the deck as the soldiers went about their drills. They were a cocky bunch, proud of their new uniforms, proud of their country, proud to be soldiers. One fellow noted Tom's tender smile and joked, 'You could still enlist, sir.'

'My son is with the South African Heavy Artillery, a bombardier.'

'My brother's a pilot in 84 Squadron.'

'My uncle's in Palestine,' said somebody else.

'My cousin's fighting in Flanders!'

'I think my son's going to France—' The doctor paused, suddenly aware of the emotion in his voice. 'I hope to see him before he leaves.'

He took down the soldier's name and his brother's name (and the name of his second cousin) and gave Arthur's in return. This ritual was repeated many times as Tom met other soldiers; the impersonal throng was transformed into a web of acquaintances. One evening, kept awake by the deep grind of the engines, Tom imagined the millions of such exchanges among these boys, small acts of defiance against the war's fundamental purpose – to transform millions of vital souls into mere numbers of winners or losers.

At Portsmouth, Tom disembarked and took a room in a hotel for the night. In the morning he boarded a train to London, arriving at Victoria Station in time to see newsboys hawking the headlines of the day.

'Ship torpedoed off Cornwall!' cried one. 'Forty drowned! *Allerton Castle* sunk by U-boat!'

His own ship had been sunk off Bishop Rock on its way to join a southbound convoy. Tom sat down on his bags in the centre of the station, surrounded by the warm glow of its new incandescent lights, and wept for the random slaughter and the stark incongruity of his survival.

AS TOM EMERGED from the bustling terminus, he was seized with shock. Motorcars sputtered past, issuing clouds of blue smoke. The rare clatter of hooves on cobbled streets was drowned by the cacophonic roar of trucks and motorcycles. Above the London skyline, he counted fifteen balloons suspended like enormous teardrops.

Where were the gas lamps and the lamplighters with their ladders and sticks? Where were the barrows pushed by fruit sellers, the carts, and the rich smell of manure? All gone. This wasn't the London of his youth; this was a city in the grip of progress. The window glass of a nearby shop rattled as a biplane flew overhead, the hostile throb of its engine reminding him that the air had joined earth and water as a venue for battle.

Electric lightbulbs surrounded the theatre marquees – *Chu, Chin, Chow* was playing at His Majesty's, *The Maid of the Mountains* at Daly's Theatre. The women queuing for tickets wore slender, unflattering clothes and seemed, in Tom's view, underdressed. Gone were the full skirts, the bustles, the leg-of-mutton sleeves and wide hats. Perhaps war shortages meant that women could no longer claim yards of fabric for fashion. This was an austere new world. How provincial Gantrytown had been – the styles there were years out of date, and judging from a group of women in WAAC uniforms, so were the views on women's service.

Outside the public houses, young men in uniform clustered in groups. Every one resembled Arthur, in Tom's eyes. Then, in Trafalgar Square, the doctor noticed groups of people marching together in black coats with lavender piping on their lapels and sleeves. A banner sported an alarmingly familiar slogan: THE END IS NEAR. REJOICE!

The Pendletons seemed to have taken over the city. Groups of them greeted young people, and bands paraded the streets singing 'Glory, glory, hallelujah' with bass drums and trumpets. Tom anxiously surveyed the marchers' listless faces. He hoped for a glimpse of Charity – she'd not written in months.

Several times, he stopped people to inquire about his daughter. One young woman told him there were thousands of Pendletons in London. 'I'm sure she's here,' she said. 'It's almost *time*, you know.'

'Time?'

'Judgment Day.' She smiled.

If Judgment Day was indeed less than two months away, Tom thought it would be quite normal for those who believed so to weep, to mourn, to tear out their hair, and to rend their garments in compassion for the end of humanity. The serenity of the Pendletons, however, chilled him. Surely, even if they thought themselves worthy of ascendance, they must feel some misgiving about the annihilation of friends and family. As they marched past him in their smart uniforms and straight rows, he found it curious that their spiritual joy was expressed in a ritual so similar to that of warfare.

THE MAYFAIR HOTEL was a brick building with blue shutters, run by a small Portuguese proprietress with tightly bound hair and deep worry lines on her forehead. She asked if he had any friends in London, to which he replied, 'I don't know.' This prompted her sympathy. As Tom lay down for a nap, a boy appeared at his door and presented him with a cup of tea and a slice of Madeira cake.

He fell asleep that evening holding the items he would need for the next day: the address of the War Ministry and an envelope bearing Eve Mansworth's letter. He considered visiting his father's house but decided his duty to his son came first.

THE NEXT MORNING, the rosy-faced sergeant at the Civilian Queries desk was ready for the gaunt, anxious-looking fellow before him. 'We regret we cannot report the whereabouts of individual soldiers, sir. I'm sure you understand the risks to the lives of our fighting men.'

'I'm only asking whether he has been sent to the front,' replied the doctor. He realized that it was too late to excuse Arthur from service for being underage – the boy was eighteen and a half – all he wanted was to ascertain where Arthur was stationed, and to assure himself that the boy was alive.

The sergeant became contemptuous. 'There are hundreds of thousands of men at the front, sir!'

'And every one of them with a concerned father,' the doctor replied. 'Where is your compassion?'

This wiped the sergeant's smirk away. People began to peer around from their places in line behind Tom.

'Look,' said Tom, 'would you please tell me to whom I should speak in order to find my son?'

'Beg your pardon, sir, but your son knows his duty better than you do!' The sergeant dabbed his forehead with a handkerchief. *'Next!'*

Tom was a fish in the wrong current. It was three hours before he learned that there was no department equipped to help a man find such information. Nevertheless, he gave it his best try; over and over he presented his story, then waited for an answer from subsequent links in the chain of authority. As the hours passed, he studied the patterns on the linoleum floors, counted the chips and scuff marks on the wainscoting, and imagined faces in the whorls of wood grain. This ordeal prompted Tom to consider the nature of hell, and he wondered whether, instead of a fire pit, the devil's realm was a banal place filled with bureaucrats and scuffed furniture. Eventually he found a fellow sympathetic enough to give him the names of Arthur's company and commanding officer.

THE NEXT MORNING, Tom returned to the War Ministry. He had decided to go to the top floor. The oak wainscoting there was neither scuffed nor dented; the boards were varnished to a shine. Two police officers flanked the young woman seated at the threshold of the minister's office.

'May I help you, sir?'

'Yes, I'm an old friend of the minister,' said Tom.

'Have you an appointment?' She smiled.

'No,' replied Tom. 'I'm afraid not.'

'He's terribly busy this morning, sir.' But to Tom's surprise, she grasped the telephone earpiece and prepared to dial. 'May I tell the minister your name, sir?'

'Doctor—' Tom realized that Geoffrey Mansworth would recognize him only by his old name. 'Dr Tom Bedlam,' he replied.

A policeman must have sensed his hesitation. He stepped forward. 'Would you have a card, sir?' Tom noticed that the other policeman was now standing behind him.

Tom produced his wallet, then paused. 'I must explain that my name has changed since I last saw the minister.' He attempted a smile. 'We were boys at school together.'

'What is your legal name, sir?'

'Chapel.'

'I see. Chapel? *Not* Bedlam, sir?'

One wrong answer changed their expressions, and all other courtesies. In moments, Tom had been escorted out of the building, held firmly by two hands above his elbows. His papers were examined, along with his hotel receipt, by the policeman who then questioned Tom's purpose in being on English soil.

'I'm trying to get my son out of the army,' he insisted.

'Well, I suggest you stay out of the War Ministry, sir,' advised the policeman. 'People like you can say what they want at Speakers' Corner.' He gave him a wink and strode back into the building.

'For heaven's sakes, I'm not some lunatic!' Tom cried, realizing that his words provoked just such an idea in the faces of passersby.

AT ABOUT TWO O'CLOCK in the afternoon, Tom alighted from a cab alongside a row of houses in Bedford Park. A town house of crimson brickwork stood on a placid, sun-drenched lawn fringed by beeches and oaks. His heart beat faster as he approached the door and knocked. He half-expected to be met by another pair of police officers, but instead a maid greeted him. This time he asked for Mrs Mansworth, gave his name, and prepared to offer his card, but the maid left without asking for anything. He heard her footsteps retreat across a marble floor and passed the time listening to a little girl somewhere across the grounds, uttering squeals of delight.

Tom paced the foyer and noticed, at the foot of the stairs, a table bearing a silver-framed photograph of a family. Eve's features were no less striking, her raven dark hair parted in the centre, eyes glowing with familial pride. Her left hand rested in the crook of her husband's arm, while the other encircled her daughter's waist. At first glance, Tom imagined he saw himself in the picture. But soon he made out a pasty complexion and the petulant bulge of Geoffrey Mansworth's upper lip. The daughter, however, might have passed for Margaret at the age of eight – the resemblance was uncanny.

When the maid returned, she was polite but firm. 'Mrs Mansworth cannot see you now.'

'I've come a very long way. Did you tell her who I was?'

'I did, sir, but Mrs Mansworth has guests.'

Tom rose to leave, but the maid made one more remark as he turned. 'Most visitors use the *telephone* to avoid disappointment.' It seemed that this was an instruction from Mrs Mansworth, for the maid placed a card in his hand.

On the back of the card was written: 'Please telephone me.'

LA BOURSE

A NEW COMMANDING OFFICER, MAJOR WARRICK, TOOK CHARGE OF Arthur's group at Scotton Camp. Warrick was less of a patriarch, more of a bureaucrat. Anything that reduced the size of his stack of papers appealed to him. When Arthur requested a transfer to the Officers' Cadet Battalion, Warrick was happy to oblige. 'Want to go to France, Chapel? Very well. You'll go with the next draft in three days.'

Supplied with gas mask, steel helmet and a tunic with field dressings stitched into the linings, Arthur found himself with several hundred men aboard a troopship heading across the channel for Le Havre. Judging from the young faces around him, Major Warrick considered any boy who could wear boots an adequate man for the job.

One lad, Markham, was enormous – a barrel-chested fellow with hands that could span a dinner plate – though clumsy and awkward, he was clearly still a boy in a man's body. He kept company with another lanky giant, Cargill, who made comical noises to earn a laugh. The two became a sideshow, playing practical jokes on each other, but the other soldiers derided them; nobody was as naïve or foolish as Cargill and Markham.

'Fools,' remarked Arthur's sergeant, who explained that it was no virtue to be tall under fire in the trenches – one became a choice candidate for a sniper's bullet. He constantly berated the two for their juvenile behaviour.

Arthur's shoulders were broad, and his hair had darkened from the ginger of his youth; he was happier when listening rather than talking. His loping walk dipped in midstride – something he had picked up from the other men with whom he had carried hundred-pound shells at Scotton for practice in loading the howitzers. Because of Arthur's relative maturity, the sergeant assigned him the job of escorting two deserters while he was on board ship.

The prisoners were named Gibson and Sweet; they were being sent back to their battery in France as punishment. Both were incredibly polite fellows who had managed to get across the channel by exercising their charm and reached Folkestone before they were unmasked as deserters. Gibson was earnest and eager to be understood.

'I'm not a coward,' he insisted. 'Neither is Sweet.'

'Not unless going on thirty-two patrols in no-man's-land is cowardice,' added Sweet.

'Not unless bringing back dozens of wounded men under enemy fire is cowardice,' said Gibson.

'Not unless choking from gas till my buttons were green and still charging a German munitions bunker is cowardice,' continued Sweet.

'Then why were you deserting?' asked Arthur.

'Well, it's hopeless, isn't it?' said Gibson, raising his palms. 'The army's full of officers who don't know their filthy arses from the Pope's.' He raised a finger to quiet an anticipated dissent. 'Look, I've fought alongside idiots – no matter; they're my countrymen, you see, and God made them stupid for his own reasons – but I will not take orders from a fool in a lieutenant's uniform.'

'Or a captain's, or a major's,' said Sweet.

They told Arthur of a botched assault on a village east of Hazebrouck and blamed the loss of forty men on an overzealous commanding officer.

'Young man,' explained Gibson, 'a few months in officer training doesn't prepare one to send so many good men to their deaths.'

Arthur must have looked surprised at the idea of an officer being incompetent, because Gibson qualified his assertion: 'Mind you, not *all* officers are stupid fools.'

'True,' agreed Sweet. 'One or two are just idiots.'

'If you want to get out of this,' whispered Gibson to Arthur, 'let a sniper shoot you in the arm or leg. Trench foot used to be an easy way out of the front lines, but now they've run inspections to make sure nobody's letting it fester. Lice won't get you back to Blighty either.'

'Aye, but they might drive you out of your mind,' said Sweet, 'which isn't the worst way to get out of the war.' He rolled his eyes upwards, and he lolled his tongue between his teeth in hearty imitation of an imbecile.

'I recommend shaving for the lice,' said Gibson, brushing off his woollen cap to reveal a bare scalp. 'And down below,' he added, gesturing to his crotch.

'*Carefully*,' added Sweet.

'Lucky for you, the gas masks are better than they was a few years ago,' Gibson continued.

'Aye,' said Sweet. 'Used to look like the oat bags you give to a nag. Useless.'

Arthur was shocked and admiring of his charges. They had a philosophy about the war, strong opinions, a sense of self-assurance, while he felt simply ignorant. As Gibson passed a cigarette to Sweet, Arthur observed that the deserters were synchronized both by their cravings for a smoke, or a piece of chocolate, and by their disgust. They told Arthur dark jokes about soldiers' attempts to be sent home by injuring themselves and suddenly remarked wistfully on a pleasant meal of duck they'd shared in some French town just before an assault.

Their stories contradicted his training at Scotton Camp. There was no united effort, no exaltation, no camaraderie. Trench warfare was terrifying and wretched. Sweet described the stages of putrefaction of a corpse, from the bloated, unrecognizable body of a German that had terrified him during a patrol to the rat-scoured skeletal remains he had kicked to pieces while singing 'The Grand Old Duke of York' to pass the time in a bomb crater. Arthur stared from one fellow to the other with wide eyes, trying to make sense of the awful contrast between their experiences and their casual humour.

'Does the gas kill you?' he asked.

'Not the tear gas, but the mustard can, or make you as sick as a dog,' said Sweet.

'Just remember that the gas is *heavy,*' said Gibson. 'It seeps into holes and trenches. Never let your head be as low as your boots.'

'Unless you're ready to hop it,' said Sweet, slicing his neck with his forefinger.

'There's a point where you stop giving a damn,' muttered Gibson, 'but that's what the rum's for. After you stop caring about kings and countries and your C.O., you'll jump into the fight just for a tot.'

At this moment the sergeant interrupted. *'Can't you two arseholes shut your traps for five ruddy minutes?'*

'Aye, aye,' murmured Gibson, and in tandem, the deserters shifted position, slumped against each other, back to back, and promptly fell asleep.

AFTER THEY DOCKED at Le Havre, Arthur left his charges at the Harfleur transit camp. They wished him well, gave him chocolate, and advised him to shoot off his trigger finger when he had had enough of the war.

Arthur received his posting with the South Africans – the 125th Siege Battery of the Royal Garrison Artillery. He was sent with another bombardier to join his unit in a town called La Bourse. His companion, Tom Hartwell, was nineteen; he had been injured a few months before and proudly showed Arthur a shrapnel wound on his shoulder, remarking with disappointment that he had hoped for a bullet wound. 'To show the girls,' he explained. They alighted from their train at La Bourse, to be greeted by a couple of explosions. It was the first sound of the enemy Arthur had heard.

'Six-inch guns,' explained Hartwell. 'Fritz is probably trying to shake up the town. Scares the hell out of everyone, but they're not landing anywhere nearby.'

'How will I know if they're landing nearby?' asked Arthur.

'Well,' said Hartwell, 'first you'd hear a big whistle, and then a pit the size of a truck would suddenly—' He pointed ahead. 'Something like *that.*'

A massive crater had torn up the road ahead. A wheelbarrow lay flattened on the ground nearby – as if stamped by God's fist. Hartwell kept walking and whistling, but Arthur stared at the object for a few respectful moments.

When they arrived at the battery command post, a German plane had just shot at five British kite balloons that were anchored by cables to trucks on the field. The explosions were stunning – fireballs rose into an ashen sky while debris floated down. Several men parachuted from their destroyed balloons.

'Balloonatics, we call them.' Hartwell laughed. 'They spot enemy movement, gun positions, and so on. You couldn't get me up there!'

One of the other bombardiers nodded at the departing plane. 'Good shot, whoever that was,' he said, alluding to the German pilot.

Arthur wondered silently if the pilot might have been another South African, like Max Immelmann.

The howitzers in Arthur's battery group stood in a line across the open farmland, about a hundred feet apart, nestled in shallow pits and draped in camouflage netting.

Arthur was assigned the job of giving coordinates by telephone from the command post to the howitzers. A network of wires from headquarters enabled the commanders to dictate targets to each battery. Suddenly, the guns would begin firing, sometimes for as long as sixteen hours. Once Arthur counted an assault of twelve hundred shells fired from his battery. The cries of the bombardiers, the subsequent explosion and the strong odour of cordite in the air became a familiar trio of sensations. Arthur began to dream it in his sleep – even the smell.

Hartwell explained to Arthur that, after a week or two, the enemy's spotters would work out the coordinates of their battery, and it would be time to move the guns. Sometimes the Germans would pinpoint their location but wait for an opportune time to retaliate.

Arthur witnessed such a strike about two weeks after he arrived, and it was then that he realized the danger of his job compared with those of the men in the gun pits. When the shells started whistling around him, four in one minute, the commanding officer ordered his bombardiers to abandon their guns and stand in the fields until the strike was over.

Arthur was ordered to stay with Roddy Wilson at the command post to monitor the phone line from brigade headquarters. Lieutenant Vardy supervised them; his infectious laugh and jokes kept them calm during the assault. When two shells came howling towards them, blowing craters about ten yards short of the building, Vardy slurred like a drunk: 'One more like that and we're leaving the party!'

The next shell struck the roof of the house, and timbers began to fall. 'No more scotch left, lads! Everybody out!' cried Vardy. The men staggered through a cloud of plaster and smoke as the upper part of the house started to collapse. Arthur began choking in the dust and couldn't see his way out.

'C'mon, Chapel, no time for a last drink,' Vardy chuckled, pushing him through a doorway. Another shell screamed overhead, and the explosion collapsed the house. Arthur's ears rang with an endless, high-pitched whistle. Suddenly, he felt himself being dragged out of a heap of plaster.

'Are you all right, Chapel?' asked Hartwell. He nodded back at the heaping ruin of a house. 'Wilson and Vardy are dead,' he said. 'They didn't make it out.'

'But he was with me,' Arthur insisted.

Hartwell's reply was inaudible. Arthur could hear only the pounding of his heart – the machinery of life – a restless, clumsy drumming reminding him that he had prevailed while his friends had perished for no good reason. The difference between life and death had been a footstep, a half second, or Vardy's last joke.

The other members of the company parted as Arthur, dusted white from head to foot, staggered, phantomlike, back to his barracks.

VARDY AND WILSON were sewn up in blankets and laid on stretchers. The company crammed into a truck to escort them to the cemetery outside Béthune. The army graves were simple trenches of about fifty feet in length. 'What sort of dignity is this?' Hartwell complained to Arthur, looking down at a hole, yards long, with blanketed corpses huddled side by side.

A soft rain fell while the C.O. gave a short eulogy for Wilson and the lieutenant. 'Lieutenant Vardy was a good man, fine officer,' he said.

'Hear, hear,' murmured several in the company.

One of the British 'balloonatics' wandered over and sang 'Ave Maria'. He was a tenor, and for a moment his voice seemed to rise above the noise of trucks. Then a few shovelfuls of mud were thrown across the blanketed bodies. The rain stopped, and Arthur gazed across the communal burial site as more soldiers approached, bearing stretchers with blanketed bodies. He counted twenty trucks parked at the cemetery road. More dead. More holes to be dug. And more trucks arriving in the distance.

On the drive back to La Bourse, the others broke the silence. Gregory Norkin showed Arthur his good-luck charms – a saltshaker and a girlfriend's bracelet. He tossed salt over his left shoulder at every meal and kissed his thumbnail whenever Bombardier McCormick swore.

McCormick told Arthur he had joined the South African Army to avoid working for his father, a butcher. 'Pigs' feet, pigs' intestines, pigs' heads, pigs' tails – pigs as far as the eye could see. And the other day I saw Garson pissing into a bush with his trousers down, and I thought I was back on the farm!'

MCCORMICK'S PROFANITY WAS TIRESOME, Norkin's nervous habits irritated everyone, and Hartwell's willingness to risk a bullet wound seemed foolhardy to the rest of the crew. Iris would have described them as brutes, brats and dandies. Arthur, however, was constantly amused by their company, for he was privy to a world that was his alone, a world his family would never know.

One day, when two trucks arrived with a supply of shells for the howitzers, Arthur saw a familiar face. The captain in charge had a drooping moustache and a languid manner. He grinned at Arthur. 'Chapel? Is that you?' he said.

'Sir?' replied Arthur.

'Remember me, Chapel? Boyle, your Latin teacher. *Captain* Boyle, I should say!'

'What a pleasure, sir,' replied Arthur, earnestly, as he helped unload the ordnance. Watching Arthur work up a considerable sweat carrying the hundred-pound shells, Boyle advised him to slow down.

'You won't get a medal for this kind of effort, Chapel,' he said. 'Look, you're a bright lad. They could use you in one of the medical units. Why don't you leave this sort of work for the slobs? I could put in a word—'

'I don't want any help, sir,' Arthur replied. 'I got here by myself. I'll be fine.'

'Fine?' echoed Boyle, sceptically. 'I was fighting in the trenches for about three months when I was shot,' he explained, rolling up his right trouser leg. 'It wasn't funny when the infection set in. Thought I'd die.'

Hartwell stared dubiously at the small scar. 'From *that*?'

'Yes, from *that*,' snapped Boyle. 'It's not the hole that kills you, lad. It's the infection. Unfortunately for me, I recovered. The lucky ones lose a leg or a hand and go home.'

Hartwell sneered. 'Coward,' he muttered, walking away.

'Have you seen any sign of Wally Hill, sir?' said Arthur.

'He died a few weeks ago. Hit by a shell. I wrote the letter to his parents.' Boyle's tone was frank, but he didn't anticipate Arthur's shock. The boy stared, uncomprehendingly, as if he'd been punched by some unseen force.

Recognizing this reaction, Boyle reached forward and put his hands on Arthur's shoulders. 'I'm sorry, Chapel, I'd forgotten that you've only just arrived. We've lost a lot of boys like Wally. I'm afraid that's what happens here.' He glanced sharply at Hartwell. 'Heroes *and* cowards. Dying every day.'

'How about a fellow named Georgie Goode—'

The schoolmaster interrupted Arthur's question before he could finish. 'Please don't ask me about all of your acquaintances, Chapel.'

Boyle then changed the subject to the new minister of war, Geoffrey Mansworth, who was arguing in Parliament against further negotiations with the Germans. This, the captain said, would probably extend the war for another year. 'You'll see, Arthur, that we become something of an abstraction to the politicians and those' – he paused as if the words were distasteful – 'stoking the home fires – they think it's all rather fun.' He removed a mailbag from the truck and threw it into Arthur's arms, then consulted a piece of paper in his jacket pocket with a frown.

'I can recall Cicero, but I have the damnedest time remembering modern poetry. This one's by a British soldier – a fellow named Siegfried Sassoon.' He handed it to Arthur.

While you are knitting socks to send your son
His face is trodden deeper in the mud.

Boyle shrugged. 'When I hear the patriotic nonsense, I find that passage rather a relief.'

'What's the point of it?' Arthur asked.

'Well, Chapel,' Boyle replied, 'what's the significance of a man fighting for his country when he might be mown down like a blade of grass? Machine guns, bombs, chemicals. This uniform turns us from souls into statistics.'

After Boyle departed, Hartwell joined Arthur.

'Friend of yours?'

'Teacher.' Arthur nodded.

'Probably shot *himself* in the knee,' said Hartwell. 'The French Army executes men who do that. Imagine him driving around the countryside reading his poetry while others die – it makes me sick.'

Arthur said nothing. He didn't understand Hartwell's bravado any more than he understood Boyle's disgust; but he admired them both for believing in something. He yearned for some conviction of his own.

ENTRENCHED

It is one thing to be forgiven in a letter, but Tom hadn't anticipated the heat of Eve's anger in person. As he sat before her in the glorious conservatory at the Mansworth residence in Bedford Park, she served him tea with barbed generosity.

'I recall your preference for sugar in your tea, or did I misconstrue that *too* all those years ago?' she murmured. 'Forgive me,' she added, after a pause. 'That was unfair.'

Tom said nothing, deciding that she was entitled to at least one uppercut.

Eve was still the embodiment of grace. Her perfect almond eyes simmered at him as she offered the sugar from a silver tea bowl, freshly baked scones and jam tarts. A brilliant mosaic of colour emanated from the garden beyond the enormous windows; inside, the walls were painted a warm lemon, the furniture upholstered in soft yellows and golds. Eve told him that the small framed landscapes on the walls were by Corot, part of her collection. Everything in the room was carefully chosen, expensive, tasteful, and arranged to best effect. It might have been Mansworth's house, but this room was Eve's, all right.

'This is a beautiful home,' he began.

'And your home?' she asked. 'What's it like?'

'Worn,' he replied. 'Full of things needing to be repaired but comfortable. The children – they're adults now – have worn the edges down. The garden is nice,' he said, 'in a wild sort of way, though not as pretty as yours.'

This compliment failed to defuse the tension in the air. He was a living reminder now of her loss of pride, and Eve valued her pride above most things.

'I've done my best, considering . . .' she said.

'Considering?'

She tilted her head, as if he was being unspeakably dense. 'When one is deceived early in life, one is at such a disadvantage.'

'I understand,' he conceded.

'I doubt it.'

'Eve,' Tom began, 'your father told me, rather bluntly, that you would attract many better offers than I could make. Furthermore, he told me that I wasn't welcome in his house.'

'So, in deference to his edict, you chose to elope with my sister?'

'Lizzy found me at the station,' he replied. 'Would *you* have been happy to ride around some dusty little town in a dogcart, counting pennies and tending patients? Giving piano lessons to little children? Would you have been happy with such a life?'

'Did I seem so incapable of sacrifice?' Her voice broke as she said this. 'Was I so shallow, to you?'

'Eve, I loved you both. You spoke of making me a success in London, and just now, when I walked up the steps to this house, I said to myself, "This looks like the house for Eve. She must have found precisely what she wanted in life." Was I so wrong?'

'Yes!' she cried with the full force of her emotion. Her reply must have shaken the house, because Tom heard a door suddenly open and the footsteps of a child racing down a hall, followed by the hushed admonishments of an adult. Wiping her eyes clear, Eve abruptly changed her tone. 'You're probably right.' She glowered. 'I *was* better off. I married a fine man, and I have a beautiful daughter.'

From the double doors of the conservatory, a young woman's face appeared. She was about fifteen, solemn, and she stared at the two of them for a perplexed moment.

'Josephine? Come in!' said her mother. This prompted an approving sound from the governess, who appeared in profile at the doorway. So the girl entered, walked straight up to Tom, and curtsied.

'Josephine, this is your uncle,' said Eve.

'How do you do, Josephine?' said Tom.

She had high cheekbones, wild red hair and a bold stare. She looked more like Lizzy than like her mother, and she seemed to take the measure of Tom quickly, delivering a frank reply: 'I am sorry to have interrupted. I heard an argument and assumed my father had come home.'

Now Josephine turned sharply to her mother, as if to make clear to whom her remark was directed. Eve took this barbed comment without flinching. Tom guessed that she was quite proud of her daughter's spirit.

'I have a daughter named Margaret in Africa,' he said. 'You might pass for sisters. She's twenty-eight, but she was very like you at your age.'

'I should like to meet her very much,' the girl replied. 'It would be like seeing my future, or jumping ahead a few chapters to learn the ending of my own story.'

'Hardly the *ending*, Josephine,' Eve laughed. 'Don't be morbid!'

'Who knows?' insisted her daughter. 'Some people are struck down in their prime, Mother. Juliet was dead at fourteen, Joan of Arc was burned at nineteen. Anne Boleyn was beheaded at twenty-eight. Mary Queen of Scots was—' Her eyes danced at the thought of all this tragedy.

Josephine's young governess interrupted the exchange to remind her of her abandoned schoolwork.

'Say goodbye, Josephine,' said Eve.

Josephine curtsied to Tom once more, issuing a weary sigh. 'Goodbye, Uncle.'

Eve showed Tom around the house, which was full of heavy, dark antique furniture, swords and pikes crossed on the walls, and seventeenth-century paintings of generals gathered on hilltops – the sorts of pictures that honoured victories and careers. She explained how she had met Mansworth while visiting Cornell in London.

Mansworth and Cornell had been in the same London circle. Mansworth had served as an officer in the Second Battalion stationed in

Bermuda and returned when his father became too ill to run his munitions factories. The factories produced two modern innovations: cordite and lightweight carbines with rifled barrels. These two novelties would change warfare forever; men could shoot one another from greater distances without the clouds of smoke that gave away their positions.

Cornell attempted to court Eve, but Mansworth made the stronger impression, so much so that, when Professor Harding died, Eve settled her father's affairs and moved to London. She learned, however, that although Mansworth was considered a catch, many people disliked him because he was cold and aloof. Eve set to work on Mansworth; she advised him on matters of dress and encouraged him to make charitable donations, which helped broaden his social circle to include politically and socially influential friends.

At his side, Eve became Mansworth's 'charming half'. Her popularity made him a more welcome guest, just as his business acumen made him an authority on the logistics of warfare. When he proposed to her, she accepted, believing that the transformation of his character was half complete.

'The prime minister attended our wedding – he was a friend of Geoffrey's father,' Eve explained. 'But I agreed to marry Geoffrey because he reminded me of *you*, Cortez. Something about his features, his silences, his secrets. Like you, yet not like you at all. Your secrets seemed to be private sorrows, his secrets – Well,' she sighed. 'I don't know what they are. His job *requires* secrets, but since his assignment as war minister, I am privy to less of his life than ever before. Geoffrey is not the man I hoped he'd become.'

She didn't look at Tom as she said this. It was a concession of defeat, and he suddenly understood the vehemence of her earlier fury.

'Perhaps he can still redeem himself,' Tom suggested. 'I have a favour to ask you both, in this regard.'

Eve blinked at him. 'A favour? You and I have hardly reconciled, and you come to ask me a favour?'

'Will you *let* me atone for the past?' he asked.

She pressed her index finger to her lip, then smiled. 'If you'll admit that you behaved like an absolute pig by running away with my sister.'

This he did and then explained his son's situation, concluding, 'Only the minister of war could bring Arthur out of combat.'

'You're assuming that Geoffrey and I speak of such things,' she reminded him.

'Eve, I'm sure that, if not for you, he wouldn't *be* war minister.'

She raised an eyebrow. 'It's too late to flatter me, Cortez.'

'I must beg you, on behalf of your nephew—'

'You're not in a position to beg me for anything,' she cried. 'Every one of Lizzy's letters was like a stab to my heart! How happy she was with you!'

She put her hand to her mouth in embarrassment for this outburst and fled from the room. A moment later a maid appeared to escort Tom out.

RAIN WAS FALLING as Tom took a cab back to his hotel. He let one hand linger outside the window, thinking of Lizzy and Eve. Was it his fault that Eve had spent more than twenty years mourning his departure? And if Lizzy had remained in England, would she be alive now? What had he done to the Harding sisters?

As his exposed sleeve became wet, Tom drew his hand back inside the cab and imagined Arthur in his uniform, staggering through the mud somewhere in France.

The clouds passed as the cab approached Hyde Park. He noticed a few street performers trying to draw an audience from the passing crowd. There was a juggler and a weathered old woman offering palm readings. Farther on, two elderly men were drawing a chalk circle on the pavement. The first fellow had an enormous, sphinxlike head with a grave expression, thick lips, and a mane of greying hair that fell to narrow shoulders. His body, enveloped in a tattered brown woollen coat, seemed absurdly small for such a large head. The other fellow was tall, gaunt, with a straight, narrow nose and a darting smile. His hair was silvery white, and one of his legs was a wooden peg.

Tom stopped the cab, paid his fare, and approached the performers.

The two men abruptly donned tin helmets and began to march on the spot like infantrymen. In moments, a large crowd gathered as the two started singing 'Pack Up Your Troubles' in wavering baritones.

After the song was finished, the crowd applauded, and the sphinx addressed them. 'Ladies and gentlemen, we stand here, proud to remind you of the gallant spirit of our fighting men in France—'

'Belgium!' said the other fellow.

'Greece!' said the sphinx.

'Africa!'

'And other points across the globe.'

'And before we go out, we'd like to sing one more song.'

Tom watched Paddy Pendleton begin singing new lyrics to 'What a Friend We Have in Jesus'.

> When this lousy war is over, no more soldiering for me,
> When I get my civvy clothes on, oh how happy I shall be.
> No more church parades on Sunday, no more begging for a pass.
> You can tell the sergeant major to stick his passes up his—

At this moment, Bedlam broke in with the refrain—

> When this lousy war is over, no more soldiering for me,
> When I get my civvy clothes on, oh how happy I shall be . . .

Some onlookers laughed, others frowned, but everybody threw money when the old men offered their tin hats.

As the crowd broke up, both men relaxed from their poses to count the change earned from the performance.

Suddenly, Bill Bedlam's eyes strayed to Tom, who was exposed by the thinning crowd. 'Good heavens!' he murmured. 'Pinch me, Pendleton, I believe I see my son!'

Pendleton answered reproachfully. 'I've been pinching you black and blue for a quarter century, Bedlam. For once there is no need. This is most definitely your boy – a man, I should say, salted and peppered with age.'

'Thank heaven!' cried Bedlam, embracing Tom, tears rolling down his face, which he buried in his son's shoulder, making such a spectacle of himself that even Pendleton became disdainful.

'Bill Bedlam,' he remarked, 'not content with chewing half of London's scenery, must you now overact your own family reunion?'

The old man released his son and, with much dabbing of eyes, declared: 'My boy, you must be starving. Where would you care to go for a meal? Name it, and I'll take you immediately!'

'Perhaps you know a place?' Tom replied.

'Of course, of course!' Bedlam cried, adding, 'It's a good thing we found each other, or you'd be victim to the worst scoundrels in the city. There are places with fine service but small helpings, and places with large helpings and poor service, but Bill Bedlam knows where generosity and goodwill converge.'

'Yes,' murmured Pendleton. 'In his son's purse strings.'

Bedlam shot his companion a reproachful glance. 'Don't mind him, Tom,' he said. 'His liver's playing up.'

'Better the liver,' retorted Pendleton, sharply, 'than the entire man.'

A SMOKY PUBLIC HOUSE lay below the street; it was a busy place, made popular perhaps by the combination of good service and heaped plates. The diners were a boisterous lot with napkins stuffed into their collars. There was a bar dispensing ale in the dark rear of the room. The floor was gritty with salt, sprinkled to prevent the staff from slipping on the greasy boards. The establishment drew most of its light from several windows up by the rafters, which offered a view of the ankles and shins of passing Londoners. When a brief shaft of sunlight struck the glasses, tableware and cutlery, Tom was inspired to wipe the grease from his glass and give his knife and fork a careful polish with his handkerchief.

'Three girls and a boy? How lucky you are,' Bedlam sighed as Tom explained the past twenty-odd years as best he could. 'And may your wife rest in peace, poor dear,' he continued. 'I'd have sent a wedding present if I'd known of the wedding, and my condolences if I'd known of her demise.'

Pendleton twisted his neck clear of his collar in reaction to Bedlam's sentiment. 'I daresay ignorance is *always* bliss in *your* case,' he muttered.

'Silence, ruffian,' snapped Bedlam.

Tom addressed Pendleton. 'Any ignorance on his part is my fault too,' he said. Then, turning to Bedlam, 'Father, I know that I have been an ungrateful son, and I can't hope to make up for it.'

For once, Bedlam seemed not to know how to react. Before his son's eyes, the man's worn features shifted from shock to dignified entitlement. He must have imagined such a moment but never expected it to come, for he became confused. 'All is forgiven, my boy,' he said finally, in a half sob, and began to dab his eyes with a handkerchief.

The sphinx's enormous head bobbed with irritation. 'Oh, for heaven's sakes,' he cried. 'Bedlam, spare us the waterworks!'

'I weep with *sincerity*, Pendleton!' said Bedlam.

'You wouldn't know the meaning of the word,' muttered his friend.

A commotion outside suddenly interrupted all conversation. There was the crash of a bass drum and the cry of trumpets. The dining room suddenly grew dark as gathering spectators blocked the windows while the music boomed, shaking the table settings.

To the kingdom of our saviour we devoutly wish to go,
For the righteous and the meek have a place up there, I know,
The apostate and the pagan shall be burned in fires below,
His truth is marching on!
Glory! Glory! Hallelujah!
Glory! Glory! Hallelujah!
Glory! Glory! Hallelujah!
His truth is marching on!

The tune prompted the strangest response in Pendleton: the man's stately features began to quiver and contort with fury.

'Thieves!' he cried. 'How dare you parade about under my name! *Impostors!*' Rising from his seat, Pendleton staggered up the stairs of the restaurant and roared, raising his arm in outrage, spittle flying from his uneven teeth.

From their chairs, Tom and his father could see only the old man's heels rising with every expostulation while spectators edged nervously away from him to reveal the marchers in their black jackets with lavender piping. A banner read, JOIN US FOR THE END – BE BLESSED!

'Pendletons?' said Tom.

Bedlam nodded. 'Do you remember the thin fellow who was staying with us a long time ago? Isaiah Pound?'

'Yes, I remember,' said Tom. 'He opened the door when I first arrived.'

'Aye,' said Bedlam. 'Well, he stole Pendleton's livelihood.'

'How could he possibly have done that?'

Pendleton was now addressing the crowd with his orator's baritone: '*Don't listen to them! They're frauds!*' he cried. Tom had forgotten what a voice Pendleton had – the windowpanes rattled with each word he uttered.

'One day,' Bedlam explained, 'Isaiah Pound offers Paddy an arrangement. He wants to start a society dedicated to the arrival of the Apocalypse; wants to call it the Pendletons after Paddy. Well, Paddy's getting used to being waited on by this fellow, so he says yes, thinking that the boy's plan will never amount to anything. But a few weeks later, people are coming to my house. Y'see, Pound's been handing out leaflets, making his own speeches, so folk come visit, and stare at old Paddy like he's the Second Coming! And Isaiah has picked a date off the calendar, see, and promises that that's the end of it all.'

'My God,' said Tom, 'November eleventh, nineteen eighteen?'

Bedlam nodded. 'Which Paddy doesn't like, see, because once you write it down, people are going to *remember*, and you'll look like a fool come November twelfth. But Isaiah keeps making his speeches and plastering his ideas on poles, and he expects Pendleton to hold court and not to go out on the street any more. Poor old Paddy's never been told what to do by *anybody* before, and he misses his freedom, misses his pint, and even misses getting out there for a good rant. So he gets tanked, announces at the next meeting that the Pendletons are frauds, and Isaiah hires a few brutes to rough him up.'

The wind must have changed direction, because suddenly the marchers' voices seemed to carry through the restaurant with rousing clarity:

Glory! Glory! Hallelujah!
His truth is marching on!

The other diners looked up. Nobody was eating now. Down in the dark and pungent confines of the restaurant, the jubilant chorus sounded like the peal of angels.

'You see,' said Bedlam, 'Isaiah knew a thing or two from working in the novelty business. Cheap nickel crucifixes, clay nativity scenes – he sold hundreds of these things, but boxes and boxes of them added up to a small fortune just as pennies add up to pounds. Made in a factory, stamped out of a sheet, hundreds, thousands of them! Everybody's got a crucifix somewhere, y'see. Thanks to Paddy, he's founded a club, and to join the club you have to buy the suit, the badges, the Bibles, the banners. All made in a factory. All for sale. He's making a fortune. All over the world.'

'What happens when it's over?' Tom wondered.

'God willing, not the end of the world.' His father winked. 'Paddy says—'

'Paddy says what?' growled Pendleton. The sphinx had returned, flushed and breathless, to finish his meal.

'I was just explaining how you were cast off by your own admirers,' Bedlam replied.

Pendleton's stone-cut features assumed a grave sneer. 'Cast off, indeed, like Jonah from the ship, by my so-called shipmates,' he growled. 'Lazy, he called me! I was out there exhorting the throng when he was in his nappies.' Paddy leaned forward to Tom. 'Of course, when the war started, people *really* stopped to listen. Suddenly, he was *credible*! He was *sharp*! Membership *swelled*. Isaiah Pound had become God's holy trousers. And the money came rolling in. Do you know how much he's got?'

'How much?' asked Tom.

Pendleton narrowed his eyes. 'A lot more than he made selling trinkets. His people are all over the world. And he goes around giving his sermon, most of it nicked from me! He took my name, my sermon, and he's collecting money by the sackful!'

'For what?'

'Well,' Pendleton snorted, 'that's the question, isn't it? Who needs money in heaven?'

AFTER TOM HAD PAID for the meal and left a tip on the table, they rose to leave. He picked up his father's hat; this appeared to displease Bedlam, who accepted it, frowning. When they reached the door of the restaurant, Bedlam slipped back to the table for his gloves, though Tom didn't recall him wearing any. From the corner of his eye, though, he noted that Bedlam gathered up the tip he had left for the waiter.

'We must go, my boy,' said Bedlam, as they stood on the street, 'but I shall insist that you let *me* take you to dinner when next we meet.'

When Tom asked if his father still resided at his old house, Bedlam nodded, took Tom's address at the hotel, and they parted ways.

BÉTHUNE

THE BATTERY COMPANY MOVED ITS POSITION TO THE SHATTERED town of Béthune, which had been almost entirely deserted by its inhabitants. An estaminet remained; it was run by two women, a mother and daughter, who served the soldiers fried eggs, chips, or wine in china cups (all the glasses had been broken). The mother was small, dark and taciturn. Arthur greeted her once in his fluent French, and she smiled, revealing a chipped tooth, and asked if he was *Bretagne.* The daughter would not meet his eye; like her mother, she had shiny black hair, a high waist with full hips, and elegantly tapered ankles. Her eyes were impenetrably dark; Arthur couldn't help but be hypnotized by them.

'A bit horsy for my taste,' remarked Garson later. 'Not enough bosom and too much arse,' he added. 'She could show off her legs, and an occasional smile wouldn't spoil her chances.' The other soldiers agreed with this critique, which only increased Arthur's sympathy for her.

The soldiers slept on beds of chicken netting in a cellar that was fortified against shellfire by layers of brick and corrugated iron. Arthur's days could be tedious, long periods spent waiting by the telephone for orders from headquarters, then frantic hours of shouting target coordinates to the bomb crews as the howitzers blasted away. In their spare moments, Arthur and Hartwell hopped on bicycles and explored the cellars of the deserted buildings in town. Once, Hartwell stumbled on a cache of champagne and vintage cognac while Arthur discovered a treasure trove of cheese. The soldiers rode back with baskets balanced on their handlebars and passed the two French women – they were dressed in black and walking to mass. Arthur felt a wave of shame as he rode with this bounty of theft on his handlebars.

He tipped his hat to the mother, who replied with her chipped smile. The younger woman avoided his glance. Arthur noted that her black hair was braided and bound by a tricolour ribbon. After they had passed the women, he muttered to Hartwell, 'Look at us, we're thieves. And on Sunday, no less.'

'Aye, and for them we risk getting our heads blown off every day. Sundays *included*,' his companion replied. 'I wouldn't put it past those ladies to steal from their own neighbours. Where do you think they get the wine they serve at the estaminet, eh?' He laughed carelessly and struck a bump, knocking a chunk of Mimolette into the bushes. Arthur stopped to retrieve the cheese. He glanced back at the women; the mother had paused to remove a pebble from her shoe. Her daughter folded a strand of hair behind her ear and surveyed the fields, the sun, and the swoop of a magpie. As Arthur admired her shiny black hair and narrow waist, she sensed his gaze and raised her chin defiantly at him. This is my land, she seemed to be thinking. And you'll all be gone soon.

ARTHUR MADE MANY subsequent visits to the café in spite of the weak coffee and weaker tea. Once, when the daughter dropped change into his palm, their eyes met briefly. A few days later she murmured a wary greeting to him, her voice low and raspy.

One evening, a soldier refused to leave at closing time. Sensing the women's anxiety, Arthur talked the fellow out of his chair. 'Come,' he said, 'I'll walk home with you.'

The soldier was too drunk to move. 'Don't touch me,' he warned. 'I'll kill anyone who touches me. I want another drink.'

'Come, I'll walk with you,' said Arthur. 'Let the women go to sleep. They're not running a hotel. Look at them, they're exhausted. You're keeping them up.'

These gentle reproaches eventually prompted the soldier to go back to his barracks. The next time Arthur visited the estaminet, he was welcomed with gratitude.

The mother introduced herself as Madame d'Usseau. Her daughter's name was Martine. Martine's father had been a farmer; he'd died of pneumonia when she was five. Madame d'Usseau had sold the property and bought the small town house with the estaminet below it. The furniture from her sprawling farmhouse was stacked in the small rooms – a sewing table balanced upon a bureau, which rested upon a linen chest. Dining chairs hung from the walls. The furniture had been from her dowry, and Madame d'Usseau couldn't bear to part with any of it.

One evening Arthur went upstairs for more teacups and discovered a toy piano atop the china cabinet. He brought it down and played 'The Marseillaise' while Martine sang the words. Her deep, gravelly voice against the plinkety-plunkety sound of the toy piano gave the song a haunting dissonance.

The next morning a salvo of shells began bursting around the howitzers, so the gun crews were sent out into the fields until things quieted down. Arthur spent his shift beside the telephones at the command post. He tried to make a call to Martine, but the lines were damaged. As plaster and wood splinters showered around him, his knees shook, and a chill crawled up his back and around his neck. There was a rattling sound on the desk, which turned out to be his hand, trembling as it held a pencil. Shells seemed suddenly to fall in a rhythm, *boom-boomity-boomity – boom.* Perhaps it was just his fear, seeking rationality in the terrifying chaos. Suddenly the Number 1 gun, which lay nearest to the command post, blew to pieces.

When the bombardment stopped, Arthur burst out of the office and asked permission to check the estaminet. His C.O. assured him that the attack had not reached Béthune, then remarked tactfully on the wet stain between Arthur's legs and dismissed him for twenty-four hours.

That night Arthur buried his face in his pillow for shame. His body had failed him; he was in love with Martine and fearful of losing her. He had found something to believe in, but it had nothing to do with war or politics. It was the love of a raspy-voiced French girl in Béthune. Without the war, he would never have found her, and because of the war, he feared losing her at any moment.

The bombardment of the German guns commenced every night. Arthur comforted himself with the thought of Martine's dark, soulful eyes. As the shells whistled overhead, he imagined her low voice whispering in his ear. When mustard gas was detected, he slept with his gas mask on. Stifled by the oppressive rubber cocoon, Arthur pictured himself in Martine's naked embrace; the thought of her wide hips and deep voice could distract him from almost any discomfort.

Over several days he woke from these fantasies with his underpants sticky from a wet dream, while the buttons of his tunic were tarnished green from the mustard gas and his clothing covered with toxic yellow dust.

ONE AFTERNOON ANDREW BOYLE appeared with supplies. The two giants, Cargill and Markham, were working for him now. Arthur guessed that the former schoolmaster had taken them under his wing as hopeless cases. Boyle considered him thoughtfully. 'Everything all right, Chapel?'

'Yes, sir,' Arthur replied.

The schoolmaster's gaze lingered. 'Any excitement lately?' he asked.

Arthur nodded. 'It's noisy at night.'

'Chapel, I could still probably get you into one of the medical units. Your experience—'

'No,' Arthur interrupted. 'I'm happy here.'

'Happy?' Boyle looked alarmed. 'Here?'

Arthur couldn't explain it. The prospect of losing his life was never as awful as the thought of losing Martine.

THOUGH THEY RARELY HAD a private moment together, Martine began to make her interest in Arthur abundantly clear. She exerted a tender pressure against him when they stood side by side, and on one occasion, when Arthur was speaking to Madame d'Usseau, Martine passed between them, facing her mother so that her bottom brushed against him provocatively. Because Madame never let Martine out of her sight, their encounters were choreographed within the confines of the town house.

Once, when Martine balanced on a stepladder to retrieve a jar of peaches on a high shelf, she asked Arthur to steady her. He placed his hands on her hips, but she corrected his grip, moving his hands beneath her breasts.

When they returned downstairs, Madame d'Usseau stared at their flushed faces with bewilderment. *'C'était difficile de descendre les pêches?'*

Martine seemed unable to prepare the midday sandwiches without Arthur's assistance in the cluttered kitchen upstairs. With great speed and dexterity, they would throw the sandwiches together, load the food upon a plate, brace themselves on the only part of the floor that wouldn't creak, and fondle each other – Arthur's hand buried between Martine's legs while she stroked him until they were both in ecstasy.

'Good heavens,' cried Madame d'Usseau when they returned. 'These are the worst sandwiches I've ever seen. Did you make them with your feet?'

One evening, after sweeping the floor, they shared a cigarette outside.

'Run away with me,' said Arthur.

'I can't leave my mother,' Martine replied.

'We'll take her with us.'

'She would never leave her furniture,' the girl sighed.

'We could drug her coffee and take her to England or Africa.'

'Oh, Arthur.' Martine smiled. 'What a romantic you are.' She pressed against him gently. 'You don't seem English at all.'

'Run away with me.' There was more desperation in his voice this time.

She answered with a frail smile. 'You'll be sent to prison, or shot for desertion.'

'To hell with them all!' he cried.

Madame d'Usseau watched them embrace from her window upstairs. She didn't mind her daughter's affection for this man. As first romances go, it was suitably innocent, though she worried about the effect his death would have on the girl; for he would surely die.

HOLLOWAY

THE WOMEN'S PRISON HAD A GRAND POSTCARD FAÇADE OF PARAPETS, towers and wrought-iron gates. Inside, however, there was no mistaking its purpose: the narrow windows, iron catwalks, and rows of doors reminded all who entered that this was the domain of miscreants and murderers.

Audrey Limpkin had earned her twenty-eight years of imprisonment for refusing to show any regret for her crime – shocking the jury, the newspapers and society at large. At each parole hearing she repeated her innocence and showed no remorse (in spite of Oscar's advice that she do so simply to shorten her sentence). Since she couldn't be reformed, it was a relief to civilized society that she lay behind a three-foot-thick wall of stone.

The visitor from far-off Gantrytown who hesitated at Holloway's entrance feared not Audrey's influence but an attack of conscience from within. He had betrayed Arthur Pigeon and reaped from his betrayal an education, a family and a comfortable existence. In supporting her mother and sisters, Audrey had had to fight off the attack of a violent predator and garnered society's harsher rebuke, a long prison sentence. The inequity of their fates was simply staggering.

Tom took his seat in Holloway's waiting room, a heavily overpainted basement chamber with pipes running along the ceiling and a series of worn oaken pews where visitors waited until the inmates were summoned. It was a slow process. Every twenty minutes a prison officer would approach the podium at the front of the room and send the next visitor into the meeting room while repeating an admonishment against physical contact.

Tom passed the time thinking about his visits to three Pendleton lodging houses in search of Charity. Nobody would acknowledge her existence – they were such secretive people. He left notes but suspected that they would never reach her. He recalled his daughter's little clothes-peg family and wondered if the Pendletons were a more formidable substitute – blank faces, rigid convictions, matching clothes and matching dogma. Was she happy? He doubted it.

As for Iris, well, he had found her company's lodgings, but was informed by a surly woman that nobody was up before two in the afternoon. 'Come back later,' she said, 'or go to the revue!'

'Dr Chapel?'

Tom snapped out of his reverie. An inmate wearing a tidy green serge uniform with a white cap and checked apron stood before him.

He mouthed her name.

'Yes, Tom,' she replied. 'It's me.'

Unable to speak for the sight of her, Tom reached out, but checked himself, remembering the officer's warning. But Audrey embraced him, then steered him past the officer's forgiving nod.

'Dearest Tom,' she said. 'It is so good to see you.'

Words failed him again. The sight of her face, her warmth, her gentle spirit – at once he felt the urge to laugh in joyous relief. Oh, dear Audrey! She was still his sweet Audrey, safe and sound.

'I'm taking you on a tour. It's one of the privileges of a wardswoman.' She led him past the interview tables, along a corridor, through a door, and suddenly the prison opened up into a broad, sunlit chamber containing three levels of steel catwalks, a skylight above, and a concrete exercise area below.

'Welcome to my home,' she said, without irony.

He noticed that her walk was awkward. One of her feet splayed slightly.

'That's my hip. It never quite healed properly.'

Tears suddenly welled in his eyes; his emotions seemed to veer from one extreme to another. He dabbed his cheeks with a handkerchief, not saying anything for fear she would think him utterly unhinged.

'It's all right,' she assured him. 'I'm perfectly fine. And it doesn't hurt, I just walk a bit like a duck now.'

Audrey told him about the prison's history. She spoke quickly and confidently, slipping into a routine she must have conducted many times before for visitors. At times Tom was aware that she stole glances at him; he imagined she was reconciling her memory of young Tom Bedlam with the man before her, and he wondered what she must think of him now.

'Many suffragettes were incarcerated here. Emmeline Pankhurst would come for a month, go on a hunger strike, then be released until she recovered,' she explained.

'Why was she arrested?'

'Arson and other acts of civil disobedience – anything to call attention to the cause. The authorities here responded by force-feeding her and others very brutally. My heart went out to them. When Newgate closed in nineteen-oh-two, I was brought here; I saw them suffering *my* ordeal—'

'You mean incarceration?'

'No, Tom, I mean *rape*.'

'Rape?' Tom exclaimed. 'How?'

'With a tube forced into one's mouth, rectum or vagina. That's how they made them eat. What else would you call such a ghastly violation?'

He winced and averted his eyes. 'I didn't know they did such things.'

'Oh, yes,' said Audrey. 'I worked in the infirmary. Some women never recovered from the experience. Many were so badly hurt that they had to be released.' She sighed. 'Then the war came along, and that was the end of *that*.'

'The abuse, you mean?'

For the first time, Audrey looked despairingly at him. 'No, Tom, I mean the *cause*,' she replied. 'You see, when Mrs Pankhurst turned her attention to the war effort, beating the Huns became more important than giving half the country the vote. Everything the suffragettes had done seemed forgotten, and something so important to so many people slipped from the public mind.' She shook her head. 'God, we might not have *gone* to war if women had the vote.'

As they went back to the meeting room, Audrey's pace slowed. They walked side by side now, talking of family news.

Audrey had heard from the Orfling that Iris had inspired the company to do a war revue. 'She has wonderful pluck, Tom,' she said. 'You should be proud. The Orfling thinks she's brilliant. You must see the show and tell me all about it!'

Audrey's face was lined now, and her hair was turning grey beneath her cap. Her eyes, as she looked at him, were still warm and generous, which provoked Tom's shame again.

'Audrey,' he began, 'I'm so sorry for all these years, for being so angry with you. For behaving so badly—'

Audrey's closed smile appeared, but she looked pained.

'I must say it, I've been unfair—'

'I accept my lot,' she interrupted. 'I'm stubborn, Tom. Oscar says so all the time. I will not let you apologize. I had your letter, that was enough.'

Surprised, Tom looked at her. 'But you never answered it.'

'Oh, Tom, *of course* you had my forgiveness,' she whispered. 'I still love you.'

'I love you too,' he said.

It was a relief to him to say those words. In some way it was an acknowledgment, perhaps, that he could love a woman again. Later he would wonder whether the bitterness he had harboured towards Audrey for so many years was his own affection – misunderstood, misdirected and misspent. The dark offspring of unrequited love is hatred.

Audrey explained that she was to be released in two weeks' time.

'I will be there,' Tom promised.

Audrey blew him a kiss as she rose from the table, and Tom stared after her, feeling, again, the dizzy intoxication of her presence.

BEDFORD PARK

The message waiting for him at the hotel desk was written on War Ministry stationery. The handwriting was large, the signature enormous.

Chapel,

I understand from my wife that we are now related. We must meet again. Please join us for dinner tonight at my residence in Bedford Park.

G. Mansworth

P.S. Bring this letter.

Mansworth's house and lawn were illuminated with bright lights that evening. Policemen walked the perimeter, conveying a sense that the more humble world that lay a few feet beyond the minister's fence was a dark and insignificant domain.

Tom wondered how much this perception was shared by his host as he alighted from a cab and surveyed the security around him. Several policemen examined his invitation while an officer apologetically patted down the doctor's pockets, explaining that there had been threats to the minister's life. Apparently, Geoffrey Mansworth, minister of war, leader of the armed forces, and the man who could bring Arthur Chapel home, enjoyed precisely the kind of importance and public loathing he had achieved as a schoolboy at Hammer Hall.

Eve met Tom at the door. Her face and shoulders were powdered and pale, like those of an alabaster goddess.

'Thank you for this,' he said softly.

Though anxious, Eve looked pleased. 'Geoffrey can't wait to see you. He remembers you very well from school. How odd,' she went on, 'since you knew each other for only a year.'

'It was a *memorable* year,' Tom replied cautiously.

'He's engaged with a meeting in the library at the minute, but he'll be with us shortly.'

How much did Mansworth remember? Tom recalled his dreadful smile at the summit of Hammer Peak after Arthur Pigeon's fall. Had time changed him at all? It seemed unlikely. Audrey had reminded Tom that Mansworth was still contesting his father's will and was staunchly determined to prevent his sister and Oscar from sharing the family fortune.

Another couple was waiting in the sitting room.

'You've inspired me to bring the family together, Tom,' said Eve. 'This is my sister-in-law, Penelope, and her husband, Oscar Limpkin.'

'Tom!' Oscar shot up from his chair. Now fifty-one, with a broad, unforgettable grin and a greying red moustache, he simultaneously shook and embraced Tom. 'Is it really *you*? Good heavens, isn't this a peach! I never thought I'd see you again, Tom, *never*! Penny, this is Tom!'

Last seen by Tom through a bedroom window in Kensington, Penelope Limpkin's pretty face had become frail over the years. She offered him a timid but earnest smile. 'Hello, Tom,' she said. 'I'm so glad to meet you. Isn't it so very kind of Eve to invite us here? Geoffrey and I haven't spoken for years.'

What a price she had paid for marrying Oscar, Tom thought.

'I told you our luck would improve, Penny!' Oscar's eyes danced, and Tom could see his old friend concocting a plan. 'Tom, I *must* have a private word with you! Please excuse us!' He took Tom's arm and steered him out of Eve's earshot. 'You are precisely the man I need to speak to,' he whispered. 'My next biography is about Geoffrey Mansworth, and as I remember, you knew him as a boy.'

'I did,' Tom replied.

'Well, I shan't hold back this time, Tom. The public will know the truth about him. No more chummy biographies for me. I'm going to write the facts!'

'Is that prudent,' Tom said, 'given your kinship?'

Oscar squinted at Tom indignantly. 'He is a warmonger, a profiteer, and he has denied his own sister her birthright! People must know what kind of a man—'

'*What kind of a man, indeed!*' boomed a voice.

Tom turned to see a figure standing at the threshold. The eyes were puffy, and the skin was pale and blotched with bruises. One hand clutched a silver-handled stick. He was a mere shadow of the man pictured in the silver frame. He stepped into the room with painful, cautious movements, his whitened knuckles pressing the stick for support. This was a very sick man, Tom guessed.

'I knew you would come,' said Mansworth, without addressing Tom by name. He sat slowly before the group, gasped and gestured for a glass. Eve was ready with the sherry and placed it in his hand. Mansworth nodded his thanks, but Eve hung behind him, more like an attendant, Tom thought, than a wife.

'Oscar? Penelope? What a pleasant surprise. Eve, you've put together quite a committee for me.'

His wife looked slightly wounded by his remark. 'It's a nice change, isn't it, to see *family*?'

Mansworth's eyes skated warily to Eve, then to Tom. 'Yes. Well, at the very least, my past has caught up with me.'

'Yes, Geoffrey,' said Oscar, gloating. 'Tom is going to tell me about your childhood for my new biography!'

Mansworth answered Oscar's remark with a dead stare. 'My childhood? How convenient,' he said finally. 'Between Penelope, Tom and my wife, you won't need to consult *me* at all!'

When his sarcasm produced no amusement, Mansworth looked disappointed. He studied his sherry for a moment.

'The book will be *authentic*, Geoffrey.' Oscar savoured his next words, clearly wishing to irritate the man. 'People will be able to weigh your past deeds against your aspiration to be prime minister. Tom and I are old friends. He'll tell me *everything*.'

Mansworth eyed Tom over the rim of his sherry glass, and remarked with mock sorrow: 'Are my secrets no longer safe with you?'

'For a price, perhaps,' Tom replied.

Mansworth's smile faded. 'What brings you here?' he growled. 'Surely it can't be the weather.'

'The war,' Tom replied.

'The war,' echoed Mansworth. 'I advise keeping at a safe distance from it.' He smiled. 'Go south, Bedlam. Go south.'

'My son has been shipped to La Bourse, in northern France. I'd like to have him back. Perhaps you can win the war without him.'

Mansworth nodded gravely. 'Well, my friend, at the beginning of the war we took soldiers no shorter than five foot eight. Now we'll take them at five foot three. They're *all* needed now. What's his rank?'

'He's an assistant bombardier in the South African Heavy Artillery.'

'Artillery?' Mansworth gave a sniff. 'I wouldn't move him from the artillery. His chances there are better than in the trenches.'

His casual indifference brought sudden tears to Tom's eyes. He sat down. Eve saw his reaction, and she put her hand on his shoulder in consolation. Mansworth's eyes met hers, but she kept her hand where it was, as if in defiance of him.

'Penny and I also have a son in the war, Tom,' said Oscar brightly. 'He was at Suez, and at the fall of Jerusalem. An officer; a captain, actually, and only twenty!'

'So has Audrey,' said Tom.

'Audrey, yes,' said Oscar. 'Poor Audrey.'

The group's shared sympathy caused Mansworth to wince. He interrupted the ensuing silence. 'Well, every war needs soldiers,' he said. 'And sacrifices. Losses too.'

'All the more reason to end it,' said Oscar.

Mansworth glared at him. 'It keeps our economy going. It is paying for your dinner and the wine in your glass. So spare me a lecture, Oscar. Those are the terms of my hospitality.'

Mansworth turned his eye to the dining room. At once, the kitchen maid appeared to welcome the guests to dinner.

Eve glanced apologetically at her guests and ushered them into the dining room. Amid the silver settings and candlelight, the conversation seemed to wander aimlessly, as it invariably does when the subject on everyone's mind has been banned. By the time dessert was served, Mansworth had begun to complain of pain and announced that he was retiring to bed.

Tom asked if a doctor was treating him.

'Ten doctors. *Ten doctors*, each with a different opinion!'

'Has any suggested a kidney ailment?'

'Probably,' growled Mansworth. 'I can't remember.'

'I would prescribe eight glasses of water a day and absolutely no strong drink,' Tom said.

'And I would suggest you go to hell!' Mansworth smiled, his eyes skating to his other guests. 'I have no intention of giving up the very things that make my life tolerable!'

'You have a beautiful wife, a precious daughter,' replied Tom sharply. 'What else is worth dying for?'

Mansworth flinched; sentiment was apparently more painful to him than his physical infirmities. 'Help me up the stairs, Doctor.'

With Tom flanking him, Mansworth slowly ascended the winding staircase of his mansion. He paused at the top, turned his scrutiny to the guests lingering in the dining room, and leaned closer to Tom. 'I have something to say to you in confidence,' he said. 'I shall look into bringing your son back. It may take some time. In return, I would appreciate it if you would do me the favour of resisting Oscar's inquiries. I won't have him blacken my name.'

Tom stared at Mansworth. 'Very well,' he said. 'If you bring my son home.'

'What's the boy's name?'

'Arthur Chapel.'

'Arthur?' Mansworth frowned. 'You didn't name him after Arthur Pigeon, did you?'

'I did.'

'Why?'

'I did it to remember him,' replied Tom. 'He was like a brother. I betrayed him for my own gain – and yours.'

Mansworth said nothing but led Tom into his lavish bedroom. Tom recognized Eve's touches – a small framed Corot of the Grand Canal hung at her side of the bed, and a photograph of Josephine stood on the table. A heavy brass telephone sat on the table at Mansworth's side.

The war minister removed his jacket, wrapped a silk robe around his bloated frame, and lay down on the bed. He looked at Tom. 'Arthur Pigeon,' he mused. 'How *far* we've come since then. Think of the good you've done, Tom. You're a doctor. You've saved lives, I'm sure. My father gave you that education.' He smiled. 'I'm war minister.' He nodded slyly. 'Your role in my destiny has not been forgotten, Tom. Look what we've achieved together!'

'Together?' Tom stared at him.

'I think Eve loved you once,' replied Mansworth. 'We married sisters. You must admit that our lives are curiously linked.'

'There is no comparison between us,' Tom replied. 'I heal the sick. You commit men to *die.* My son is at war. Your daughter is safe at home. If you had any compassion, Mansworth, you would end the war. End it tomorrow. Bring them all home. Pass the order. Retire. You'll change the lives of thousands in a day. Give back the sons to their mothers, the husbands to their wives, the children to their families.'

Mansworth chuckled, amused by Tom's fervour.

'How *poetic* you sound,' he murmured. 'First you ask me to save your son, then you ask me to save every boy in uniform. Don't you know, Bedlam, that half of the country would tar and feather me if I brought our men back without victory?'

'The other half would thank you.'

Mansworth closed his eyes. 'I'd like to be prime minister one day. You see, I have to do more than run the war effort. I have to make sure we do it with honour.'

'How many more men will die while you manoeuvre your political career?'

Mansworth grunted. 'Remember our bargain, Doctor,' he replied, smiling faintly, and then he began to snore. A dark shadow crossed the doorway; it was the valet, coming to pick up the clothes and hang them in the wardrobe. For a quiet moment, Tom marvelled at a missed opportunity: if only he'd brought his medical bag, he could have given the wretched man an overdose of morphine and ended the debate for good. But he had made a bargain for the life of his son.

AT THE TOP OF THE STAIRS, Eve was waiting for him.

'Is he dying?' she asked.

Tom knew better than to reply to such a direct question. 'You must encourage him to go to hospital. He's very ill.'

Eve shook her head. 'He'll never agree to that,' she replied. 'To enter a hospital would be an invitation to his enemies to bring about his retirement from government.'

'Eve,' Tom began, 'I understand that you wish him to succeed, but he will not live to be prime minister if he doesn't receive treatment.'

She flinched at his words. 'Can you truly believe I'm that ambitious? I have no influence upon him. I've proposed many dinner guests, but you're the first person he's agreed to see. *He* suggested inviting Oscar and Penelope. What did he ask of you? There must have been something. Some favour.'

Tom noticed that Eve's alabaster makeup faded at the base of her neck to reveal her true skin colour. Under the circumstances it seemed an appropriate flaw. 'Was it about me?' she continued. 'I told him I loved you once. Did he show any concern? Any jealousy? He's a possessive man.'

The poor woman, Tom thought. Had she invited him merely to light some jealous spark in her husband? How mercenary we are in the name of family. But he couldn't lie to her about Geoffrey Mansworth. He had lived with one devastating lie for thirty-five years.

'Eve,' he replied. 'Geoffrey doesn't want me to tell Oscar about events in his childhood. He's afraid it will ruin his political prospects.'

Eve paused; then her composure snapped. 'Damn him,' she sobbed. 'God help me, Cortez,' she whispered. 'If it were not for Josephine, I'd wish him dead.'

MARTINE

Many nights after dinner at the barracks they played brag, a game of poker with three cards. One evening, Garson had the bank and was telling a joke when they heard a gas shell whistling overhead. Everybody tumbled down the steps of the cellar as it burst. They emerged a few minutes later to find Garson still seated, covered with dust, his arms spread across the table, protecting the cards and the money. The fumes had blown away quickly in the breeze. The men cheered Garson for his bravery, though McCormick took a different view.

'You're a blasted *idiot*, Garson,' he said.

All Arthur had thought about during those few minutes in the cellar was Martine's safety. 'I worry about you during the attacks,' he told her later.

'When the bombs fall, we go to the church of Saint-Agnant.'

'What makes you think it is safe?' he asked.

'It hasn't been touched yet,' she replied, 'and the crypt is deep and made of stone. Everybody still in the town goes there. They have beds, food, everything.' She put her lips close to his ear and whispered lustily, 'Maybe I'll take *you* there sometime.'

The next week the company was moved to Vermelles, a small town seven miles from Béthune. Arthur could visit Martine only once a week, but Madame d'Usseau permitted her daughter to leave the estaminet in his company for an hour. It was enough time to walk to the wheat fields, disappear among the swaying stalks, cautiously arouse each other, and lie in each other's arms, staring at the limitless sky and entertaining daydreams of life after the war. But with each week that went by, their moments together became darker and more desperate.

Without Madame d'Usseau as an impediment to their lovemaking, their encounters became serious. They made love, then argued. The tension stemmed from their frustration, a desire for stability, a yearning for an existence beyond food shortages, thunderous barrages, shattered houses and heaps of rubble.

Once, when Arthur whistled 'Rule, Britannia' after Martine reached her climax, she cried, 'Be serious! I love you!'

As they threw on their clothes, he promised her everything would be all right, but his assurances meant nothing. *Nothing* would be all right.

On the fourth weekend, Martine led him silently into the fields, and when he put his hand playfully over her breast, she struck his cheek. 'Make love to me as a husband makes love to his wife,' she said. They had never done this before; she had been afraid of becoming pregnant.

'Are you sure?' said Arthur.

Martine led him into the middle of a field of golden sheaves beneath a sky of puffy storybook clouds. They removed all of their clothes. His army coat served as a mattress and her shawl as a blanket. Arthur hadn't seen Martine's bare shoulders before, and he was astonished that she looked so pallid and vulnerable beneath him.

'You're covered with freckles,' she remarked, caressing his arm with similar astonishment.

Arthur paused, as if their nakedness might put her off the whole venture, but she pivoted her hips impatiently, and in a few moments he had penetrated her, and they forgot the swooping magpies and the soaring cumuli above them, imagining themselves as husband and wife in another place, far away. When Martine didn't reach climax, Arthur made an effort to change position, but she insisted that he enter her again. She kept her hands on his back, digging her fingernails into him. Finally, he reached a third, painful climax. Martine indicated that he should stay inside her. As they lay together, her eyes filled with tears.

'Martine,' he said.

'Again,' she replied.

'This is not pleasure,' he began.

'*Again,*' she insisted. 'Fuck me.'

It was then that he realized she had an entirely different motive. 'I want to be finished with you. I want not to *want* you any more!'

They walked back to town in silence. Martine wouldn't look at him; her hair was loose and wild, and she wouldn't speak. Arthur felt sick to his stomach. He begged her to talk to him, but in her torment she remained silent. He worried about returning her to Madame d'Usseau in such a state.

'I would rather be alone,' she answered, when he offered to see her to her door.

'Next week, then?' he asked.

'No. Don't come again,' she answered, adding, 'Don't come ever again. It's over. I can't stand it any more.'

MARGARET'S LETTER

October 1, 1918

Dear Father,

I am doing my best to cope with your patients. They all want to know when you are coming back, as I do.

Dr Green is doing an adequate job as your substitute, though he is a little timid. When old Mrs Muerling came in with an infection (below the waist), he insisted that I conduct the examination while he stood at the far end of the consulting room and stared at the wall. I had to walk back and forth, whispering in his ear, then re-examining her, then answering his questions. All the while, the poor woman had terror on her face because the doctor wouldn't go near her.

Yesterday the little Coxton boy came in with a rubber duck stuffed up his you-know-what. This must be the fourth time. I don't know how the boy walks around comfortably. His mother simply shakes her head when I inquire what inspired him to do this.

I asked John to speak to him, and he wisely told the boy that God wouldn't have given us pockets if he meant us to keep things in our you-know-whats. Have no idea whether this made an impression.

We are very excited about the wedding. You will remember that it is on November 11th. It is my hope that you will bring my sisters back with you. They both claim to be in London (addresses enclosed).

No news from Arthur. I pray that our fighting forces may be victorious.

Sincerely,
Margaret

THE END IS NEAR~REJOICE!

It was a squalid existence. Charity's room was five feet wide and eight feet long. The Pendleton philosophy dictated that people sleep alone but spend all the rest of their time in the company of the group. Charity had lost twenty-five pounds. She knew this only because she had to take in her dresses by inches every few months; her only personal possession was her sewing box, stowed secretly beneath her bed. The hall sister allowed her to keep it so that she could secure the loose buttons of her brothers and sisters. 'Remember, Sister Charity, vanity is a sin,' she reminded her.

She had been in London for six months but had seen little of it besides her lodgings off Piccadilly Circus and the mission hall. She played with the chorus every evening at the rallies and then there were the trips around the country. Birmingham, Leeds, Sheffield, Bristol – the rallies attracted the solitary, the lonely, and those who had lost loved ones to the war. There were plenty of those. Time was running out, and there were so many people to be saved.

Charity didn't have much of an appetite lately. Perhaps it was the food, which wasn't very good, or perhaps it was simply that the days had a wearying banality. Reading the newspaper was discouraged. 'Let us not be distracted from *our purpose*,' Isaiah Pound reminded them. Books, newspapers, letters, postcards were all distractions.

Sometimes she couldn't bear it, and would try to slip out for a walk, but someone always joined her – Sister Amelia, usually. She always seemed to be on the lookout for Charity. She often peered into her room, and always turned up to eat with her. Once Charity asked Amelia if she had sisters.

'*You're* my sister.' Sister Amelia smiled.

'But what about your family?'

'*This* is my family,' Sister Amelia replied matter-of-factly. 'No other family matters.'

Sometimes they walked together around Piccadilly Circus, looking for people to invite to the rallies. Solitary souls were the most receptive. One evening Sister Amelia spotted a nurse who appeared to be talking to herself; she wore a uniform, with white shoes and a white cap that draped to her shoulders.

When Sister Amelia greeted her, the woman's lips seemed to stop in midconversation. Startled, she stared at the two young women and abruptly buried her trembling hands in her pockets.

'I'm Sister Amelia, and this is Sister Charity. Are you lost?'

'No,' replied the woman. 'My husband's lost, but I'm not.'

'Is there anything we can do to help?' said Charity.

The woman's chin bobbed with emotion, and she shook her head. 'He died.'

'Oh, you poor dear,' said Sister Amelia. 'You must be so lonely.'

The woman's eyebrows rose pitifully.

'Do you need somewhere to stay? Something to eat, perhaps?'

The woman shook her head. 'I *have* a home. I have a job. I'm a nurse.'

'Sometimes it's comforting to share your feelings,' said Amelia.

They bought her a cup of tea and inquired gently about her life. The woman explained that she worked at a local hospital, that she used to nurse children, and that she wanted children, but that was impossible now.

'We all seek to fill a void,' Isaiah Pound repeatedly reminded his followers. This nurse was a potential Pendleton. If they could get her to a rally, she would probably join.

The sisters offered the woman gentle sympathy. 'I'm so sorry about your husband. Was it an accident?'

The nurse hesitated. 'Oh, no, dear, it was murder.'

'Murder?' cried Sister Amelia. 'How terrible!'

'Yes.' The woman nodded. 'It was a terrible way to die. He was pushed off a mountain when he was just a little boy. The shepherds found him. Poor thing.'

Sister Amelia smiled nervously. 'A little boy? But I thought he was your husband—'

'Yes, dear,' said the woman, as though there was no apparent contradiction in this logic. 'And one day I'll avenge his death. The minister of war killed him, you know – Geoffrey Mansworth.'

It was evident that the woman was a little confused, so the two Pendletons quickly wished her well and parted ways with her.

'Poor dear,' said Sister Amelia. 'I didn't know what to believe of her story. And such a strange name – Polly Pigeon.'

SANCTUARY

Vermelles stood a mile from Loos, which had suffered intense destruction at the beginning of the war. Norkin said that the British had accidentally poisoned many of their own troops there during a botched gas attack. Because of their exposure on the flat plain, the C.O. directed camouflage netting to be strung in front of the artillery placements. It did little to assuage the soldiers' sense of exposure in the flat countryside. Strict orders were issued to extinguish all lights at dusk for fear of giving the Germans a mark.

Arthur's melancholy provoked sympathy from the others. Garson tried to commiserate with a little speech about the duplicity of women, but Arthur believed Martine was simply trying to protect herself.

The devastation in Vermelles echoed his despair; houses stood without roofs and walls, just the leaden window frames intact. An enormous stone crucifix stood at the entrance to the town graveyard, and the many crosses marking the graves stood upright in orderly rows – a stark contrast to the shambles in town.

One morning Arthur was awoken by Hartwell yelling in his ear: 'Chapel! The Fritzes are on the move!'

Arthur staggered out of the barracks to see the street full of a battalion of Highlanders marching in formation on their way back from Loos. The skirl of bagpipes filled his ears; each piper led a platoon in steel helmets and full battle gear. The sight of their grimly magnificent faces filled him with a burst of envy. These men didn't piss in their trousers, he was sure of it.

Behind the Highlanders, black smoke rose and guns thundered.

The artillery group met to discuss strategy. 'We suspect that the Germans will advance today,' explained the C.O. 'Our company will keep firing until they appear a quarter mile away. If they advance, we cannot let them claim our artillery. We need four men to destroy them while the rest of the company leaves.'

Arthur volunteered with Hartwell, Norkin and Garson.

'You'll have to blow up the guns by inserting one shell into the breech,' explained the gunner, 'and another into the muzzle, fuse first. Then you fire the gun with a lanyard from about fifty feet away. The gun will blow itself to pieces.'

The gunner gave Arthur a length of telephone wire for the lanyard, and Arthur took a service rifle and a few clips of ammunition, and waited with the other men.

At 4.00 p.m., beneath a sunless, grey sky, the German advance commenced with a salvo of woolly bears – soldier slang for shells that explode overhead in billowing clouds, raining shrapnel on their victims. The company cleared out, leaving one truck for the last four men. Suddenly, the Number 1 and 4 guns exploded in direct hits. Both Norkin and Garson died instantly. Arthur and Hartwell dragged their bodies to the trucks and set about detonating the remaining two guns. As Arthur put the first shell into Number 3 gun, he saw movement on the horizon – an eerie column of men merged with machinery.

'Almost ready?' Hartwell shouted. Arthur nodded as his companion, having secured a cable to his howitzer, scrambled backwards to set it off from behind a small standing wall.

Arthur hoisted the second shell into the open muzzle of Number 3 gun, then ran to his position to set it off. His heart was beating loudly, and his senses seemed to sharpen with the impending urgency of his task – his footsteps crunched on pulverized brick, he heard the sharp report of rifle fire in the distance, and his left knee began shaking uncontrollably. To calm himself, he listed the simple order of his tasks: detonate gun, sprint to truck with Hartwell, drive towards Annequin. Which way was Annequin? Was it to the left or right? Never mind, he thought, Hartwell will know.

Another sound broke his concentration: a German biplane swooped over the dun landscape. Arthur guessed it was probably assessing the Allied retreat.

Hartwell's gun suddenly exploded with an unfamiliar crack. The assembly blew to pieces, sending a wheel spinning out of the pit while a large piece of the howitzer barrel revolved upwards. Arthur watched it rise slowly to its apogee. Then, as it fell, he realized it was going to land precisely where Hartwell lay.

'Hartwell!' he cried.

But no sooner had his warning been spoken than the howitzer's barrel struck the small wall, creating a dust cloud.

'Hartwell?'

There was no reply. Arthur tugged his telephone wire, ducked as his gun exploded, then without thinking to look overhead, ran to his friend. Halfway to the wall, he recognized part of Hartwell's torso in the dust. Then, he heard the vigorous chatter of the biplane's machine gun.

A strafe of bullets tore into the truck, igniting it with a thunderous pop, followed by a rain of metal. The plane veered up and around for a second run. Arthur stood still, confused. The order of his tasks had been sabotaged.

His throat stung from the burning cloud enveloping the truck. Something hot landed on his back, and he felt his tunic burning. He tore off his jacket with his satchel, seized a bicycle, and pedalled away, counting his own shrill breaths. When the road passed through a copse of fir trees, he felt the sublime relief of a rabbit in the undergrowth. In the pines, he couldn't hear the rifles. The whine of the plane subsided. There was a blessed and petrifying silence.

He emerged from the wood at a crossroads. The sun was now impossible to see behind a blanket of clouds. Arthur's compass had been in the satchel he had cast off. Not only might he run into the advancing German infantry but he had left his rifle behind. Where was Annequin? Perhaps he was riding to Sailly, or Noyelles. It was impossible to know, so he proceeded, hoping he would eventually see some familiar landmark.

After a few miles, Arthur entered a devastated town and spotted a steeple. The church appeared to be the only untouched structure. He remembered Martine's remark: *Everybody still in the town goes there.* Was this the church she attended on Sundays? It was a limestone structure, with Gothic windows and a central, stained-glass window – still gloriously intact.

Suddenly, he heard the sound of an axe hacking into wood.

'Halt,' cried a voice. Arthur turned and saw a soldier in a khaki serge uniform. A cigarette hung from his lower lip.

'Georgie?' he cried.

The soldier grinned. 'Arthur Chapel! What the hell are you doing here?'

'I've lost my way. All the signs are gone!'

The debonair soldier grinned. 'That's my job, chum. Destroy the signs to obstruct the enemy advance.' Georgie Goode indicated a sign he had hacked from the church wall. He offered Arthur a ride on his motorcycle back to the rest of his company.

'If you'll wait, I'll pick you up in ten minutes. I have one more sign on the Sailly road to take down.'

Arthur agreed to meet Georgie at the church of Saint-Agnant. He pedalled towards the church and rested his bicycle below the saints that stood above the Gothic doorway. Their grey faces seemed focused on the devastated city and the mournful column of black smoke on the horizon. Martine had told him that this church's crypt was the safest place to be during an attack. Arthur hesitated at the door and looked up – thinking of Martine, hoping to see one stone face with an expression of compassion. He needed to believe that fortune had brought him here for a reason.

He entered, and a cool breeze enveloped him. How blessedly peaceful it was. An anguished, life-size statue of Jesus hung above the altar, gnarled toes nailed together with an iron spike. A phalanx of tin pipes marked the organ on the second level, to the right. The battered pews had cushions of worn velvet. The floorboards were dull and bowed.

Behind the apse, a small chamber lay with a desk and several shelves of books; a priest's black cassock was draped over a chair. A circular staircase led up to the organ but none to the crypt. Arthur circled the pews. After a second circuit, he noticed a rug behind the altar. He lifted a corner, but it was tacked to the floorboards. Spying a ring, Arthur pulled at it, and a hatch rose to reveal steps.

Scores of faces in the darkness peered up at him, but before he could react, he heard the growl of a truck. Arthur let the hatch fall and, running past the pews, peered through the stained-glass windows to see the progress of a vehicle manned with German soldiers, a machine gun mounted on its roof.

It halted outside the church. The soldier at the machine gun scanned the church, then spun around to survey the landscape behind him. Almost as soon as Arthur thought of Georgie Goode, he heard the rattle of a motorcycle speeding back along the Sailly road. In a moment, the two drivers spied each other.

Through the window Arthur saw a German lieutenant wave Georgie down. Georgie stopped and raised his hands, with the motorcycle still idling. As the German opened his door to climb out, Georgie tore forward, kicking the truck's door shut, and accelerated. The machine gunner spun around and fired at his back.

It happened so slowly: Georgie seemed to tumble from his motorcycle as if he had simply fallen asleep. The cigarette fell from his lips. His body slumped gently into a heap on the road while the machine continued forward until its front wheel twisted and the cycle spun side over side and struck a post.

Arthur ran to the apse, kneeled to the carpet, and pulled at the ring of the hatch, but it had been bolted. He considered pleading with the people below to open the hatch but knew he would imperil Martine and the others hiding down there. His eyes shifted to the cassock that was draped upon the chair. Quickly, he shed his uniform and slipped it on. Before he could appraise his appearance, he heard a voice call from the front of the church.

'*Ist da jemand?*' cried a helmeted silhouette.

UNFINISHED BUSINESS

'WHY NOT?' OSCAR REPLIED.

Tom had refused to discuss Mansworth's past.

'Because he is going to bring Arthur back from France.'

Oscar burst into laughter. 'He *promised* that?'

'I have no choice but to believe him.'

'He's a liar,' said Oscar bitterly. 'You'd be a fool to believe him. Don't you see, Tom? This is how he manipulates people. He's protecting his political future by silencing me. The last thing he'll do is bring Arthur back, because then you'd have no need of him.'

'I'm sorry, Oscar,' said Tom, 'but Mansworth's my only hope.'

Oscar's amusement faded. 'Look, I've a son in uniform too,' he said. 'I know the desperation you feel, so I'll try to find out if Arthur's safe.'

TOM TOOK A NAP that afternoon, but something caused him to sit bolt upright, eyes wide open, heart thumping in his chest. A fearsome panic gripped his throat. He couldn't speak, yet a torrent of awful thoughts gripped him. Which of his children was in danger?

He staggered about his room, drank water, unbuttoned his collar, threw open the window and peered at the skyline. A dirigible hung over St Paul's Cathedral. A horn blared, the sound ricocheting against the buildings. Was it a motorcar, or the Pendletons marching again?

There was a sudden knock at his door, and a note was pushed under it to announce the presence of a visitor downstairs.

Tom found his father filling his pockets with pencils, matches and any other items on the proprietress's counter.

'My boy! I thought I might propose dinner, if you are so inclined.'

Tom escorted the old man out of the hotel lobby while the other patrons stared at the carnival apparition with ramrod nose, wooden leg and broad grin.

'Do I embarrass you, Tom?' Bedlam asked, as his son steered him across the street.

'Immensely,' replied Tom.

Bedlam chuckled. 'When you are my age, you won't care about appearances or attitudes. People are stunted by their own prejudices,' he said merrily. 'I hate no man, Tom. I am a man at peace. I expect nothing from anybody.'

'You expect me to pay for dinner,' Tom replied.

After a wounded silence, Bedlam admitted that he was famished and begged his son not to insult him when his stomach was empty.

Tom chose the restaurant this time, an establishment with white linen tablecloths and attentive waiters. They were placed at a window table. Immediately Bedlam complained of the small helpings at London's finer restaurants.

'Have you eaten here before?' asked Tom.

'Well, no,' admitted his father.

'Then your complaint is premature,' replied Tom.

'In truth, it's not the size of the helpings that troubles me,' began Bedlam, 'but that you owe me much more than dinner.'

'Oh?' said Tom. 'What do I owe you?'

The old actor preened the strands of silver hair that fell to his shoulders and adopted a grave expression to match his words. 'Forgiveness, of course.'

'Forgiveness?' Tom repeated.

Bedlam nodded, and his face took on a sentimental cast:

When thou dost ask me blessing, I'll kneel down,
and ask of thee forgiveness: and we'll live,
and pray, and sing, and tell old tales.

He put his hands together and looked his son in the eye. '*Forgive me*, my boy. Make peace with me.'

Tom regarded the man with astonishment. 'Father, you love no one but yourself. You're conceited and conniving. You've exploited me at every occasion. And, most of all, you ask for redemption without offering to change in any way!'

Bedlam shrugged. 'I admit, my boy, I am incapable of reform. I'm old, Tom, and too set in my ways.'

Then, to Tom's horror, the old man began to weep. His face took on a pitiful cast, tears rolled down his cheeks, and his shrill sobs turned the heads of the other restaurant patrons. 'I dominate all conversations and draw every subject to myself. I consider my needs above all others.' He groaned. 'I crave an audience, and adore the sound of my own voice. I'm a wretch, conceited, selfish, slothful.' He blew his nose on a table napkin. 'Now, old Paddy claims these are vices, but I maintain they are an actor's *strengths*!' Bedlam dabbed at his eyes and summoned his pride with a heaving gasp. 'But, I ask you, what sort of actor would I be if I didn't think myself worthy of an audience? What kind of actor hides his light under a bushel? Hmm? I would be a *mussel*, silent in the clay, *buried* among other mussels, in a vast mussel bed – still, silent and ignored.'

Now he leaned forward to his son imploringly. 'Accept me for my conceits, Tom. Please, if I die without redemption, without relief from my burden, what a tragedy it will be!'

Tom heard Audrey's voice in his head, counselling reconciliation, but how could he dispense with an anger nursed since boyhood? How *could* he forgive his father? The outrage that had burned in his chest for all these years was a vital sustaining force; it had driven him to bring up his children in defiance of his father's shabby betrayals and powered his convictions about marriage and moral decency. It was his very foundation. For all he knew, to forgive this man might rob his heart of the ability to beat.

'I cannot.'

'I beg you, Tom. *I beg you.*' The face across the table implored, eyes wide, mouth contorted like the mask of tragedy. 'Give an old man what he asks.'

'What will you give me in return?'

'In return?' Now Bedlam looked startled. 'What can I possibly give you?' he asked. 'What have I to give?'

Tom brooded in silence. Eventually he replied, 'I want to know what you did with my brother.'

'I would never have hurt a hair on that boy's head. I gave him to an esteemed gentleman who promised to find him a good home. That's all I know of him!'

'What esteemed gentleman?'

'You've met him: Tobias Griff.'

'Did Mr Griff tell you where the baby went? Did he know his name? Was it Arthur Pigeon?'

Bedlam shook his head. 'I never knew the name. Never wanted to know.'

'Why not?'

'I had failed, hadn't I?' The old man averted his eyes to study the tablecloth. 'What father gives away his son? Hmmm? Better not to know. Mr Griff said it was best that only he knew the child's origin and destination.' A feeble smile returned to the actor's face. 'In my experience, the truth of *any* matter is a disappointment. Box office receipts, audience in attendance, income per annum. Best not to know. Ignorance is bliss.'

'I'd come to believe that my brother had perished, most probably of a broken heart,' said Tom. 'If I am mistaken, I promise you, Father, I shall be delighted. I shall visit Mr Griff forthwith!'

SUCH A GIFT

GOD HAD TAKEN SECOND LIEUTENANT DIETER WEEKS.

The captain had lost thirteen of his men in that day's advance, but his grief was spent mourning one man, the man who epitomized the spirit of the company, the man who had elevated the idiots, the vulgar scoundrels, the weak and the dim-witted into a respectable group of fighters. It was a shameful admission, but just as a teacher has his pet, the captain had Dieter Weeks. The second lieutenant was as strong as a bull, argumentative (especially on the virtues of Schubert and Goethe), and insistent that Handel's Baroque operas were superior to anything written by an Italian. He was absurdly built, with an enormous trunk, a swelling gut, no buttocks to speak of, and a walk that was more stagger than stride. Malformed, stubborn and noisy when he joined the company, Dieter Weeks had seemed a prime candidate to supervise the trench-digging crew. His surname, after all, was not even German.

One drizzling night he was sent on patrol to find a few men who were missing after an assault. The enemy began a fusillade to cut him down, and the man vanished in the fog. They had given him up for lost after three hours, but suddenly, out of the darkness, the captain heard someone whistling 'Ombra mai fu'. When he whistled the tune back, the second lieutenant had sprung up with four other men and sprinted through enemy fire to the safety of their trench.

What a wondrous fool the fellow was! When every other man was shitting in his trousers before an attack, the second lieutenant's tuneless voice would start a melody, and soon the entire company would be humming. He was the mascot, the bumpkin and the bravest of them all.

How many times had Weeks brought back a wounded man on his shoulders? Too many to count. He was no figure of beauty, but he was nimble and fast with his hands. He cheated at cards and could finish off the plate of an unwary cadet as it sat in his lap. And he was stubborn: he had once driven a sergeant into a fury by arguing that the world was flat. Dieter Weeks believed that God was a fiction and churches were a conceit built by the many for the elevation of the few. Furthermore, he claimed that meat sapped a man of his prowess, and a diet of potato and cabbage would give a fellow a mighty hard-on. His flatulence was legendary. No one would sit with him after dinner. Rumour was he once lit a fart that burned so brightly he was demoted for exposing his company's position to the enemy. Yet he earned his rank back a week later by rescuing a lieutenant trapped between trenches.

Why on earth would any God take a man like that?

When machine-gun fire ripped into him that morning, Weeks tumbled like a sack of potatoes, his belly spilling its contents into the mud. Oh, the awful sight of such a titan collapsing into meat and bones! When he cried out, his throat turned scarlet and red bubbles burst from the black maw of his gaping neck. That was the end of the music. That was the end of the farting, whistling contrarian, and the end of his brothers' fighting spirit. Even the sergeant who lost the argument about the shape of the world wept for Dieter Weeks.

It was hard to feel victorious with Weeks gone. They were all sheep now. They would continue to sleep, salvage and shore up their defensive line, like good soldiers, but the captain had no doubt that the enemy would come back for Béthune in a week or two, the lines would change again, and there would be plenty more Germans buried beside the second lieutenant.

But the sight of this church spire brought back the captain's fury – this tribute to the God who had let Dieter Weeks fall. With vengeance burning in his throat, the captain circled the buttresses and stonework, choking with renewed grief. Why should a structure dedicated to an indifferent God be intact when every man's home was shattered, every school, every hospital, every museum and library was in shambles?

Well, the first apostle of Dieter Weeks wouldn't tolerate it. The captain vowed to eat no more meat; it would be potatoes and cabbage for dinner. God was dead. And the earth was as flat as a mess plate.

'I want this building taken down,' he told his sergeant.

'The church, sir?'

'Yes, the church. I want it blown to pieces.'

The sergeant dusted one of the carved faces of the saints on the massive door with his woollen cap. 'Imagine what people will say about us if we destroy it. It must be more than five hundred years old.'

But the captain was resolute. What better memorial to Dieter Weeks than to turn a monstrosity like this to rubble?

The sergeant made a final plea: 'Let me warn the priest if he's here. We don't want to leave them with a martyr.'

The captain granted him five minutes to find the man and ordered a crew to rig the central columns with explosives.

It took the sergeant fifteen minutes to reappear. And when he did, he was flushed and in despair.

'He's inside. He refuses to leave. He says we cannot touch the church. "It's a sanctuary," he says.'

'Take two men and *carry* him out!'

'Impossible, sir. He is upstairs playing the organ. The stair doors are thick and old, locked from inside the stairwell.'

The captain drew his pistol and entered the church, with the sergeant following anxiously behind him.

The interior was dark and grand, and the low hum of the organ sent a chill up the captain's spine. A few bare lightbulbs hung from the ceiling – the ugly intrusion of modernity on a Baroque masterpiece. Yes, he admitted that it was a masterpiece – the vaulted ceilings; the dark chapels with their sleeping lords, recumbent hounds at their feet; the anguished monsters peeking from their stone pillars; the heartbreaking splendour of the stained-glass saints, their beatific faces and beseeching palms – all Christian hokum.

The agonized Christ stared reproachfully at the captain's piercing footsteps.

Forgive me, thought the captain, but I'm a disciple of Dieter Weeks now. I'll take your priest as my first sacrifice.

The priest sat before the Baroque organ, with its carved wooden façade and vast array of tin pipes. He pressed a key. A deep note echoed through the church, and the electric lights dimmed.

The captain raised his gun, preparing to fire a bullet through the man's head.

Then a melody emerged from the organ, and the captain gasped.

It was a Schubert impromptu. Strange to hear it played on an organ, especially such a familiar melody; the captain was used to hearing it whistled crudely by the second lieutenant, but it was unmistakable. The phrases sprang sweetly into the vaulted ceiling, and the grandeur of the organ's resonant notes drew the strength from the captain's legs. He sank into a pew, lips trembling.

Out of the corner of his eye, Arthur saw the captain lower his pistol. He hadn't performed this piece in years; he couldn't even call it to mind, but it seemed to leap from his fingers the moment he touched the keys. Arthur didn't know any church music, that was Charity's domain. But this melody always reminded him of church. It was the piece his mother used to play most often, the piece Charity had played at the wake. That was the amazing thing about music. It could reside, dormant, in one's fingertips. Arthur couldn't remember his mother's last day clearly, just a glimpse of the doorway to her bedroom and the knowledge that she was gone. But he knew the *feeling* – the grief bursting out of his chest in helpless sobs, his loneliness, the ache of wishing to see her face again at his bedside, or beckoning to him from the dogcart in her white linens, or smiling with astonishment when he first played the piano for her. In the same way that his fingers had never forgotten this melody, his eyes still expected to see his mother again.

As the German captain sat in his pew, rigid and still, Arthur stole a glance at him and wondered if he was to be shot as he played the impromptu's last note. Perhaps these last minutes were a gift from his mother and the music had prolonged his life a few moments longer. Perhaps life is just a series of last chances.

When the organ music subsided, the young priest turned cautiously to the captain below.

'Play!'

Arthur glanced briefly at the captain. The man looked haggard; the expression on his face was stricken and miserable. To his left, two soldiers were wrapping sticks of dynamite on the church's columns. Suddenly, one man dropped his pliers on the stone floor; the echo provoked the captain to dismiss them with an angry wave. He gestured for Arthur to continue.

As the second impromptu began, the captain sat back against his seat and gazed at the vaulted ceiling. The melody was another of the second lieutenant's favourites. But the priest couldn't have known this. Was it a message? The captain was not a superstitious man, but how many coincidences could he ignore? He looked at Christ's anguished face: he saw no reproach there this time. It seemed kindly now – an expression of condolence, perhaps.

The captain noticed that the priest was almost a boy, yet he seemed gripped by emotion, as if he too were moved to tears for this fallen soldier. So be it, he decided. Dieter Weeks had received his memorial in a church. To destroy the site would be sacrilege.

When Arthur finished the piece, he kept staring forward, expecting that the bullet from the captain's gun would strike the back of his head. But all he heard were footsteps, and the sound of the great doors closing.

WHEN IT SEEMED CLEAR that he had been permitted to live, Arthur unbolted the door and walked down the steps. Through the leaden panes he saw that the truck had driven away. He knocked at the hatch behind the altar and heard a bolt being slid aside. The faces of about twenty people appeared, blinking in the light of the stained-glass window above them.

'Martine?' he asked. He repeated her name a few times until one woman replied.

'Martine d'Usseau? Her house was destroyed two days ago in a bombing raid. She was found with her mother. Both dead.'

Arthur staggered away from the hatch. How could Martine be dead? He loved her so much. He had believed that his bond with her would deter bombs and bullets, just as his thoughts of her had tided him through the gas attacks. What power was stronger than their love? Even when she had sent him away, he'd been sure the bond between them was immutable. He sank to the floor.

The refugees assumed that the priest was now praying for them. They clambered out of the crypt, thirty of them, some carrying children.

Oh, Martine. If there were forces more powerful than love, if a person could be snuffed out like a candle flame, what was the point of living? Arthur looked up at the Christ and understood what he looked so upset about: he was writhing at the agony of existence. *That* was life: pain in an indifferent world.

What was he to do now? The one thing he believed in was gone. He was marooned.

A man in a postman's uniform shuffled towards him. 'Are you our new priest? We've been waiting for weeks.'

Arthur didn't answer. He unbuttoned the cassock.

Another man approached, carrying a blanketed bundle in his arms. 'Please, Father,' he appealed, in French, 'do you know of a doctor nearby? My baby is sick.'

Arthur gazed into the man's imploring face. 'What's the point?' he replied bitterly.

The man didn't understand him but smiled hopefully and unwrapped the bundle to reveal the baby.

Arthur looked at the child. 'When did she last eat?'

The man stared, confused.

Arthur repeated his words in French, adding, 'Perhaps there is some condensed milk in the kitchen next door.' As he examined her, another woman brought her two children for him to see. Then an old woman moved behind them, and the postman took a place in line behind her.

THE GOAT'S HEAD

ALTHOUGH LONDONERS WERE SWAYED DAILY BY THE WAR HEADlines and accommodated the marching doomsayers on their streets with mounting concern, the partners of Griff & Winshell remained unimpressed. The law was their Bible; the courts were their battlefield; and the gavel was more powerful than any cannon. The clerks remained perched at their desks (now equipped with typewriters rather than inkwells and blotting sand), their spines still arched like those of jockeys atop steeds. The atmosphere of urgency remained, as did the crackling inferno tended by Mr Tobias Griff with his shining brass goat-headed tongs. The only obvious change was that Mr Griff's divergent eyebrows were now snowy white, as was his goatee.

When Tom requested a private moment, Mr Griff deposited a lump of coal on the fire and led him to his office, leaning against the brass tongs for support.

'Perhaps you don't remember me,' Tom began.

'On the contrary, it is my curse to remember *everything*, Tom Bedlam or, I should say, Dr *Chapel*?' muttered Mr Griff. 'Though I cannot remember where I put my spectacles five minutes ago, I do recall the breakfast I enjoyed moments before you first walked into my office. I believe—'

'Then you may recall,' Tom interrupted, 'that a baby was brought to you by my father, William Bedlam, about fifty-two years ago. I wish to know what became of him.'

The old solicitor looked momentarily shaken by Tom's inquiry.

'It was half of a cold meat pie, peppered until it was black,' he murmured, for this was the answer to the question he had expected – he prided himself on anticipating his clients' questions.

'Please, I need to confirm the identity of my brother!' Tom cried.

Mr Griff embarked on a complicated justification for the necessity of privileged information, but Tom cut him short. 'Surely you have wished, on occasion, to unburden yourself of the many secrets you carry with you?'

'I have, yes!' replied Mr Griff. Raising his tongs, he struck the floorboard, and Tom noticed that the floor was pitted with scores of little indentations from such a gesture. 'Nevertheless, such information is sacrosanct. My practice depends upon it. My *reputation*!'

Tom sighed. 'Mr Griff, please. I must know what happened to my brother. Are you aware of his identity?'

Mr Griff nodded. 'I sympathize deeply,' he replied. 'But as I said, I have sworn not to let such information pass my lips.'

'I see,' Tom replied, and he sank miserably into his chair.

Mr Griff turned the tongs in his hand, glanced briefly at his interlocutor, and wrapped his hand below the brass goat's head.

'Imagine if *this* fellow could talk; there'd be no stopping him. Oh, the things he's heard. Shocking things. Deplorable things. And, of course, things of great *illumination*.'

Tom looked grimly at Mr Griff, then down at the goat's head. What nonsense was this?

'Of course, goats cannot talk,' Mr Griff added casually, 'though I've heard tell of animals that could signify an *aye* or a *no* with one tap or two taps of the hoof.'

The lawyer raised the tongs and struck the floor loudly. Tom looked down at the indentations. There were hundreds, perhaps even thousands. It was a wonder that the boards remained intact. Then it occurred to him that these were not exclamations of Mr Griff's reputation at all but perhaps the *aye*s and *no*s of the past fifty or sixty years.

'Mr Griff,' Tom began, 'would *this* fellow happen to know the identity of my brother?'

The lawyer peered through the glass window of his door at the clerks bent over their desks. He stroked his chin and slowly grasped the goat's head.

Suddenly, the tongs struck the floor with a loud thump.

'Was his name Arthur Pigeon?' Tom asked.

The tongs rose and struck the floor twice.

Tom gasped. '*Not* Arthur Pigeon? Then he was someone else?'

Another tap from the tongs indicated the affirmative.

Not Arthur Pigeon? Then who could it be? Tom wondered. How could he possibly pose the question in such a way as to discover the truth? He was baffled.

'Is he alive?'

The tongs struck the floor once.

'Have I ever met this man?'

The goat's head repeated its answer.

Tom put his hands to his head in frustration. Griff sat back in his seat, his hand wrapped firmly around the goat's head. Tom thought of Todderman & Sons, the billowing smoke, the fiery furnaces, and his acquaintances in the tenement building.

'Brandy Oxmire?'

The tongs struck the floor twice.

'Oscar Limpkin?'

The previous answer was repeated.

Forgetting London, Tom thought of all the boys at Hammer Hall, but it seemed too much of a coincidence for any boy there to have been his brother. He thought of his peers at Holyrood; was it possible that he and his brother shared the same occupation? Then he considered Mr Griff's role in his life. If Bill Bedlam had been a client of Griff & Winshell, perhaps the recipient of the baby had been a client too, and there was only one other client Tom was aware of: the man with wiry black muttonchops who had swept out of the establishment like a tornado in a black morning coat, the man who had paid for Tom's education as a bribe for remaining silent about the murder of Arthur Pigeon, the magnate who had thought nothing of using his influence for the benefit of his son.

'Is my brother Geoffrey Mansworth?'

THE REVELATIONS

THAT EVENING, AFTER AN ENORMOUS RALLY IN MANCHESTER, THE Pendletons waited for the crowds to dissipate before making their trip back to London. The theatre was still hot with the energy of so many bodies in such an enclosed space. Charity stood by the open door at the back of the stage as a breeze swept by. For a moment, she imagined herself carried off by the wind, free from the gravity of her brothers and sisters and their mission. Suddenly Isaiah Pound slipped his hand around Charity's arm and steered her swiftly past his circle of admirers.

She was terrified. What had she done wrong? She wondered if he might even have sensed her rebellious thoughts. Perhaps her tailored skirt and jacket had given her away. 'We are Pendletons, Sister Charity, not peacocks,' the hall sister had once reminded her. His grip remained strong and steady as he took Charity into the cool alley behind the building.

'Sister Chapel, may I tell you something?' he said quietly.

Charity hesitated, her heart turning leaden.

'If all of our members had your devotion, your virtue, your spirit, I have no doubt that we could make every man, woman and child on this earth a Pendleton. You see, I believe we teach by example. I've watched you over this past year, and you are a beacon—' He paused, withdrawing his hand from her arm. 'Does this seem rude or unseemly?'

'Not at all,' gasped Charity. 'I'm very flattered.'

'It pleases me to hear you say so,' he replied. 'Of course, it is my wish not to flatter you but to speak of my admiration and respect.'

He presented her with a pendant – a silver symbol of the illuminati, the all-seeing eye – and asked her to wear it from now on. Charity kept it buttoned beneath her blouse. This token changed everything. Starved by the cold, impersonal atmosphere of her lodgings, she took Isaiah Pound's gesture as a sweet, consoling indication of his friendship.

In subsequent days, as they conducted rallies in smaller towns, Pound made a point of visiting Charity in the late evening in her hotel room. He would chat for ten minutes, sharing some detail of his day, then leave. Though these visits were as innocent as they were brief, she became sleepless with anticipation of his next appearance. In Newcastle he knocked just before dawn. She was furious with him for making her wait but almost immediately felt gratitude, relief, even, for the consummation of her evening – she felt special, distinct, *chosen.*

Once she wore the pendant to bed and lay there naked, thinking of him. She imagined sleeping with him, and although ashamed of such thoughts, she couldn't resist them.

Pound was not a conventionally attractive man. His features were gaunt, and his hair, prematurely grey, was dyed a deep black, which contrasted unnaturally with his face. But there was no doubting his powerful charisma. He drew attention whenever he entered a room, his potency fuelled by self-assurance and the awesome horror of his predictions of the Apocalypse.

He had once touched the arch of her back, and she felt an electric jolt through her body. Was it the touch of a prophet or her own fearful passion for him?

The cycle of anticipation, anxiety and relief at his visits caused her appetite to vanish, and though she reminded herself to be strong, her dependence on seeing him became overwhelming. At the rallies, she wept as she played the organ, exhausted, smitten and bereft.

Pound's visits stretched to an hour; he flattered her by sharing his personal concerns. 'Oh, these newspaper reporters, Sister Chapel,' he muttered. 'They seem more interested in putting their *own* opinions into their articles. They never quote me accurately.'

'At least the rallies allow you to make your point directly to people,' she replied.

'*Our* point, Charity. *Our* point,' he corrected her.

He admitted that he had doubts, that his calculations indicated November 11 to be the day of reckoning, but God hadn't spoken to him with clarity. 'Perhaps the day will fall later, perhaps if we enrol enough souls in God's army, we may forestall Armageddon. Wouldn't that be an achievement?'

'I wouldn't have imagined it possible to forestall such a thing,' Charity replied.

'One cannot imagine the unimaginable,' he replied.

Charity veered between awe at his confidence and admiration for his humility. These rendezvous convinced her that she was, in some way, his partner. And she felt gratitude for this. She was fortunate, she reminded herself, perhaps the most fortunate woman on earth.

BROTHERS

TOM TROD A STUNNED AND BITTER PATH BACK TO HIS HOTEL, BY turns feeling sick then perplexed by the certainty of Mr Griff's information. William Bedlam had been right, the truth of the matter *was* a disappointment. All his life he had yearned for a brotherly alliance, but Geoffrey Mansworth was more of a Cain to his Abel.

He felt compelled to reveal this news to Mansworth, but before he did, he took steps to confirm the facts. The next day he visited the General Register Office. He waited another day, expecting to savour the satisfaction of a mystery solved, but his disgust grew all the more intense in consideration of this kinship. It was bad enough to be related by blood to a murderer, but this murderer had been blessed with all the advantages of wealth and class. Geoffrey Mansworth's privilege, his education, even the fatherly efforts of Bronson Mansworth (a more doting parent, indeed, than William Bedlam) had produced a villain with the blackest heart.

TOM SENT MANSWORTH a telegram asking to see him. The reply came quickly.

As he hailed a cab to Bedford Park, he noticed a man pacing outside the hotel. His loud, checkered suit was familiar.

'Oscar? What are you doing here?'

Oscar Limpkin looked startled to see him. 'Oh, hello, Tom. On your way somewhere?'

'Mansworth's house.'

'Oh?' Oscar averted his eyes. 'News of your son, perhaps?'

'As far as I know, there hasn't been any news about Arthur,' Tom replied.

Oscar frowned. 'Mansworth is a liar. *Ask* him about Arthur,' he said. 'See what he says. *Press* him, Tom. He owes you that.'

Alarmed by Oscar's tone, Tom dismissed the cab. He studied his old friend. 'Oscar, what are you doing here? Were you coming to see me? What do you *know*?'

Oscar groaned. 'Look,' he said. 'I've the worst news. Arthur may be dead, Tom. A fellow I know heard that they found some of Arthur's kit after an explosion near Vermelles. It's most likely that he's been killed.'

Tom stared at his old friend. 'Oscar,' he said. 'Lie to me. Tell me my son is coming home. Spare me this misery.'

Oscar looked feebly back at Tom and shook his head. 'I'd like to be wrong, Tom, you know that.'

TOM WAS USHERED into Mansworth's study without being aware of his cab ride to Bedford Park or the greetings of the police officers. Grief stricken, he clung to one source of hope – the man Mr Griff had identified as his brother.

'Eve has taken Josephine to the theatre,' Mansworth explained; he was looking particularly vulnerable this evening. His ankles were bloated and swelled around the edges of his shoes. His eyes were puffy, his skin pale.

'Brandy?'

'No, thank you,' said Tom. 'And *you* shouldn't have any either.'

'Good heavens, you're not here to discuss my health again, are you?'

Tom searched Mansworth's face. He was looking for some shared trait, some signal of their kinship, some reason to *like* the man. 'Have you a birthmark here?' he inquired, pointing to his own collar.

Mansworth mirrored Tom's gesture and revealed a faint red spot. 'Yes, why?'

'I have it on good authority that we are brothers. Geoffrey, you were given away by my father shortly after you were born in a Vauxhall slum. Bronson Mansworth adopted you.'

Mansworth laughed softly. 'Oscar didn't tell you this, did he? It sounds like something he would dredge up.'

'No, not Oscar – your adoption certificate at the General Register Office, with a small notation of your former parents, William and Emily Bedlam. Were you ever told of your adoption?'

The war minister paused – it seemed an implicit acknowledgment. 'How long have you known?' he growled.

'Just a few days,' Tom replied.

Mansworth nodded. 'We should toast. But you wouldn't approve, would you, Doctor?' He sat down and rubbed his ankles. 'As a boy, walking with my father, I sometimes passed the time looking for kinship in passing faces. It was a careless pastime. I had a fine home, everything I could want. I never wished for a brother – or a sister, for that matter. Now I have both. How lucky I am.' The detachment in his voice belied this last remark.

Tom stood, rigid and unamused. 'How lucky, indeed.'

Mansworth's smile faded. 'You can always count on me, Tom; you know that, don't you?'

'I'm glad to hear it,' Tom replied. 'Have you any news?'

'News?'

'Of my son.'

Mansworth took a cautious sip of brandy and issued a nod. 'As a matter of fact, I've learned that Arthur is safe and well.'

'He is?' Tom felt a sickly wave of relief – it was not conviction but desperate hope. 'Can you bring him back?'

Mansworth examined his brandy glass. 'No, but I assure you, he's perfectly safe. You have nothing to worry about.'

'Where is he?'

'I've no idea, but my sources guarantee that he's perfectly safe. *Perfectly safe.*'

The odd repetition was dismaying. It reminded Tom of Bill Bedlam's assurances of his brother's safety. Then, he became struck by

Mansworth's expression: it harkened back to the summit of Hammer Peak, that same starkly calculating stare, waiting for Tom to believe that Arthur was safe. But now, he was assuring him of his own son's safety. It was just as transparent.

'You're a liar, Geoffrey. I think you're leading me on. You haven't a clue where my son is.'

'Tom, honestly, you can count on me.'

'I've learned from Oscar that Arthur probably died in an explosion in Vermelles.'

Mansworth looked away. 'Well, Oscar is hardly a reliable source. His books are pure fabrications!'

'I should believe you, then?'

'Well' – Mansworth smiled – 'I'm responsible for thousands of soldiers, a nation at war, our collective future—'

Tom could bear it no longer. 'Spare me the hustings speech, Geoffrey!' he cried. 'You're a murderous scoundrel and a liar. Oscar would never lie to me. He's more of a brother to me than you could ever be.'

Mansworth shifted uneasily. 'How dare you? I made you a promise. That should count for something. Oscar and I have our differences, but you and I are bound, now, as *brothers*—'

'Bound, yes, but by lies. By a murder you committed! And Oscar can rely on me as a knowledgeable source. People must know what a wretched creature you are, Geoffrey. God help us if you become prime minister.'

CHARISMA

IN A NARROW MUSIC HALL, ON A STAGE BATHED IN WARM INCANDESCENCE, Iris sang her paean to peace before an audience of scruffy and youthful Londoners – students, teachers, actors, poets, artists and other good-for-nothings. She was dressed as Victory, her breasts barely concealed by bandoliers, her hips draped in pistol belts. In a soaring soprano, she sang—

When this lousy war is over,
Oh, how happy I shall be,
I will welcome all you soldiers,
Bid you sleep awhile with me.
Lie with me on England's hilltops,
Cast your guns into the sea,
We'll make love for e'er and always,
Make the war a memory . . .

Tom guessed that Iris had recrafted the song's lyrics herself: it had her bawdy touch. Just in case anybody missed the point, the dead soldiers who were lying onstage rose to reveal white wings on their backs. They hoisted Iris onto their shoulders, while she casually shed her helmet, sword, bandoliers, and pistol belts, and was carried naked – save for a pair of large, feathery white wings – offstage.

The audience stamped, whistled and cheered lustfully. Tom admired his daughter's considerable stage presence, though he wished she had worn some vestige of clothing when she was marched offstage. He knew it wasn't great theatre, but she had rallied the youthful idealism of her audience. After the curtain fell, the cast came out to take a bow. Iris received whistles and cries of 'I love you!'

She beamed, delighted with the fuss, and Tom wondered if the sight of all those boys from St Peter's cheering at Margaret on the hockey field had inspired his second daughter's desire to become a figure of lust herself.

'Oh, Papa,' Iris insisted later in the hallway as she dressed, 'the audiences are *always* with us! People are tired of having their children coming home in bandages and boxes. The war will be over very soon. Mark my words! Arthur will be back before—'

'Iris, please listen to me.' Tom steadied himself by putting a hand to her shoulder. 'I've had news that Arthur has been killed. There was an explosion, and some of his clothing was found; his company has assumed the worst.'

Iris blinked at her father. It took a few moments for the information to register. 'His *clothes*? You mean, they haven't actually found a body? How can they assume—'

'Iris, please. This is very hard for me to accept, but—'

She shook her head. 'I refuse to believe it.'

'They conducted a service for him; they seem sure—'

'I don't care,' she interrupted. 'Piglet was *always* getting into trouble, but he had a funny way of turning up all right in the end.'

'Yes, he did. But this is a *war*!' Tom stared at her, angry now that she was challenging him on a point he had been struggling with for some time already. 'Iris, I have to go back for Margaret. The wedding is in two days, but I hoped that you and Charity might come with me.'

'Papa! You can't give up!'

Perhaps somewhere else, Tom might have tolerated Iris's protest. But not in a theatre corridor full of grown men and women darting about in greasepaint and silly clothing. Enough artifice, enough nonsense, he thought. 'Iris, you *must* be realistic!' he cried. 'Your brother is dead. You and I have a responsibility to the family we *have*, not the one we wish we had.'

Though his admonishment was directed as much at himself as at his daughter, Iris suddenly burst into tears. It seemed to make her all the more obstinate. 'Well, then, I *must* keep performing,' she cried angrily. 'And Margaret should keep her knickers on until the war is over. What's her hurry, anyway?' she added fiercely. 'She's only going to make that poor man miserable for the rest of his life!'

'Iris, be reasonable. Your mother would expect us to look after each other.'

Iris blushed at the invocation of her mother's memory. 'Papa, I must be at a festival in Brighton this weekend. It's very important. Artists, musicians, church groups – it's a chance to get the word across to thousands!'

An actor dressed in a flowing robe, a white wig, and a beard that hung to his knees nodded agreeably to Tom. He put down two stone tablets and removed the beard, revealing a familiar pink face.

'I saw your sister last week,' Tom told him.

The Orfling gave him an appreciative nod and planted a wet kiss on the top of his head.

TOM MADE ANOTHER ATTEMPT to see Charity at her lodgings. Sister Amelia heard him asking about his daughter and joined the other Pendletons at the counter to explain that Charity was on tour on the coast and that she wouldn't be back for a while.

'On what day will she return?'

Sister Amelia hesitated to answer this question. 'It doesn't really matter,' she replied finally.

'It matters to *me*,' Tom replied. 'She's my daughter, and I haven't seen her for a very long time.'

'She returns on Monday, November eleventh, which happens to be humanity's last day on earth.'

Tom looked at their serious faces. 'Well' – he smiled – 'just in case, expect me on Tuesday,' he said.

The Pendletons stared at the man who clung foolishly to the philosophy of the damned.

'God save you,' one called after him.

NOVEMBER 10, 1918

On the evening before the apocalypse, the Pendletons' rally at Brighton's Palace Pier drew their largest crowd ever. They held a mass prayer between the arcades and flashing lights; hundreds were baptized in the water below. Joyous faces clambered to the shore, freed by Isaiah Pound and ready for the Rapture.

In the bingo hall, a company of actors performed a dramatic protest against the war. A man dressed as Moses presented a woman dressed as Winged Victory with a tablet carved with the words THOU SHALT NOT KILL; Victory put down her weapons and gave up her garments in an extended striptease as she led the crowd along the pier until they spilled into the streets of the seaside town singing 'When This Lousy War Is Over' into the wee hours.

It was a warm evening for November. The water lapped gently at the pilings while a salty breeze provoked lovers to cling together and friends to cluster in tight groups, savouring the energy in the air and the hope and faith provoked by the festivities. There were stragglers in the streets, chattering, joking and singing in the twilight, waiting for something important to happen – love at first sight, perhaps, or a quick encounter with a stranger beneath the pier, or even news of the war's cessation or the opening of heaven's gates.

Anything seemed possible tonight.

Charity sat in her hotel room, hungry, tired, dizzy from the rally, and most of all anxious that she should see Isaiah Pound before the trumpet of angels and the drumbeat of the Apocalypse.

Outside her door, she heard people singing.

When this lousy war is over,
Oh, how happy I shall be,
I will welcome all you soldiers,
Bid you sleep awhile with me.

It must have been those actors. They were walking the streets, laughing and chattering the night away. One of them sounded like Iris, but that could only be wishful thinking. Charity missed her family dearly – the banter, Margaret's temper, Iris's wit, Arthur's gentle presence, even her father's strangely placid glow as he witnessed their most energetic and furious arguments. This familial turmoil suddenly appeared wrenchingly preferable to the cool ritual friendship of the Pendletons.

Charity shivered and considered her four-walled cell. There was a knock at the door. Brother Isaiah smiled at her; he was holding two glasses and a bottle of wine.

'I thought we were not allowed to drink,' she began.

'On the eve of Armageddon, I think it's permissible,' he replied, pouring a glass for each of them. 'The war might be over tomorrow,' he told her. 'This, Charity, is an evening of portent for the world.'

She stared at her glass.

'Join me, Charity,' he said, raising his glass. 'God has led us this far, but tomorrow is a mystery, even to me.'

She took a reluctant sip, but Pound insisted that she drink more.

'I admire your self-discipline, Charity, but this is a special moment for us both.'

'How so?'

'I consider myself lucky to have you by my side. You're a remarkable woman, one of my pillars. You have no flaws.'

Outside, there was a burst of laughter. Charity thought again that she recognized the voice. Then that silly song began again, with new lyrics.

Lie with me on England's hilltops,
Cast your guns into the sea,
We'll make love for e'er and always,
Make the war a memory . . .

'Flaws? Of course I have flaws,' she replied, taking another sip. 'I'm vain, and I indulge in foolish thoughts.'

Pound poured more wine into her glass. 'Foolish thoughts? Of what foolishness might you be guilty?'

Charity paused. Her hunger combined with the wine was having a peculiar effect. She felt irritated; his flattery struck her now as condescending. If he admired her, why would he tempt her like this?

'Impure thoughts,' she replied.

'You? I doubt it.' He laughed. 'Tell me.'

Charity shook her head, wrestling with a desire to shock the amusement off his face. 'I would be ashamed,' she said. 'And you would be embarrassed.'

'You have nothing to be ashamed of,' Pound insisted with a half smile. 'Nothing you say will surprise me.'

'Very well,' said Charity, taking another sip of her wine. 'Once I removed my clothes, wearing only the pendant you gave me. Then I imagined myself in your arms.' She wiped a drop of wine from her chin and looked at him.

Pound refilled his glass and nodded, as if the fantasy didn't surprise him. 'Symbolically, you are opening your soul to me.'

'Am I?' she said.

He poured more wine for her, but she set down her glass. 'No more,' she said. She was feeling dizzy; the wine was turning her hunger to nausea.

Pound put the bottle down, satisfied with its effect. 'Charity,' he began, 'we are souls locked in a mission before God. Are we not?'

'Of course,' she replied.

'Flesh means nothing. Besides, tomorrow we may not even *be* flesh, just the essence of the human spirit.'

'I suppose,' said Charity, rubbing her temples as her head began to throb.

'You have nothing to be ashamed of, Charity.'

'I'm not ashamed,' she replied. 'It's just that my head is hurting.'

'Indulge my point for one more moment. Remove your clothes, and I shall remove mine, and you will see how little it means.'

Charity stared at him for a long moment. Her clothes? Her clothes had always been her pride. She stared at the stark walls of the room, the wineglasses, and reconsidered his request. 'I beg your pardon?'

'Show me that you have no shame.'

'Shame? I need something to eat. I'm tired,' she answered. 'I have no desire to – I don't care about *shame*.'

He smiled again. 'Remove your clothes.'

Despite the haze of her nausea, Charity couldn't mistake the shift in his tone. It was a command. His stare had become predatory, his small eyes piercing, and she was aware now of his hairline, white at the scalp, black at the tips.

'We've been leading up to this moment, Charity,' he said. 'I've sensed your desire. God has plans for us.'

She looked at Pound with disbelief. 'What?'

'I am Adam and you are Eve.'

He leaned forward and kissed her.

Charity held her breath as he kissed her mouth, her neck, and unbuttoned her blouse at the collar. He kissed her shoulder and the spot between her breasts. A tear rolled down her cheek.

'It's all right,' he assured her.

But it wasn't all right, she thought. She felt no desire. A fantasy was one thing, but now, she felt disappointed. He ran his finger down her neck, and she shivered.

Was something wrong with her? Should she submit? Did love come *after* a conquest? Then another question struck her: had he been preparing her for a seduction? The pendant, the long waits, the confessions, and finally, tonight, the wine. His clumsy effort to compromise her was compounded by this idiotic attempt to get her to remove her clothes, a ploy no less awkward than a youth's first grope. It was maddening. Pathetic. Humiliating.

'I shall leave,' she said, trying to stand, but he pushed her back roughly, planting his palm at the base of her throat. Suddenly Charity felt she was going to be sick.

'You will stay until I say you may go,' he replied.

Charity searched his face. She had always forgiven the cruelty in his features as the unfortunate luck of birth (she'd never felt that she deserved her face either), but now it seemed true to the mark, and she felt a fool.

'Brother Isaiah, please,' she murmured, shifting her tone to conciliation and imagining that he couldn't possibly *want* to hurt her.

His fingers adjusted around her throat. 'Take off your clothes.'

'I'm sorry, I misunderstood your feelings.' She gasped. 'And I'm sorry if I'm to blame, but it's late, and perhaps I misspoke. Let's just let it be and forget that it ever happened. Please?'

Any dormant compassion in the man refused to appear in his eyes. *'If you do as I say, Sister Charity, everything will be fine.'*

She shook her head. 'No. I confessed something inappropriate. Please, forgive me.'

It was too late. He leaned forward, pinning her down upon the floor while he seized the fastening at the side of her skirt. He tore it so violently that she was lifted, then thrown down upon the carpet.

Gasping, Charity freed one arm and hit his nose from below with the heel of her hand. Enraged by this, Pound seized her stray shoe and struck her head with the wooden heel; he wanted her to give up, or pass out.

Charity rolled on her hips to protect her face. Her movement caught Pound by surprise; he lost his balance on top of her and fell. Charity staggered to her feet, making for the door, but Pound grabbed her ankle.

Now she thought of nothing but escape. She clawed at the firm grip around her leg, but Pound wouldn't let go. She peered around and spotted the wine bottle. Seizing it, she swung wildly behind her. Pound ducked its first two arcs, but misjudged the third; it struck his jaw, shattering the bone. He uttered a cry and released her.

AS SHE STAGGERED DOWN the corridor, gasping, several Pendletons emerged from their rooms, startled by the noise. They stared at her.

'He tried to violate me,' she cried.

The doubt on their faces was obvious. 'Who?'

'Brother Pound! Brother Pound tried to violate me.'

'What?'

'Sister Charity has been drinking!'

It was Pound, at the end of the hall, pointing at her with condemnation. He held up the bottle.

Charity broke into a run. She hurried down the staircase that circled the lift and, still wearing only one shoe, tore across the hotel foyer into the dark street. The early morning air was thick, salty, and she gasped for breath, her lungs whistling. She touched her forehead and saw blood on her fingers. Her skirt was ripped at the waist. The bitter taste of wine lingered on her tongue. Who would help her in this state? Who would believe her? She saw a figure emerge from the hotel, and panic struck again. She ran down the street, past the dark awnings of souvenir shops, public houses and ice-cream signs, following the incline in the darkness until her feet were slowed by sand and her remaining shoe became mired in a tangle of seaweed. Above her, the great glittering Palace Pier, illuminated by thousands of lightbulbs, loomed.

Charity staggered to the water and collapsed. She vomited, then lay in the dark surf, heaving, helpless and sobbing.

The cheery pier lights melted into streams of tears. Charity lay in the water, her hair streaked with vomit, her faint weeping drowned out by the noisy crawl of waves upon the beach. *Take me,* she prayed. *End it all now. There's no place for me in this world.*

She must have passed out for a little while. Suddenly, she was startled by voices. Silhouettes were crossing the beach: soldiers, she thought, for they wore tin helmets, but there were wings on their backs. In the half-light, they looked fearsome and vengeful. They slowed when they saw her and approached. A woman clad in a war helmet and bandoliers, like some warrior angel, emerged from among the group. Charity shrank in terror. Was it the end of the world? She turned her face into the water, expecting the awful trumpet call of Armageddon. Suddenly, an old man in flowing robes, with white hair and a white beard, reached down and picked her up out of the water. She fainted in his arms.

'Charity?' Iris whispered to her sister. 'It's only me, darling. Didn't mean to scare you.'

THE END OF THE WORLD

THE ARMISTICE WAS DECLARED EFFECTIVE ON THE ELEVENTH DAY of the eleventh month at precisely 11.00 a.m. Although the treaty had actually been signed at 5.00 that morning, hostilities continued until the final minute.

One might have expected those last hours before 11.00 to be quiet, placid, ghostly even, but this was not so. That morning the men of Arthur's battery company fired off as many shells as possible. It was a thunderous, terrifying barrage, that echoed along the lines as soldiers tried to use up every last ounce of ammunition, perhaps as a way of ensuring that this was, indeed, *la fin de la guerre.* Markham, the barrel-chested fool, shot a German who poked his head over a trench wall at 11.16 a.m. An anguished cry of protest burst from the enemy trenches, several white flags went up, and Markham would suffer many nightmares about taking the man's life sixteen minutes after the cease-fire.

In Paris it was said no soldier could avoid kisses that day. The champagne flowed freely, and soldiers of every nationality – Italians, Belgians, Americans, Greeks, Poles, Czechs, Brazilians, Jocks, Tommies and Aussies – traded hats and helmets and walked down the Champs-Elysées arm in arm. It was a good day to be drunk, to be joyous, to cheer, to cry and to hug each and every stranger.

That evening, the remaining members of Arthur's company were given a double issue of rum, but that was the extent of the celebration. They were ordered to keep their position on the farm near the River Schelde. A few men strayed across the river to search a château near which the Germans had positioned a machine gun. It was deserted now.

A farmer and his wife appeared the following day on a wagon loaded with their possessions. The soldiers had made a mess of their house. Several bombardiers carried cheeses and bottles of the farmer's ale in their kit bags. The couple protested, but it did no good.

'Tough bloody luck,' replied the C.O., offering no apologies. The old Roman adage applied: To the victors go the spoils.

In London celebrants walked the streets arm in arm and piled into cars to parade down the Strand. The lights stayed on all night across the city. People's voices could be heard chattering and cheering at every street corner until dawn.

All across the Western Front, soldiers were told to remain with their companies until they were sent home. But they were still prey to the angel of death. She had a new name: la Grippe. She killed many of Arthur's former comrades, following them through the trenches, the towns, the embarkation camps and ships across the sea, wiping out those who had survived bullets, bombs, gas and the loss of their wits. Compared with the 9 million who had died because of the war, influenza killed, by some counts, as many as 22 million across the world in half the time.

In the living rooms, the public houses, pulpits and presses, there were, of course, endless debates about the war. Who had started it, who had ended it, who had *really* won, who had *really* lost. Credit was given to the ceaseless negotiations of the gallant leaders, the courage of the soldiers, the fortitude of the common people, the brilliance of the officers, the spirit of mankind, and of course, the will of God.

It came as no surprise to anyone that Isaiah Pound took full credit for Armistice Day. Some of the Pendletons who woke up on November 11 to find the world intact, its blasphemers still walking the filthy streets, took solace in the theory that their missionary zeal had ended the Great War; others, however, questioned the integrity of their leader.

Tom received a call from Iris informing him that she had found Charity, and she was recuperating in Brighton Hospital.

Pound announced a rally on the evening of November 13 to celebrate his achievement. Though his most ardent supporters cheered him at the podium, the vast majority of his brethren failed to attend. Without the Apocalypse to distract them, they had focused their concerns on his leadership, sharing rumours of his depravity and the stories of several attacks he had made on women in his inner circle. After years of being admired for his words, Isaiah Pound was finally being judged by his deeds, and they condemned him.

MARGARET SENT A TELEGRAM to her father. Its woeful tone, in the light of world events, would become a family joke.

PAPA,

WEDDING POSTPONED.

WAR OVER.

JOHN AND I DEEPLY DISAPPOINTED.

MARGARET

In celebration of the cease-fire, the Holloway prison authorities released Audrey a week earlier than planned. Tom met her at the gate, as he had promised. She emerged from the building to see a bleak rim of naked horse chestnut trees and an overcast sky.

'I would have wanted a better day for your release,' Tom said.

'I can't think of a more beautiful day,' Audrey sighed. 'The war is over, and you are here.'

'There's a big party for you this afternoon,' Tom explained. 'I'm to take you to Oscar's house.'

'Could we just *wander*, Tom?' she asked. After almost three decades of strict order, what Audrey most desired was the experience of an unplanned moment. From the moment she woke in the morning to the last bell before lights were turned out, she had missed those indulgent pauses, the choices, the whimsical silences.

They took the Caledonian Road south to King's Cross. Audrey invited Tom to tell her about Arthur. With pride, he described the progress of his son's musical talent, his imaginary language and his make-believe games with Iris. It was only when he got to the subject of the lead grenadiers that Tom stopped talking.

Audrey filled in the silence with news of Jonah's exploits. He was in the Australian Second Division, had survived Gallipoli and fought to victory in the battle of Mont St Quentin. His letters to her were full of bravado and spirit, though he was frequently charged with and punished for infractions. Scrappy, cunning, his schemes invariably got him into more trouble than they were worth. Like Oscar, Jonah was full of himself and never looked back. Audrey couldn't wait to see him but worried that he might jeopardize his lucky military career with some foolish deed.

'Audrey, Margaret has picked another wedding date,' said Tom, 'and this time I must be there. I wondered or, rather, I should say that I hoped you might consider coming with me.'

She didn't answer at first. 'The thought of being able to go where I please is still unfamiliar,' she confessed. 'But I must see Jonah before anything else. I'm hoping he'll pass through London on his way home to Melbourne. I hope you understand.'

'Of course,' Tom replied.

They rested on a park bench and watched people pass by – a luxury Audrey missed from her days when, dressed as a man, she would study the crowds outside the Mercantile Exchange.

Audrey was silent for some time, though she held Tom's hand. He guessed that she was trying to reconcile a lifetime's worth of wishes with this first day of liberation.

'Come,' she said, finally. 'Oscar will be furious if we are late.'

A cab drove them the remaining distance to Oscar's house. As Audrey pressed the doorbell, Tom wondered silently whether he should excuse himself now. He didn't want to share Audrey with others. It was a jealous impulse – he wanted her to himself and feared losing her as she found her footing in the world again.

She clutched his arm, however, and murmured, 'Stay with me, Tom.'

Oscar, red-faced, appeared at the door. 'Well, finally! We were becoming damned worried about you!'

'Oh, Oscar, what sort of a greeting is that? Kiss me! Where's Penny?' Audrey cried.

Oscar did as he was told, while Tom stood at Audrey's side feeling her tight grip on his arm. She was terrified.

It was a warm gathering, with many of Audrey's old friends from Newgate and a few suffragettes from the early days at Holloway. Audrey kept Tom by her side, introducing him and explaining the stories of these many friends. It became clear to him that her imprisonment had sustained a vital and intense series of friendships.

'What a lot of friends, Audrey!' Oscar remarked. 'When you sent me the list of people to contact, I began to wonder if you'd been attending tea parties for twenty-eight years instead of living behind bars.'

'Oh, Oscar, I wasn't the Count of Monte Cristo, for heaven's sake, I was in a London prison,' Audrey replied. 'You aren't really going to write that book about Mansworth, are you?' she inquired.

'I must, Audrey, I owe it to my country!' Oscar replied. 'And Tom is going to help me. It turns out that Mansworth murdered one of his classmates at school. It's a wretched story – highly inappropriate behaviour for a man who wishes to be the next prime minister. The public *must* know!'

'But what about Penelope's inheritance?' said Audrey.

Oscar took his wife's hand. 'We have filed a countersuit. Thanks to Tom here, we know the facts of Mansworth's adoption. His sole claim to the family fortune is invalid. Thus, Geoffrey Mansworth must live by the dictates of his father's will or give up his fortune to his adoptive sister.'

AFTER HE HAD RETURNED to the hotel, Tom received a call from Mansworth; he sounded very sick. 'I'm in a hospital, Tom. I need your help, as a brother.'

To say that Tom was surprised would be an understatement. Of what tactical use could he be to Mansworth now? Oscar would write his book, Mansworth's sins would be exposed, and the results of the election would be anyone's guess. Tom had never expected to see the man again;

certainly not for sentimental reasons. Nevertheless, he threw on his clothes, cognizant of Audrey's opinion on one's duty to family and aware that he still owed his father a debt of forgiveness. Perhaps Geoffrey too sought redemption of some sort.

I need your help, as a brother.

Tom took a cab to the hospital in the early morning darkness. The barren city streets were shiny, and the cab's windscreen wiper moaned; it was a time when babies were born and old souls departed. Charity would be released from the hospital in Brighton today. Iris was accompanying her; it gratified Tom to think of his children caring for each other. He wondered if anyone had cared for Arthur, or if the boy had simply been felled, like a blade of grass, in that vast conflict.

Two police officers flanked the hospital entrance, and two more greeted Tom in the private ward reserved for the minister of war.

The walls of the room were suffused with the same blue light Tom recalled from his mother's last minutes all those years ago. Beyond the window he saw London before dawn, her dark buildings pressed together like biscuits, her ships berthed, her gardens empty, her church spires pointing upwards, her clock hands pointing down, while the millions slept in a peace they had not known for four long years.

'How are you, Geoffrey?' Tom whispered.

'I am ruined, thanks to you.' Mansworth took a difficult breath and added, 'That I am dying is the least of my troubles.'

Tom frowned. 'I'm sorry to be the cause of them.'

'And Oscar, with his book. And my wretched sister, for marrying him.'

'Perhaps, Geoffrey, if you settle the matter of the will, Oscar might reconsider.'

'Never.'

Tom sat down. 'Are you in pain?'

'Of course I am,' came the reply. 'I asked for more morphine. They won't give it to me. You're a doctor. Help me.'

Tom examined the chart at the foot of Mansworth's bed. 'Any more morphine would kill you.'

'Pity me,' Mansworth groaned. 'Help me.'

'I do pity you,' said Tom, 'but to give you more morphine would be murder.'

Dismayed by his reply, Mansworth glowered at Tom. 'Answer me this. What sort of a brother are you to let me suffer like this? You're a sadist. You envy me my good fortune, and you wish to see me suffer as much as possible.'

'I don't envy you,' Tom replied. 'I pity your greed and your callous regard for the people around you and the damage you've done, but there's nothing I can do to remedy that.'

Mansworth shook his head. 'I am finished. My career is finished. I'm damned if I'll live out my life in a wheelchair while gadflies like Oscar blacken and deride my name.'

'You have a wife and child. Tomorrow you will feel differently.'

A spasm of pain silenced Mansworth for a moment, and when it was over, he looked at Tom wearily. 'Give me the morphine. *Give me the morphine!*'

'I'm sorry, Geoffrey.'

Mansworth's eyes rolled bitterly, and the words that issued from his raw breath were a blast of hatred. 'Then go to hell and be damned, Tom Bedlam. Damn your children and *their* children. Damn your goodwill, your high notions and your brotherhood. You *disgust* me! I hope you die alone, wretched and poor!'

IN THE CORRIDOR, Tom searched for an exit, but he was too shaken to find his way out; Mansworth's last words rang in his ears. Soon, however, another sound pierced the silence of the corridor – the rattle of a glass bottle on an enamel tray. A nurse walked by; beneath her cap her hair was streaked with grey, and her chin bobbed nervously. She held a kidney dish with the bottle and a hypodermic. Her eyes regarded Tom with a start, but her task drew her towards the policemen flanking Mansworth's doorway.

It wasn't until Tom set foot outside the hospital that he connected the bobbing chin, the unsteady hands and the face of Polly Peckam with the nurse who had passed by. The bottle, he realized, contained morphine.

'I'm too late,' he murmured. 'Too late again.' He buttoned his coat. 'Too late to save Mansworth, just as I was too late to save Arthur Pigeon.'

Reconciled to his many failures, Tom walked back towards the hotel. The same eerie blue light suffused the city. It began to rain, and he felt the hems of his trousers stick to his ankles as the downpour intensified. He kept walking, however, past his hotel, through Mayfair, Hyde Park and Knightsbridge until, finally, he became lost. He remembered Charity, Iris and Audrey, and turned back.

GOODBYE

EVE ARRANGED THE FUNERAL WITH THE SAME PANACHE THAT HAD served Geoffrey Mansworth to such good effect in his career. She gave him a hero's farewell. The Allied nations sent representatives for the occasion. The prime minister and some of Mansworth's political supporters gave eulogies. Many grand statements were made about the minister's achievements – statements he would never have heard made about him in his lifetime: 'He delivered our brave soldiers from servitude.' 'He freed Britain from the enemy's iron yoke.' 'Without him, the war would still be raging.'

Some funerals become joyous celebrations of a man's character – real or imaginary – but Mansworth's was less about the man than about the war's cessation. The strangers who wept did not weep for him but for their loved ones and the lives that would never be the same. The figure carried through London would be forgotten quickly by most, though his fanfare would linger in the memories of a generation as a milestone of grief and a marker of the next era.

Eve wept for Josephine because she knew what it meant to grow up with the loss of a parent; Mansworth's absence would change her daughter's life in unimaginable ways.

Tom suffered through the service – embittered by the pomp accorded a man like Geoffrey Mansworth and disgusted at the power of the strong over the weak, the well-placed over the rank and file, and the evil over the good.

As for William Bedlam, he made a spectacle of himself, weeping copious tears, wailing and shaking his head. If he had known of his first son's vast wealth, he might have convinced him to pay for his return to the legitimate stage. It was a tragedy indeed.

Paddy Pendleton did not weep. His stoic grimace endured throughout the eulogies, the procession, and the sombre embraces. He had been waiting for the end of the world his entire life, and it insisted on eluding him. Surely now, he thought, after such a war, people would show a little wisdom, mend their ways, follow the commandments and respect their elders.

Iris and Charity attended their uncle's funeral. Charity's face was swollen from her injuries, but she looked much improved from the night when Iris had found her.

Iris kept up a steady banter during the service. 'Mark my words, Arthur is wandering Europe. Perhaps he's suffering from amnesia, or he's joined the circus, or been taken into slavery.'

'Perhaps he's become religious,' Charity added.

Iris shot her sister a cautious glance. Religion had been a taboo subject; the Pendletons had not been discussed since the newspapers announced that Isaiah Pound had fled overseas with a fortune stolen from the Pendletons' bank accounts.

'Perhaps he has,' said Iris.

Charity shuddered. 'God forbid.'

Then Iris issued a riotious shriek, and the two daughters ducked their heads in silent hysterics.

EVE HELD A FAREWELL party for the Chapels and the Limpkins in Bedford Park. It was an opportunity for William Bedlam to meet his granddaughters, Eve to meet her nieces, and of course, Tom to give his father what the old man had yearned for – a chance to take centre seat, surrounded by his progeny, and be showered with respect, gratitude and forgiveness.

Tom feared that his daughters might be appalled by his father's monstrous ego, his shabby manners and his inflated sense of importance (now he considered himself father to the late minister of war), but for most of the evening, people mistook Paddy Pendleton for Tom's father. The colporteur claimed a comfortable chair and was greeted, welcomed, served wine and delicacies on a fine china plate, admired for the resonance of his baritone voice and the gravity of his features.

Meanwhile, Bedlam surveyed the ornate plasterwork and paintings like a pauper in Ali Baba's cave, oblivious to his family. Beneath the ruddy cheeks and straight nose, a wide smile acknowledged his potential good fortune. After his second drink, he began to hover near Eve, determined to charm his daughter-in-law into some act of generosity. His charisma, however, had become coarsened by so many performances on London's streets. When he asked for Eve's shoe so that he could perform a juggling act involving an apple and a wine bottle, she demurred.

Hastily Tom drew his father away and reminded him that he was not obliged to entertain the crowd and should show some dignity.

'Dignity? Well, it appears that Paddy has cornered *that* act! Look at him swilling the posh brandy! What better company could she have than her father-in-law? I've known suffering and loss, haven't I? Besides, she might want company now she's left with nothing but her daughter and a generous inheritance from my late son!'

'I wouldn't get your hopes up about her money,' Tom warned him.

'Her *money*? How dare you!' cried Bedlam, his white hackles quivering with indignation. 'I am not as shallow as all that! But even if I was, the fact remains that I am her daughter's grandfather! Where is *her* gratitude?'

'As I said, I wouldn't get your hopes up,' Tom replied. 'You've been no more doting a grandfather to *my* children than you were a father.'

'I thought we'd let bygones be bygones!' the old man roared.

Tom steered his father into the dining room in an effort to calm him down. 'Look, Father, you know you have my forgiveness, but let us be frank. Your motives are suspect. Eve is taking her daughter to America,' he explained, 'and I'm returning to Gantrytown. Iris and Charity are coming with me for Margaret's wedding. You must accompany us.'

'Africa?' Bedlam wilted. 'Why would I want to go there?'

'Because it's the most beautiful place in the world,' Tom replied. 'And because your family will be there: your grandchildren, your son. I'd like you to come, Father.'

'But what would I *do* there?' The old man stared at his son, mouth open in despair, while his hands stuffed food from the buffet table into his coat pocket. 'I'm sorry, my boy,' he concluded. 'I'm a Londoner. I'd be a fish out of water anywhere else!'

IRIS AND CHARITY were introduced to Audrey by Tom. They didn't know what to make of her – this small, crippled woman with large eyes who seemed to wield such intense power over their father. Tom stood beside her, his frame tilted down as if to bend his ear to anything she said. His dependence on and deference to her peeved both daughters.

Iris, true to form, made the first strike: 'So, jail for nearly three decades. How was *that*, I wonder?'

Audrey laughed. 'Iris, thank you so much for asking! I was hoping to hear you speak your mind. I've admired your poetry for such a long time. One of my regrets is that I missed seeing you perform.'

'You didn't answer the question,' Charity replied.

'Jail, you mean?' Audrey met the girl's sceptical eye with a candid frown. 'It was torment, Charity. It was rigid, it was unending, but it was predictable – and sometimes predictability is a comfort. I don't know if you've ever wondered about your place in the world, but as a young woman, I was torn in two directions. Then, suddenly, a judge decided my place. For twenty-eight years, it was no longer a matter of debate.

'Today, I'm happy to leave that question unanswered.'

THE GREY SEA

THE *EDINBURGH CASTLE* WAS PART OF THE FLEET OF THE UNION-Castle Line. She had been fitted with defence armaments during the war and had carried troops and mail in the convoys between Port Elizabeth and Southampton. Thinking the ship's name was a good omen, Tom booked three second-class cabins for the trip home in December 1918.

A good omen for what? He dared not think it, even. Iris kept mentioning the newspaper items she found about soldiers who turned up after being presumed dead. She never mentioned Arthur, of course. Tom wouldn't allow it. He had declared the matter closed. Arthur's fate, however, was scarcely out of their minds.

Audrey had received a shocking letter from her son. Apparently he had lived up to his reputation as a ne'er-do-well. While celebrating the cease-fire in France, Jonah had made friends with a few South Africans, who captivated him with stories of the fortunes to be made mining in the Transvaal. Lured by a dream of making millions, Jonah convinced them to lend him a uniform from the Transvaal Scottish Regiment and smuggle him aboard a South African troopship bound for Port Elizabeth. This meant, of course, that he would be branded a deserter by his own army and face a long jail term if caught.

Audrey saw this news as a sign that she should accept Tom's invitation to visit Gantrytown, contact her son, and set him back on the right course.

When Tom stood upon the *Edinburgh Castle*, watching the green and pleasant coastline recede, he silently bade farewell to Arthur for the last time. Gravely, he looked across the deck at his daughters and took stock of them. They were an odd pair, to be sure: Iris wore red slippers and tights, an enormous bearskin coat, a green scarf wrapped around her head like a turban, and one solitary peacock feather twitching above the whole ridiculous ensemble. What an eccentric she had become. Dressed in Chinese silks she drove death from the Chapels' door; she stole her sister's first love; and crossed continents clad (or unclad) as Victory. Iris, Tom concluded, would always stage dramas – or provoke them. By contrast, Charity was a figure of modesty and taste, haunted with yearning. She altered the black woollen coat Tom bought for her in London, taking in the waist and flaring the hem. Her small and pretty face had healed well, but it evoked disenchantment. Though Charity might regard all subsequent prophets with scepticism, Tom feared she would never kick her attraction to them, or quash a desire to find the real thing.

In short, neither daughter would find satisfaction in Gantrytown. He would have to make the most of their company during Margaret's wedding.

'GOODBYE, ENGLAND!' CRIED IRIS. 'Farewell, France!' she added, scanning the faint rim of land to the east of the railing. 'Piglet, I know you're there . . . somewhere!'

'Poor Arthur,' sighed Charity to her sister. 'I was so unkind to him all through his childhood. I shall carry that shame with me forever.'

Iris tipped her head, as if to cast her own misgivings into the water. 'I suppose it would be callous to wish for another war. I had *such* a good time.'

'Poor Papa, what a sad life he's had,' said Charity. 'He's lost so many people – a mother, a brother, a wife, a child.'

'Yes, for that reason I shall conduct my life as a comedy, *not* a tragedy,' Iris resolved.

The women looked across the deck at their father. He wore a thick black coat with the collar pulled up to his ears. His hair seemed almost silvery in the diffuse light of this overcast day. His arm was tucked in Audrey's.

'Do you think he'll marry the *murderess*?' said Iris.

Charity frowned at her sister. 'Don't say that,' she whispered.

'Well, that's what she *is*.' Iris shrugged. 'I'd *love* to be called a murderess.'

'WHAT ARE YOU thinking, Tom?' Audrey inquired, slipping her fingers between his.

'Arthur,' Tom admitted. 'Iris sold him to the Horvaths one afternoon as a piglet; for the rest of the evening he squealed and scampered across the floor. Arthur always tried to be the person that people *expected* him to be. I wonder if his death is merely another accommodation.'

'What do you mean?' replied Audrey.

Tom paused, waiting for his emotion to subside. 'Foolish of me, I know,' he gasped, 'but I still can't believe he's dead.'

THE CHAPEL DAUGHTERS watched Audrey console Tom.

'Well,' conceded Iris, 'he's entitled to a little affection, isn't he?'

Charity nodded. 'Yes, I suppose so. We're *all* entitled to a little affection.'

'Yes,' Iris agreed with a doomed expression.

'Still,' added Charity, 'I hope he doesn't marry her.'

'It's just one more murderer in the family,' said Iris with a casual yawn. 'Have you forgotten about his brother?'

Charity looked startled. 'Of course not. I meant that I'd be jealous if both Margaret and Papa suddenly got married, leaving us—'

'Oh.' Iris frowned. 'Well, I won't stay in Gantrytown! Charity, I'd go mad. I can't believe Margaret is marrying that man. *I'll* never find a man there. Oh, God!' she lamented. 'What if the best days of my life are over?'

'I don't believe mine are,' Charity replied.

Her expression was defiant, and Iris regarded her with surprise.

'I'm so glad to hear you say that. When I found you that night in

Brighton, I felt as if it was all *meant* to be – the end of the war, you there on the beach, my finding you, it all had a purpose, there was a *point.* We were brought together by . . . Providence.'

Charity looked at her sister thoughtfully.

'One night,' she said, 'I think it was near Newcastle, we had a rally in a field, and everybody in the audience was given candles and told to spread out in the darkness while Isaiah stood onstage and looked over us for some message from God in the arrangement of all of those little points of light. There was a breeze, I remember, and my candle suddenly blew out. After a moment, Isaiah told us that he saw the all-seeing eye, clear as it could be, and everybody got very excited, because this was a sign, a message that our mission was part of God's plan.

'I was quite upset. I felt excluded from the mission because my candle was out; and perhaps my faith was corrupt. So I got back on the stage and stood there, behind Isaiah, and I looked out over his shoulder, but I saw no picture, no all-seeing eye, nothing like it – just all the pretty lights, the amazing beauty of this gathering, everybody wanting to get along with one another. Being happy. It was sublime but not portentous. That was when I began to think that perhaps the Rapture was nonsense but that anything that stops people tearing one another to pieces is probably a good thing.'

Iris looked shocked. 'Darling, don't you believe there's such a thing as Providence?'

'Not really.' Charity looked ashamed; she considered her lack of conviction a personal failure. 'I'd like to believe such a thing, but I don't think I *can* any more.'

The sisters leaned against the railing with their arms around each other's waists. The *Edinburgh Castle*'s engines began to throb. An endless horizon surrounded them.

'I'll miss the soldiers most of all,' fretted Iris. 'They were always my *best* audience.' She tapped the railing. 'What a wretched journey this will be. Weeks with nothing to do!'

As they contemplated their bleak prospects, a chorus of voices struck up in the distance:

Wash me in the water that you washed your dirty daughter in
And I shall be whiter than the whitewash on the wall!

'OH, MY GOODNESS,' Iris gasped. 'Charity, I do believe there are soldiers on board!'

Quickly, she led Charity down the stairs to the lower deck and circled to a platform from which they could look down upon the rear deck.

Several thousand troops – a sea of khaki uniforms – were gathered for their journey home, chatting, joking, singing. It was an assortment of the healthy, the wounded and the shell-shocked.

Iris stuck one red stockinged leg through the railings and addressed the men nearest to her. 'I beg your pardon,' she said innocently, 'but can anyone tell me what time it is?'

Twenty men surged forward, offering the time as well as their names. She might as well have been onstage, for the company swelled around her. Charity covered her mouth, amazed to see how adroitly her sister sized up a willing audience.

'I am Iris, and this is my little sister, Charity! Say hello, Charity!'

Charity issued a timid wave and received a chorus of whistles in return.

'Now, now!' said Iris, in a tone of mock reproach. 'You must be kind to Charity,' she said. 'She's just been released from a convent, and she's a little afraid of men!'

Overhead, seagulls swooped and cried in competition with the sympathetic noises from the troops, but it was impossible to break the magic between two young women and a company of soldiers with a long ocean voyage ahead.

ON THE DECK ABOVE, Tom was in a reverie of his own. Had he accomplished anything by making this journey? His adult life had been directed by a fierce determination to be the man William Bedlam had failed to be – a doting, committed father. Perhaps that had been Tom's mistake, to live with a backward eye, intent on repairing his past instead of preparing Arthur for the world at hand. Would his children now throw themselves into an effort to better his mistakes? How else do generations proceed?

As the soldiers began singing 'Pack Up Your Troubles', Tom remembered his father's performance with Paddy Pendleton on the street and wondered, now that the war was over, whether the sentiment of the battlefield would wear thin, and what the fellow would do to raise a crowd.

No matter, he decided. There is peace between us.

IRIS'S REEDY SOPRANO rose above the voices of the soldiers, and Tom noticed that many other passengers were gathering at the railings to witness her performance.

He and Audrey walked away to escape the crush. Overhead, smoke billowed from the single funnel of the ship. Tom watched it blend with the wintry sky, a shade of grey all too familiar – the stain of Todderman's smokestacks over London, the eyes of Sissy Grimes, the smudge of fingerprints on a tenement wall, the coal ash on a furnace boy's boots and the rolling Atlantic.

Tom tightened his grip on Audrey's arm and left his memories on the deck, for a frigid wind was picking up and there were many miles to go before Africa's warm shores welcomed him back.

BALLYDORP DAILY MAIL

GANTRYTOWN HERO!

BÉTHUNE, FRANCE—February 1, 1919. Monsignor Marcenat visited his Béthune diocese after hearing reports of a heroic priest and found, to his astonishment, a lad from Gantrytown.

Several reports had come to the French prelate of a man who had persuaded a German bombing party not to destroy the town's only standing church, Saint-Agnant, a minor masterpiece of Gothic architecture built in 1255.

The stories were hard to believe; not only was this priest a virtuoso on the organ and a capable doctor but he was fluent in several languages. A local postal officer claimed that the priest had cured his gout. A teacher attested to the man's familiarity with Bach's preludes and fugues. Many claimed that his prayer and expert medical care had saved their loved ones from the devastating influenza that had wiped out thousands in this war-torn region.

The monsignor decided to pay an unannounced visit to the church during the Sunday mass to meet this amazing man. But to his astonishment, the words he heard spoken by the priest during the mass were not Latin nor, in fact, of any recognizable language at all! Furthermore, the famed priest of Saint-Agnant was barely twenty.

When confronted, the young fellow freely admitted that he had attended no seminary and held no qualifications as either a doctor or a man of the cloth. His name was Arthur Chapel, and he was an assistant bombardier in the South African Heavy Artillery. It was then that the monsignor, in spite of the cries of the laity, called for the priest's arrest.

The residents of Saint-Agnant have appealed to the authorities to release their priest and petitioned the monsignor to send him back to the parish. Four marriages stand to be annulled; three christenings and ten burials in this small region will have to be performed again if he is proved to be an impostor.

When Dr Tom Chapel of Gantrytown was informed by this reporter that his son had been found in France, he confessed that this was the best news a father could hope to hear. 'I feel very fortunate and have no doubt that Arthur felt an obligation to help these people,' he said. 'I believe in Arthur, and am sure that he is the hero they believe him to be.'

ACKNOWLEDGMENTS

This book could not have been written without the remarkable first-hand experiences of my grandfather, Aldhelm Joseph Slater. His unpublished memoir, *The Recollections of a Johannesburg Man*, provided me with invaluable details about life in colonial South Africa and on the battlefields of World War I. I would like to thank my wife, Terri Seligman, for her patient reading and insight, Henry Dunow for his inspirational counsel, Carole Welch for her sharp attention to character and dramatic integrity, and Hazel Orme, whose scrutiny of my characters' words and deeds was invaluable. All subsequent lapses in judgment are mine alone. Finally, my appreciation goes to Ann Brown, Laura Ford for her aid and early support, and my editor, Jennifer Hershey, whose enthusiasm and focus helped to bring the story alive.